# my LITTLE PONY
## Friendship is Magic

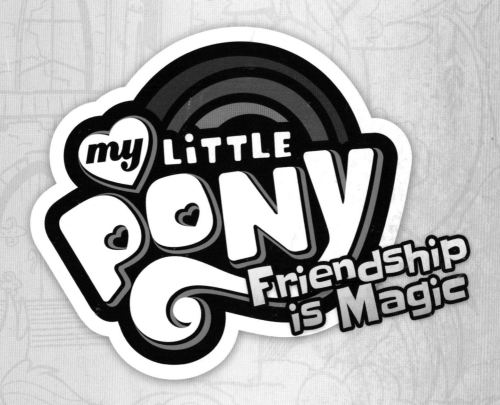

# My Little Pony: Friendship is Magic

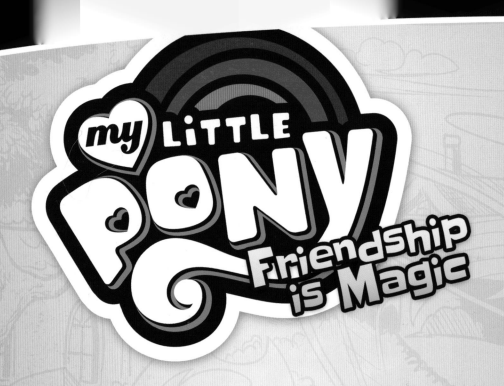

COVER BY
**Andy Price**

SERIES ASSISTANT EDITS BY
**Megan Brown**

SERIES EDITS BY
**Bobby Curnow**

COLLECTION EDITS BY
**Justin Eisinger and Alonzo Simon**

COLLECTION DESIGN BY
**Neil Uyetake**

Special thanks to Meghan McCarthy, Eliza Hart, Ed Lane, Beth Artale, and Michael Kelly.

For international rights, contact **licensing@idwpublishing.com**

ISBN: 978-1-68405-428-2

22 21 20 19 1 2 3 4

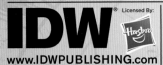

IDW® Licensed By: Hasbro

www.IDWPUBLISHING.com

**Chris Ryall**, President & Publisher/CCO • **John Barber**, Editor-in-Chief • **Robbie Robbins**, EVP/Sr. Art Director • **Cara Morrison**, Chief Financial Officer • **Matthew Ruzicka**, Chief Accounting Officer • **Anita Frazier**, SVP of Sales and Marketing • **David Hedgecock**, Associate Publisher • **Jerry Bennington**, VP of New Product Development • **Lorelei Bunjes**, VP of Digital Services • **Justin Eisinger**, Editorial Director, Graphic Novels and Collections • **Eric Moss**, Sr Director, Licensing & Business Development

**Ted Adams**, IDW Founder

Facebook: **facebook.com/idwpublishing** • Twitter: **@idwpublishing** • YouTube: **youtube.com/idwpublishing**
Tumblr: **tumblr.idwpublishing.com** • Instagram: **instagram.com/idwpublishing**



Originally published as MY LITTLE PONY: FRIENDSHIP IS MAGIC issues #69–73.

# Magical Apple

WRITTEN BY
Paul Allor

ART BY
Toni Kuusisto

# Extreme Bingo

WRITTEN BY
Jeremy Whitley

ART BY
Toni Kuusisto

# Nightmare Night

WRITTEN BY
Ted Anderson

ART BY
Andy Price

# Pie in the Sky

WRITTEN BY
Thom Zahler

ART BY
Agnes Garbowska

# Copycats

WRITTEN BY
Thom Zahler

ART BY
Toni Kuusisto

COLORS BY
Heather Breckel

LETTERS BY
Neil Uyetake

art by Toni Kuusisto

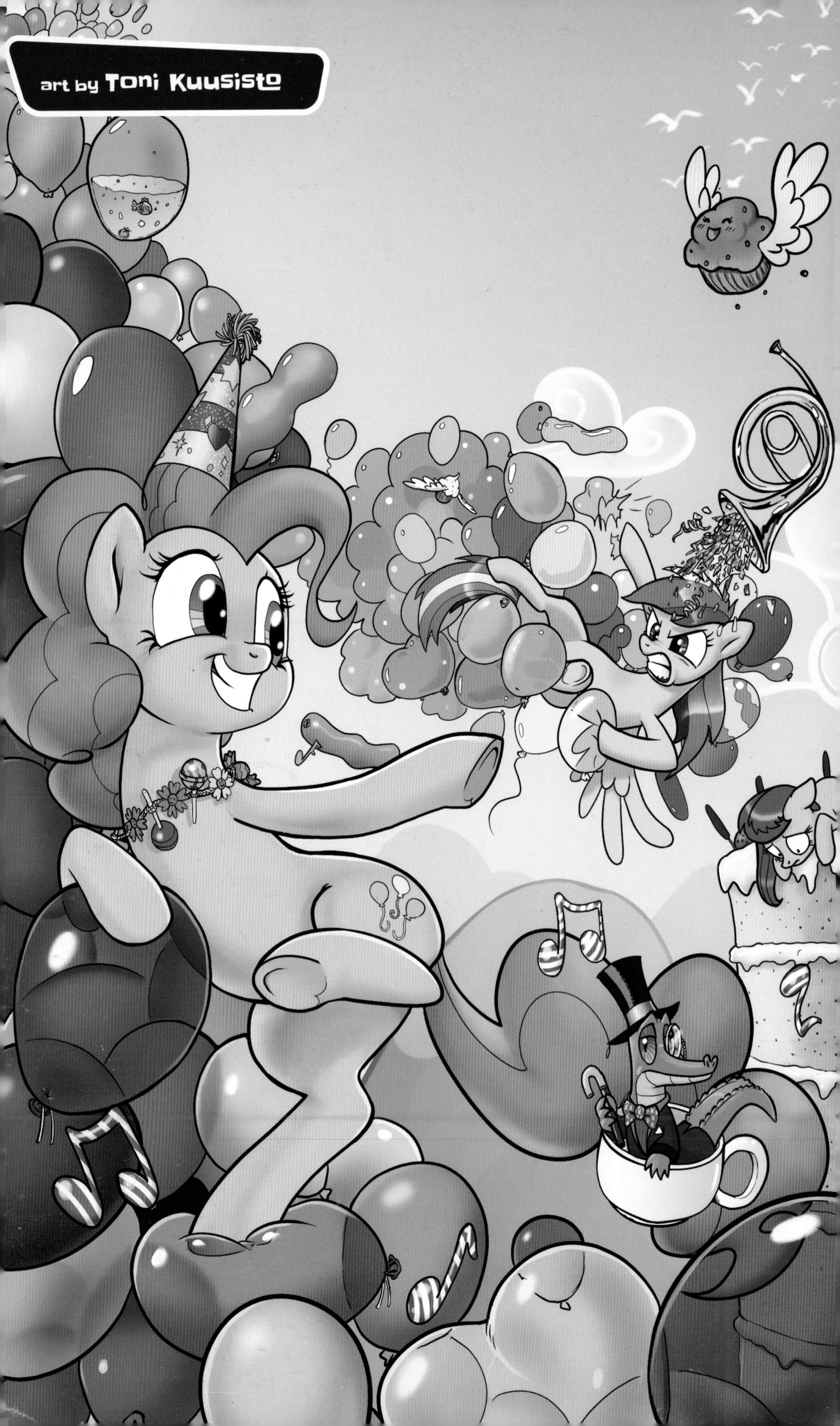

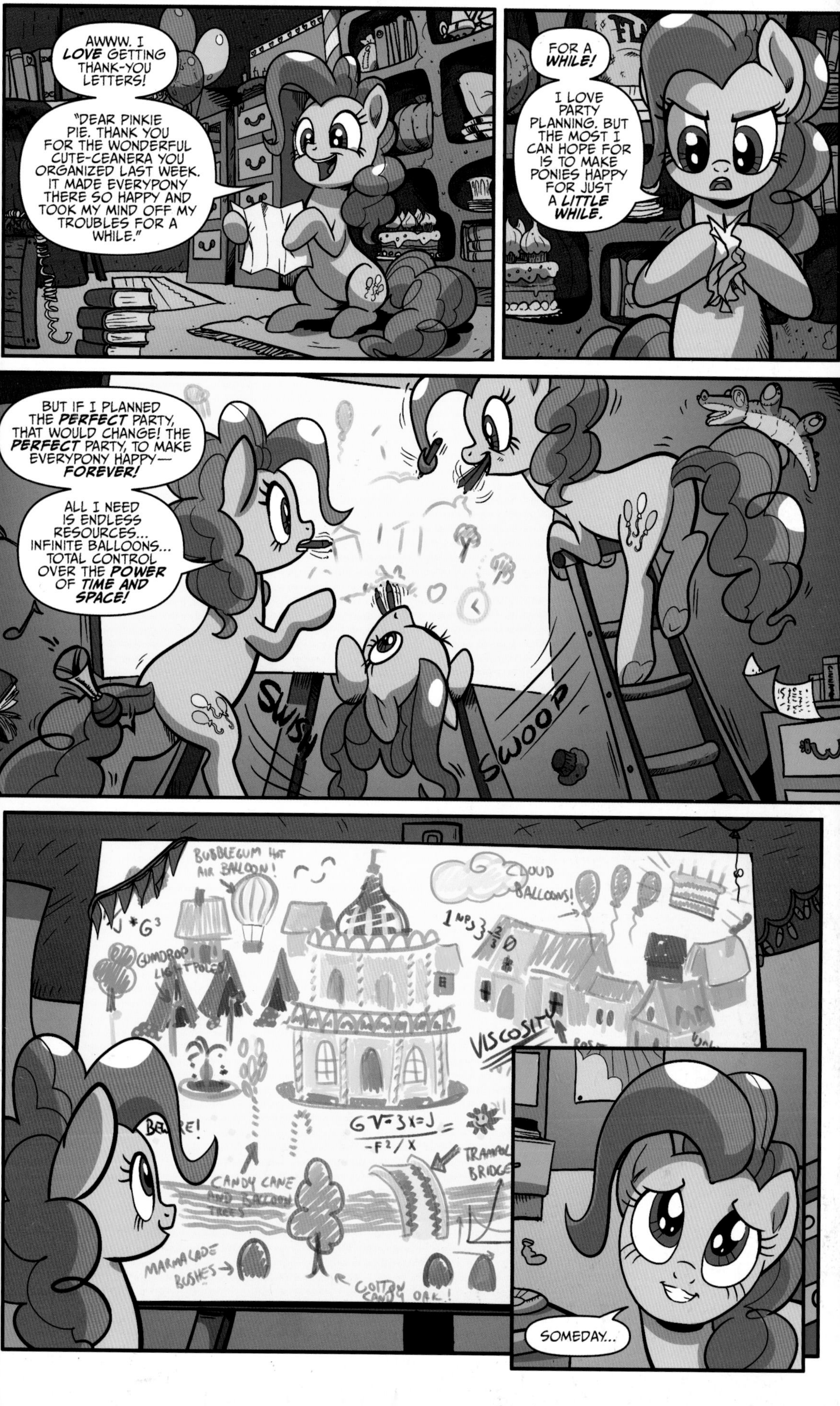
AWWW. I *LOVE* GETTING THANK-YOU LETTERS!
"DEAR PINKIE PIE. THANK YOU FOR THE WONDERFUL CUTE-CEANERA YOU ORGANIZED LAST WEEK. IT MADE EVERYPONY THERE SO HAPPY AND TOOK MY MIND OFF MY TROUBLES FOR A WHILE."
FOR A *WHILE!*
I LOVE PARTY PLANNING. BUT THE MOST I CAN HOPE FOR IS TO MAKE PONIES HAPPY FOR JUST A *LITTLE WHILE.*
BUT IF I PLANNED THE *PERFECT* PARTY, THAT WOULD CHANGE! THE *PERFECT* PARTY, TO MAKE EVERYPONY HAPPY— *FOREVER!*
ALL I NEED IS ENDLESS RESOURCES... INFINITE BALLOONS... TOTAL CONTROL OVER THE *POWER* OF *TIME AND SPACE!*
SWISH
SWOOP
BUBBLEGUM HOT AIR BALLOON!
CLOUD BALLOONS!
GUMDROP LIGHTPOLES
VISCOSITY
BEWARE!
CANDY CANE AND BALLOON TREES
MARMALADE BUSHES
COTTON CANDY OAK!
SOMEDAY...

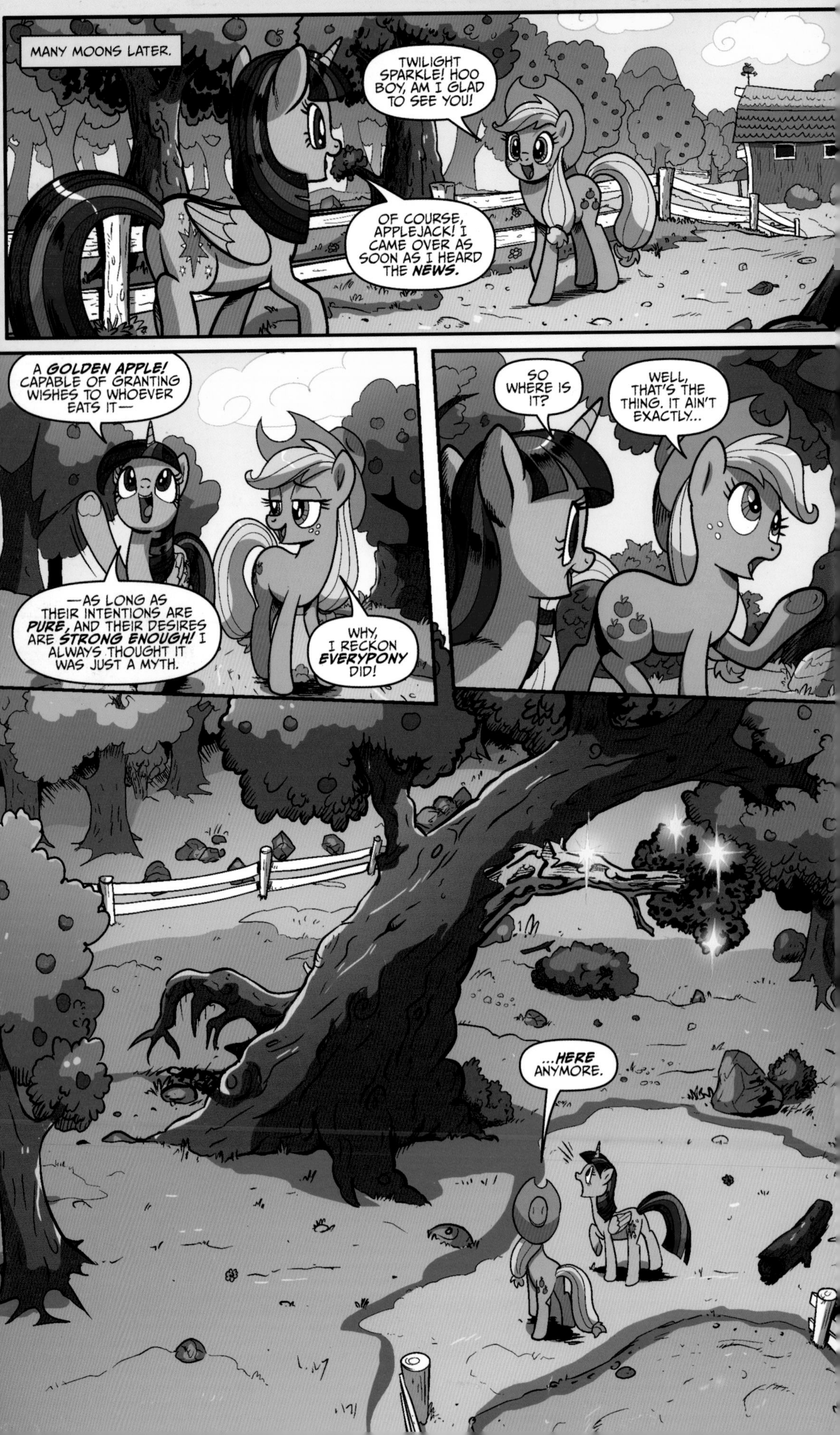
MANY MOONS LATER.
TWILIGHT SPARKLE! HOO BOY, AM I GLAD TO SEE YOU!
OF COURSE, APPLEJACK! I CAME OVER AS SOON AS I HEARD THE NEWS.
A GOLDEN APPLE! CAPABLE OF GRANTING WISHES TO WHOEVER EATS IT—
—AS LONG AS THEIR INTENTIONS ARE PURE, AND THEIR DESIRES ARE STRONG ENOUGH! I ALWAYS THOUGHT IT WAS JUST A MYTH.
WHY, I RECKON EVERYPONY DID!
SO WHERE IS IT?
WELL, THAT'S THE THING. IT AIN'T EXACTLY...
...HERE ANYMORE.

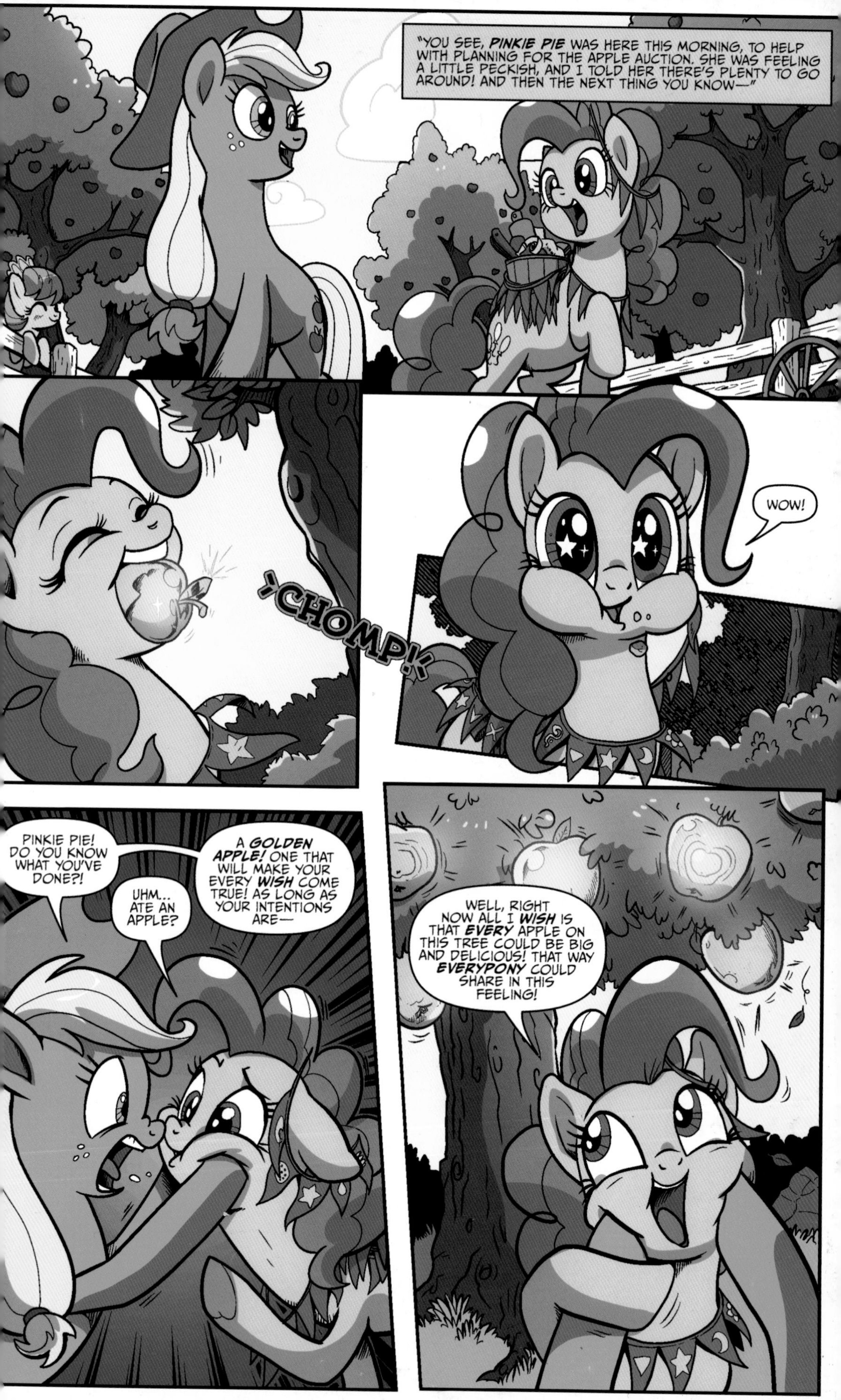
"YOU SEE, PINKIE PIE WAS HERE THIS MORNING, TO HELP WITH PLANNING FOR THE APPLE AUCTION. SHE WAS FEELING A LITTLE PECKISH, AND I TOLD HER THERE'S PLENTY TO GO AROUND! AND THEN THE NEXT THING YOU KNOW—"
*CHOMP!*
WOW!
PINKIE PIE! DO YOU KNOW WHAT YOU'VE DONE?!
UHM... ATE AN APPLE?
A GOLDEN APPLE! ONE THAT WILL MAKE YOUR EVERY WISH COME TRUE! AS LONG AS YOUR INTENTIONS ARE—
WELL, RIGHT NOW ALL I WISH IS THAT EVERY APPLE ON THIS TREE COULD BE BIG AND DELICIOUS! THAT WAY EVERYPONY COULD SHARE IN THIS FEELING!

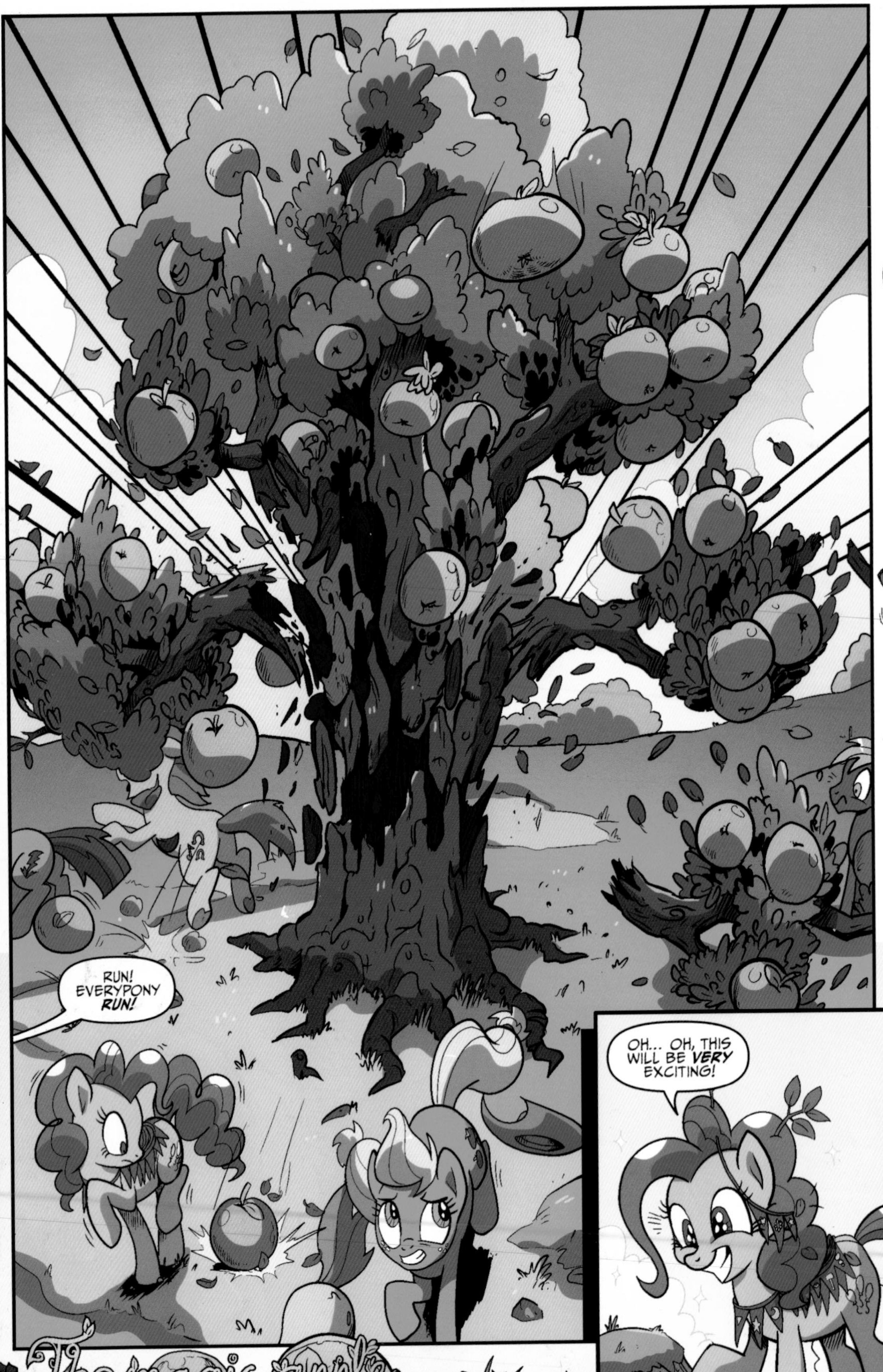
RUN! EVERYPONY RUN!
The magic apple
OH... OH, THIS WILL BE VERY EXCITING!

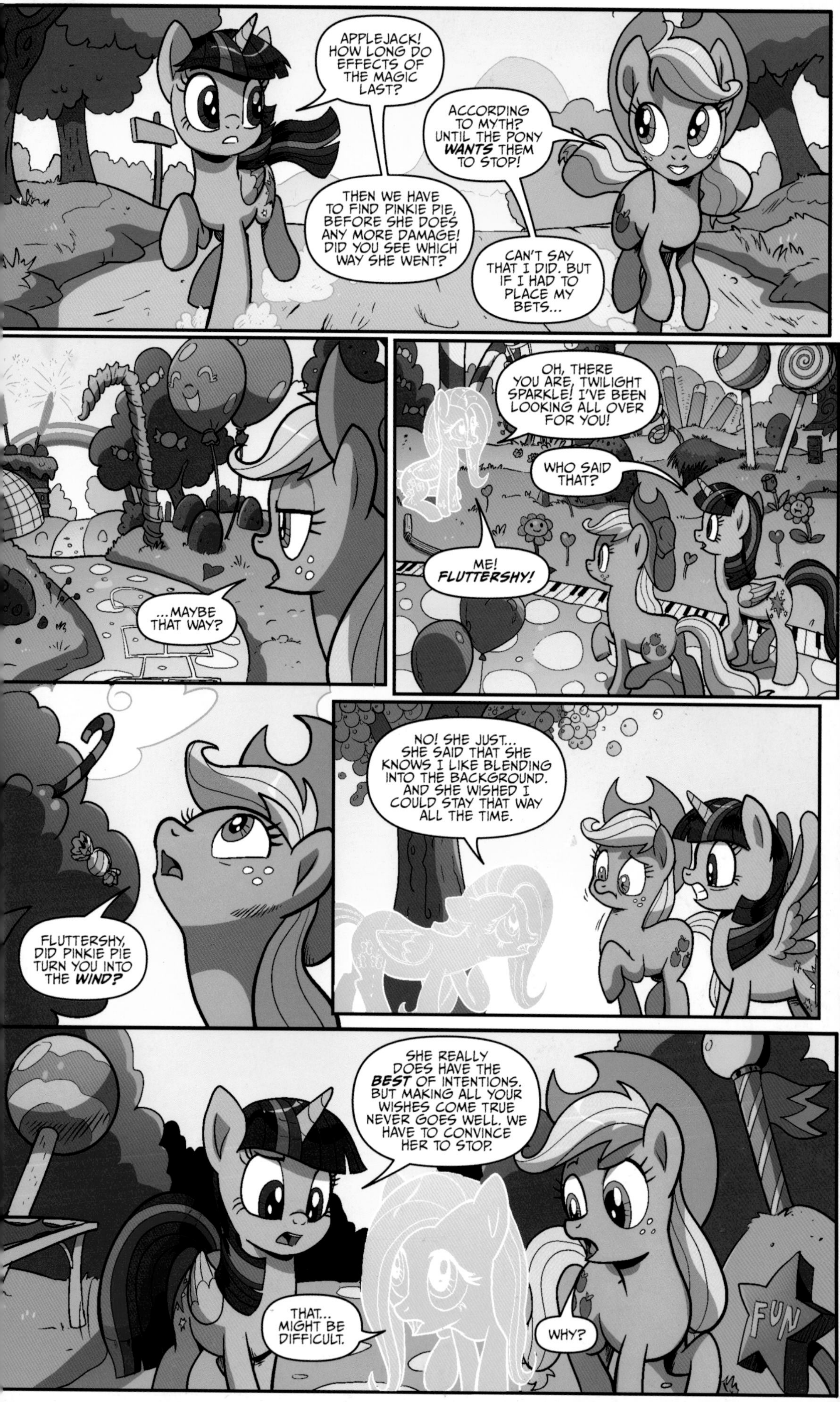
APPLEJACK! HOW LONG DO EFFECTS OF THE MAGIC LAST?
ACCORDING TO MYTH? UNTIL THE PONY *WANTS* THEM TO STOP!
THEN WE HAVE TO FIND PINKIE PIE, BEFORE SHE DOES ANY MORE DAMAGE! DID YOU SEE WHICH WAY SHE WENT?
CAN'T SAY THAT I DID. BUT IF I HAD TO PLACE MY BETS...
...MAYBE THAT WAY?
OH, THERE YOU ARE, TWILIGHT SPARKLE! I'VE BEEN LOOKING ALL OVER FOR YOU!
WHO SAID THAT?
ME! *FLUTTERSHY!*
FLUTTERSHY, DID PINKIE PIE TURN YOU INTO THE *WIND?*
NO! SHE JUST... SHE SAID THAT SHE KNOWS I LIKE BLENDING INTO THE BACKGROUND. AND SHE WISHED I COULD STAY THAT WAY ALL THE TIME.
SHE REALLY DOES HAVE THE *BEST* OF INTENTIONS. BUT MAKING ALL YOUR WISHES COME TRUE NEVER GOES WELL. WE HAVE TO CONVINCE HER TO STOP.
THAT... MIGHT BE DIFFICULT.
WHY?
FUN

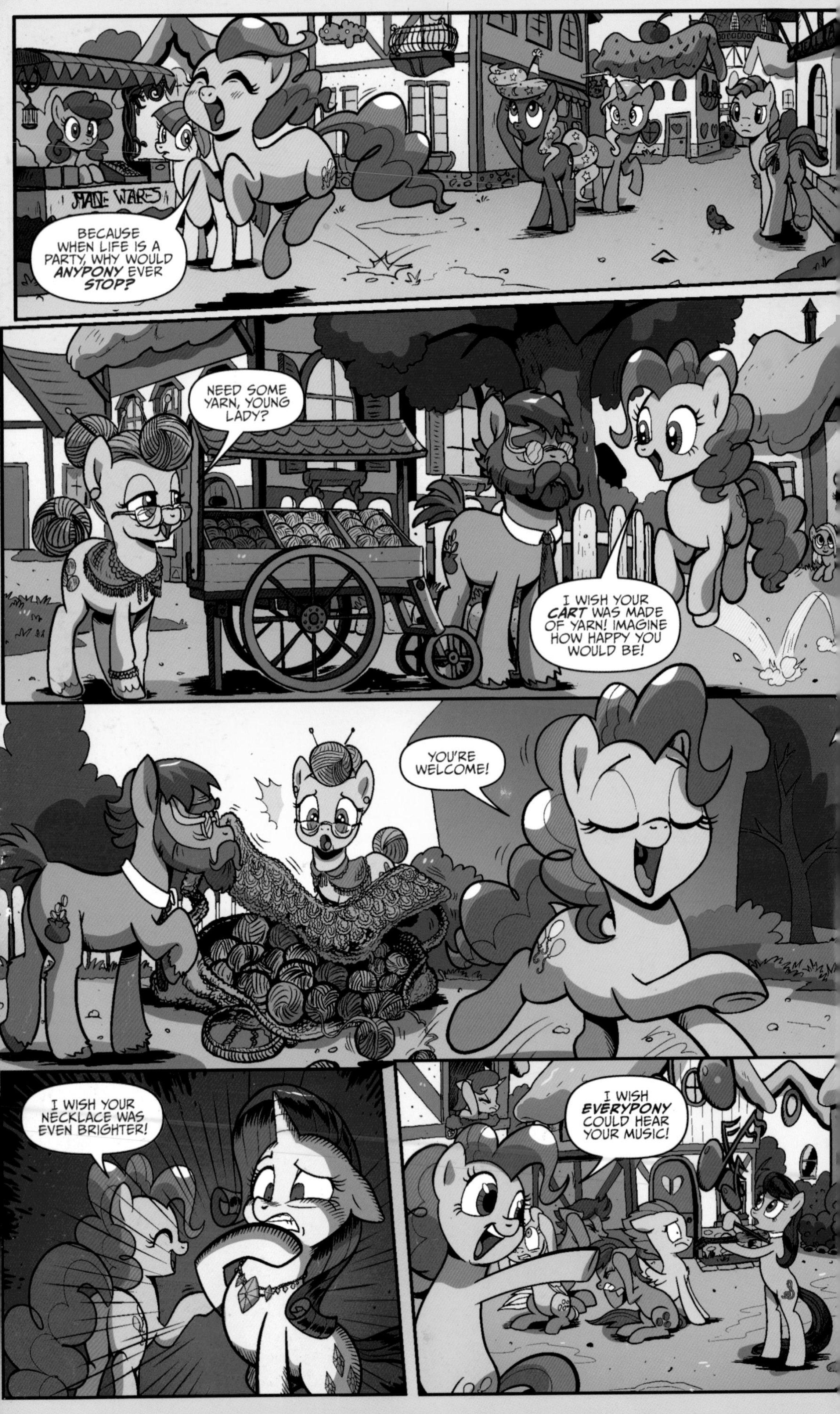
MANE WARES
BECAUSE WHEN LIFE IS A PARTY, WHY WOULD ANYPONY EVER STOP?
NEED SOME YARN, YOUNG LADY?
I WISH YOUR CART WAS MADE OF YARN! IMAGINE HOW HAPPY YOU WOULD BE!
YOU'RE WELCOME!
I WISH YOUR NECKLACE WAS EVEN BRIGHTER!
I WISH EVERYPONY COULD HEAR YOUR MUSIC!

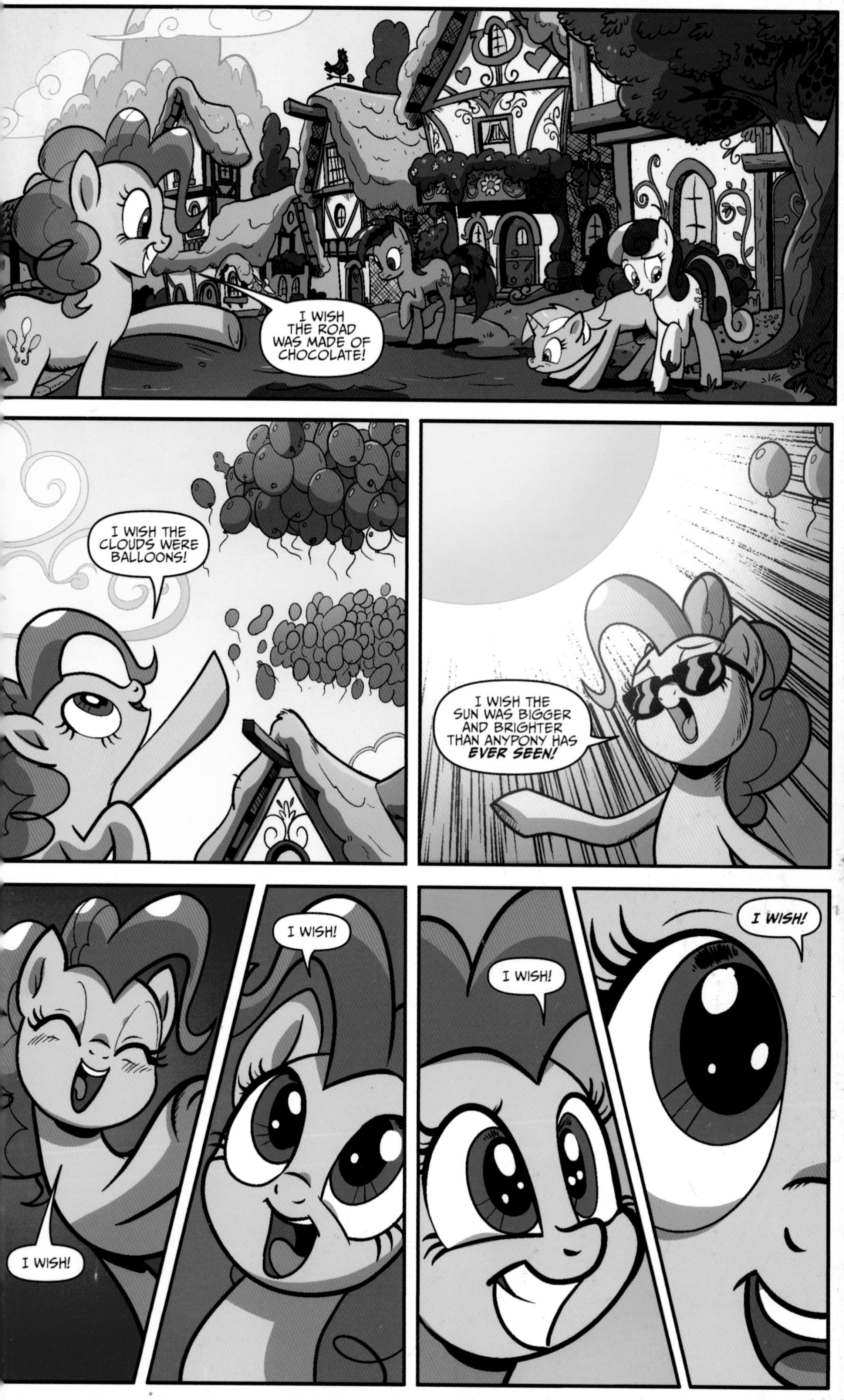
I WISH THE ROAD WAS MADE OF CHOCOLATE!
I WISH THE CLOUDS WERE BALLOONS!
I WISH THE SUN WAS BIGGER AND BRIGHTER THAN ANYPONY HAS EVER SEEN!
I WISH!
I WISH!
I WISH!
I WISH!

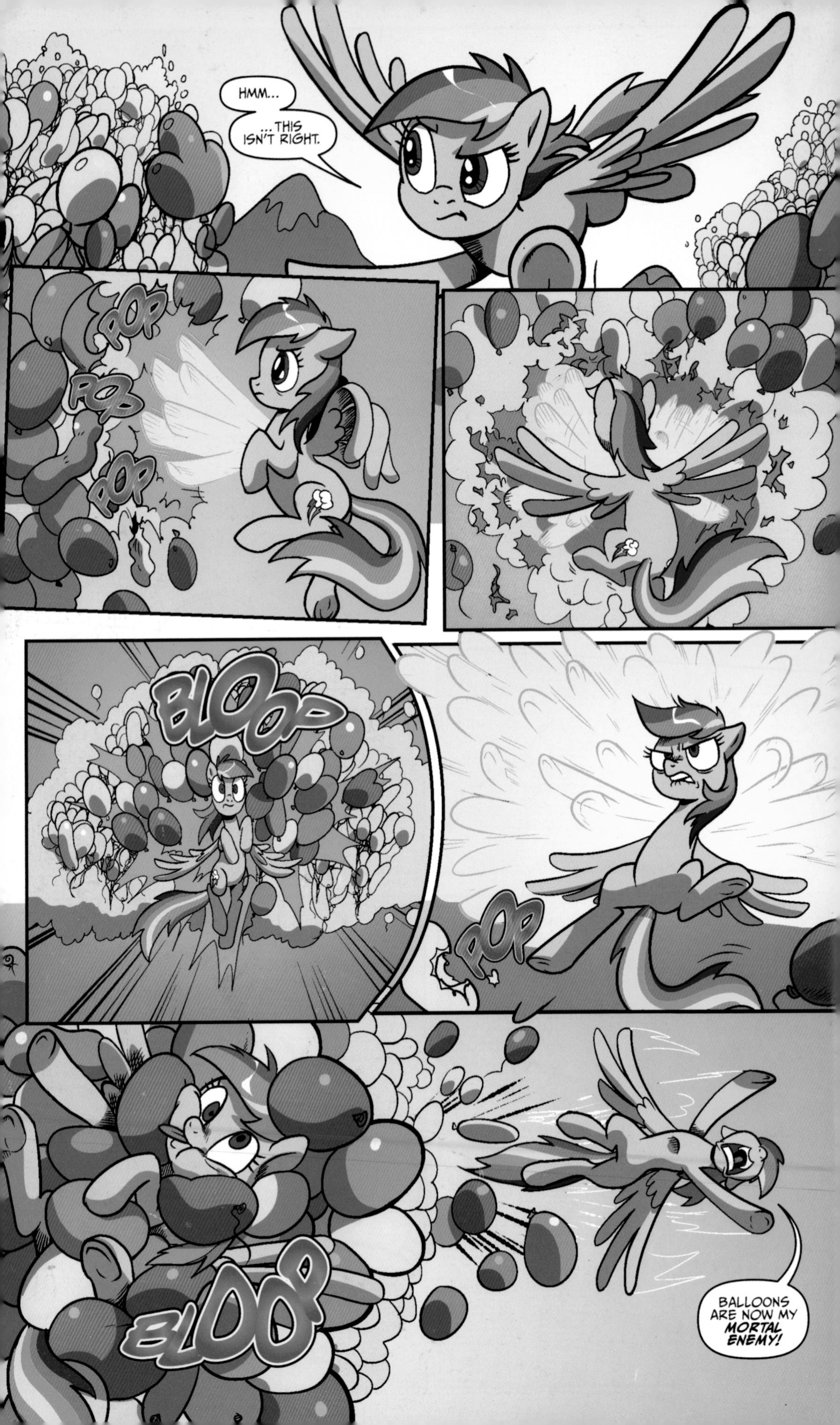
HMM...
...THIS ISN'T RIGHT.
POP
POP
POP
BLOOP
POP
BLOOP
BALLOONS ARE NOW MY ***MORTAL ENEMY!***

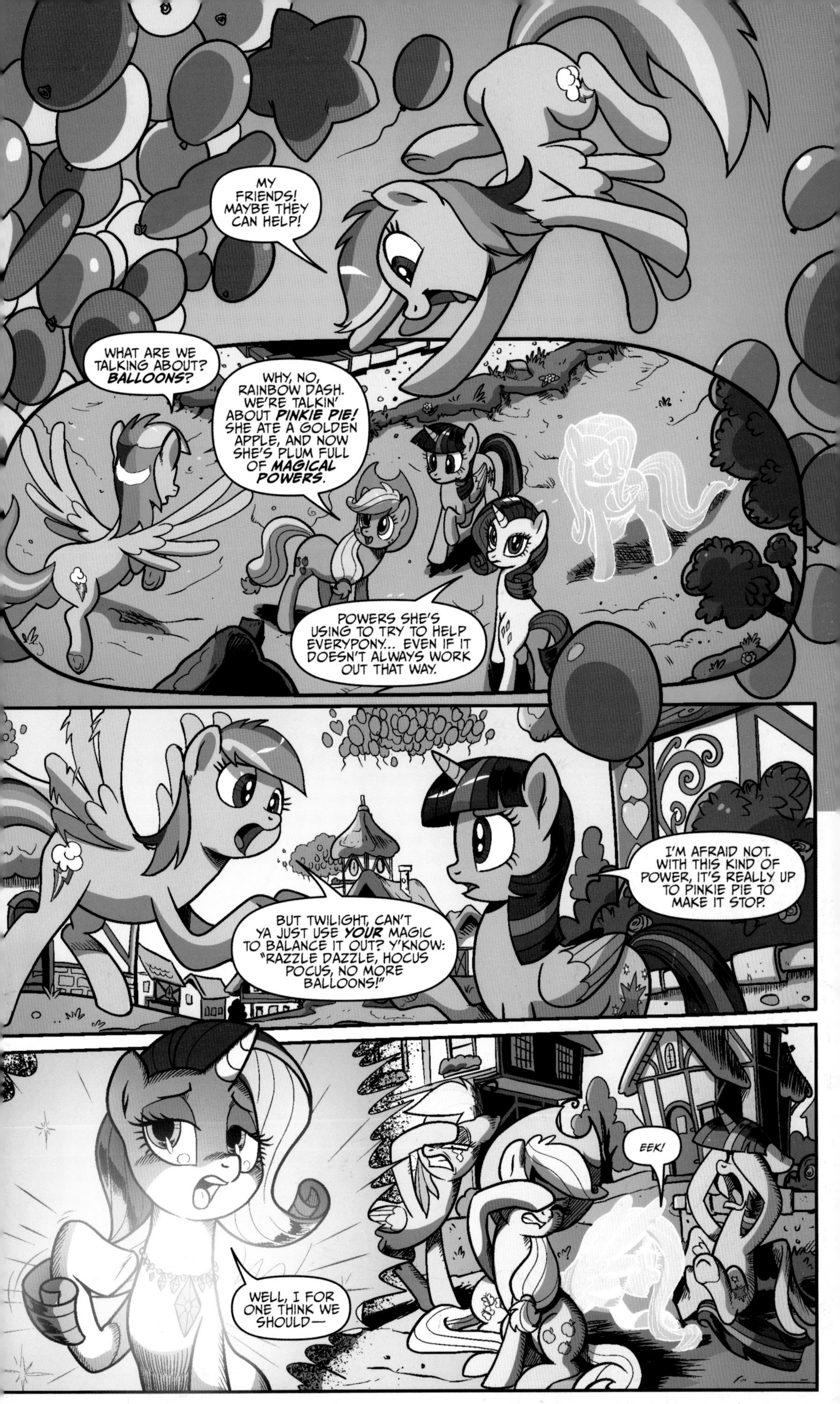
MY FRIENDS! MAYBE THEY CAN HELP!
WHAT ARE WE TALKING ABOUT? ***BALLOONS***?
WHY, NO, RAINBOW DASH. WE'RE TALKIN' ABOUT ***PINKIE PIE!*** SHE ATE A GOLDEN APPLE, AND NOW SHE'S PLUM FULL OF ***MAGICAL POWERS***.
POWERS SHE'S USING TO TRY TO HELP EVERYPONY... EVEN IF IT DOESN'T ALWAYS WORK OUT THAT WAY.
BUT TWILIGHT, CAN'T YA JUST USE ***YOUR*** MAGIC TO BALANCE IT OUT? Y'KNOW: "RAZZLE DAZZLE, HOCUS POCUS, NO MORE BALLOONS!"
I'M AFRAID NOT. WITH THIS KIND OF POWER, IT'S REALLY UP TO PINKIE PIE TO MAKE IT STOP.
WELL, I FOR ONE THINK WE SHOULD—
*EEK!*

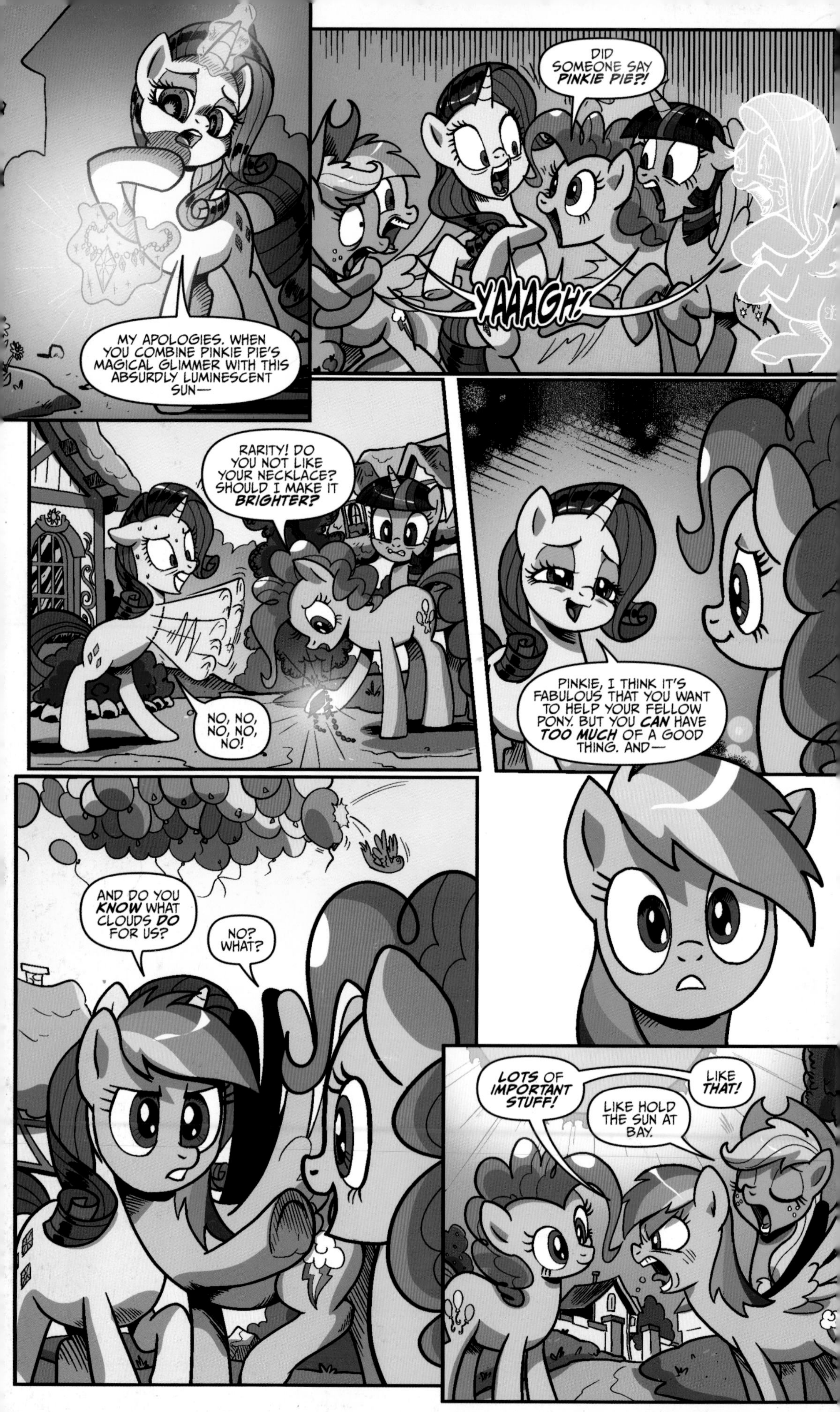

MY APOLOGIES. WHEN YOU COMBINE PINKIE PIE'S MAGICAL GLIMMER WITH THIS ABSURDLY LUMINESCENT SUN—
DID SOMEONE SAY PINKIE PIE?!
YAAAGH!
RARITY! DO YOU NOT LIKE YOUR NECKLACE? SHOULD I MAKE IT BRIGHTER?
NO, NO, NO, NO, NO!
PINKIE, I THINK IT'S FABULOUS THAT YOU WANT TO HELP YOUR FELLOW PONY. BUT YOU CAN HAVE TOO MUCH OF A GOOD THING. AND—
AND DO YOU KNOW WHAT CLOUDS DO FOR US?
NO? WHAT?
LOTS OF IMPORTANT STUFF!
LIKE HOLD THE SUN AT BAY.
LIKE THAT!

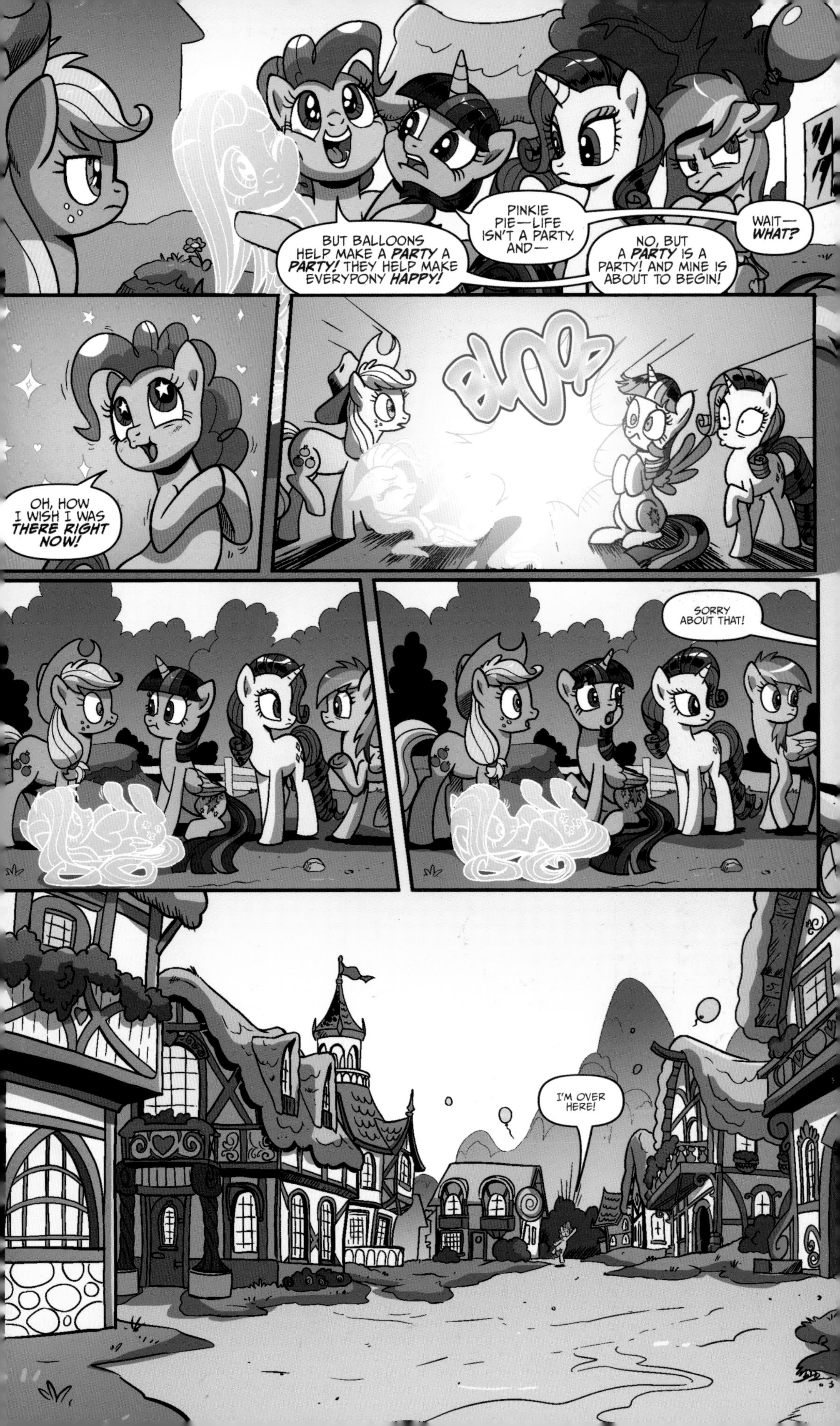
BUT BALLOONS HELP MAKE A **PARTY** A **PARTY!** THEY HELP MAKE EVERYPONY **HAPPY!**
PINKIE PIE—LIFE ISN'T A PARTY. AND—
NO, BUT A **PARTY** IS A PARTY! AND MINE IS ABOUT TO BEGIN!
WAIT— **WHAT?**
OH, HOW I WISH I WAS **THERE RIGHT NOW!**
BLOOP
SORRY ABOUT THAT!
I'M OVER HERE!

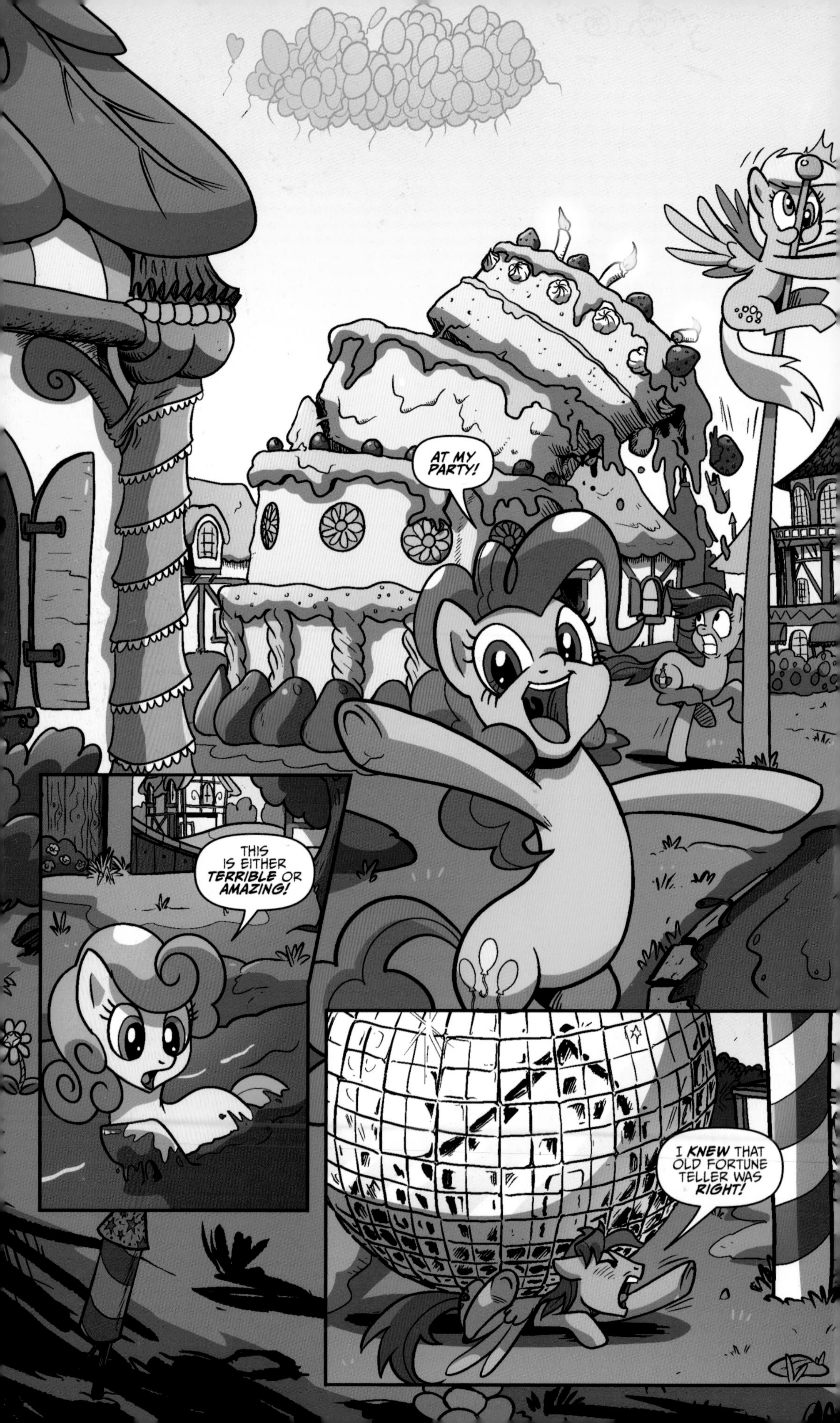
AT MY PARTY!
THIS IS EITHER TERRIBLE OR AMAZING!
I KNEW THAT OLD FORTUNE TELLER WAS RIGHT!

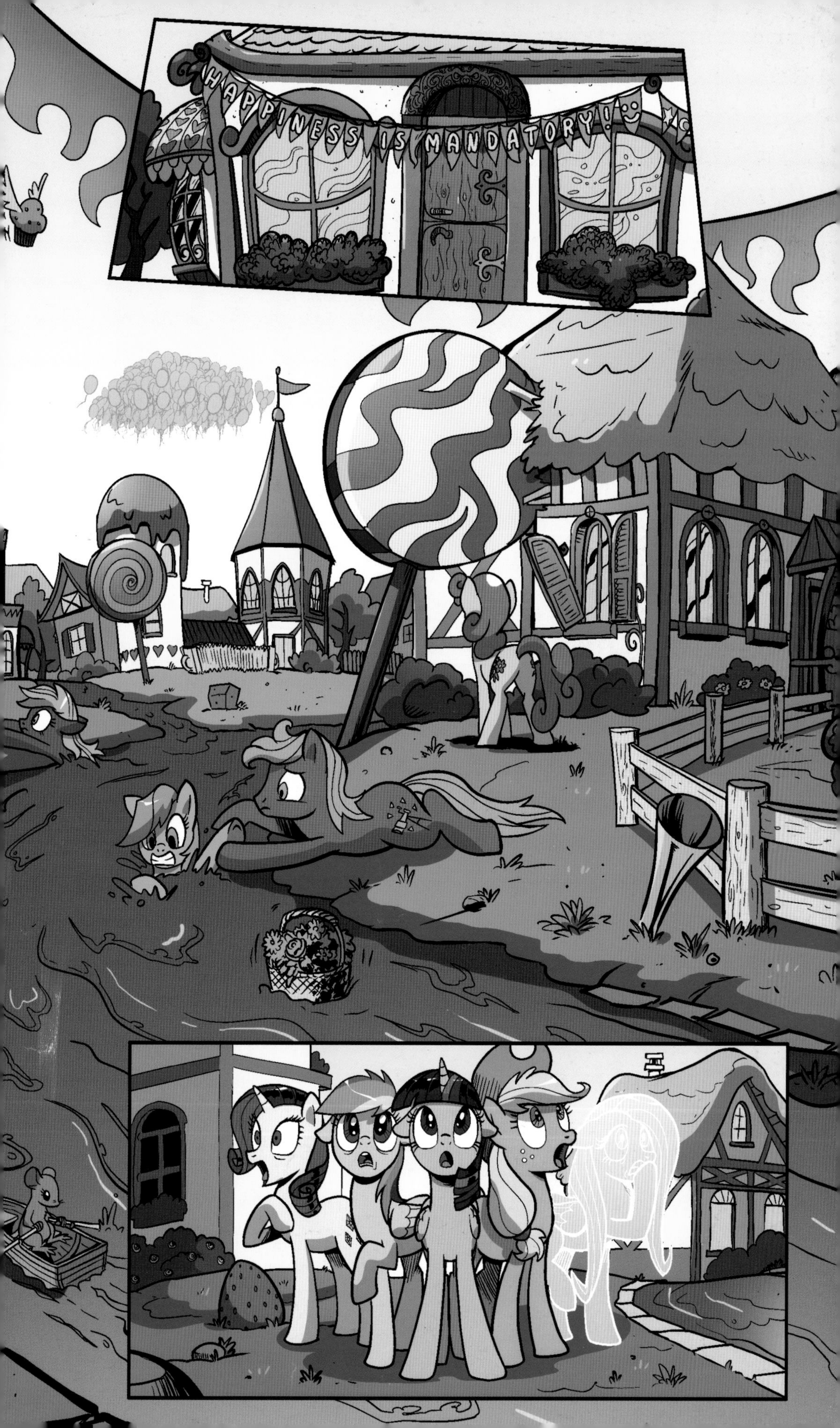
HAPPINESS IS MANDATORY!

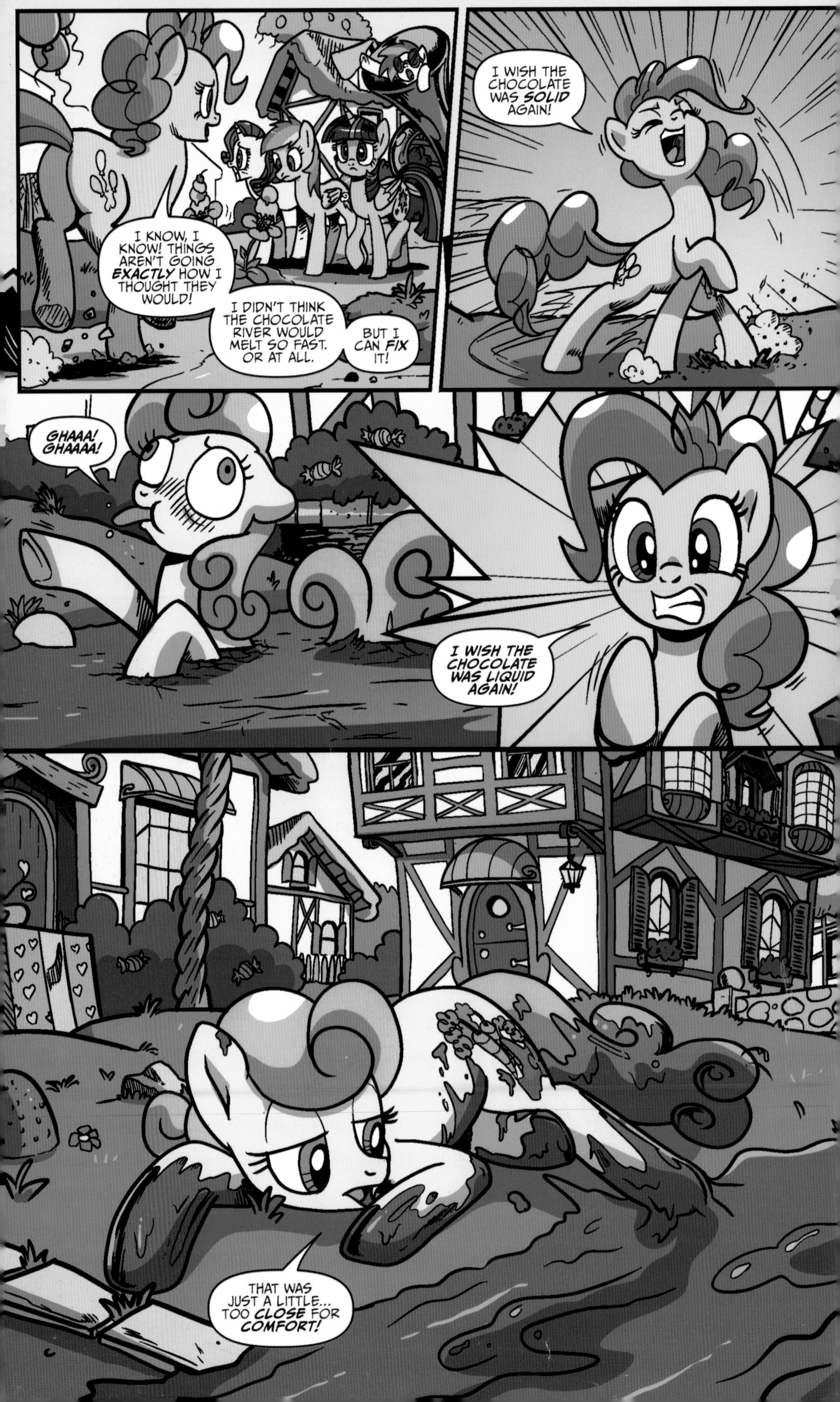
I KNOW, I KNOW! THINGS AREN'T GOING **EXACTLY** HOW I THOUGHT THEY WOULD!
I DIDN'T THINK THE CHOCOLATE RIVER WOULD MELT SO FAST. OR AT ALL.
BUT I CAN **FIX** IT!
I WISH THE CHOCOLATE WAS **SOLID** AGAIN!
GHAAA! GHAAAA!
I WISH THE CHOCOLATE WAS LIQUID AGAIN!
THAT WAS JUST A LITTLE... TOO **CLOSE** FOR **COMFORT!**

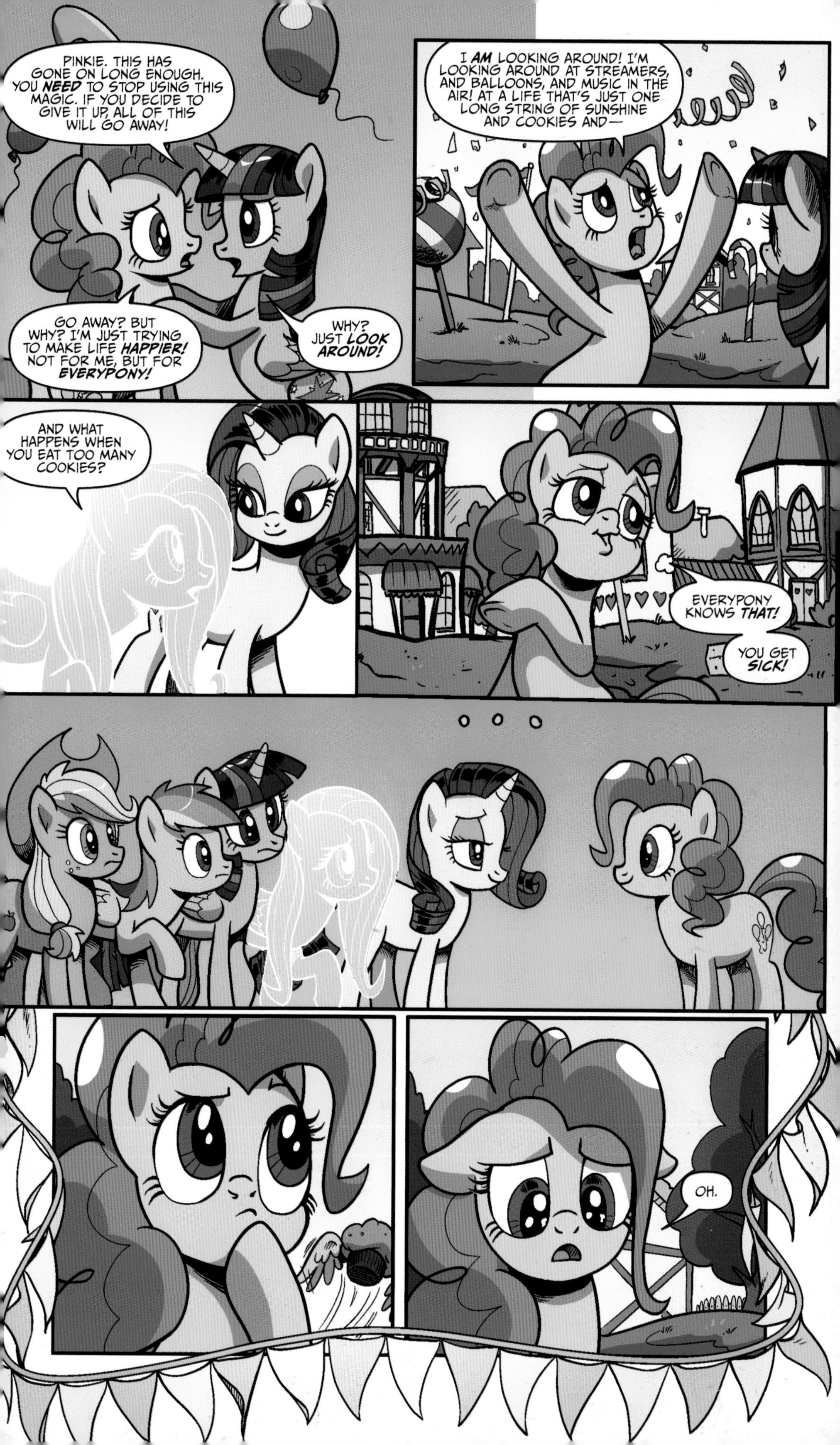
PINKIE. THIS HAS GONE ON LONG ENOUGH. YOU NEED TO STOP USING THIS MAGIC. IF YOU DECIDE TO GIVE IT UP, ALL OF THIS WILL GO AWAY!
GO AWAY? BUT WHY? I'M JUST TRYING TO MAKE LIFE HAPPIER! NOT FOR ME, BUT FOR EVERYPONY!
WHY? JUST LOOK AROUND!
I AM LOOKING AROUND! I'M LOOKING AROUND AT STREAMERS, AND BALLOONS, AND MUSIC IN THE AIR! AT A LIFE THAT'S JUST ONE LONG STRING OF SUNSHINE AND COOKIES AND—
AND WHAT HAPPENS WHEN YOU EAT TOO MANY COOKIES?
EVERYPONY KNOWS THAT!
YOU GET SICK!
OH.

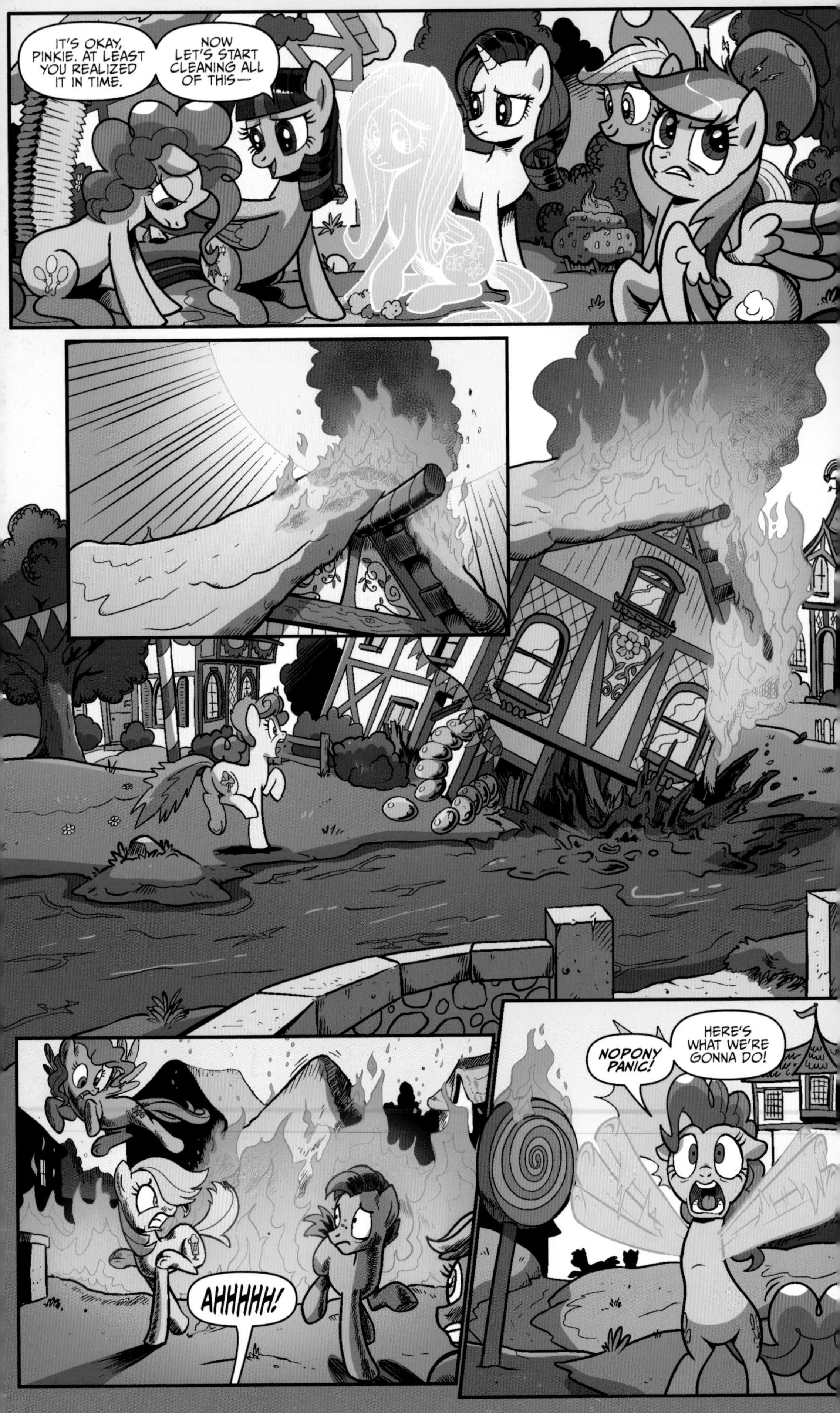
IT'S OKAY, PINKIE. AT LEAST YOU REALIZED IT IN TIME.
NOW LET'S START CLEANING ALL OF THIS—
AHHHHH!
NOPONY PANIC!
HERE'S WHAT WE'RE GONNA DO!

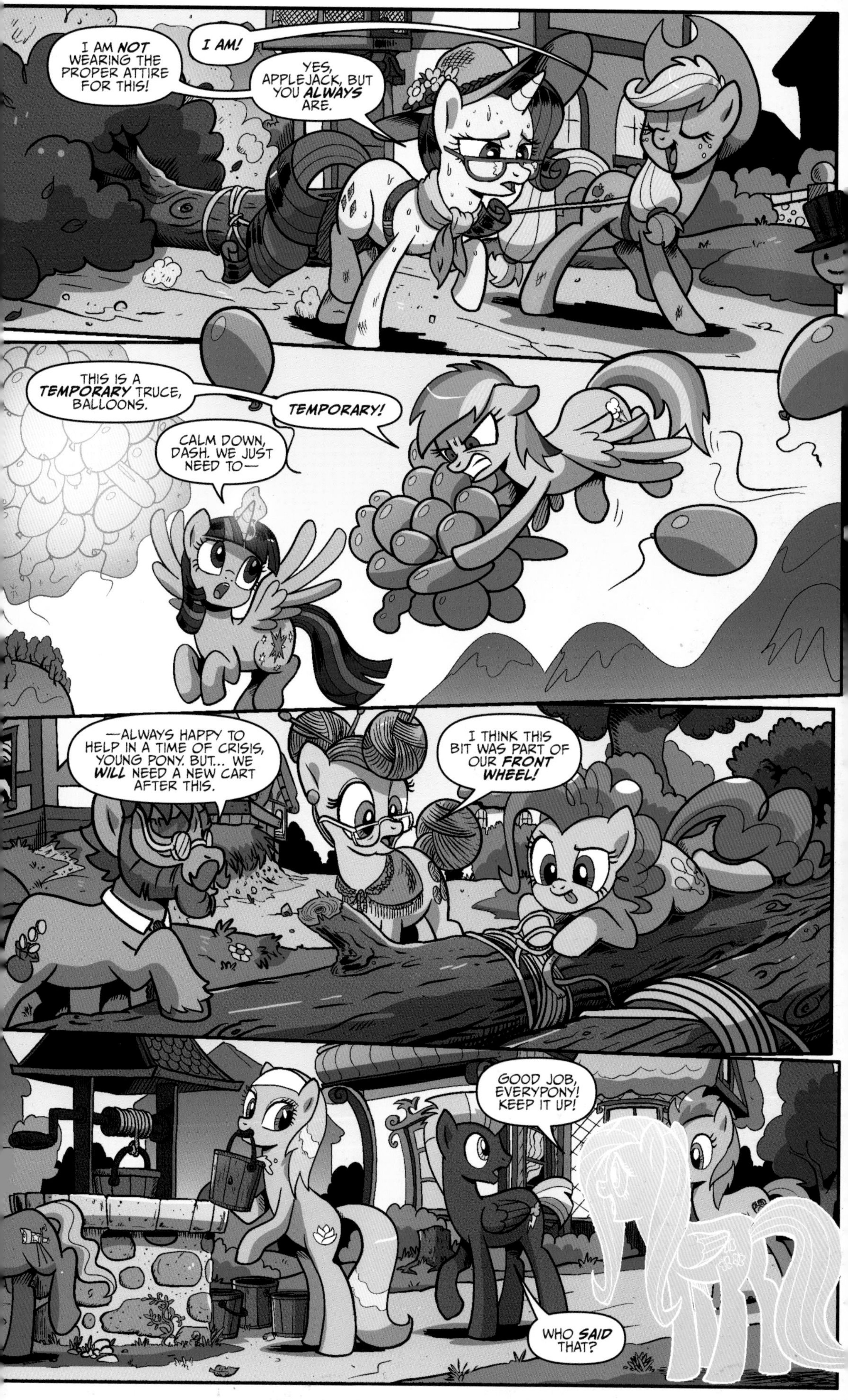

I AM NOT WEARING THE PROPER ATTIRE FOR THIS!
I AM!
YES, APPLEJACK, BUT YOU ALWAYS ARE.
THIS IS A TEMPORARY TRUCE, BALLOONS.
TEMPORARY!
CALM DOWN, DASH. WE JUST NEED TO—
—ALWAYS HAPPY TO HELP IN A TIME OF CRISIS, YOUNG PONY. BUT... WE WILL NEED A NEW CART AFTER THIS.
I THINK THIS BIT WAS PART OF OUR FRONT WHEEL!
GOOD JOB, EVERYPONY! KEEP IT UP!
WHO SAID THAT?

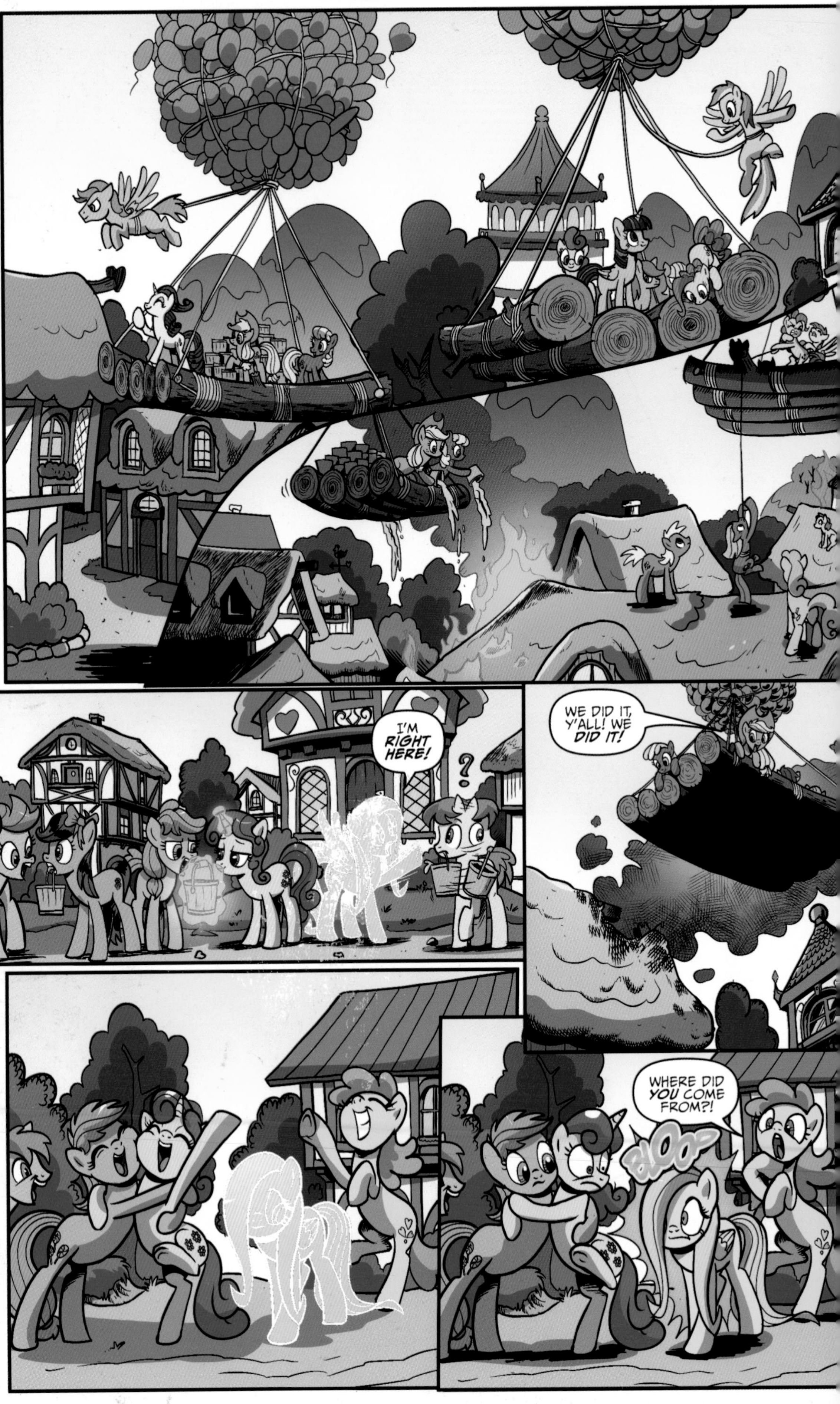
I'M RIGHT HERE!
?
WE DID IT, Y'ALL! WE DID IT!
BLOOP
WHERE DID YOU COME FROM?!

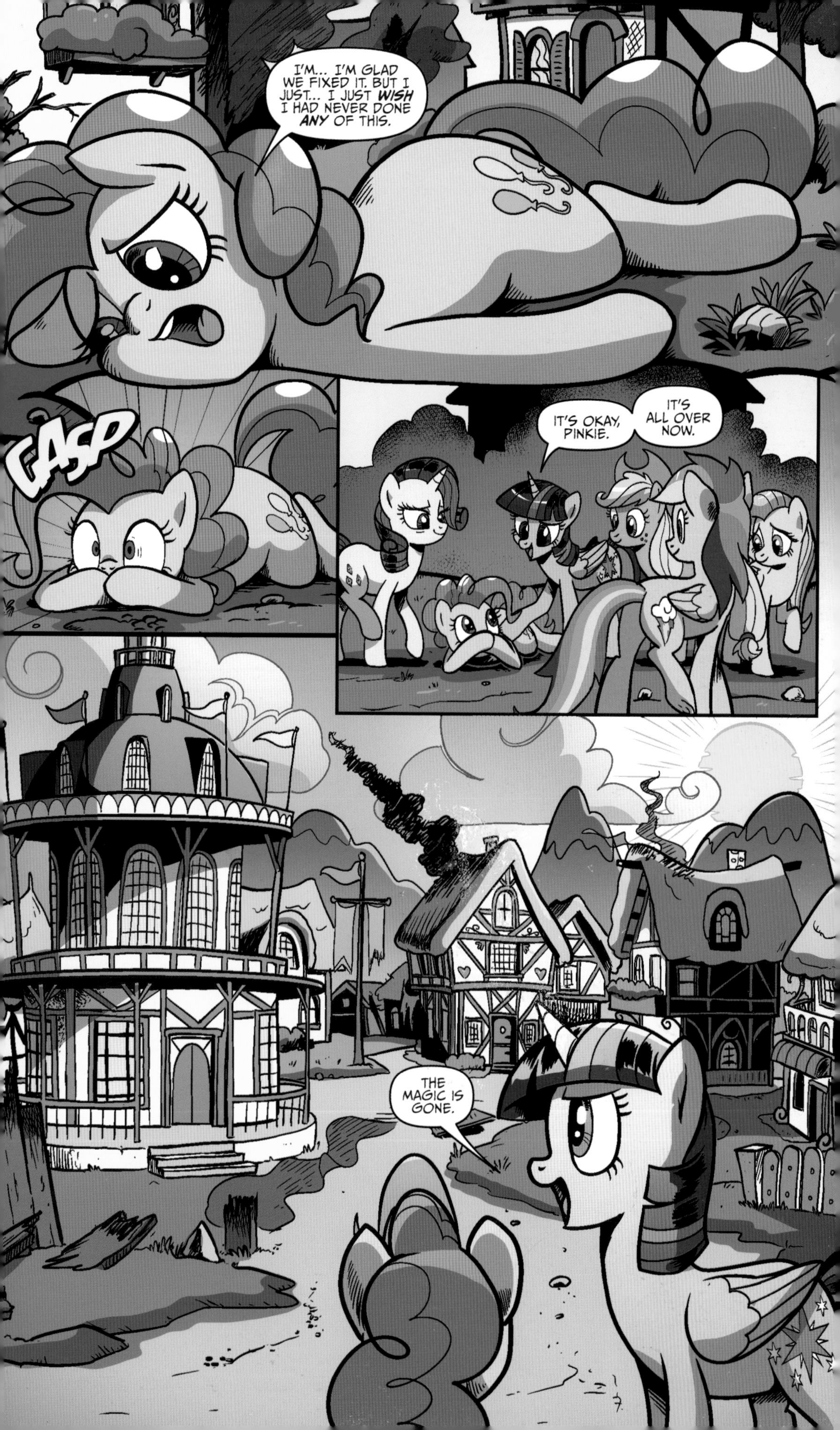
I'M... I'M GLAD WE FIXED IT. BUT I JUST... I JUST WISH I HAD NEVER DONE ANY OF THIS.
GASP
IT'S OKAY, PINKIE.
IT'S ALL OVER NOW.
THE MAGIC IS GONE.

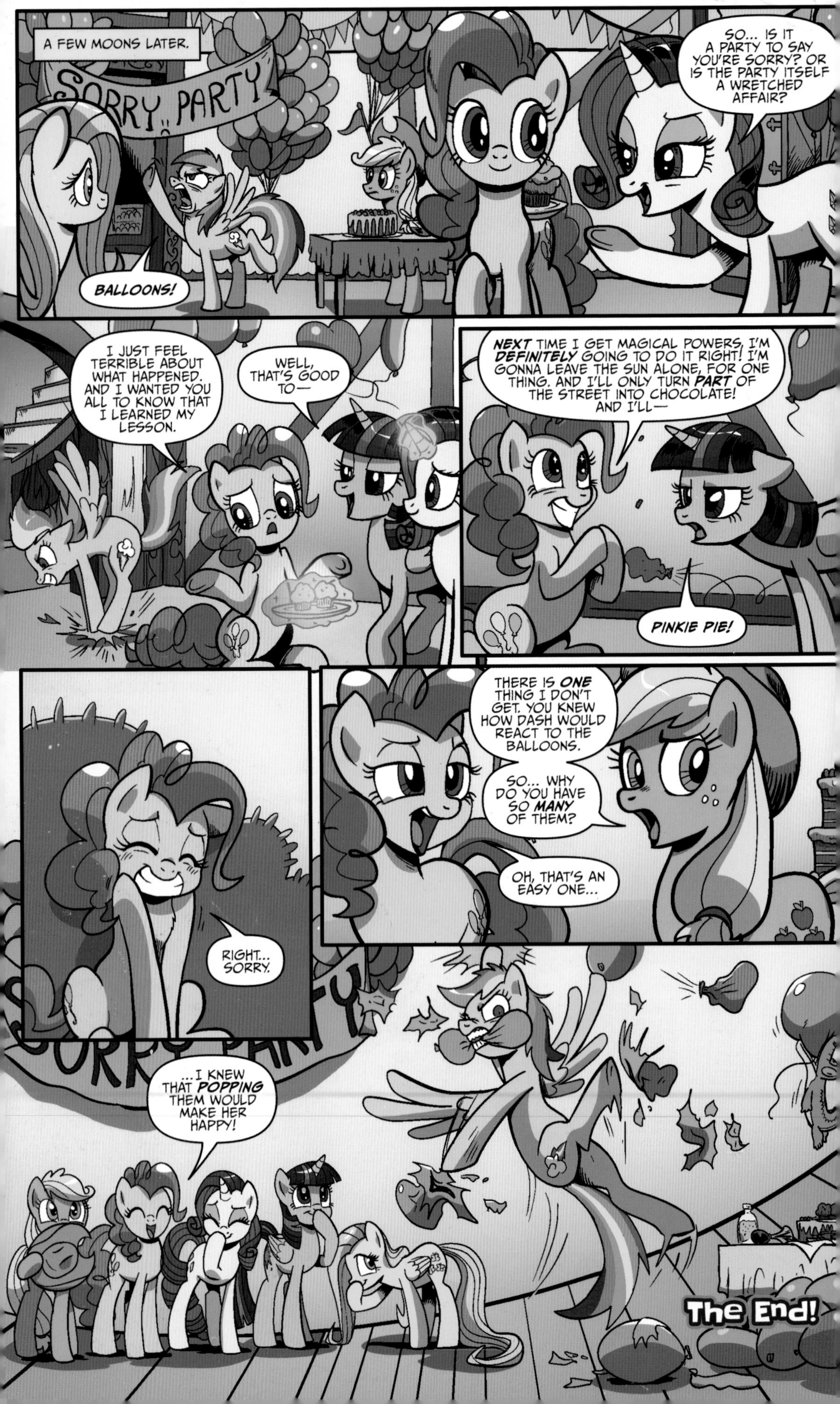
A FEW MOONS LATER.
SORRY PARTY
SO... IS IT A PARTY TO SAY YOU'RE SORRY? OR IS THE PARTY ITSELF A WRETCHED AFFAIR?
BALLOONS!
I JUST FEEL TERRIBLE ABOUT WHAT HAPPENED. AND I WANTED YOU ALL TO KNOW THAT I LEARNED MY LESSON.
WELL, THAT'S GOOD TO—
NEXT TIME I GET MAGICAL POWERS, I'M DEFINITELY GOING TO DO IT RIGHT! I'M GONNA LEAVE THE SUN ALONE, FOR ONE THING. AND I'LL ONLY TURN PART OF THE STREET INTO CHOCOLATE! AND I'LL—
PINKIE PIE!
RIGHT... SORRY.
THERE IS ONE THING I DON'T GET. YOU KNEW HOW DASH WOULD REACT TO THE BALLOONS.
SO... WHY DO YOU HAVE SO MANY OF THEM?
OH, THAT'S AN EASY ONE...
...I KNEW THAT POPPING THEM WOULD MAKE HER HAPPY!
The End!

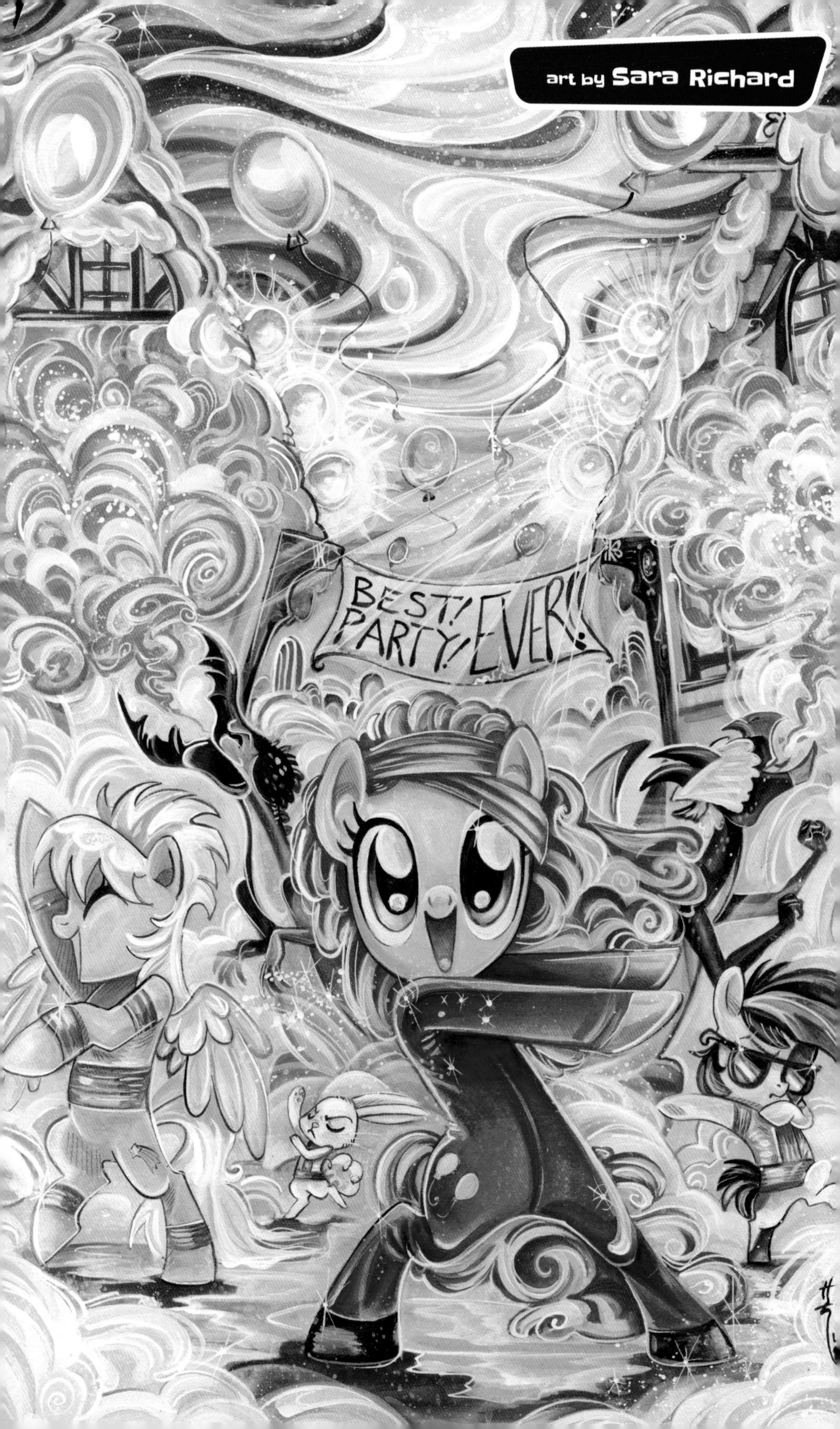
art by Sara Richard
BEST! PARTY! EVER!

art by Toni Kuusisto

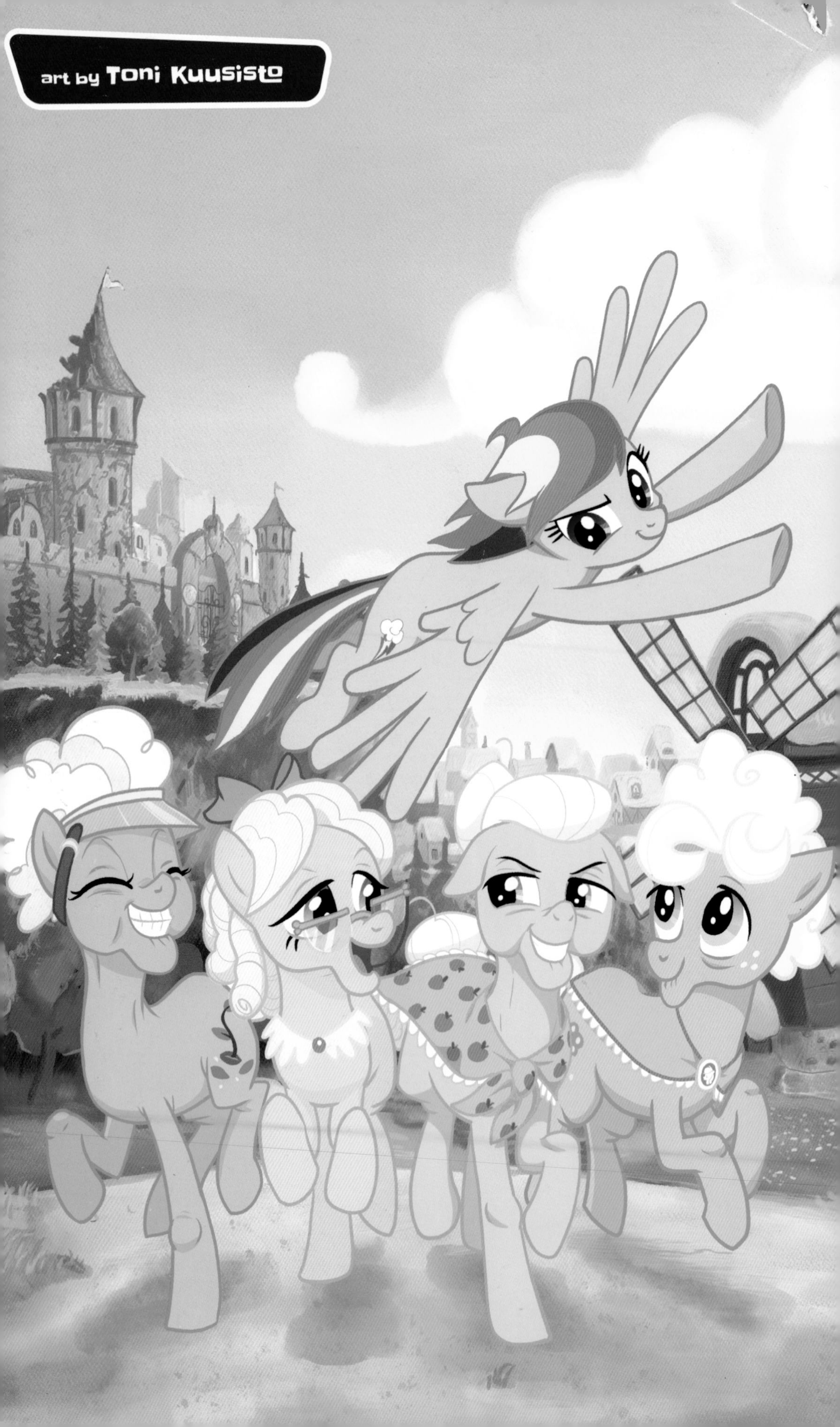

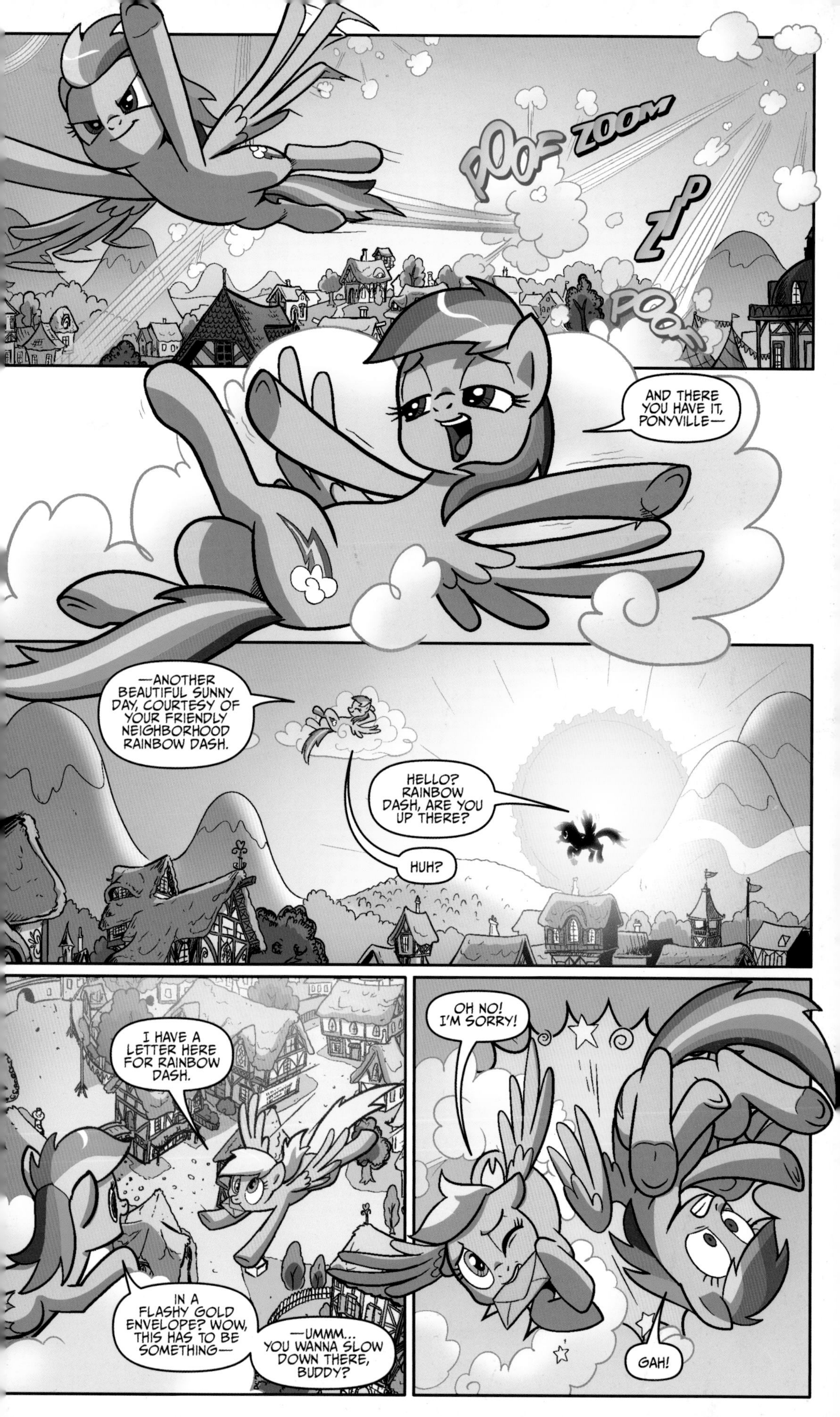
POOF
ZOOM
ZIP
POOF
AND THERE YOU HAVE IT, PONYVILLE—
—ANOTHER BEAUTIFUL SUNNY DAY, COURTESY OF YOUR FRIENDLY NEIGHBORHOOD RAINBOW DASH.
HELLO? RAINBOW DASH, ARE YOU UP THERE?
HUH?
I HAVE A LETTER HERE FOR RAINBOW DASH.
IN A FLASHY GOLD ENVELOPE? WOW, THIS HAS TO BE SOMETHING—
—UMMM... YOU WANNA SLOW DOWN THERE, BUDDY?
OH NO! I'M SORRY!
GAH!

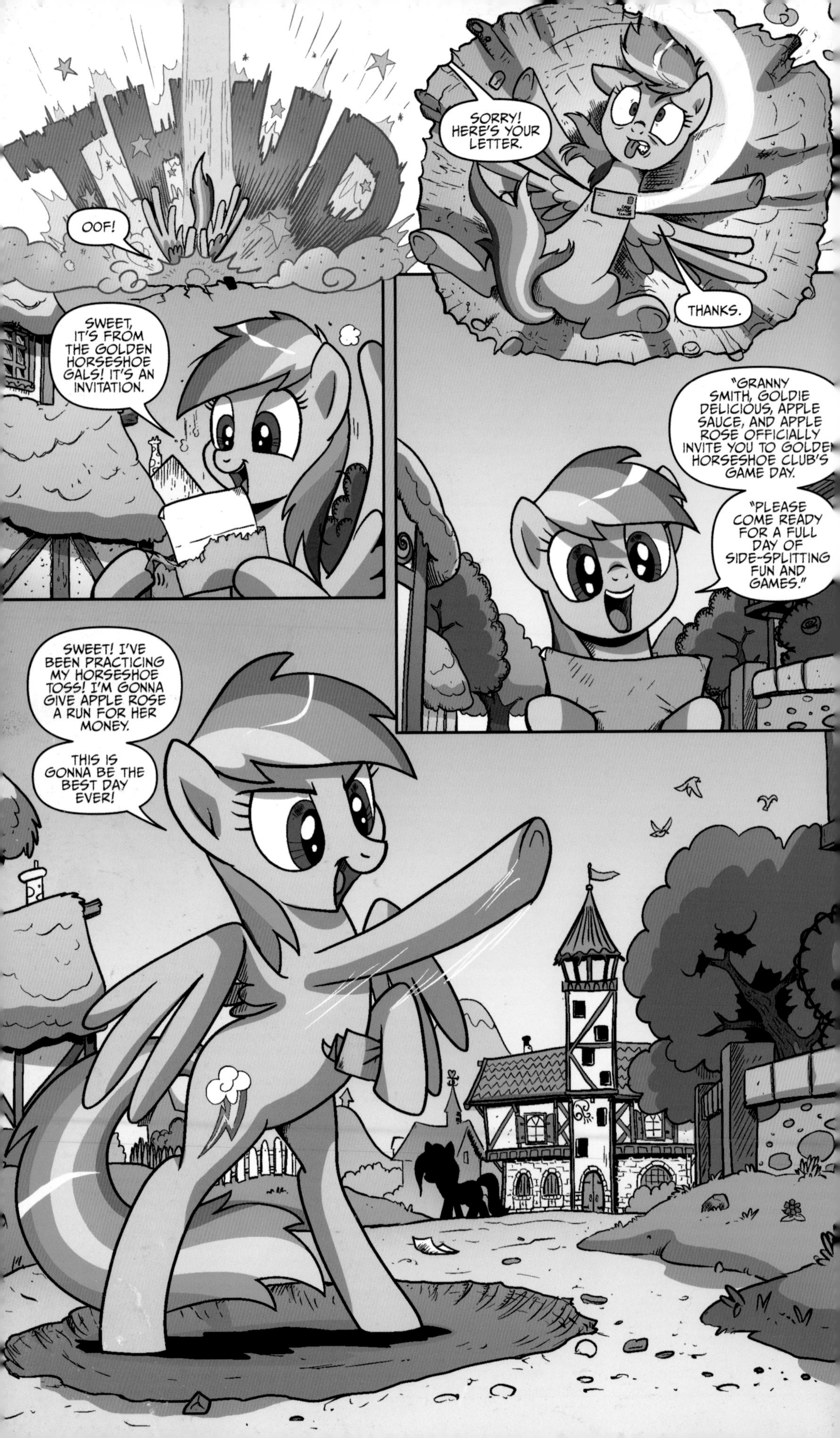
THUD
OOF!
SORRY! HERE'S YOUR LETTER.
THANKS.
SWEET, IT'S FROM THE GOLDEN HORSESHOE GALS! IT'S AN INVITATION.
"GRANNY SMITH, GOLDIE DELICIOUS, APPLE SAUCE, AND APPLE ROSE OFFICIALLY INVITE YOU TO GOLDE HORSESHOE CLUB'S GAME DAY.
"PLEASE COME READY FOR A FULL DAY OF SIDE-SPLITTING FUN AND GAMES."
SWEET! I'VE BEEN PRACTICING MY HORSESHOE TOSS! I'M GONNA GIVE APPLE ROSE A RUN FOR HER MONEY.
THIS IS GONNA BE THE BEST DAY EVER!

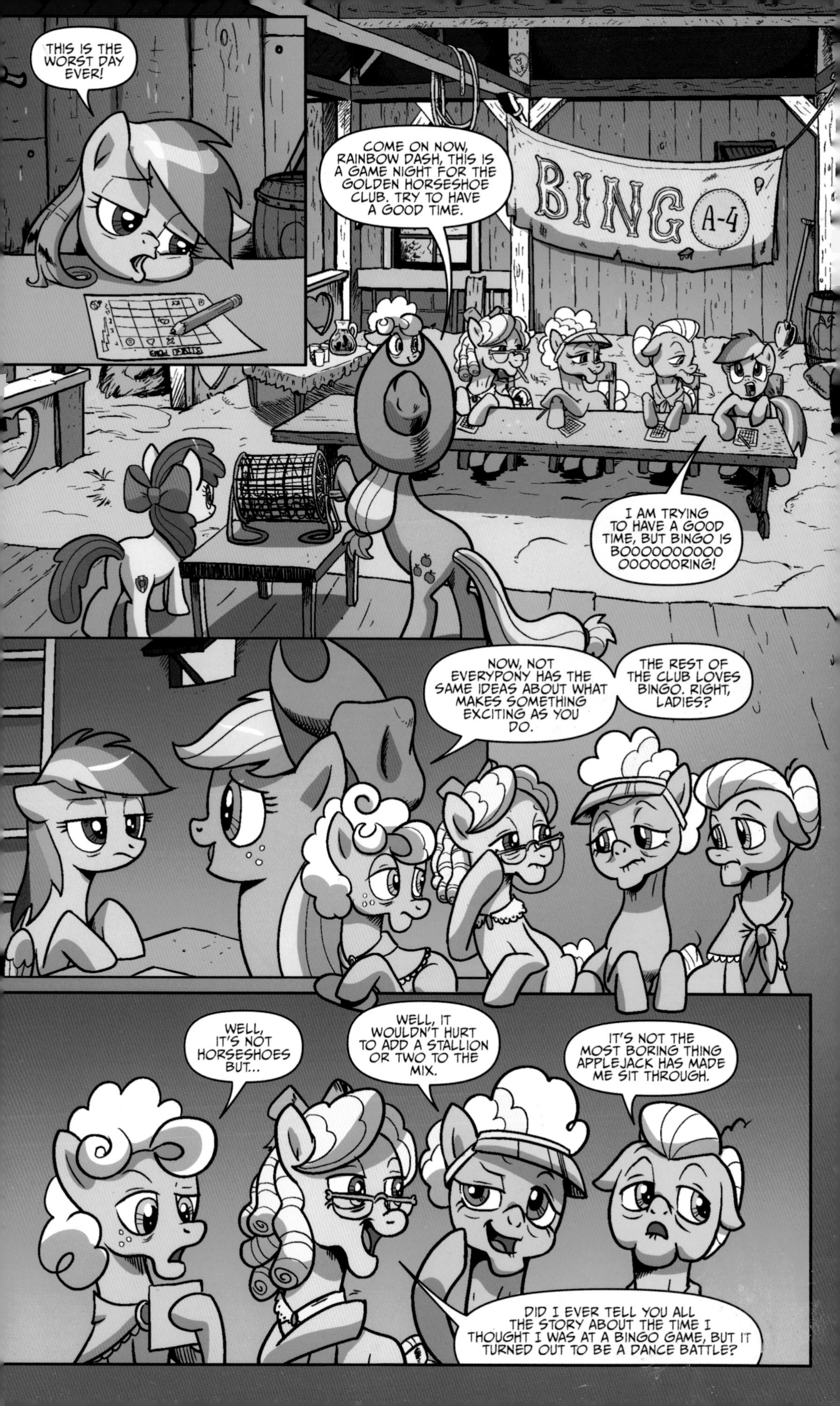
THIS IS THE WORST DAY EVER!
COME ON NOW, RAINBOW DASH, THIS IS A GAME NIGHT FOR THE GOLDEN HORSESHOE CLUB. TRY TO HAVE A GOOD TIME.
BINGO A-4
I AM TRYING TO HAVE A GOOD TIME, BUT BINGO IS BOOOOOOOOOOOOOOOORING!
NOW, NOT EVERYPONY HAS THE SAME IDEAS ABOUT WHAT MAKES SOMETHING EXCITING AS YOU DO.
THE REST OF THE CLUB LOVES BINGO. RIGHT, LADIES?
WELL, IT'S NOT HORSESHOES BUT...
WELL, IT WOULDN'T HURT TO ADD A STALLION OR TWO TO THE MIX.
IT'S NOT THE MOST BORING THING APPLEJACK HAS MADE ME SIT THROUGH.
DID I EVER TELL YOU ALL THE STORY ABOUT THE TIME I THOUGHT I WAS AT A BINGO GAME, BUT IT TURNED OUT TO BE A DANCE BATTLE?

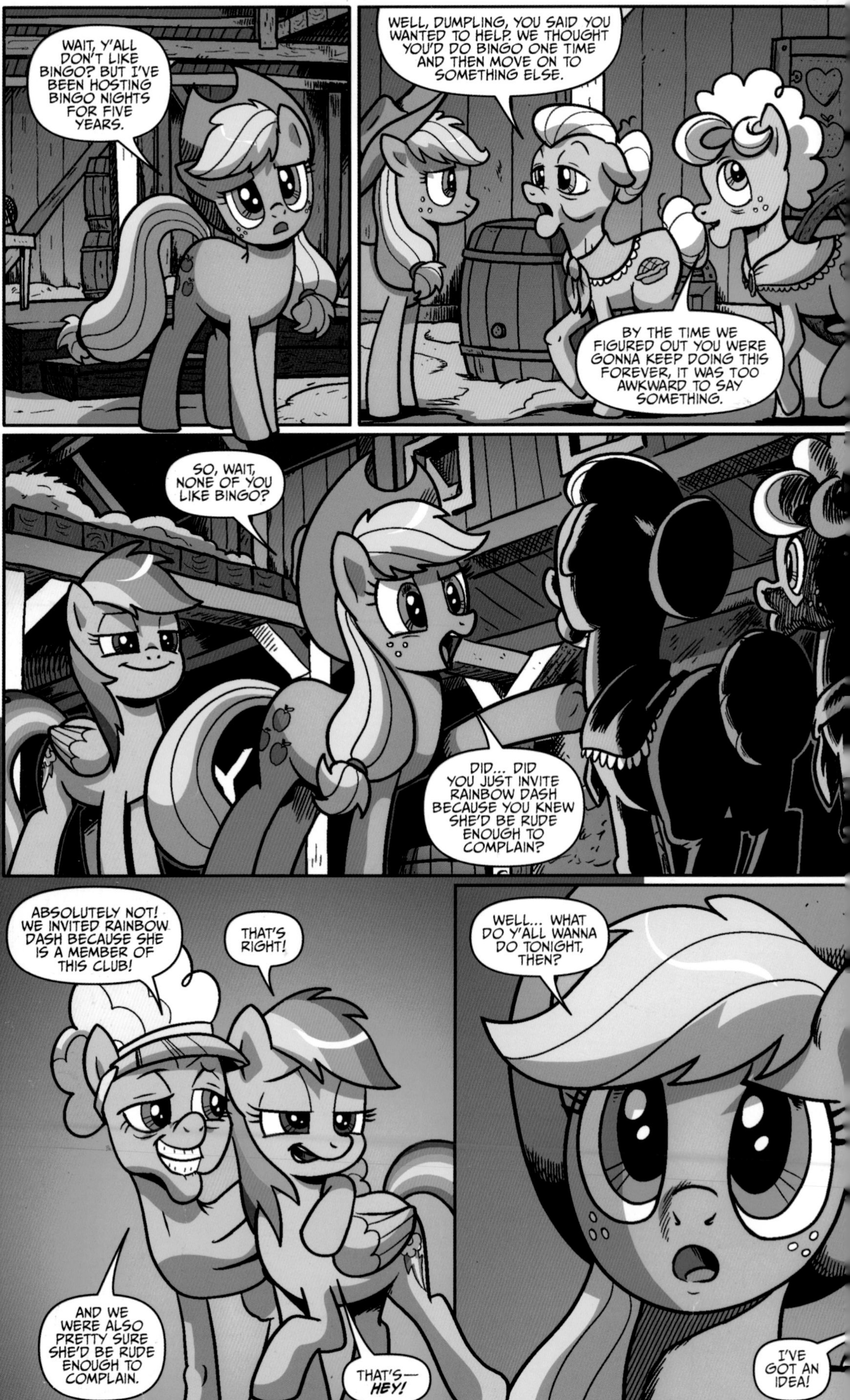
WAIT, Y'ALL DON'T LIKE BINGO? BUT I'VE BEEN HOSTING BINGO NIGHTS FOR FIVE YEARS.
WELL, DUMPLING, YOU SAID YOU WANTED TO HELP. WE THOUGHT YOU'D DO BINGO ONE TIME AND THEN MOVE ON TO SOMETHING ELSE.
BY THE TIME WE FIGURED OUT YOU WERE GONNA KEEP DOING THIS FOREVER, IT WAS TOO AWKWARD TO SAY SOMETHING.
SO, WAIT, NONE OF YOU LIKE BINGO?
DID... DID YOU JUST INVITE RAINBOW DASH BECAUSE YOU KNEW SHE'D BE RUDE ENOUGH TO COMPLAIN?
ABSOLUTELY NOT! WE INVITED RAINBOW DASH BECAUSE SHE IS A MEMBER OF THIS CLUB!
THAT'S RIGHT!
AND WE WERE ALSO PRETTY SURE SHE'D BE RUDE ENOUGH TO COMPLAIN.
THAT'S— HEY!
WELL... WHAT DO Y'ALL WANNA DO TONIGHT, THEN?
I'VE GOT AN IDEA!

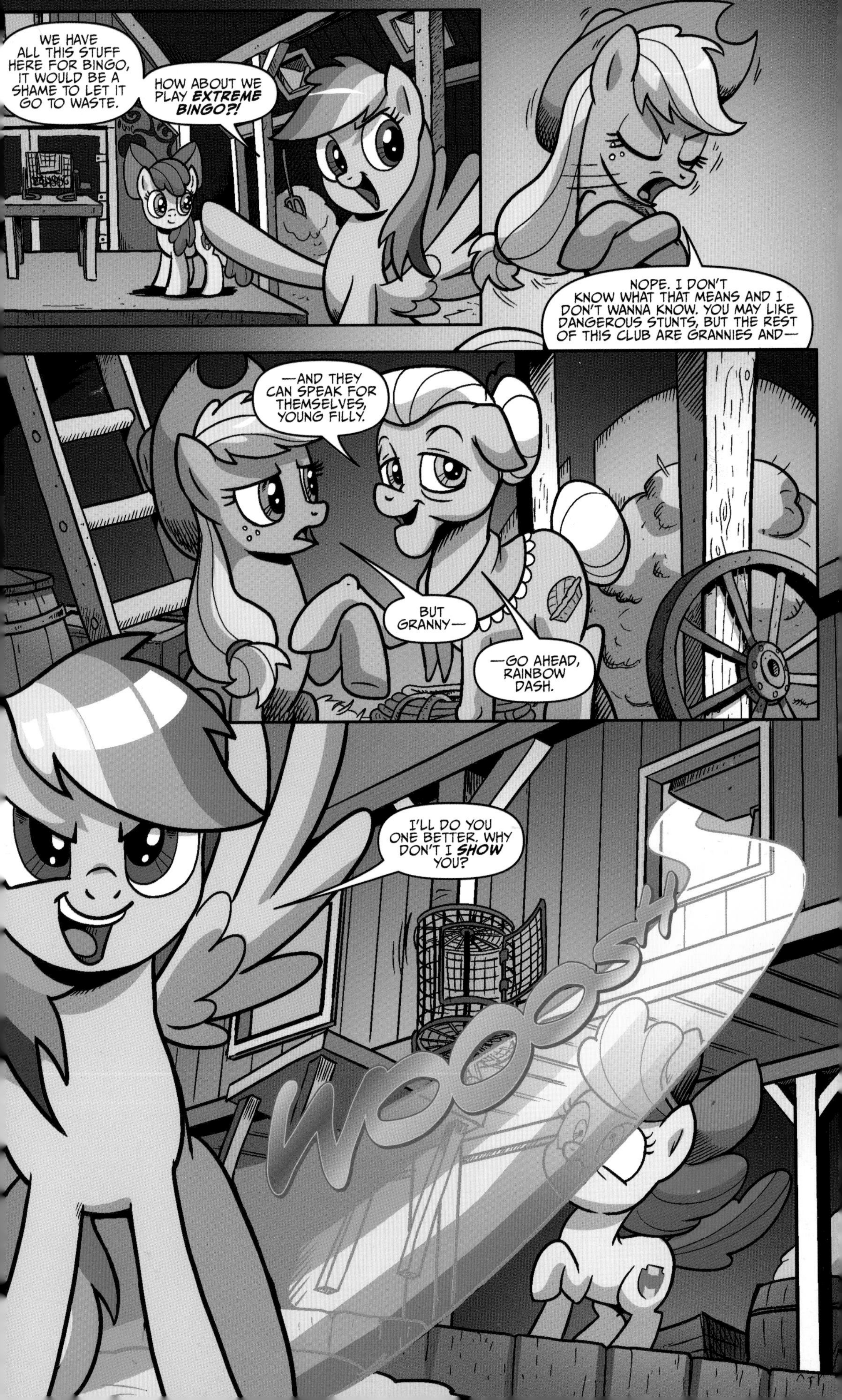

WE HAVE ALL THIS STUFF HERE FOR BINGO, IT WOULD BE A SHAME TO LET IT GO TO WASTE.
HOW ABOUT WE PLAY EXTREME BINGO?!
NOPE. I DON'T KNOW WHAT THAT MEANS AND I DON'T WANNA KNOW. YOU MAY LIKE DANGEROUS STUNTS, BUT THE REST OF THIS CLUB ARE GRANNIES AND—
—AND THEY CAN SPEAK FOR THEMSELVES, YOUNG FILLY.
BUT GRANNY—
—GO AHEAD, RAINBOW DASH.
I'LL DO YOU ONE BETTER. WHY DON'T I SHOW YOU?
WOOOOSH

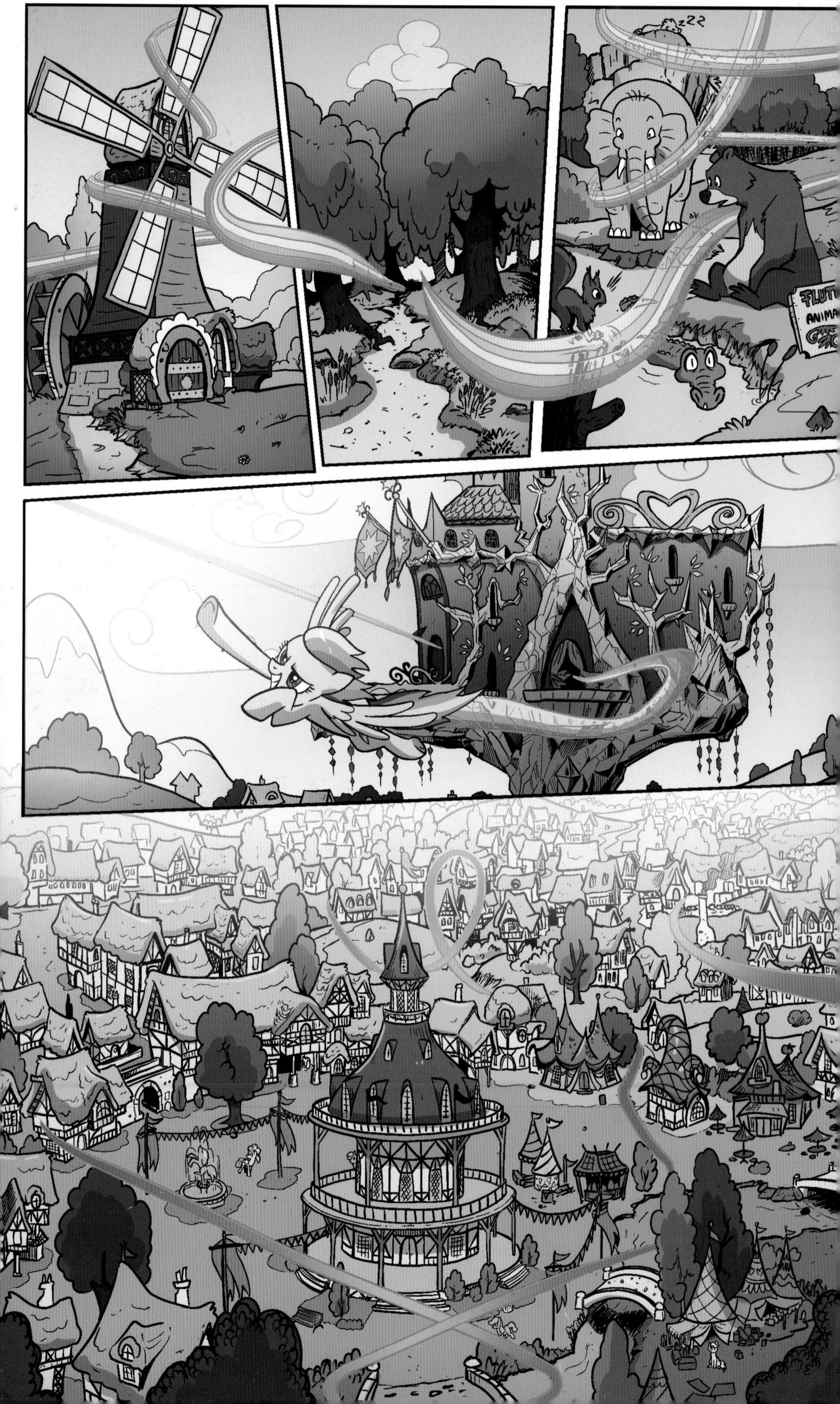
zzz

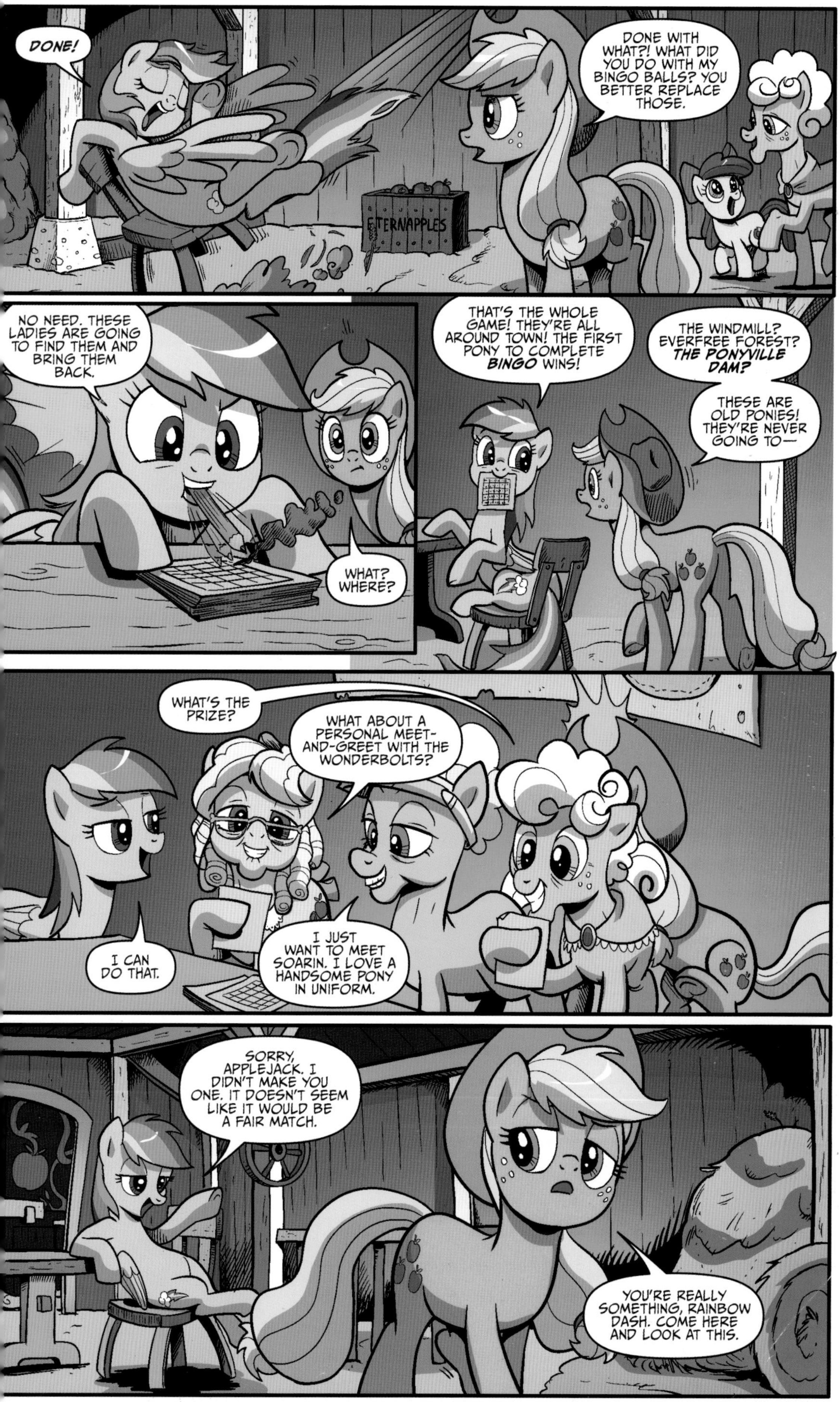
DONE!
DONE WITH WHAT?! WHAT DID YOU DO WITH MY BINGO BALLS? YOU BETTER REPLACE THOSE.
ETERNAPPLES
NO NEED. THESE LADIES ARE GOING TO FIND THEM AND BRING THEM BACK.
WHAT? WHERE?
THAT'S THE WHOLE GAME! THEY'RE ALL AROUND TOWN! THE FIRST PONY TO COMPLETE BINGO WINS!
THE WINDMILL? EVERFREE FOREST? THE PONYVILLE DAM?
THESE ARE OLD PONIES! THEY'RE NEVER GOING TO—
WHAT'S THE PRIZE?
WHAT ABOUT A PERSONAL MEET-AND-GREET WITH THE WONDERBOLTS?
I CAN DO THAT.
I JUST WANT TO MEET SOARIN. I LOVE A HANDSOME PONY IN UNIFORM.
SORRY, APPLEJACK. I DIDN'T MAKE YOU ONE. IT DOESN'T SEEM LIKE IT WOULD BE A FAIR MATCH.
YOU'RE REALLY SOMETHING, RAINBOW DASH. COME HERE AND LOOK AT THIS.

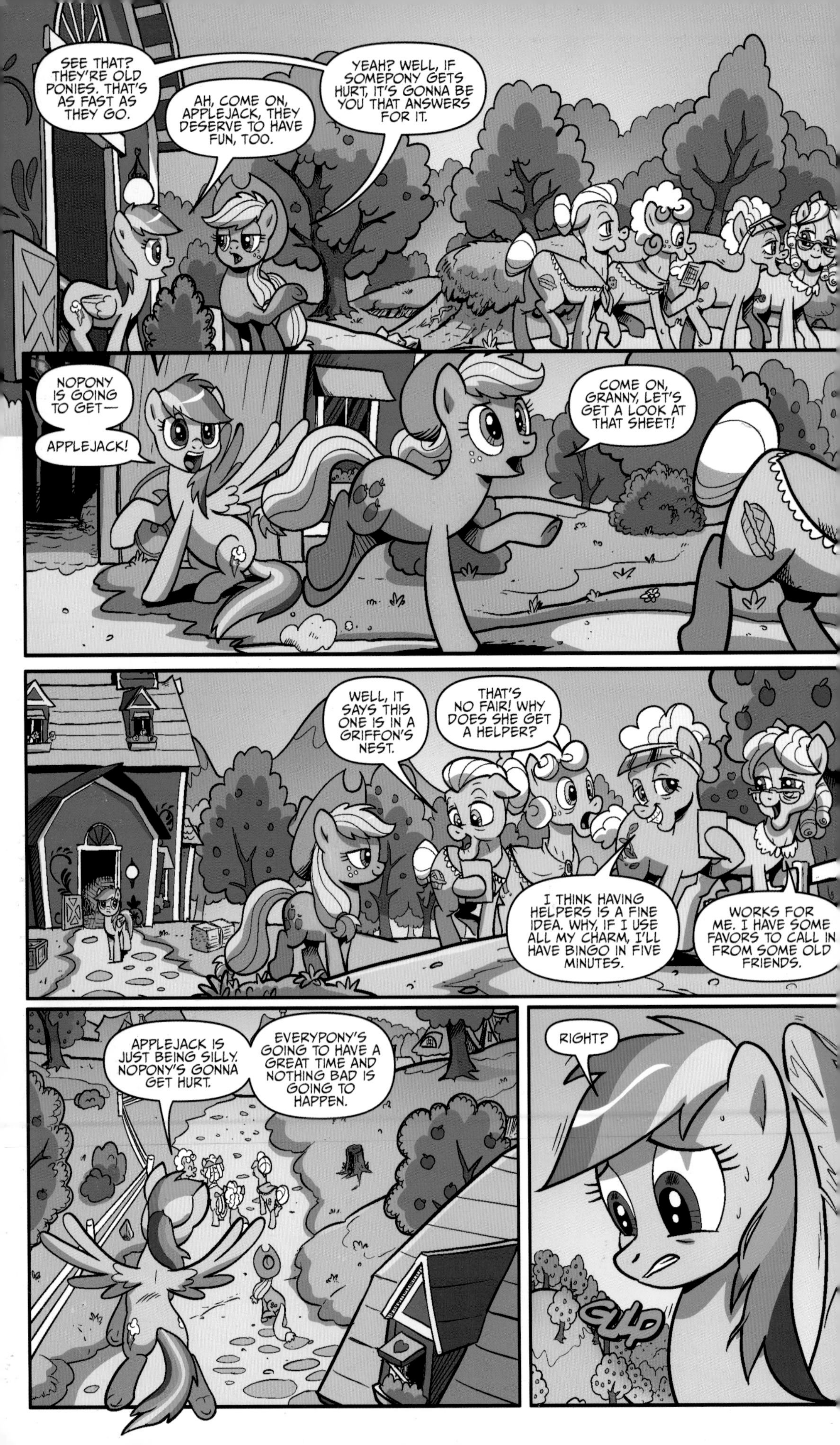

SEE THAT? THEY'RE OLD PONIES. THAT'S AS FAST AS THEY GO.
AH, COME ON, APPLEJACK, THEY DESERVE TO HAVE FUN, TOO.
YEAH? WELL, IF SOMEPONY GETS HURT, IT'S GONNA BE YOU THAT ANSWERS FOR IT.
NOPONY IS GOING TO GET—
APPLEJACK!
COME ON, GRANNY, LET'S GET A LOOK AT THAT SHEET!
WELL, IT SAYS THIS ONE IS IN A GRIFFON'S NEST.
THAT'S NO FAIR! WHY DOES SHE GET A HELPER?
I THINK HAVING HELPERS IS A FINE IDEA. WHY, IF I USE ALL MY CHARM, I'LL HAVE BINGO IN FIVE MINUTES.
WORKS FOR ME. I HAVE SOME FAVORS TO CALL IN FROM SOME OLD FRIENDS.
APPLEJACK IS JUST BEING SILLY. NOPONY'S GONNA GET HURT.
EVERYPONY'S GOING TO HAVE A GREAT TIME AND NOTHING BAD IS GOING TO HAPPEN.
RIGHT?
GULP

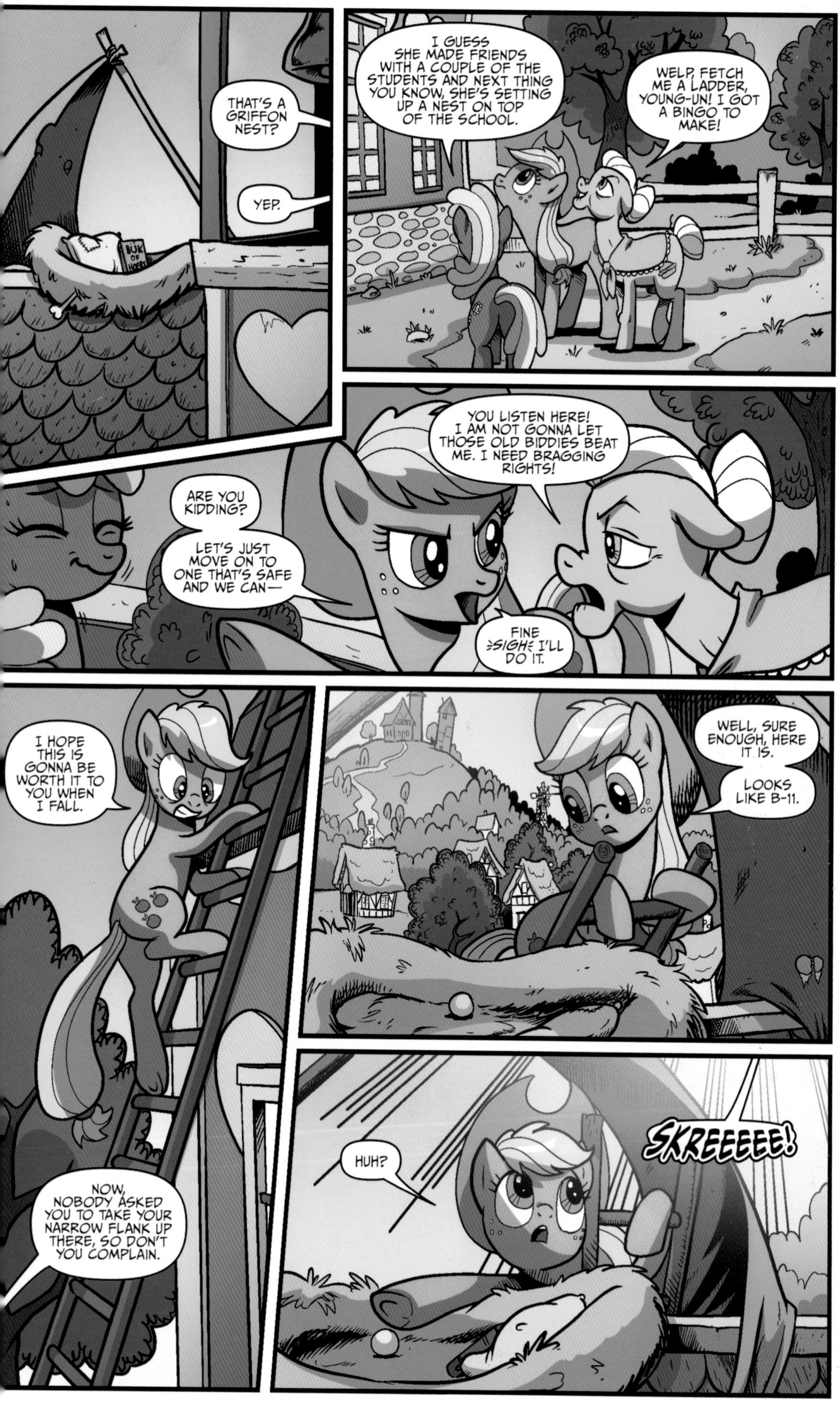
THAT'S A GRIFFON NEST?
YEP.
I GUESS SHE MADE FRIENDS WITH A COUPLE OF THE STUDENTS AND NEXT THING YOU KNOW, SHE'S SETTING UP A NEST ON TOP OF THE SCHOOL.
WELP, FETCH ME A LADDER, YOUNG-UN! I GOT A BINGO TO MAKE!
ARE YOU KIDDING?
LET'S JUST MOVE ON TO ONE THAT'S SAFE AND WE CAN—
YOU LISTEN HERE! I AM NOT GONNA LET THOSE OLD BIDDIES BEAT ME. I NEED BRAGGING RIGHTS!
FINE *SIGH* I'LL DO IT.
I HOPE THIS IS GONNA BE WORTH IT TO YOU WHEN I FALL.
NOW, NOBODY ASKED YOU TO TAKE YOUR NARROW FLANK UP THERE, SO DON'T YOU COMPLAIN.
WELL, SURE ENOUGH, HERE IT IS.
LOOKS LIKE B-11.
SKREEEEEE!
HUH?

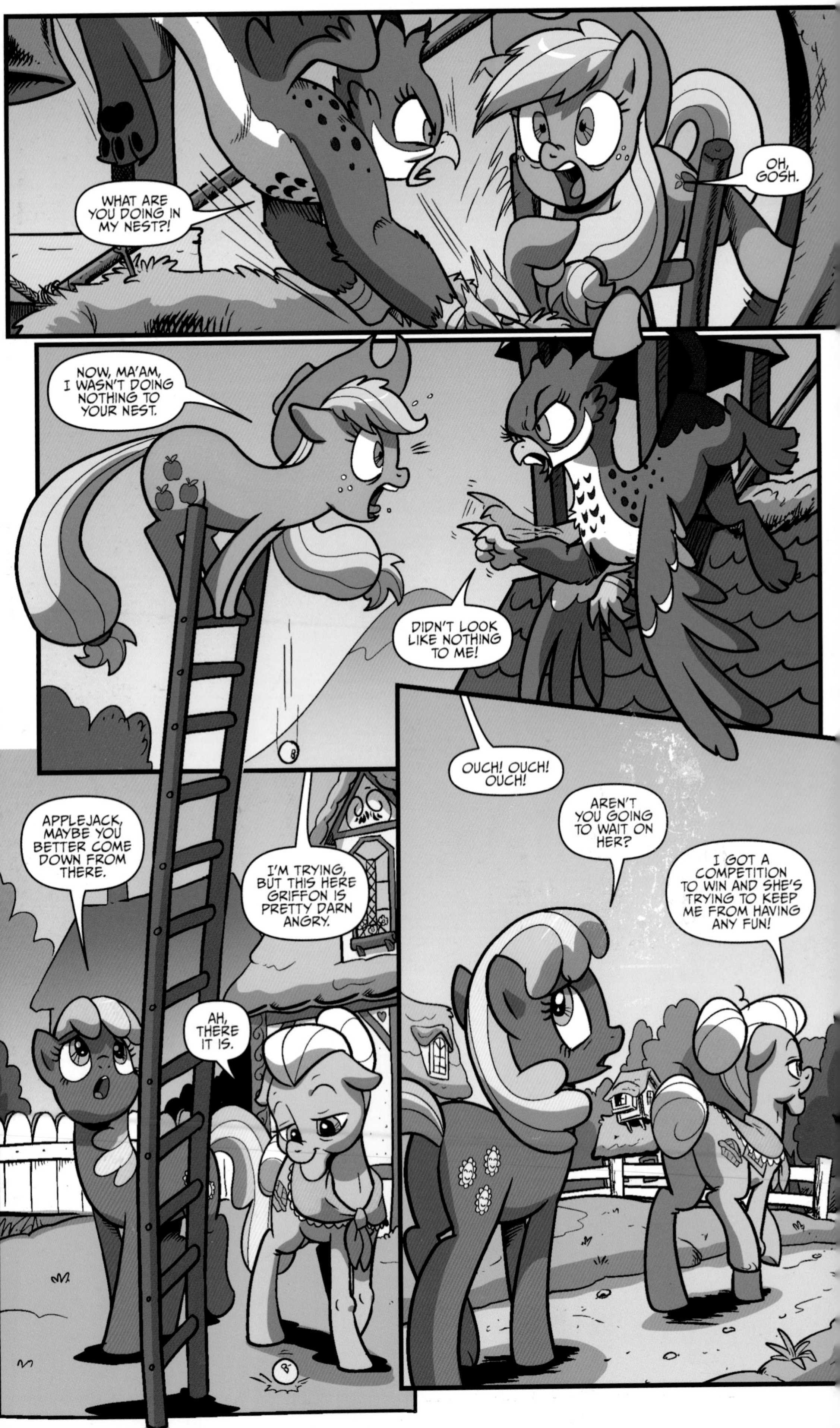
WHAT ARE YOU DOING IN MY NEST?!
OH, GOSH.
NOW, MA'AM, I WASN'T DOING NOTHING TO YOUR NEST.
DIDN'T LOOK LIKE NOTHING TO ME!
APPLEJACK, MAYBE YOU BETTER COME DOWN FROM THERE.
I'M TRYING, BUT THIS HERE GRIFFON IS PRETTY DARN ANGRY.
AH, THERE IT IS.
OUCH! OUCH! OUCH!
AREN'T YOU GOING TO WAIT ON HER?
I GOT A COMPETITION TO WIN AND SHE'S TRYING TO KEEP ME FROM HAVING ANY FUN!

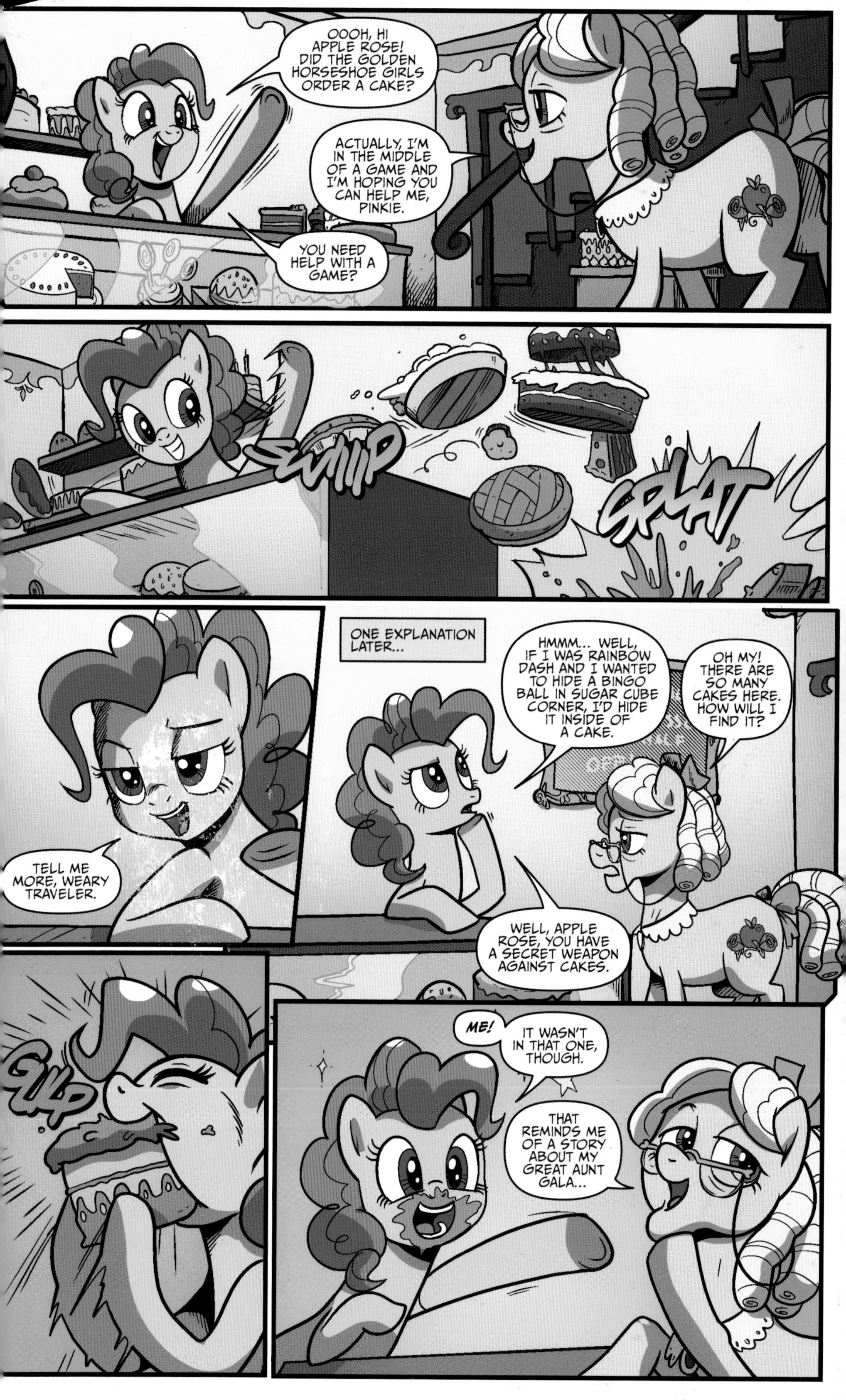
OOOH, HI APPLE ROSE! DID THE GOLDEN HORSESHOE GIRLS ORDER A CAKE?
ACTUALLY, I'M IN THE MIDDLE OF A GAME AND I'M HOPING YOU CAN HELP ME, PINKIE.
YOU NEED HELP WITH A GAME?
SWIIIP
SPLAT
TELL ME MORE, WEARY TRAVELER.
ONE EXPLANATION LATER...
HMMM... WELL, IF I WAS RAINBOW DASH AND I WANTED TO HIDE A BINGO BALL IN SUGAR CUBE CORNER, I'D HIDE IT INSIDE OF A CAKE.
OH MY! THERE ARE SO MANY CAKES HERE. HOW WILL I FIND IT?
WELL, APPLE ROSE, YOU HAVE A SECRET WEAPON AGAINST CAKES.
GULP
ME!
IT WASN'T IN THAT ONE, THOUGH.
THAT REMINDS ME OF A STORY ABOUT MY GREAT AUNT GALA...

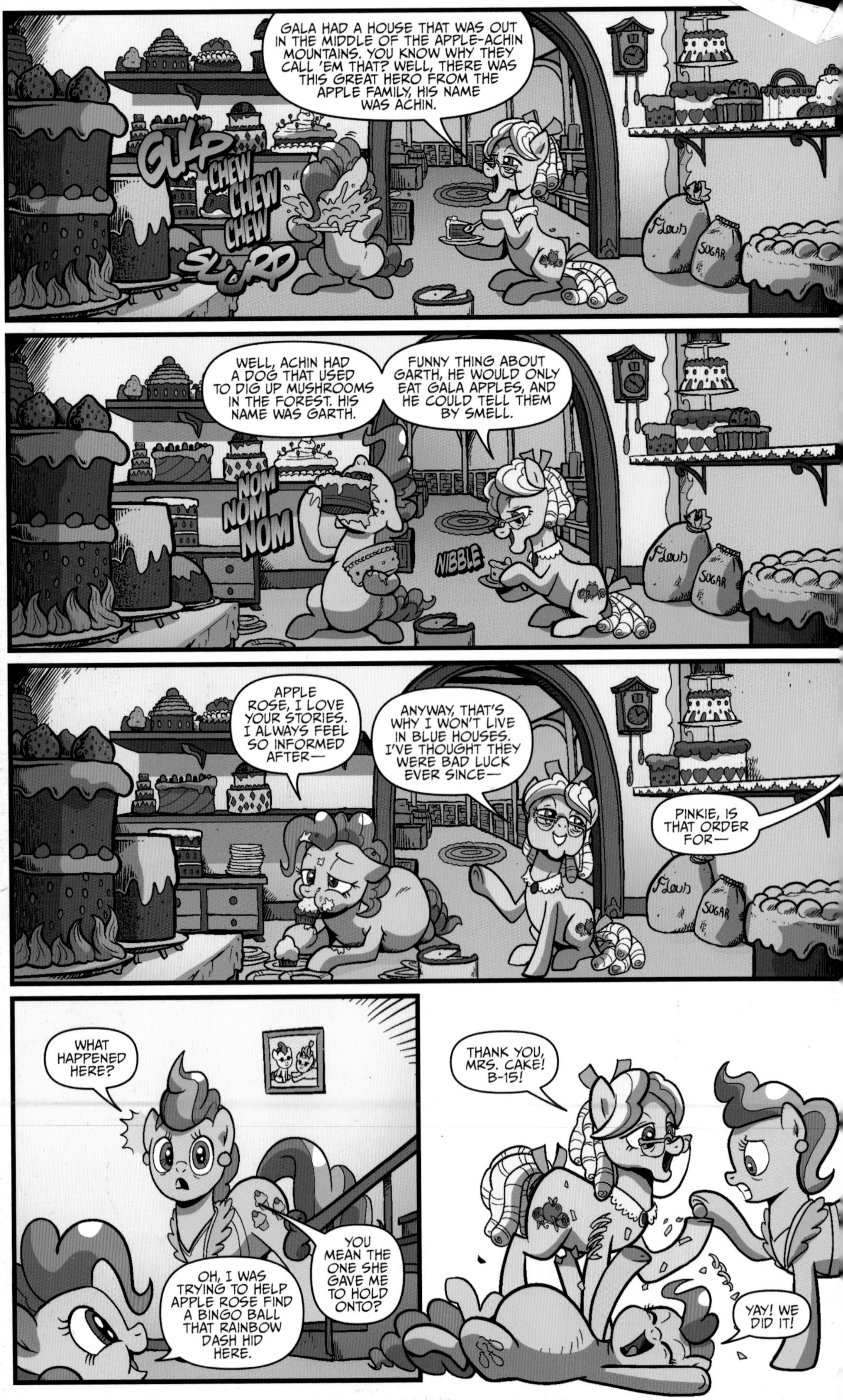
GALA HAD A HOUSE THAT WAS OUT IN THE MIDDLE OF THE APPLE-ACHIN MOUNTAINS. YOU KNOW WHY THEY CALL 'EM THAT? WELL, THERE WAS THIS GREAT HERO FROM THE APPLE FAMILY, HIS NAME WAS ACHIN.
GULP
CHEW CHEW CHEW
SLURP
FLOUR
SUGAR
WELL, ACHIN HAD A DOG THAT USED TO DIG UP MUSHROOMS IN THE FOREST. HIS NAME WAS GARTH.
FUNNY THING ABOUT GARTH, HE WOULD ONLY EAT GALA APPLES, AND HE COULD TELL THEM BY SMELL.
NOM NOM NOM
NIBBLE
APPLE ROSE, I LOVE YOUR STORIES. I ALWAYS FEEL SO INFORMED AFTER—
ANYWAY, THAT'S WHY I WON'T LIVE IN BLUE HOUSES. I'VE THOUGHT THEY WERE BAD LUCK EVER SINCE—
PINKIE, IS THAT ORDER FOR—
WHAT HAPPENED HERE?
OH, I WAS TRYING TO HELP APPLE ROSE FIND A BINGO BALL THAT RAINBOW DASH HID HERE.
YOU MEAN THE ONE SHE GAVE ME TO HOLD ONTO?
THANK YOU, MRS. CAKE! B-15!
YAY! WE DID IT!

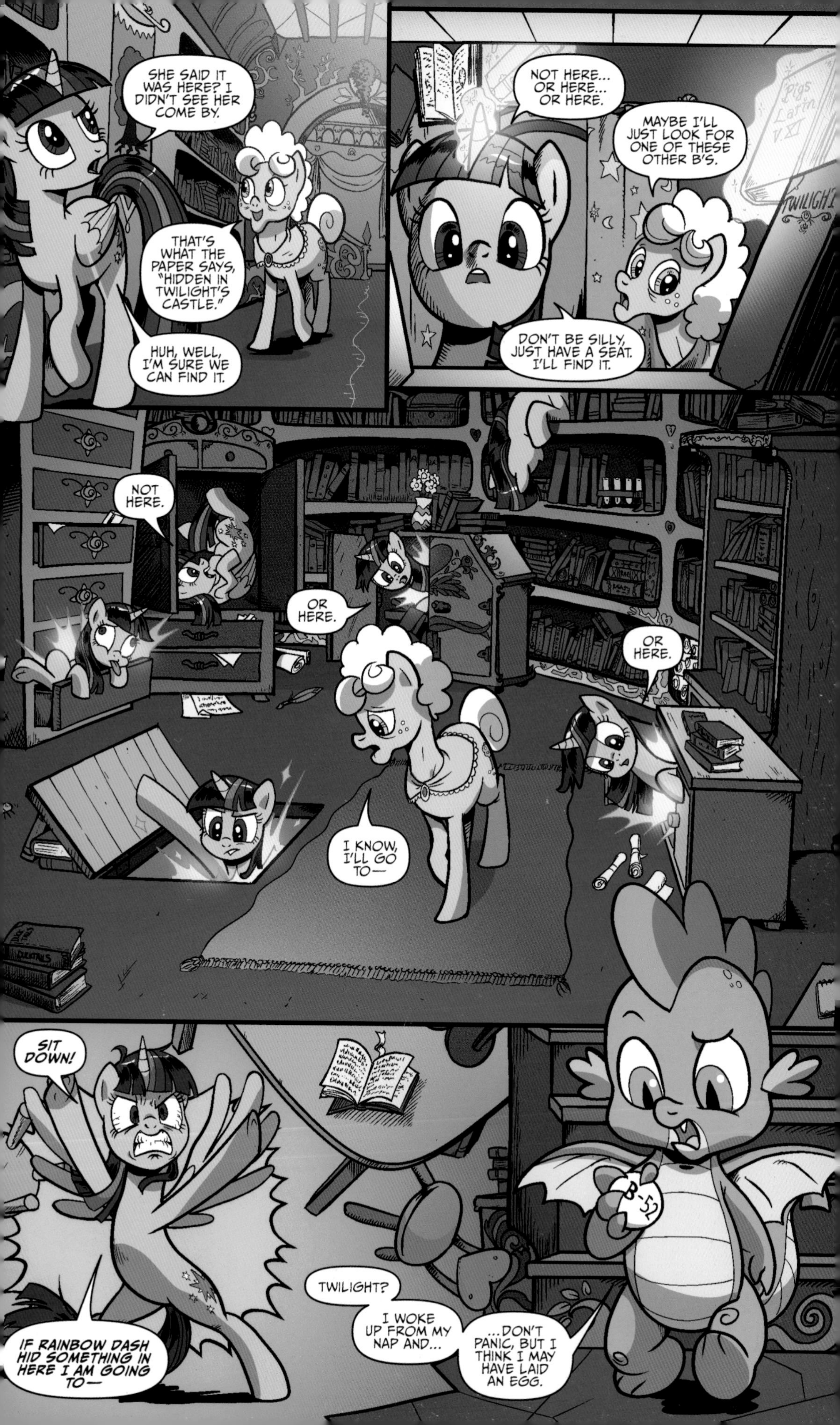
SHE SAID IT WAS HERE? I DIDN'T SEE HER COME BY.
THAT'S WHAT THE PAPER SAYS, "HIDDEN IN TWILIGHT'S CASTLE."
HUH, WELL, I'M SURE WE CAN FIND IT.
NOT HERE... OR HERE... OR HERE.
MAYBE I'LL JUST LOOK FOR ONE OF THESE OTHER B'S.
DON'T BE SILLY, JUST HAVE A SEAT. I'LL FIND IT.
NOT HERE.
OR HERE.
OR HERE.
I KNOW, I'LL GO TO—
SIT DOWN!
IF RAINBOW DASH HID SOMETHING IN HERE I AM GOING TO—
TWILIGHT?
I WOKE UP FROM MY NAP AND...
...DON'T PANIC, BUT I THINK I MAY HAVE LAID AN EGG.
B-52

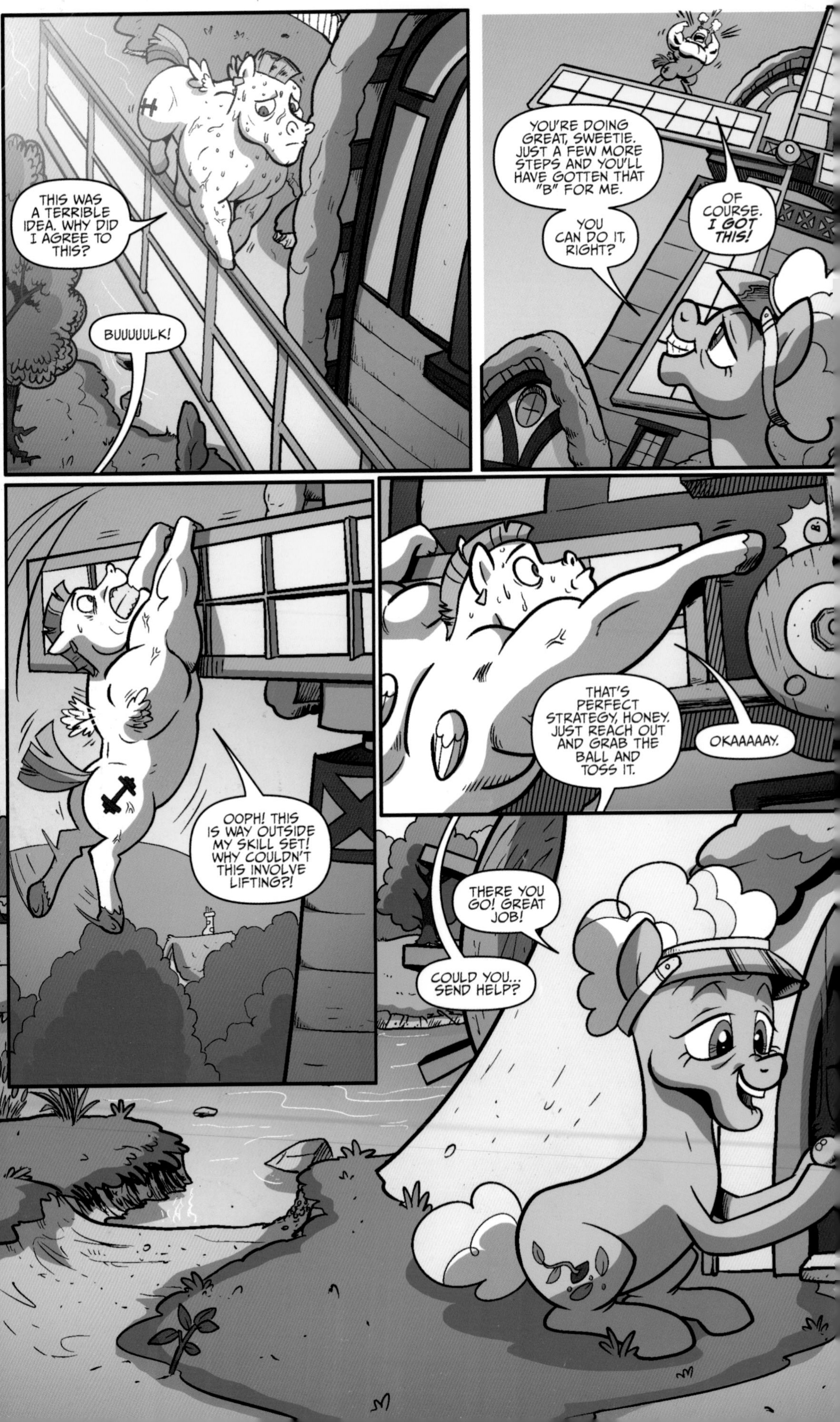

THIS WAS A TERRIBLE IDEA. WHY DID I AGREE TO THIS?
BUUUUULK!
YOU'RE DOING GREAT, SWEETIE. JUST A FEW MORE STEPS AND YOU'LL HAVE GOTTEN THAT "B" FOR ME.
YOU CAN DO IT, RIGHT?
OF COURSE. I GOT THIS!
OOPH! THIS IS WAY OUTSIDE MY SKILL SET! WHY COULDN'T THIS INVOLVE LIFTING?!
THAT'S PERFECT STRATEGY, HONEY. JUST REACH OUT AND GRAB THE BALL AND TOSS IT.
OKAAAAAY.
THERE YOU GO! GREAT JOB!
COULD YOU... SEND HELP?

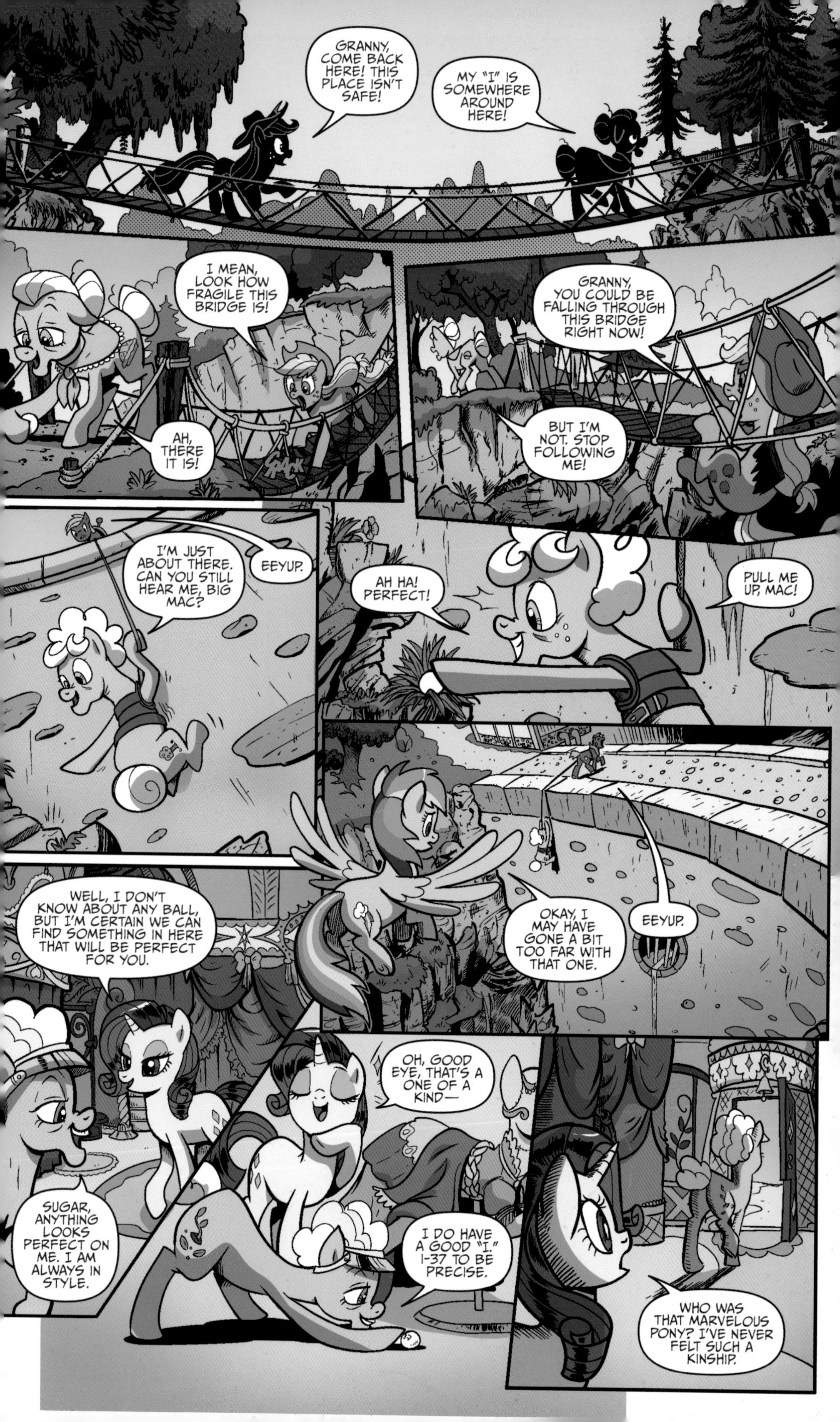
GRANNY, COME BACK HERE! THIS PLACE ISN'T SAFE!
MY "I" IS SOMEWHERE AROUND HERE!
I MEAN, LOOK HOW FRAGILE THIS BRIDGE IS!
AH, THERE IT IS!
GRANNY, YOU COULD BE FALLING THROUGH THIS BRIDGE RIGHT NOW!
BUT I'M NOT. STOP FOLLOWING ME!
I'M JUST ABOUT THERE. CAN YOU STILL HEAR ME, BIG MAC?
EEYUP.
AH HA! PERFECT!
PULL ME UP, MAC!
OKAY, I MAY HAVE GONE A BIT TOO FAR WITH THAT ONE.
EEYUP.
WELL, I DON'T KNOW ABOUT ANY BALL, BUT I'M CERTAIN WE CAN FIND SOMETHING IN HERE THAT WILL BE PERFECT FOR YOU.
SUGAR, ANYTHING LOOKS PERFECT ON ME. I AM ALWAYS IN STYLE.
OH, GOOD EYE, THAT'S A ONE OF A KIND—
I DO HAVE A GOOD "I." I-37 TO BE PRECISE.
WHO WAS THAT MARVELOUS PONY? I'VE NEVER FELT SUCH A KINSHIP.

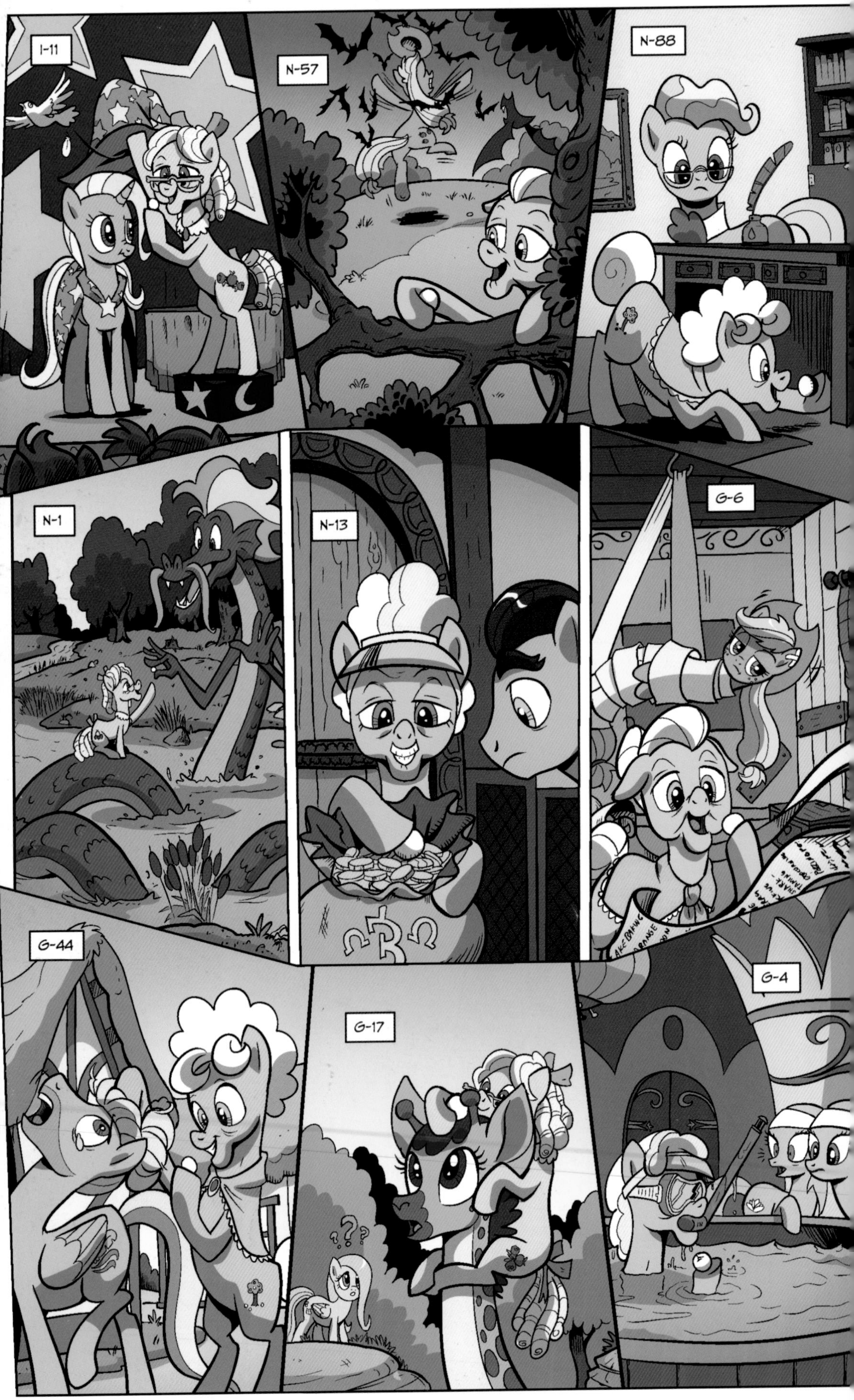
I-11
N-57
N-88
N-1
N-13
G-6
G-44
G-17
G-4

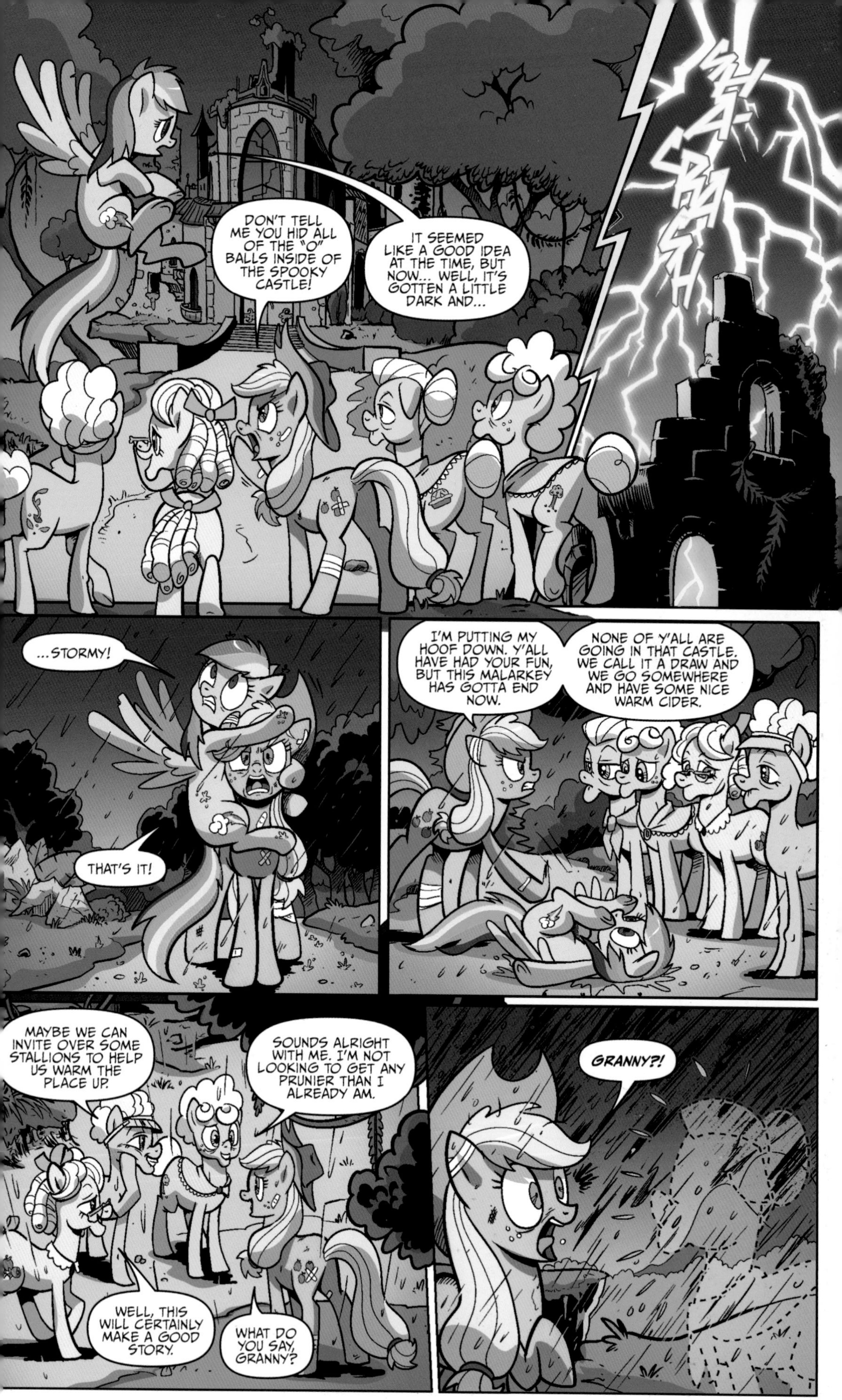
DON'T TELL ME YOU HID ALL OF THE "O" BALLS INSIDE OF THE SPOOKY CASTLE!
IT SEEMED LIKE A GOOD IDEA AT THE TIME, BUT NOW... WELL, IT'S GOTTEN A LITTLE DARK AND...
...STORMY!
THAT'S IT!
I'M PUTTING MY HOOF DOWN. Y'ALL HAVE HAD YOUR FUN, BUT THIS MALARKEY HAS GOTTA END NOW.
NONE OF Y'ALL ARE GOING IN THAT CASTLE. WE CALL IT A DRAW AND WE GO SOMEWHERE AND HAVE SOME NICE WARM CIDER.
MAYBE WE CAN INVITE OVER SOME STALLIONS TO HELP US WARM THE PLACE UP.
SOUNDS ALRIGHT WITH ME. I'M NOT LOOKING TO GET ANY PRUNIER THAN I ALREADY AM.
WELL, THIS WILL CERTAINLY MAKE A GOOD STORY.
WHAT DO YOU SAY, GRANNY?
GRANNY?!

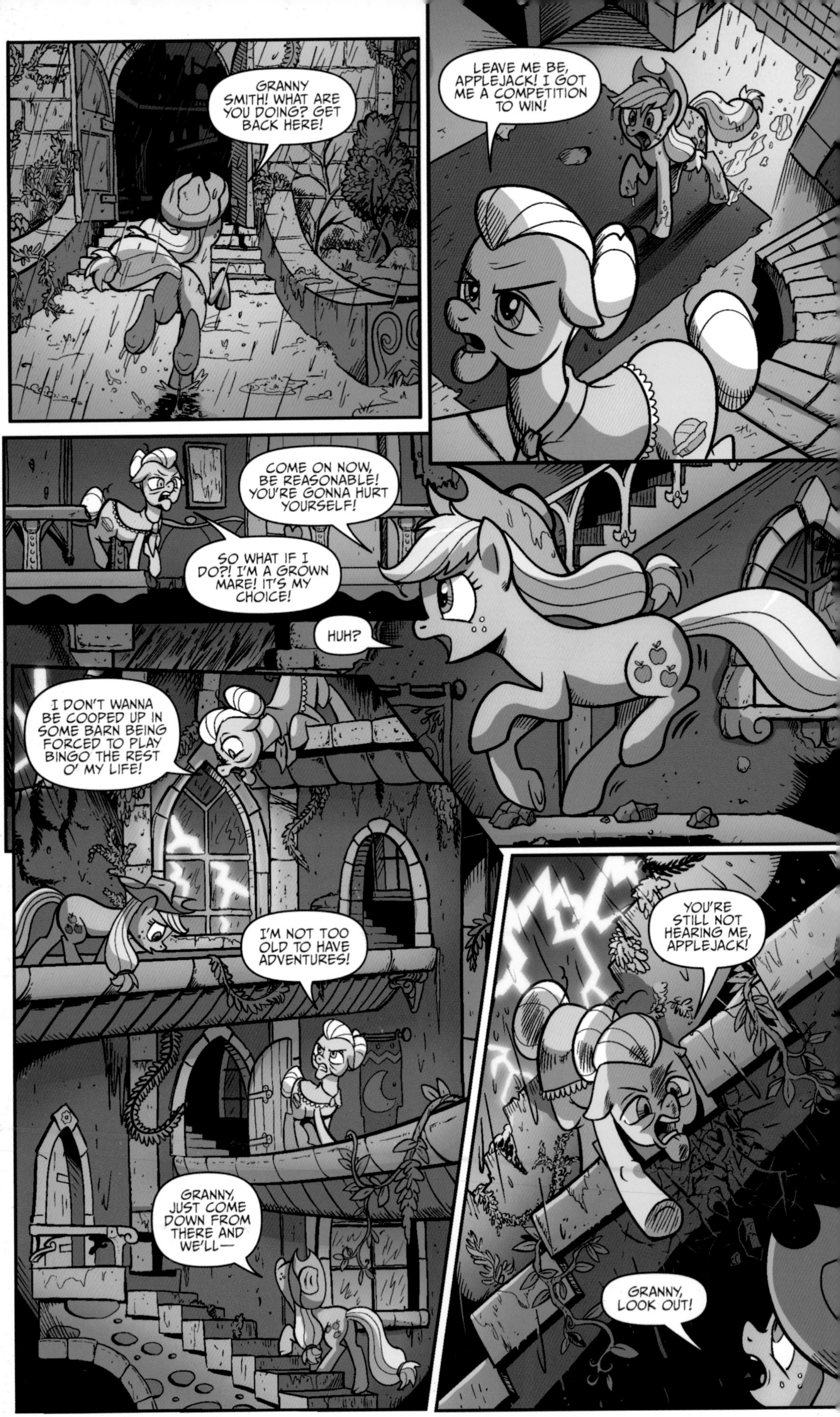
GRANNY SMITH! WHAT ARE YOU DOING? GET BACK HERE!
LEAVE ME BE, APPLEJACK! I GOT ME A COMPETITION TO WIN!
COME ON NOW, BE REASONABLE! YOU'RE GONNA HURT YOURSELF!
SO WHAT IF I DO?! I'M A GROWN MARE! IT'S MY CHOICE!
HUH?
I DON'T WANNA BE COOPED UP IN SOME BARN BEING FORCED TO PLAY BINGO THE REST O' MY LIFE!
I'M NOT TOO OLD TO HAVE ADVENTURES!
GRANNY, JUST COME DOWN FROM THERE AND WE'LL—
YOU'RE STILL NOT HEARING ME, APPLEJACK!
GRANNY, LOOK OUT!

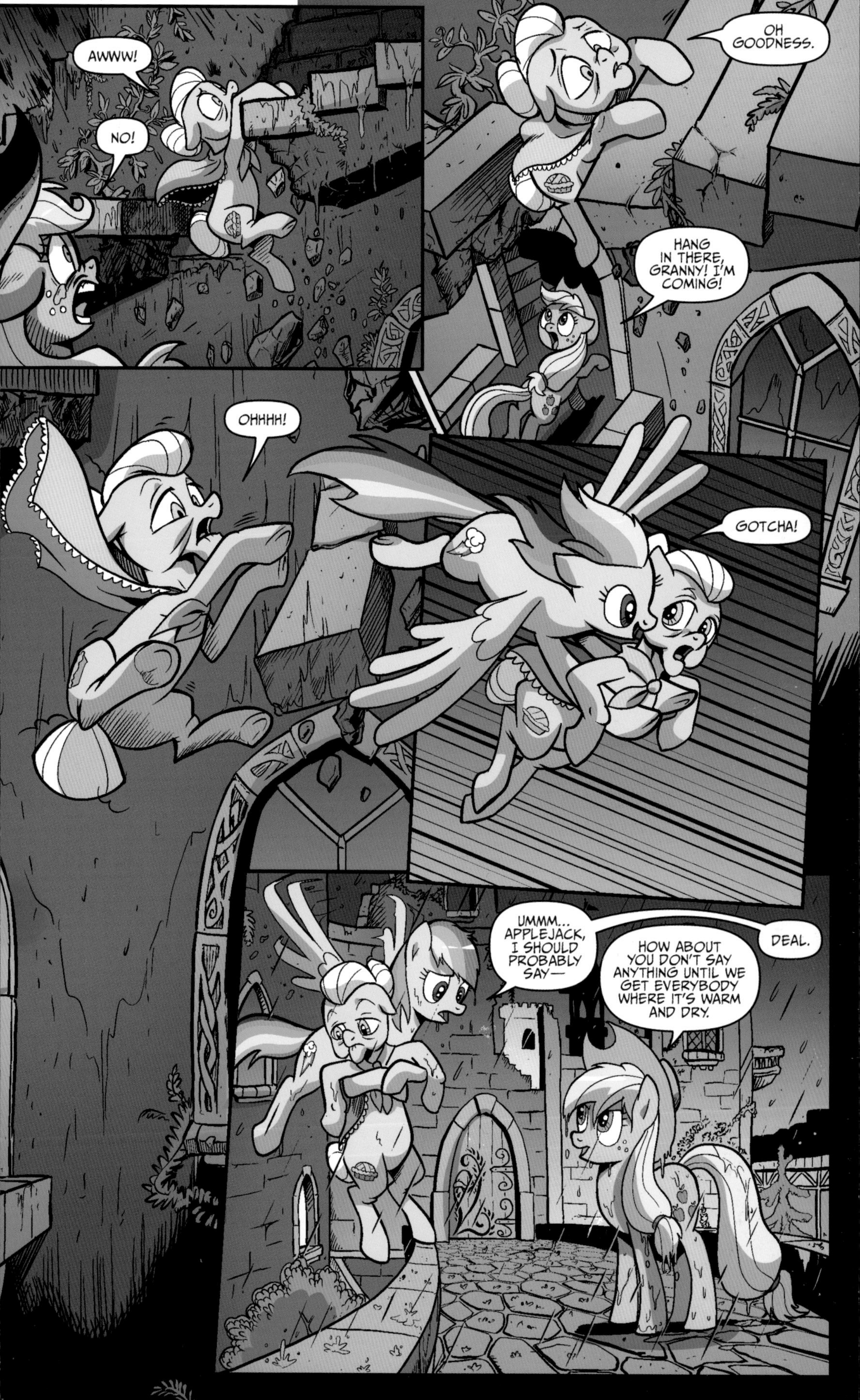
AWWW!
NO!
OH GOODNESS.
HANG IN THERE, GRANNY! I'M COMING!
OHHHH!
GOTCHA!
UMMM... APPLEJACK, I SHOULD PROBABLY SAY—
HOW ABOUT YOU DON'T SAY ANYTHING UNTIL WE GET EVERYBODY WHERE IT'S WARM AND DRY.
DEAL.

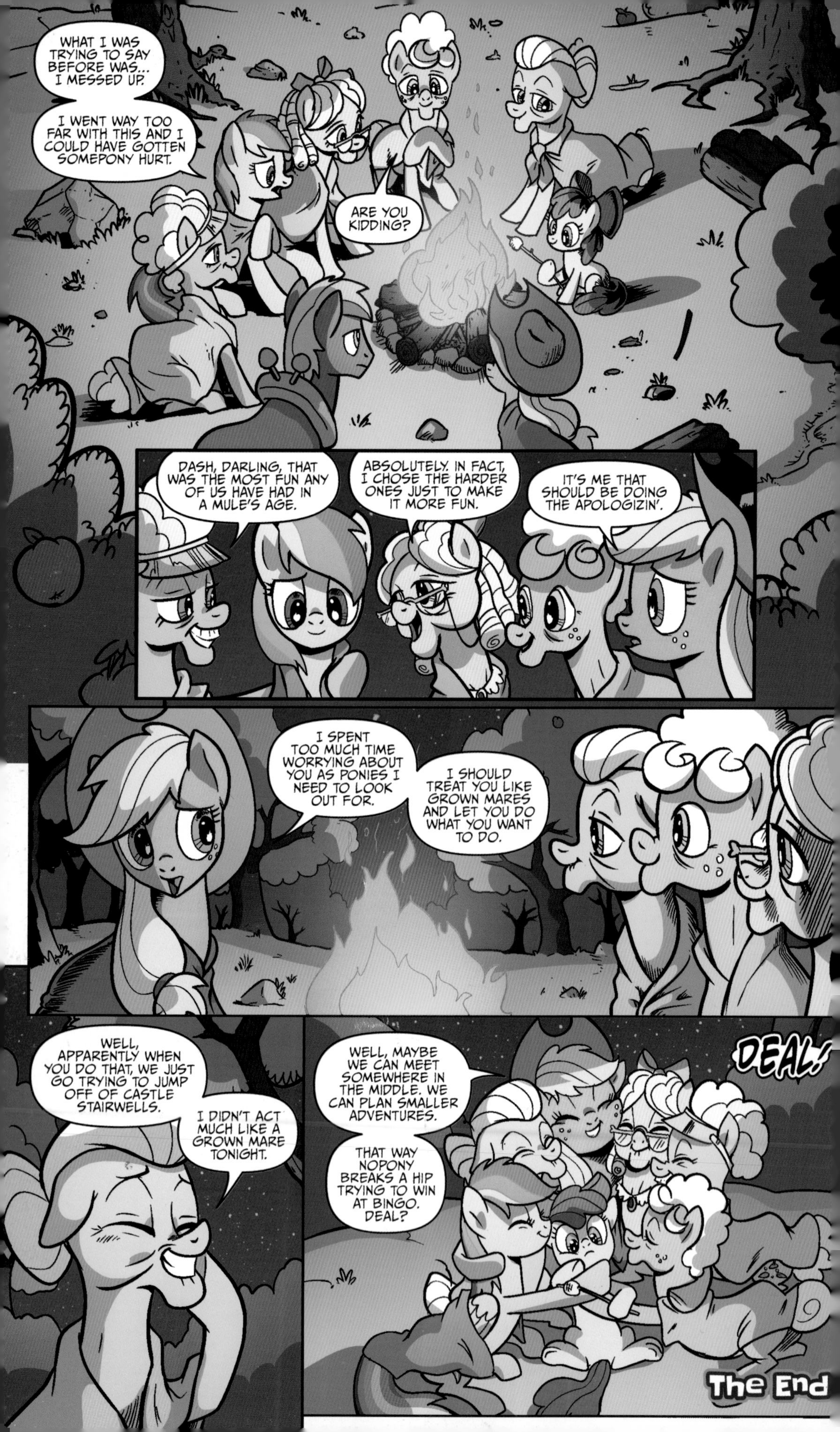
WHAT I WAS TRYING TO SAY BEFORE WAS... I MESSED UP.
I WENT WAY TOO FAR WITH THIS AND I COULD HAVE GOTTEN SOMEPONY HURT.
ARE YOU KIDDING?
DASH, DARLING, THAT WAS THE MOST FUN ANY OF US HAVE HAD IN A MULE'S AGE.
ABSOLUTELY. IN FACT, I CHOSE THE HARDER ONES JUST TO MAKE IT MORE FUN.
IT'S ME THAT SHOULD BE DOING THE APOLOGIZIN'.
I SPENT TOO MUCH TIME WORRYING ABOUT YOU AS PONIES I NEED TO LOOK OUT FOR.
I SHOULD TREAT YOU LIKE GROWN MARES AND LET YOU DO WHAT YOU WANT TO DO.
WELL, APPARENTLY WHEN YOU DO THAT, WE JUST GO TRYING TO JUMP OFF OF CASTLE STAIRWELLS.
I DIDN'T ACT MUCH LIKE A GROWN MARE TONIGHT.
WELL, MAYBE WE CAN MEET SOMEWHERE IN THE MIDDLE. WE CAN PLAN SMALLER ADVENTURES.
THAT WAY NOPONY BREAKS A HIP TRYING TO WIN AT BINGO. DEAL?
DEAL!
The End

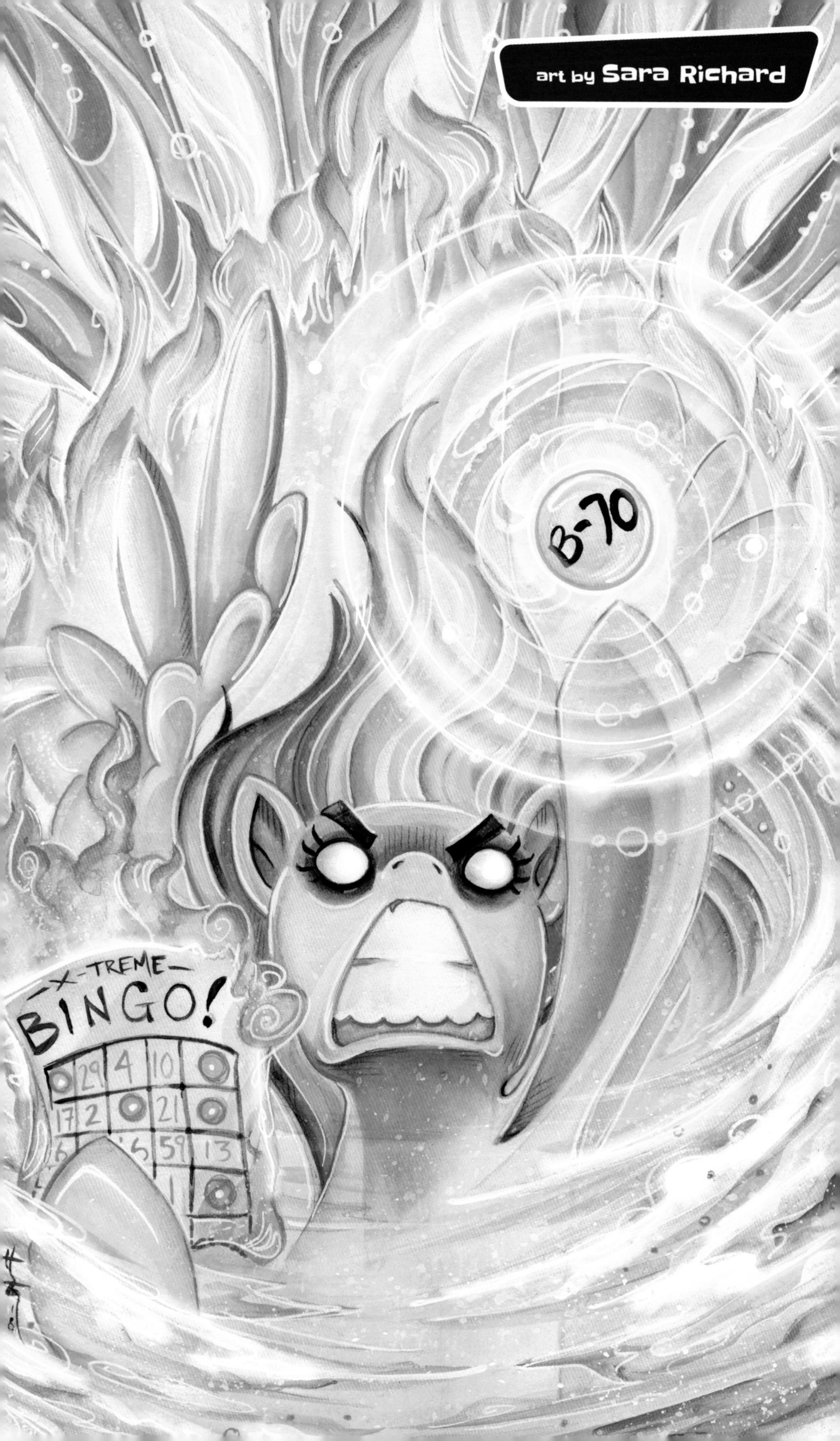
B-70
-X-TREME-
BINGO!
29 4 10
17 2 21
59 13
1
art by Sara Richard

art by Andy Price

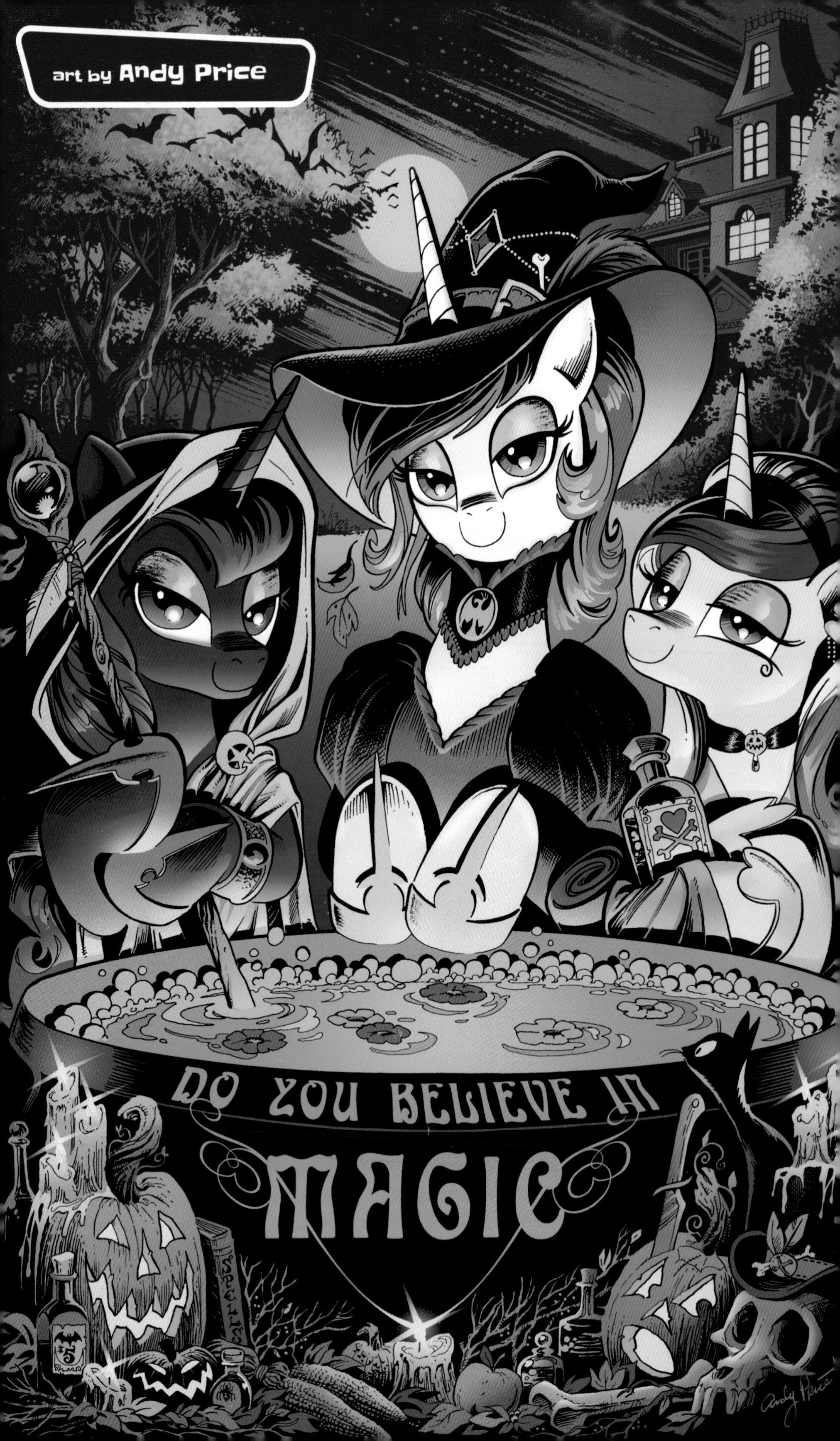
DO YOU BELIEVE IN
MAGIC
SPELLS
#5
Andy Price

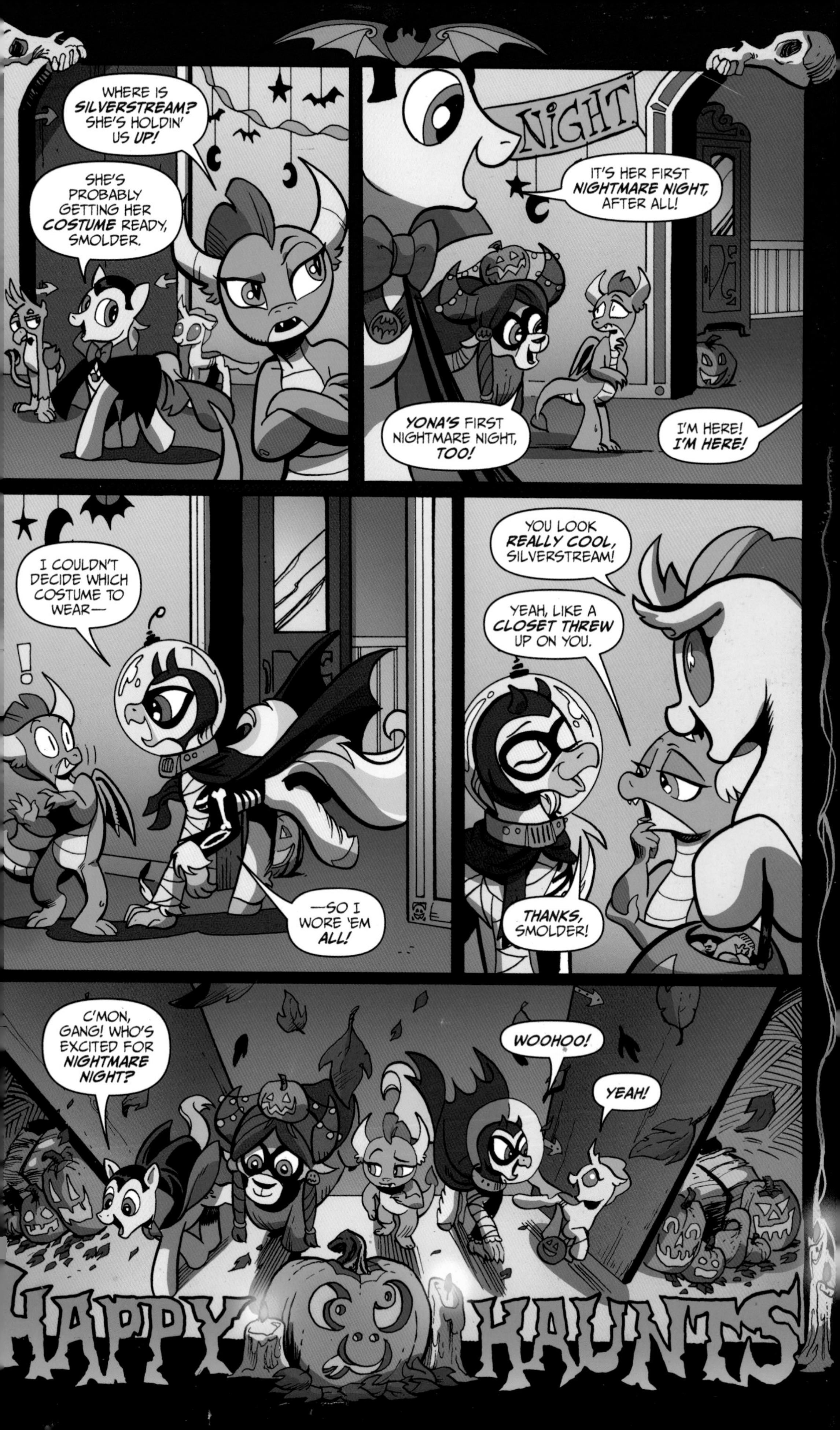
WHERE IS SILVERSTREAM? SHE'S HOLDIN' US UP!
SHE'S PROBABLY GETTING HER COSTUME READY, SMOLDER.
IT'S HER FIRST NIGHTMARE NIGHT, AFTER ALL!
NIGHT
YONA'S FIRST NIGHTMARE NIGHT, TOO!
I'M HERE! I'M HERE!
I COULDN'T DECIDE WHICH COSTUME TO WEAR—
!
—SO I WORE 'EM ALL!
YOU LOOK REALLY COOL, SILVERSTREAM!
YEAH, LIKE A CLOSET THREW UP ON YOU.
THANKS, SMOLDER!
C'MON, GANG! WHO'S EXCITED FOR NIGHTMARE NIGHT?
WOOHOO!
YEAH!
HAPPY HAUNTS

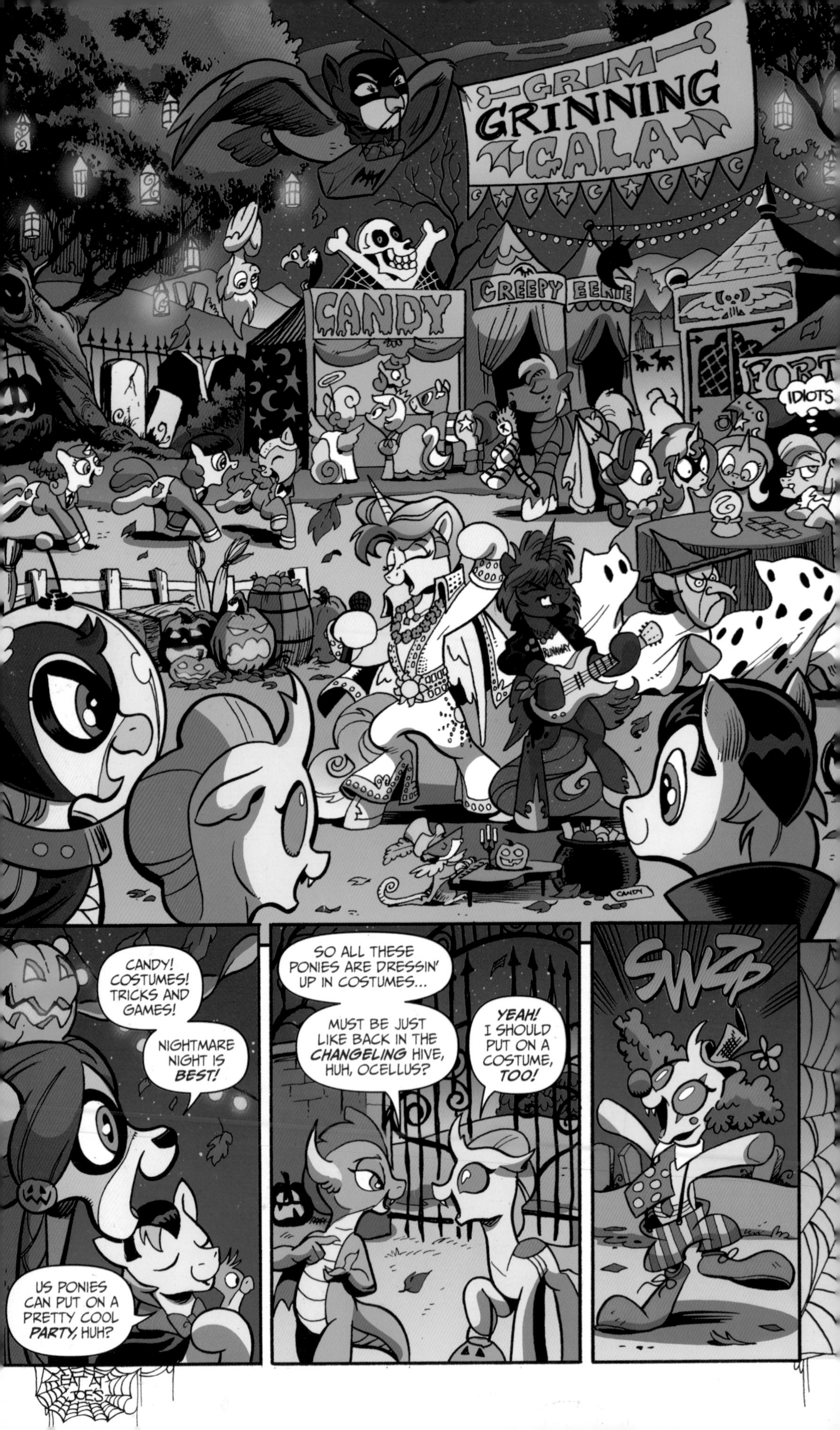
GRIM GRINNING GALA
CANDY
CREEPY EERIE
FORT
IDIOTS
RUNAWAY
CANDY
CANDY! COSTUMES! TRICKS AND GAMES!
NIGHTMARE NIGHT IS *BEST!*
US PONIES CAN PUT ON A PRETTY COOL *PARTY,* HUH?
SO ALL THESE PONIES ARE DRESSIN' UP IN COSTUMES...
MUST BE JUST LIKE BACK IN THE *CHANGELING* HIVE, HUH, OCELLUS?
*YEAH!* I SHOULD PUT ON A COSTUME, *TOO!*
SWZP
EAT AT JOE'S

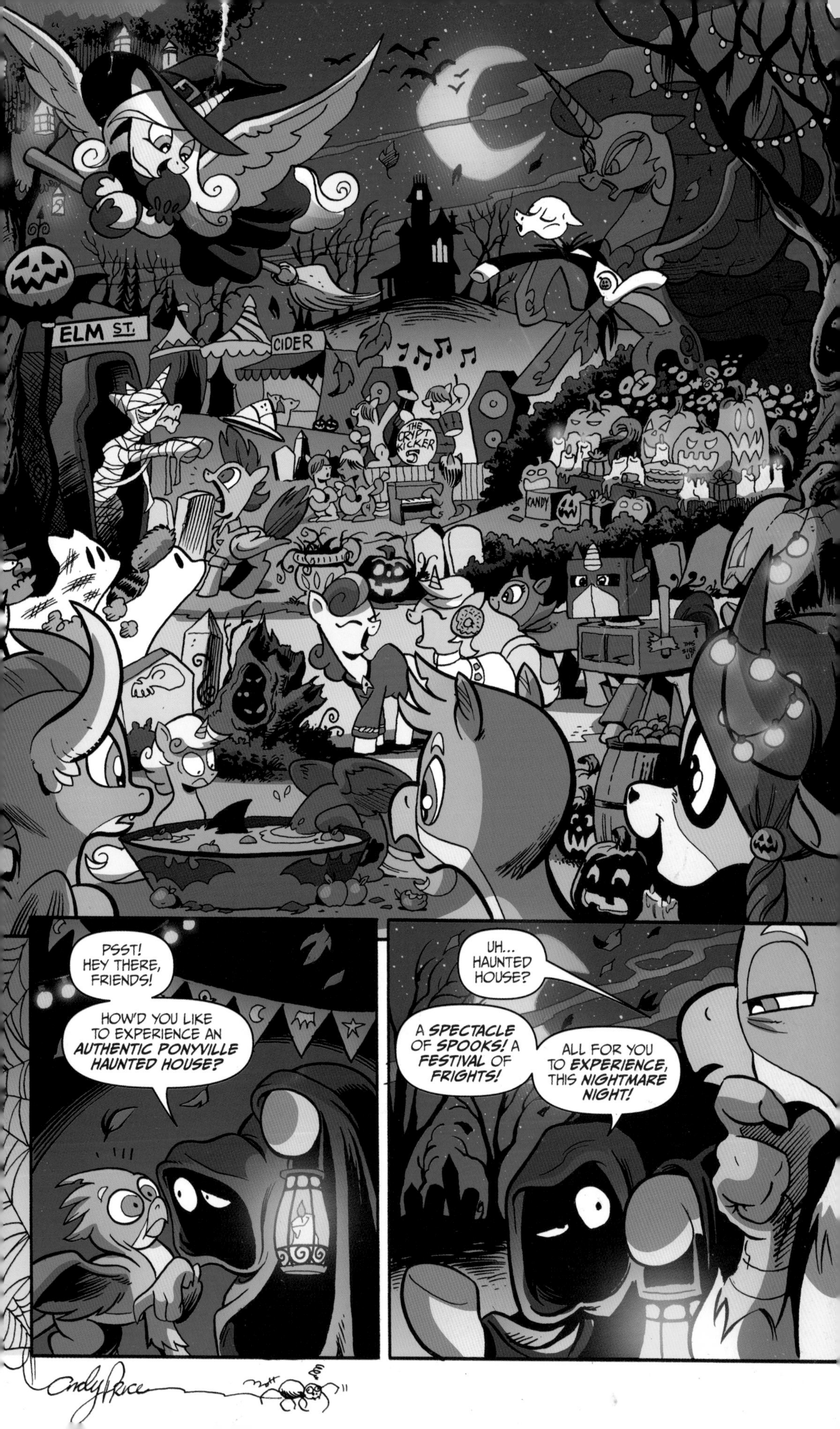

ELM ST.
CIDER
THE CRYPT KICKER 5
CANDY
THIS SIDE UP
PSST! HEY THERE, FRIENDS!
HOW'D YOU LIKE TO EXPERIENCE AN *AUTHENTIC PONYVILLE HAUNTED HOUSE?*
UH... HAUNTED HOUSE?
A *SPECTACLE* OF *SPOOKS!* A *FESTIVAL* OF *FRIGHTS!*
ALL FOR YOU TO *EXPERIENCE,* THIS *NIGHTMARE NIGHT!*

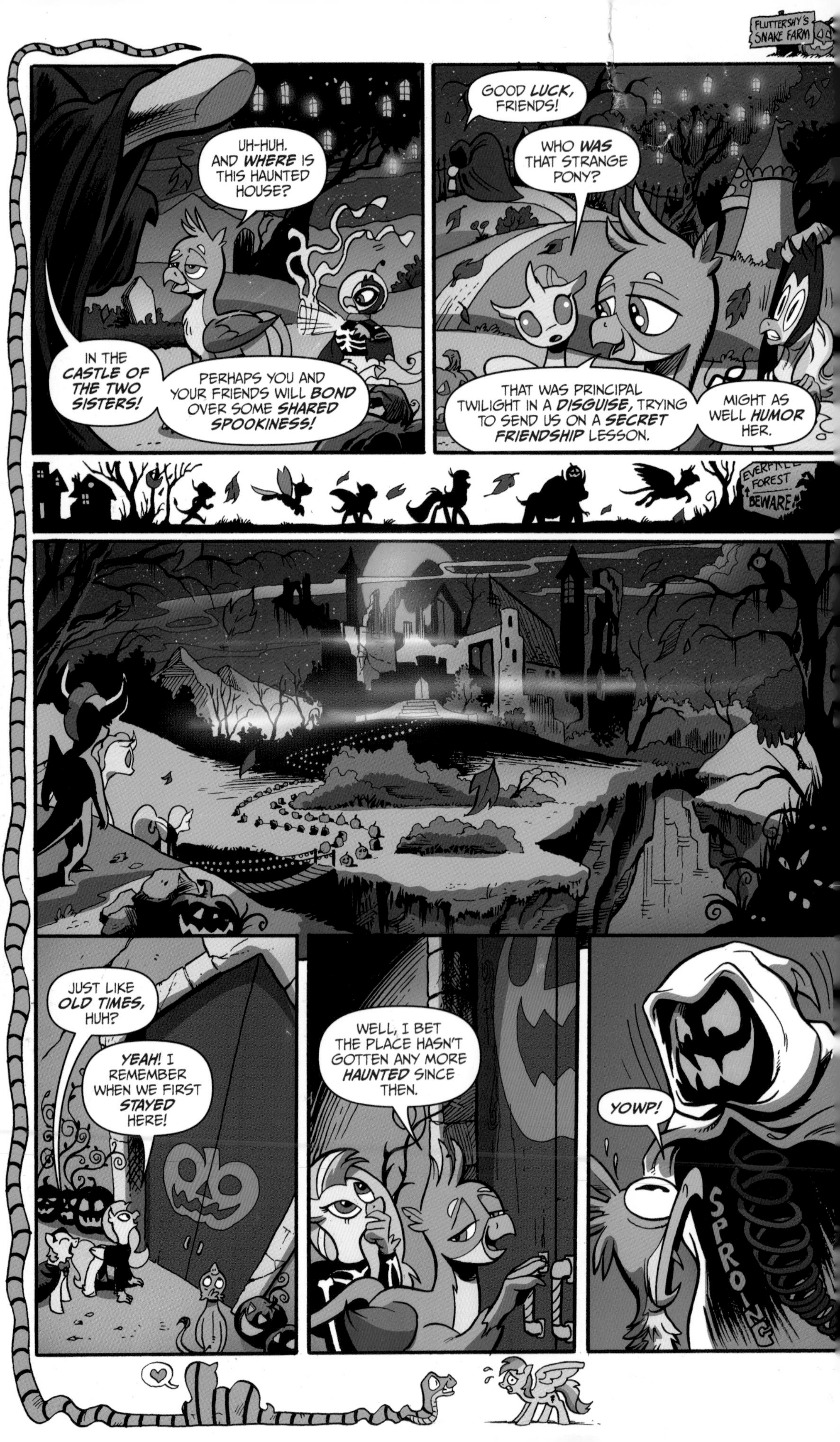
FLUTTERSHY'S SNAKE FARM
UH-HUH. AND WHERE IS THIS HAUNTED HOUSE?
IN THE CASTLE OF THE TWO SISTERS!
PERHAPS YOU AND YOUR FRIENDS WILL BOND OVER SOME SHARED SPOOKINESS!
GOOD LUCK, FRIENDS!
WHO WAS THAT STRANGE PONY?
THAT WAS PRINCIPAL TWILIGHT IN A DISGUISE, TRYING TO SEND US ON A SECRET FRIENDSHIP LESSON.
MIGHT AS WELL HUMOR HER.
EVERFREE FOREST
BEWARE
JUST LIKE OLD TIMES, HUH?
YEAH! I REMEMBER WHEN WE FIRST STAYED HERE!
WELL, I BET THE PLACE HASN'T GOTTEN ANY MORE HAUNTED SINCE THEN.
YOWP!
SPROING

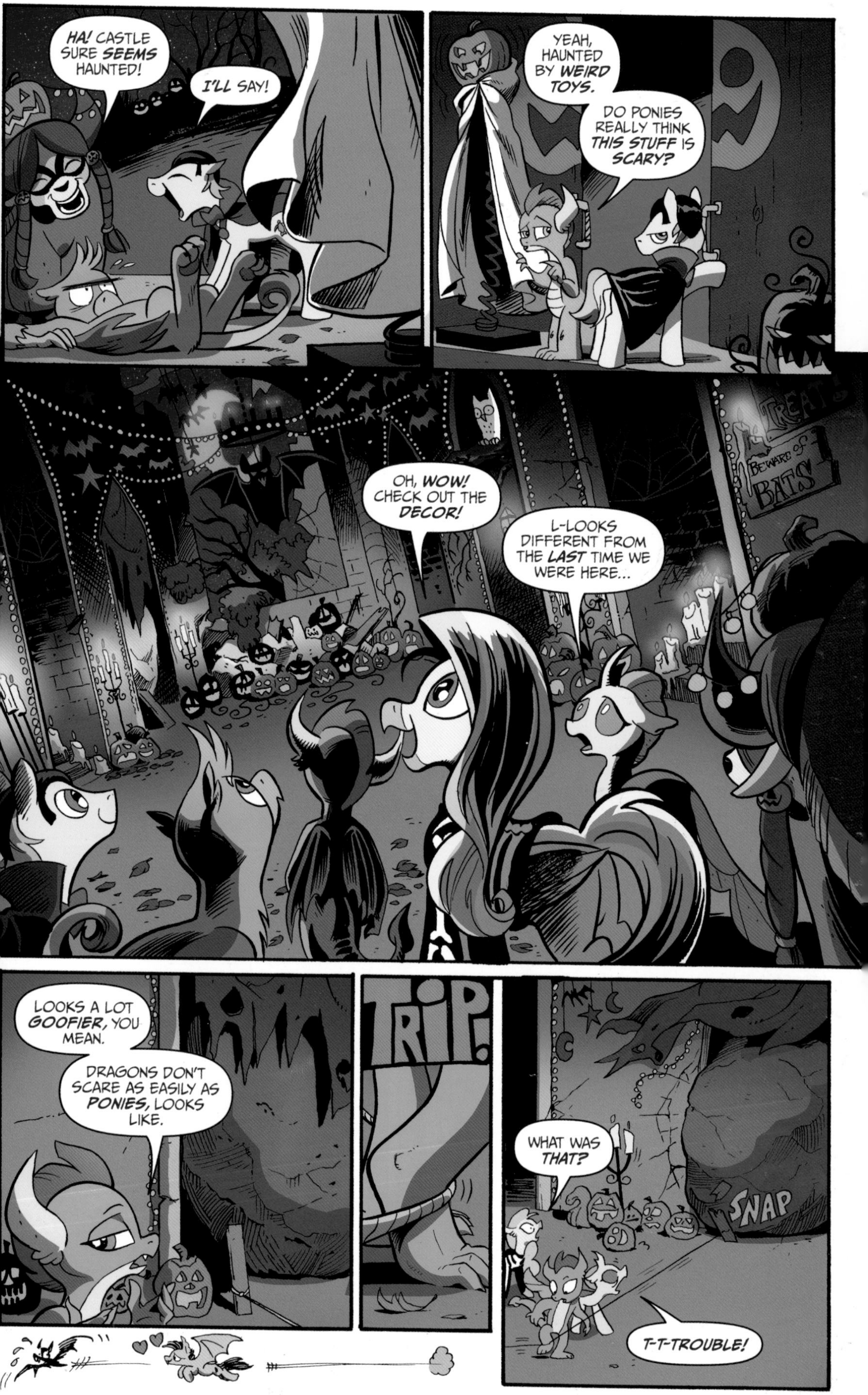
HA! CASTLE SURE SEEMS HAUNTED!
I'LL SAY!
YEAH, HAUNTED BY WEIRD TOYS.
DO PONIES REALLY THINK THIS STUFF IS SCARY?
TREAT
BEWARE OF BATS
OH, WOW! CHECK OUT THE DECOR!
L-LOOKS DIFFERENT FROM THE LAST TIME WE WERE HERE...
LOOKS A LOT GOOFIER, YOU MEAN.
DRAGONS DON'T SCARE AS EASILY AS PONIES, LOOKS LIKE.
TRIP!
WHAT WAS THAT?
SNAP
T-T-TROUBLE!

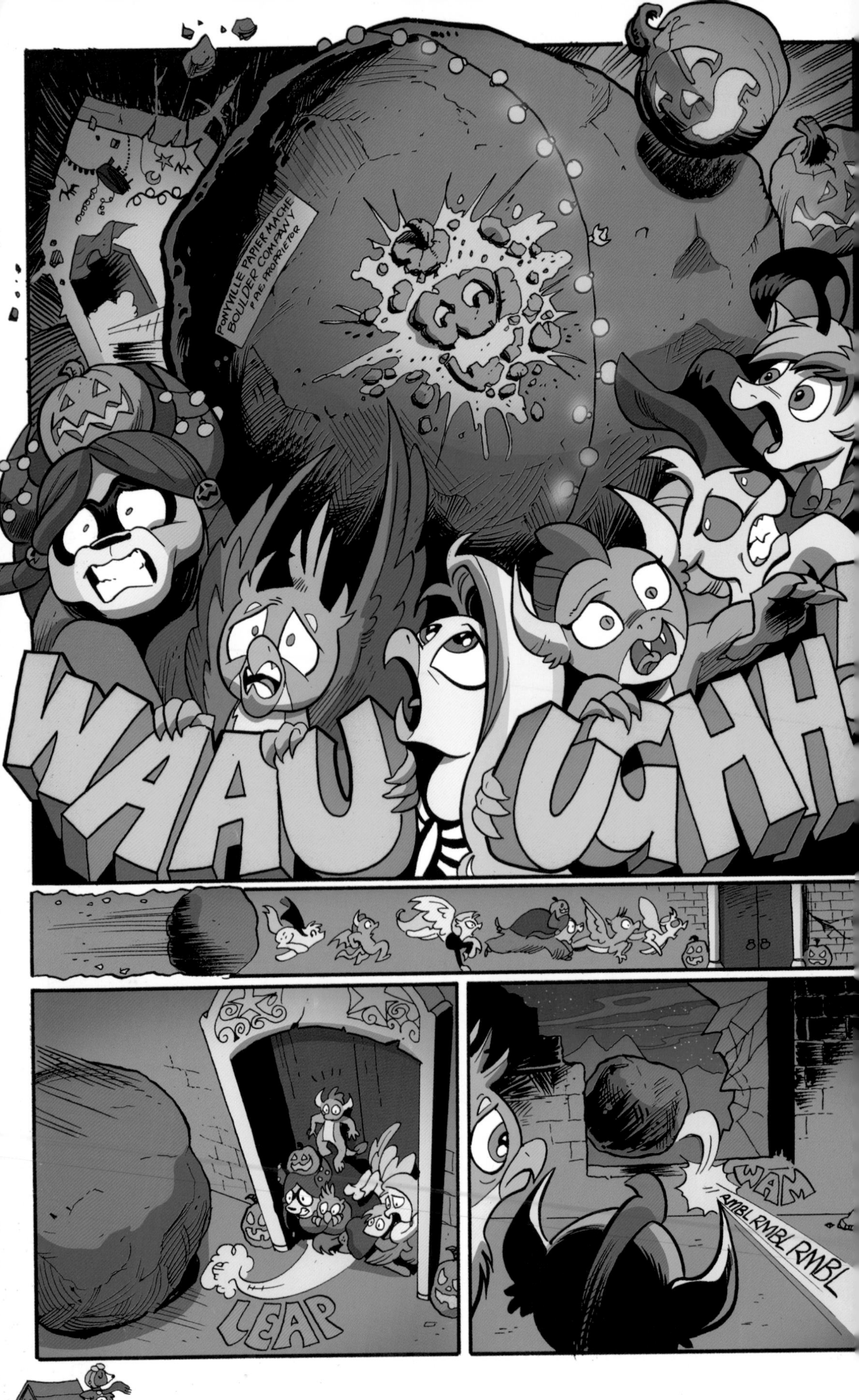
PONYVILLE PAPIER MACHE
BOULDER COMPANY
P. PIE, PROPRIETOR
WAAUUGHH
LEAP
WAM
RMBL RMBL RMBL

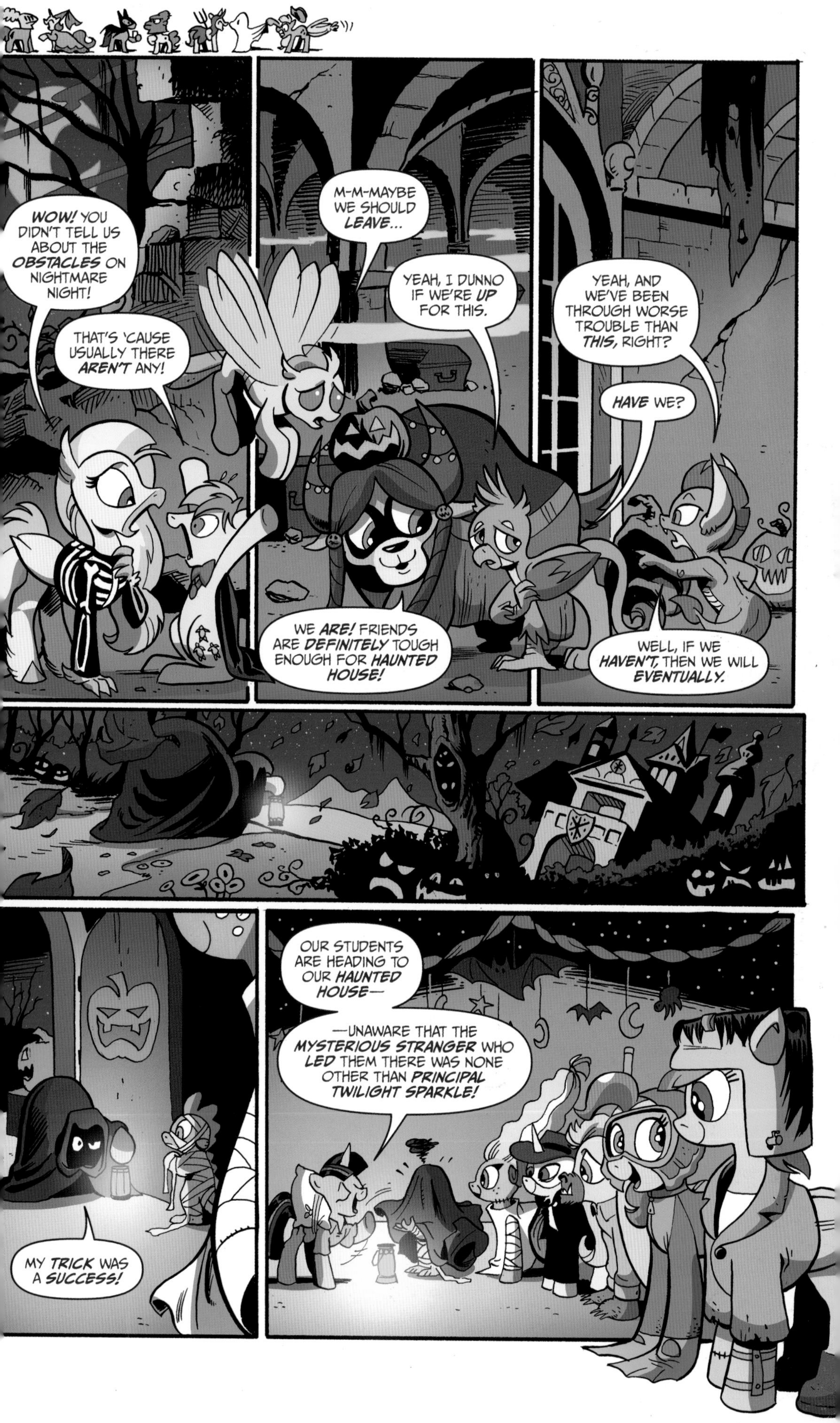
WOW! YOU DIDN'T TELL US ABOUT THE OBSTACLES ON NIGHTMARE NIGHT!
THAT'S 'CAUSE USUALLY THERE AREN'T ANY!
M-M-MAYBE WE SHOULD LEAVE...
YEAH, I DUNNO IF WE'RE UP FOR THIS.
WE ARE! FRIENDS ARE DEFINITELY TOUGH ENOUGH FOR HAUNTED HOUSE!
YEAH, AND WE'VE BEEN THROUGH WORSE TROUBLE THAN THIS, RIGHT?
HAVE WE?
WELL, IF WE HAVEN'T, THEN WE WILL EVENTUALLY.
MY TRICK WAS A SUCCESS!
OUR STUDENTS ARE HEADING TO OUR HAUNTED HOUSE—
—UNAWARE THAT THE MYSTERIOUS STRANGER WHO LED THEM THERE WAS NONE OTHER THAN PRINCIPAL TWILIGHT SPARKLE!

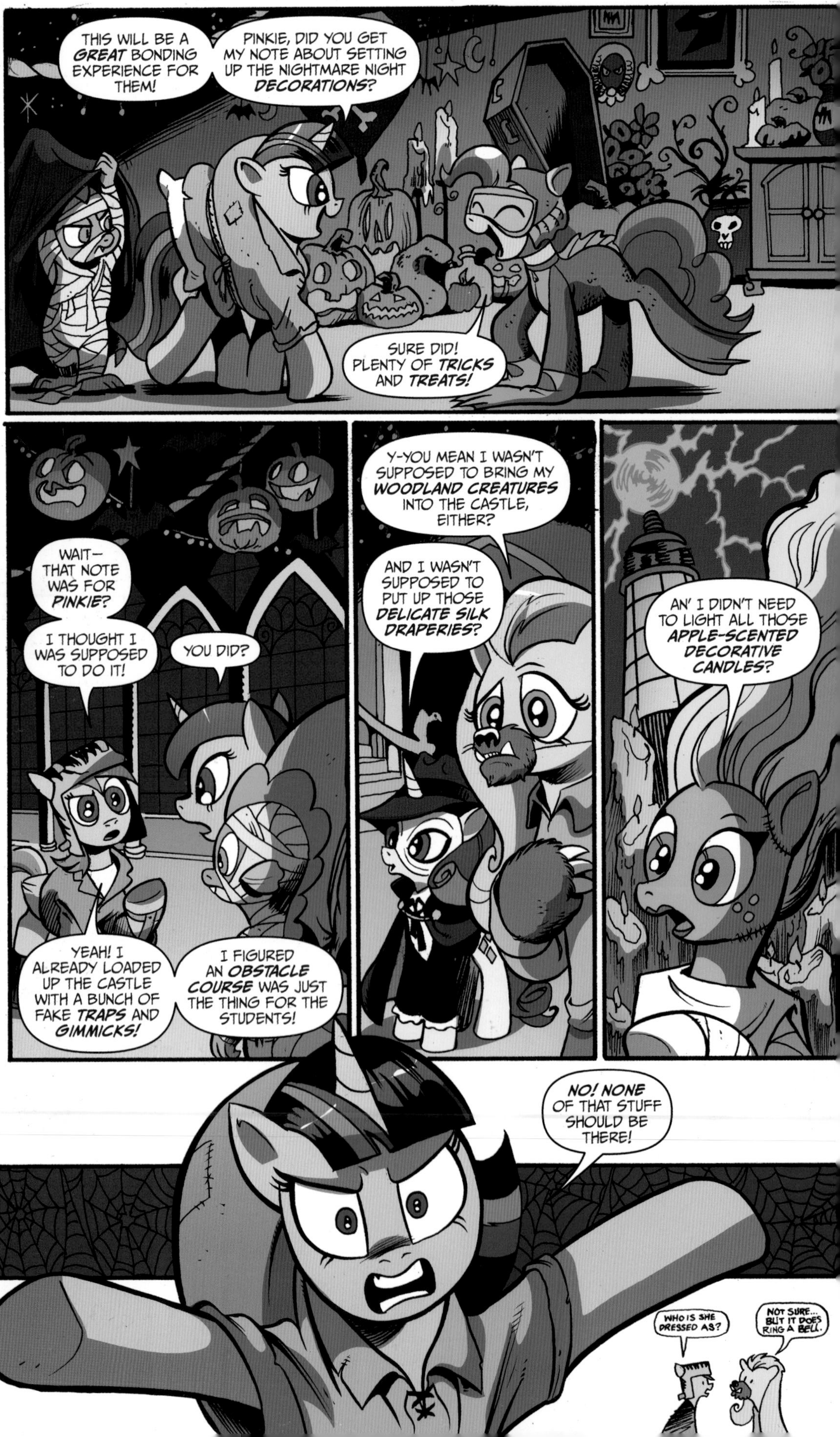
THIS WILL BE A GREAT BONDING EXPERIENCE FOR THEM!
PINKIE, DID YOU GET MY NOTE ABOUT SETTING UP THE NIGHTMARE NIGHT DECORATIONS?
SURE DID! PLENTY OF TRICKS AND TREATS!
WAIT— THAT NOTE WAS FOR PINKIE?
I THOUGHT I WAS SUPPOSED TO DO IT!
YOU DID?
YEAH! I ALREADY LOADED UP THE CASTLE WITH A BUNCH OF FAKE TRAPS AND GIMMICKS!
I FIGURED AN OBSTACLE COURSE WAS JUST THE THING FOR THE STUDENTS!
Y-YOU MEAN I WASN'T SUPPOSED TO BRING MY WOODLAND CREATURES INTO THE CASTLE, EITHER?
AND I WASN'T SUPPOSED TO PUT UP THOSE DELICATE SILK DRAPERIES?
AN' I DIDN'T NEED TO LIGHT ALL THOSE APPLE-SCENTED DECORATIVE CANDLES?
NO! NONE OF THAT STUFF SHOULD BE THERE!
WHO IS SHE DRESSED AS?
NOT SURE... BUT IT DOES RING A BELL.

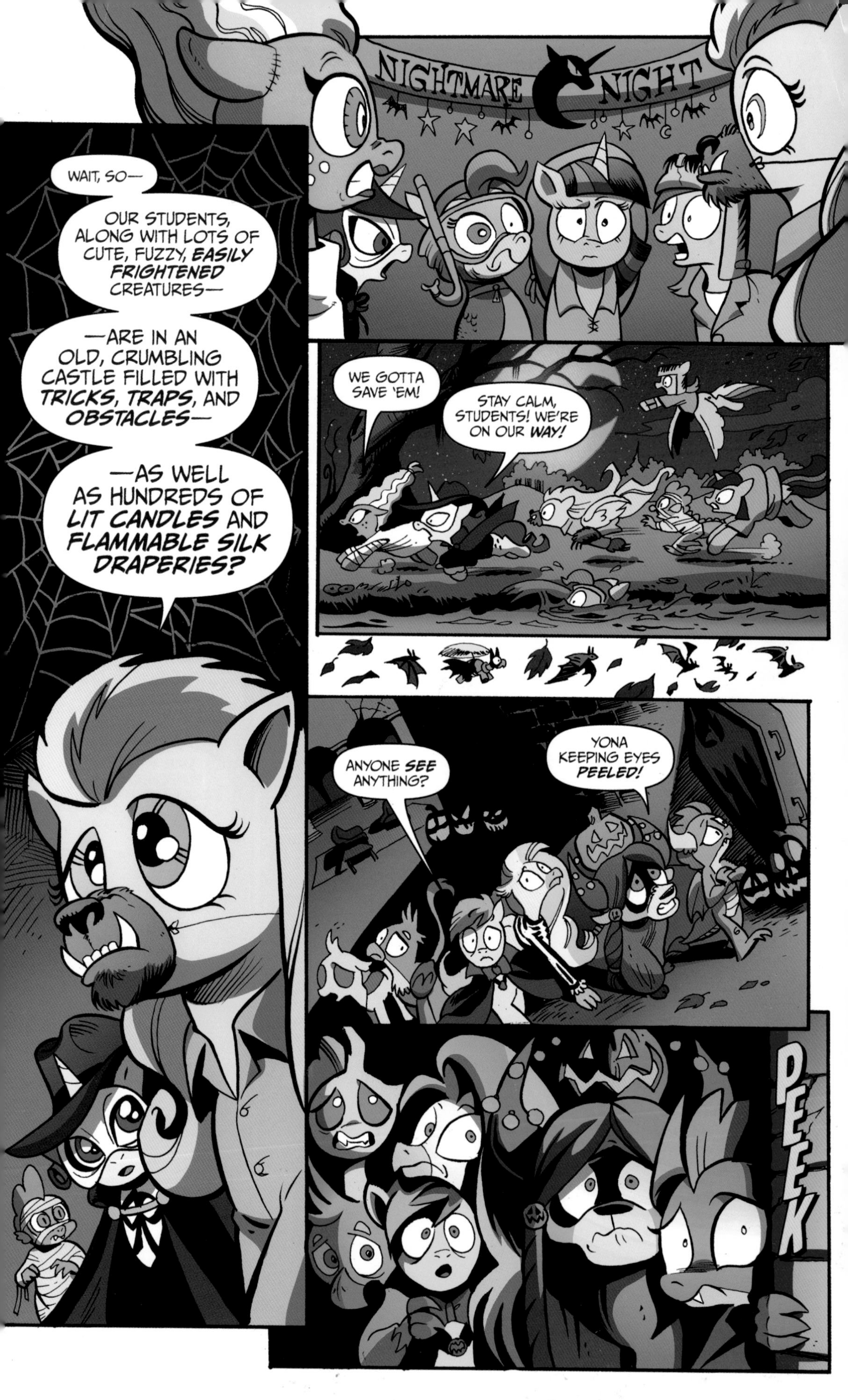
NIGHTMARE NIGHT
WAIT, SO—
OUR STUDENTS, ALONG WITH LOTS OF CUTE, FUZZY, EASILY FRIGHTENED CREATURES—
—ARE IN AN OLD, CRUMBLING CASTLE FILLED WITH TRICKS, TRAPS, AND OBSTACLES—
—AS WELL AS HUNDREDS OF LIT CANDLES AND FLAMMABLE SILK DRAPERIES?
WE GOTTA SAVE 'EM!
STAY CALM, STUDENTS! WE'RE ON OUR WAY!
ANYONE SEE ANYTHING?
YONA KEEPING EYES PEELED!
PEEK

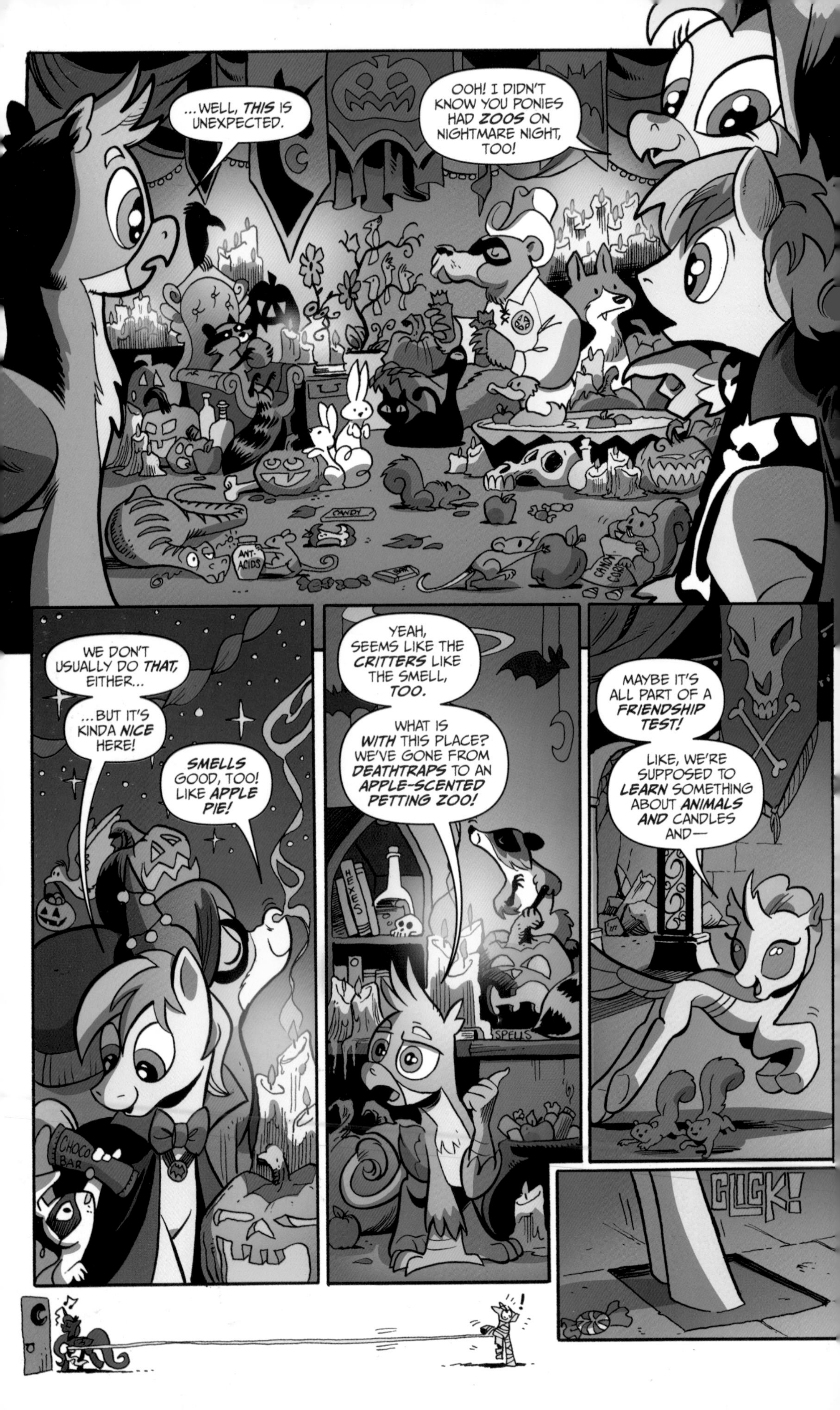
...WELL, *THIS* IS UNEXPECTED.
OOH! I DIDN'T KNOW YOU PONIES HAD *ZOOS* ON NIGHTMARE NIGHT, TOO!
ANT-ACIDS
CANDY
CANDY CORN
WE DON'T USUALLY DO *THAT,* EITHER...
...BUT IT'S KINDA *NICE* HERE!
*SMELLS* GOOD, TOO! LIKE *APPLE PIE!*
CHOCO BAR
YEAH, SEEMS LIKE THE *CRITTERS* LIKE THE SMELL, *TOO.*
WHAT IS *WITH* THIS PLACE? WE'VE GONE FROM *DEATHTRAPS* TO AN *APPLE-SCENTED PETTING ZOO!*
HEXES
SPELLS
MAYBE IT'S ALL PART OF A *FRIENDSHIP TEST!*
LIKE, WE'RE SUPPOSED TO *LEARN* SOMETHING ABOUT *ANIMALS AND* CANDLES AND—
CLICK!

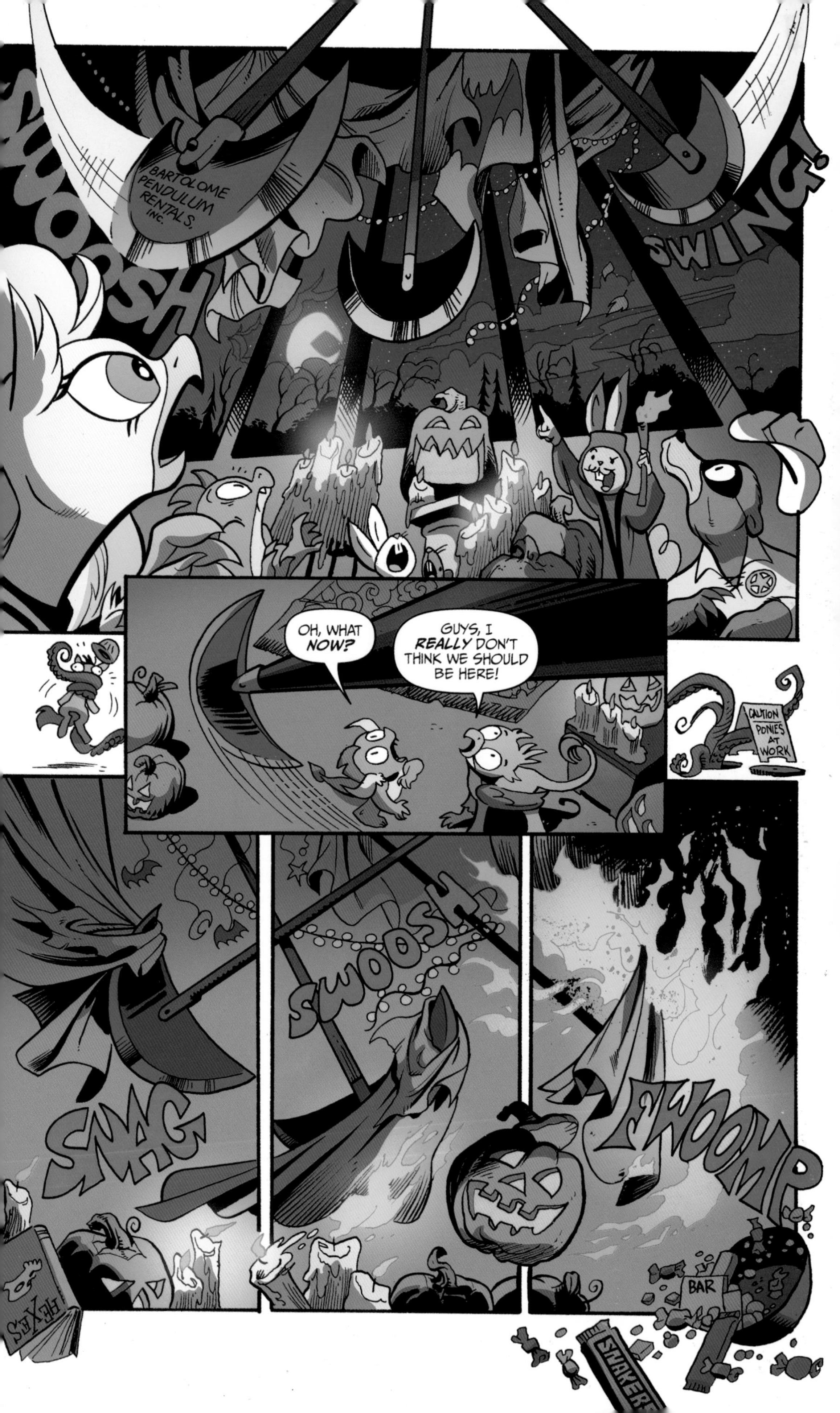
SWOOSH
BARTOLOME PENDULUM RENTALS INC.
SWING!
OH, WHAT NOW?
GUYS, I REALLY DON'T THINK WE SHOULD BE HERE!
CAUTION PONIES AT WORK
SWOOSH
SNAG
FWOOMP
HEXES
BAR

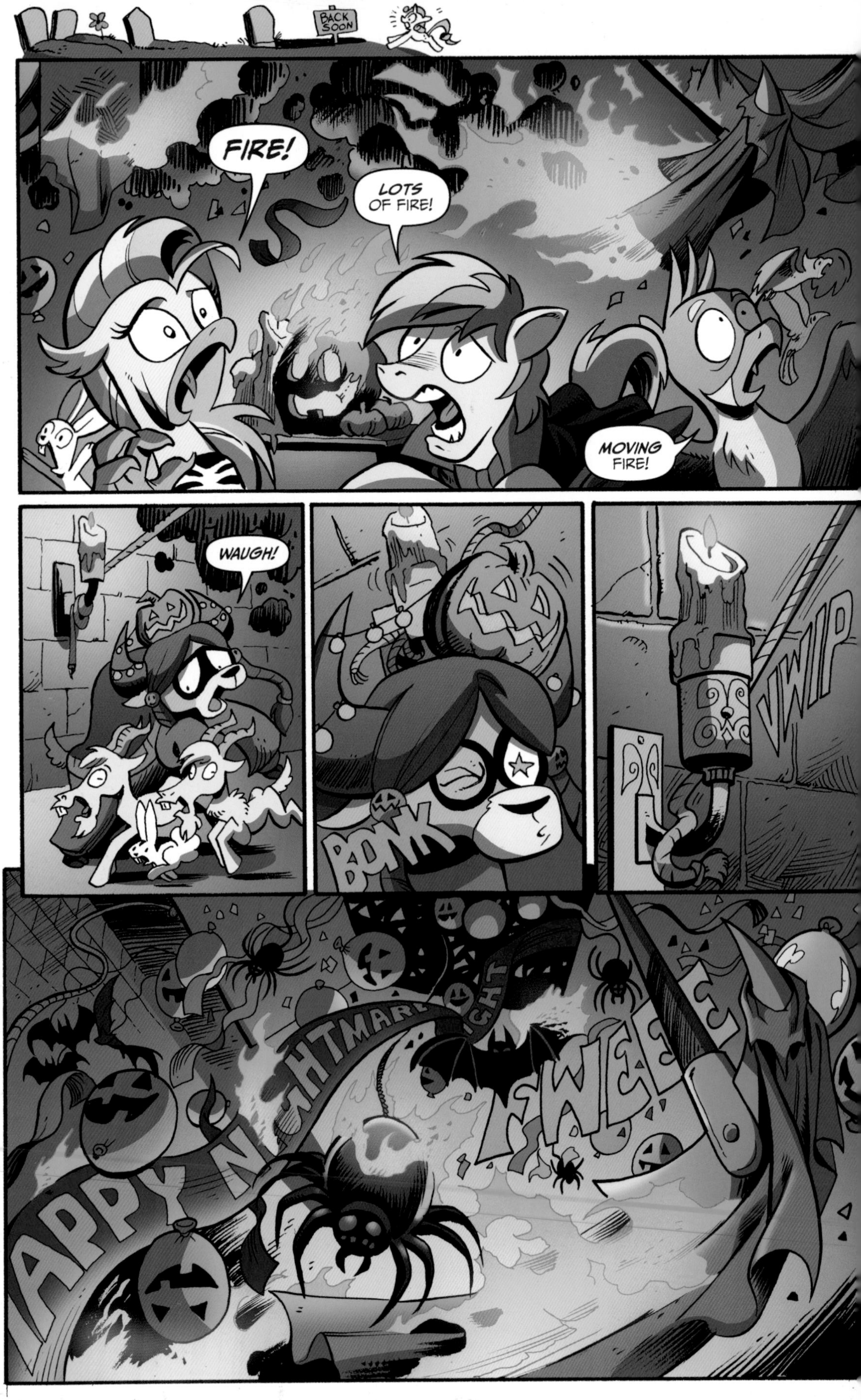
BACK SOON
FIRE!
LOTS OF FIRE!
MOVING FIRE!
WAUGH!
BONK
VWIP
APPY NIGHTMARE NIGHT

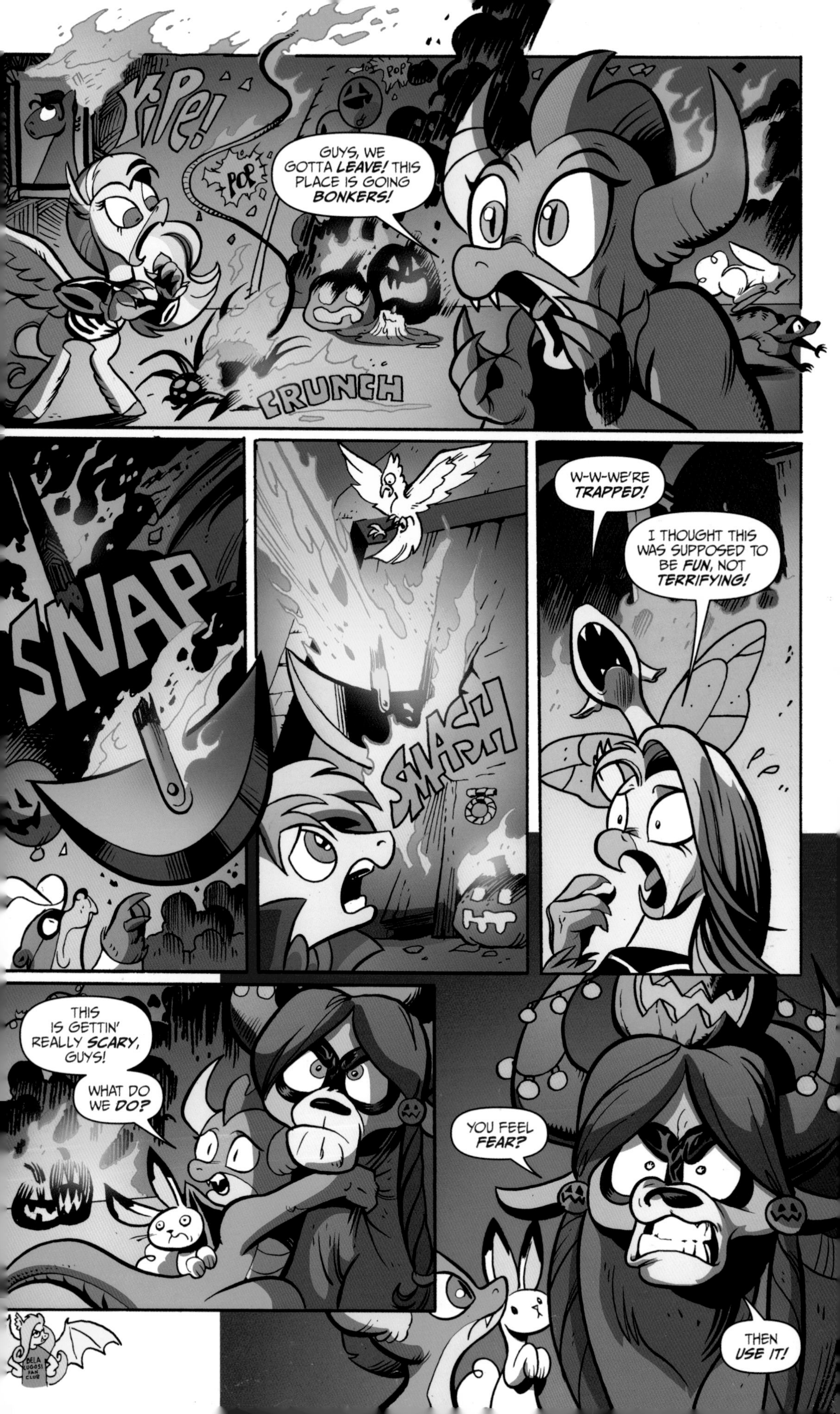
YIPE!
POP
POP
GUYS, WE GOTTA LEAVE! THIS PLACE IS GOING BONKERS!
CRUNCH
SNAP
SMASH
W-W-WE'RE TRAPPED!
I THOUGHT THIS WAS SUPPOSED TO BE FUN, NOT TERRIFYING!
THIS IS GETTIN' REALLY SCARY, GUYS!
WHAT DO WE DO?
YOU FEEL FEAR?
THEN USE IT!
BELA LUGOSI FAN CLUB

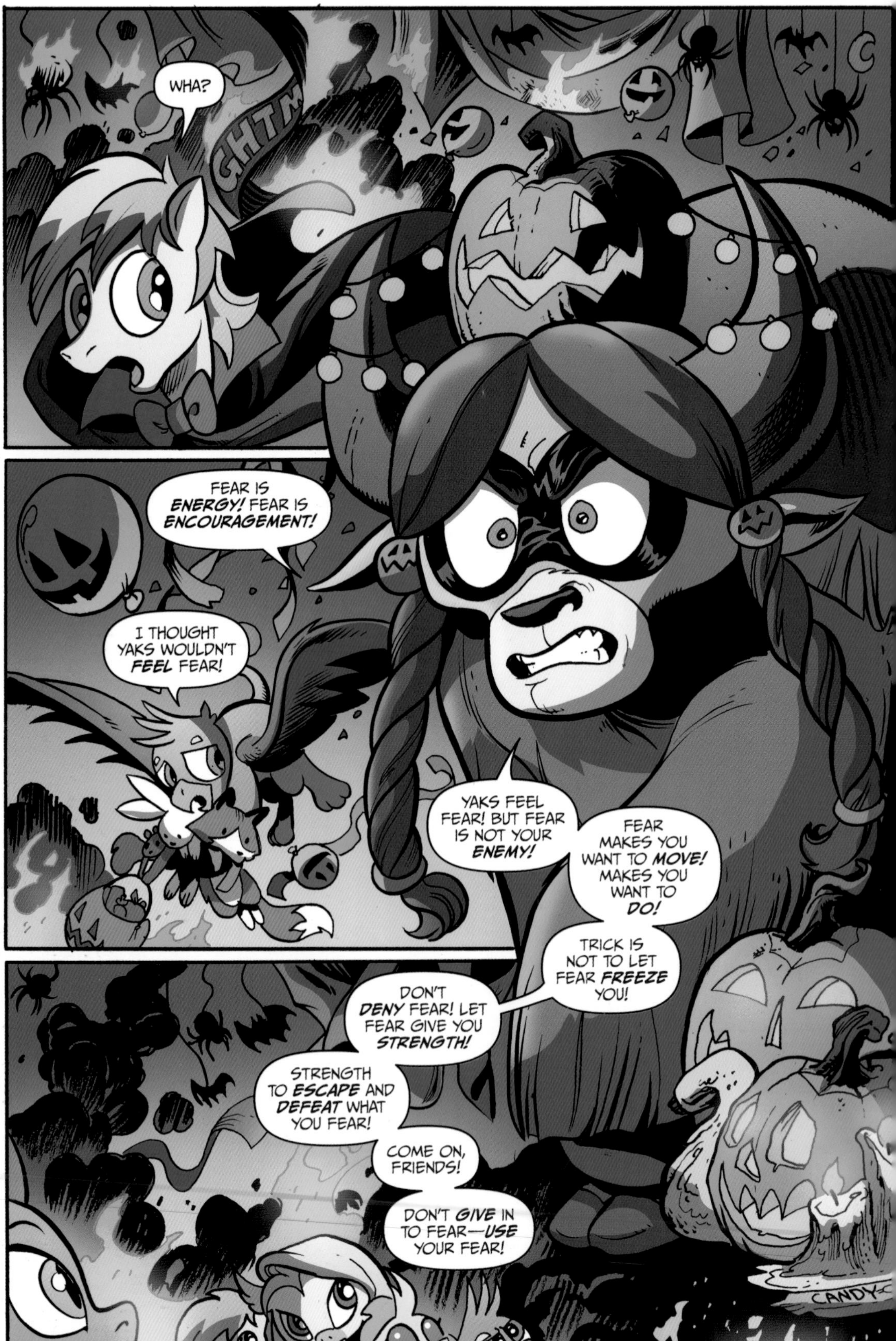
WHA?
GHTM
FEAR IS ENERGY! FEAR IS ENCOURAGEMENT!
I THOUGHT YAKS WOULDN'T FEEL FEAR!
YAKS FEEL FEAR! BUT FEAR IS NOT YOUR ENEMY!
FEAR MAKES YOU WANT TO MOVE! MAKES YOU WANT TO DO!
TRICK IS NOT TO LET FEAR FREEZE YOU!
DON'T DENY FEAR! LET FEAR GIVE YOU STRENGTH!
STRENGTH TO ESCAPE AND DEFEAT WHAT YOU FEAR!
COME ON, FRIENDS!
DON'T GIVE IN TO FEAR—USE YOUR FEAR!
CANDY
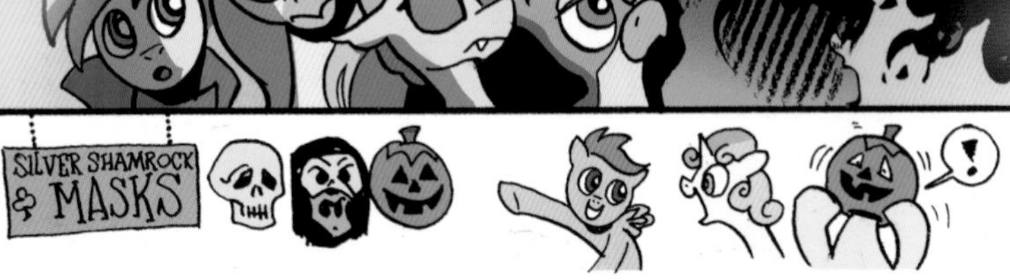
SILVER SHAMROCK & MASKS
!

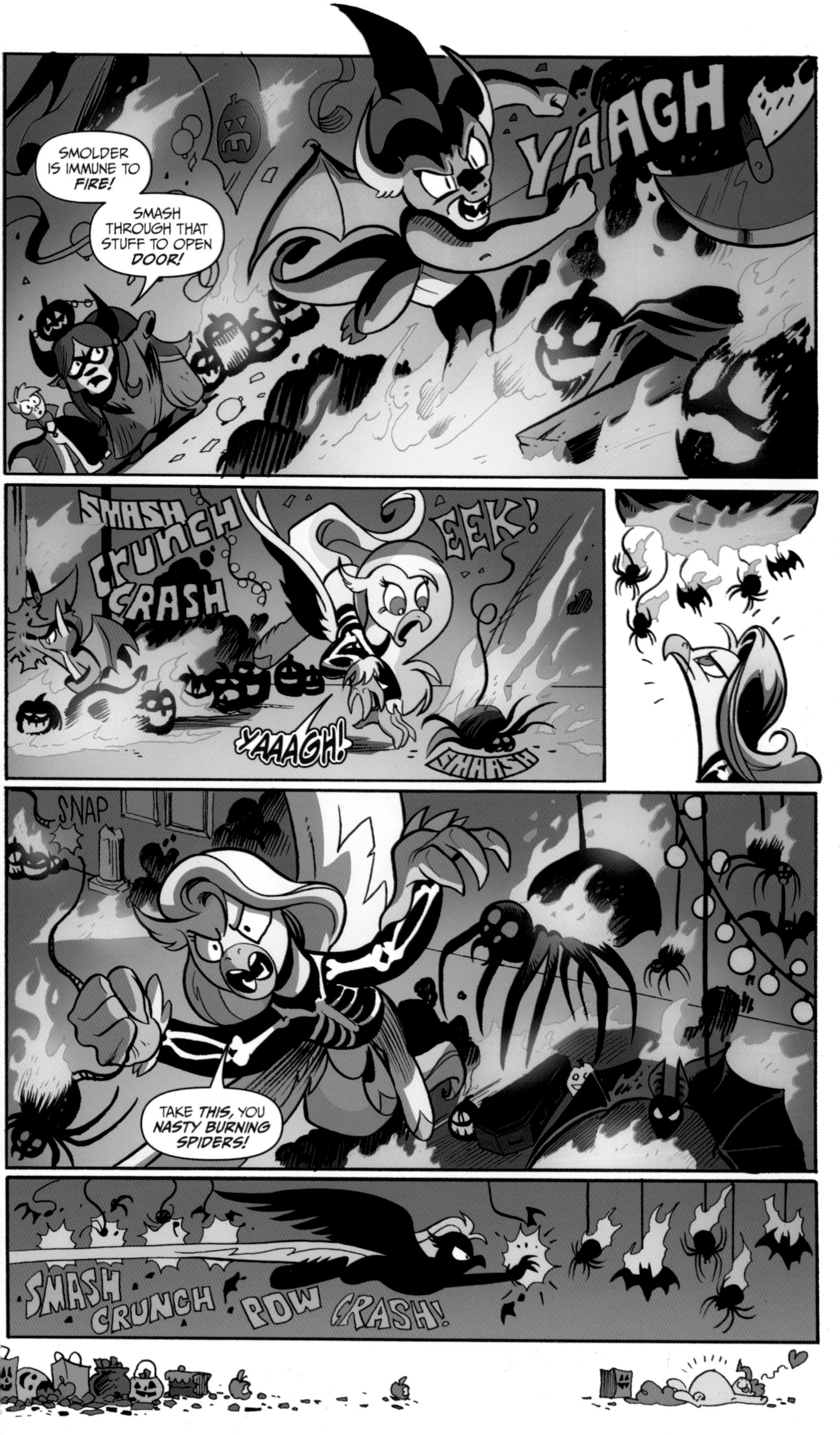
SMOLDER IS IMMUNE TO FIRE!
SMASH THROUGH THAT STUFF TO OPEN DOOR!
YAAGH
SMASH
CRUNCH
CRASH
EEK!
YAAAGH!
SMAASH
SNAP
TAKE THIS, YOU NASTY BURNING SPIDERS!
SMASH
CRUNCH
POW
CRASH!

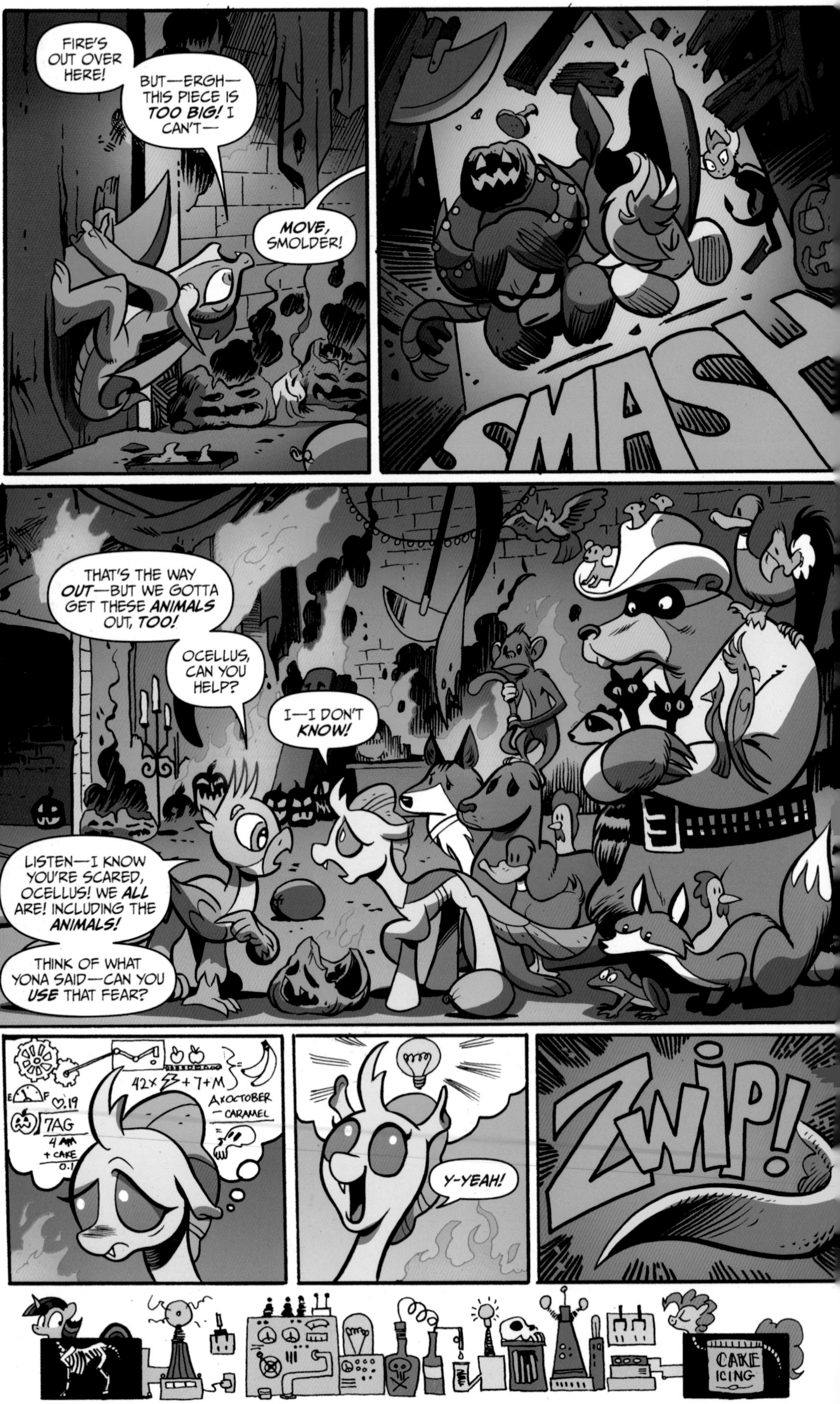

FIRE'S OUT OVER HERE!
BUT—ERGH—THIS PIECE IS TOO BIG! I CAN'T—
MOVE, SMOLDER!
SMASH
THAT'S THE WAY OUT—BUT WE GOTTA GET THESE ANIMALS OUT, TOO!
OCELLUS, CAN YOU HELP?
I—I DON'T KNOW!
LISTEN—I KNOW YOU'RE SCARED, OCELLUS! WE ALL ARE! INCLUDING THE ANIMALS!
THINK OF WHAT YONA SAID—CAN YOU USE THAT FEAR?
42x + 7 + M
OCTOBER
CARAMEL
7AG
+ CAKE
Y-YEAH!
ZWIP!
CAKE ICING

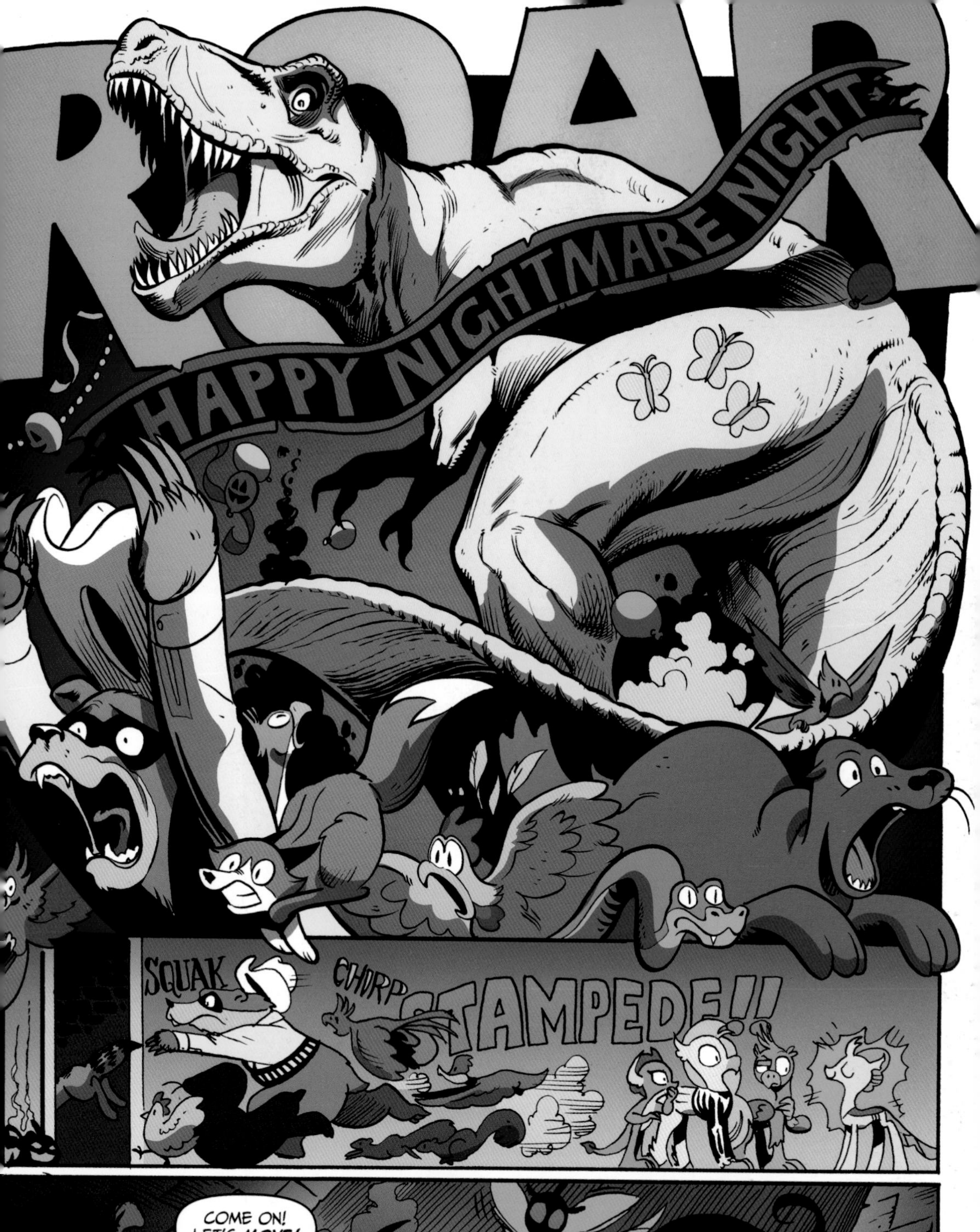
ROAR
HAPPY NIGHTMARE NIGHT
SQUAK
CHORP
STAMPEDE!!
COME ON! LET'S *MOVE*!

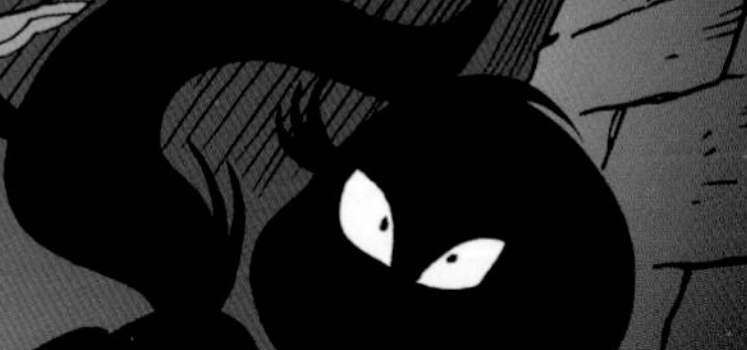
?

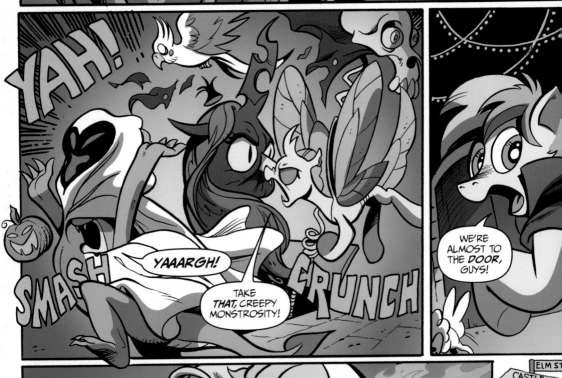

SPROING

YAH!

SMASH

CRUNCH

YAAARGH!

TAKE *THAT*, CREEPY MONSTROSITY!

WE'RE ALMOST TO THE *DOOR*, GUYS!

TO FREEDOM!

YAAARGH!

ELM ST

CASTLE ROCK

HADDONFIELD

CRYSTAL LAKE

SALEM'S LOT

LODGING
BATES MOTEL
DOLPHIN HOTEL
OVERLOOK HOTEL

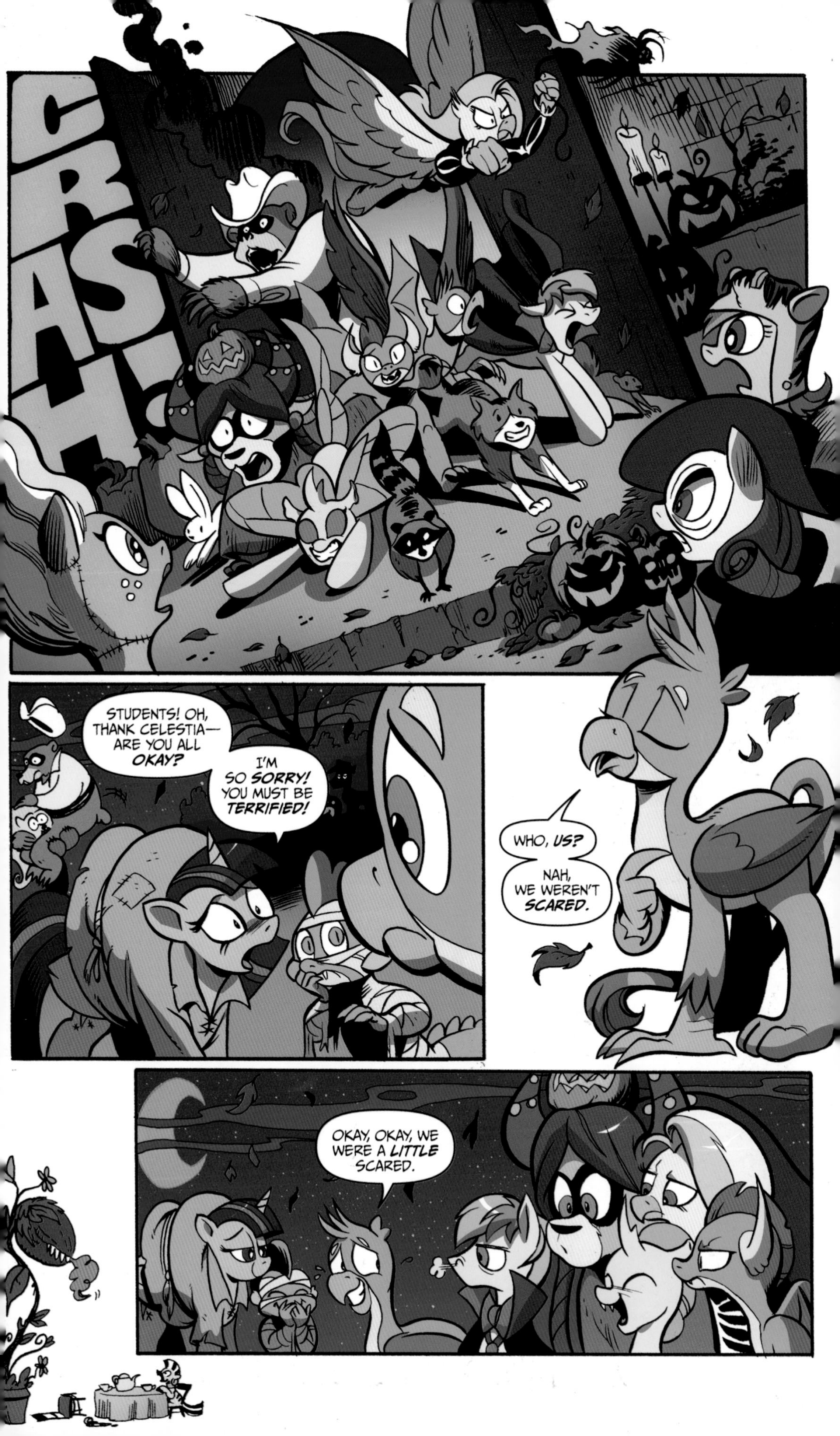
CRASH
STUDENTS! OH, THANK CELESTIA— ARE YOU ALL OKAY?
I'M SO SORRY! YOU MUST BE TERRIFIED!
WHO, US?
NAH, WE WEREN'T SCARED.
OKAY, OKAY, WE WERE A LITTLE SCARED.

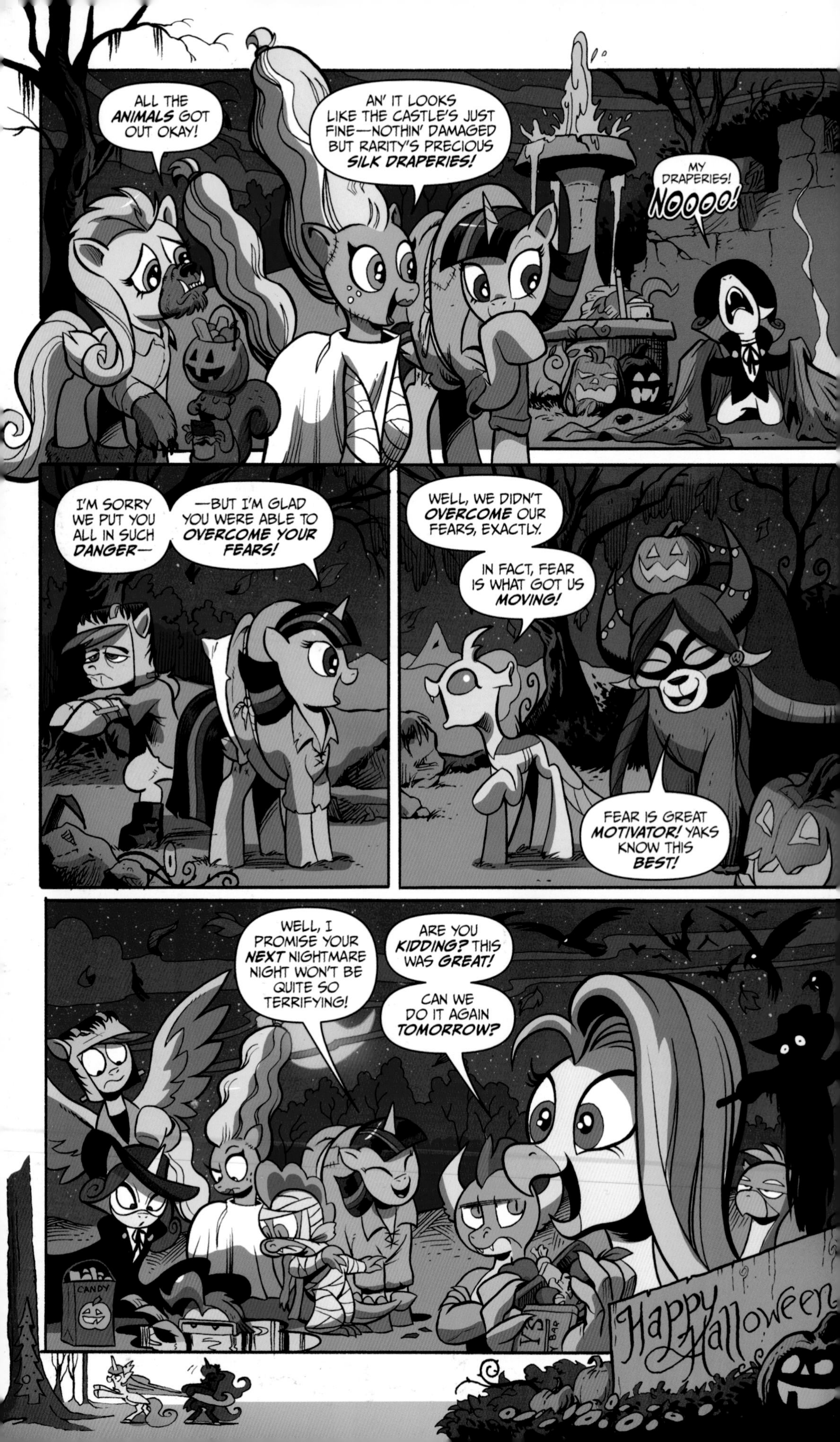
ALL THE ANIMALS GOT OUT OKAY!
AN' IT LOOKS LIKE THE CASTLE'S JUST FINE—NOTHIN' DAMAGED BUT RARITY'S PRECIOUS SILK DRAPERIES!
MY DRAPERIES! NOOOO!
I'M SORRY WE PUT YOU ALL IN SUCH DANGER—
—BUT I'M GLAD YOU WERE ABLE TO OVERCOME YOUR FEARS!
WELL, WE DIDN'T OVERCOME OUR FEARS, EXACTLY.
IN FACT, FEAR IS WHAT GOT US MOVING!
FEAR IS GREAT MOTIVATOR! YAKS KNOW THIS BEST!
WELL, I PROMISE YOUR NEXT NIGHTMARE NIGHT WON'T BE QUITE SO TERRIFYING!
ARE YOU KIDDING? THIS WAS GREAT!
CAN WE DO IT AGAIN TOMORROW?
CANDY
Happy Halloween

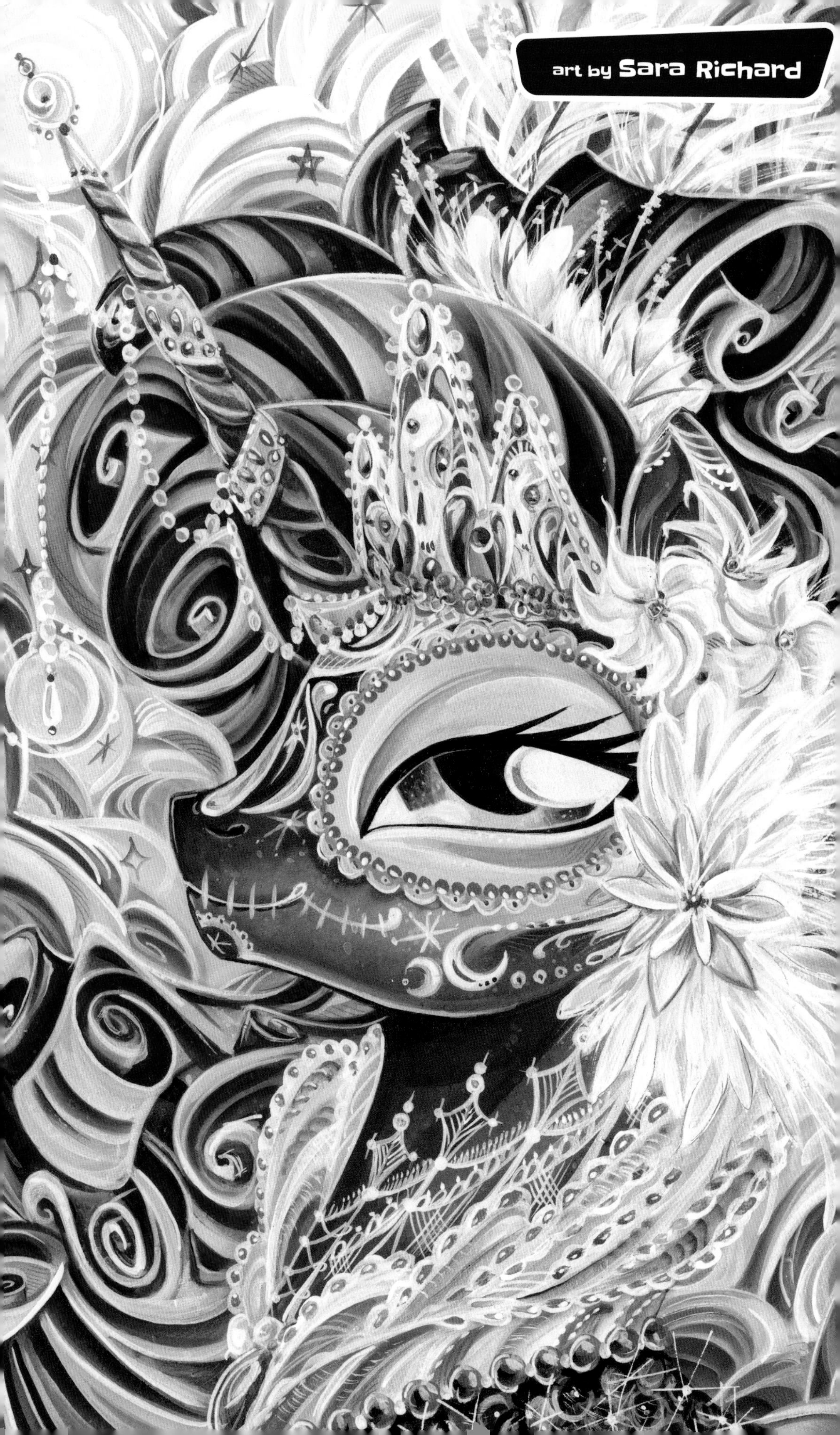
art by Sara Richard

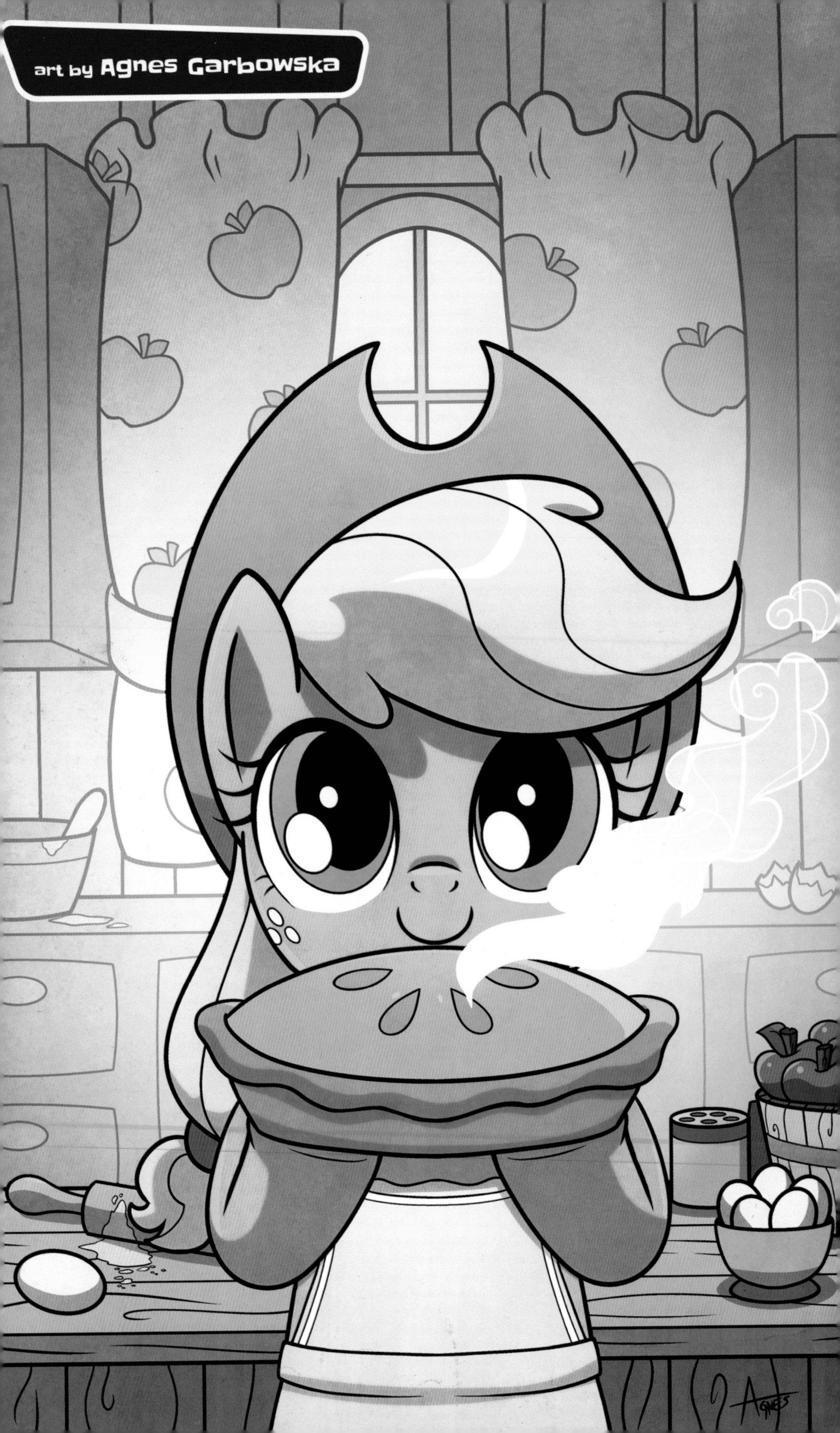

art by Agnes Garbowska

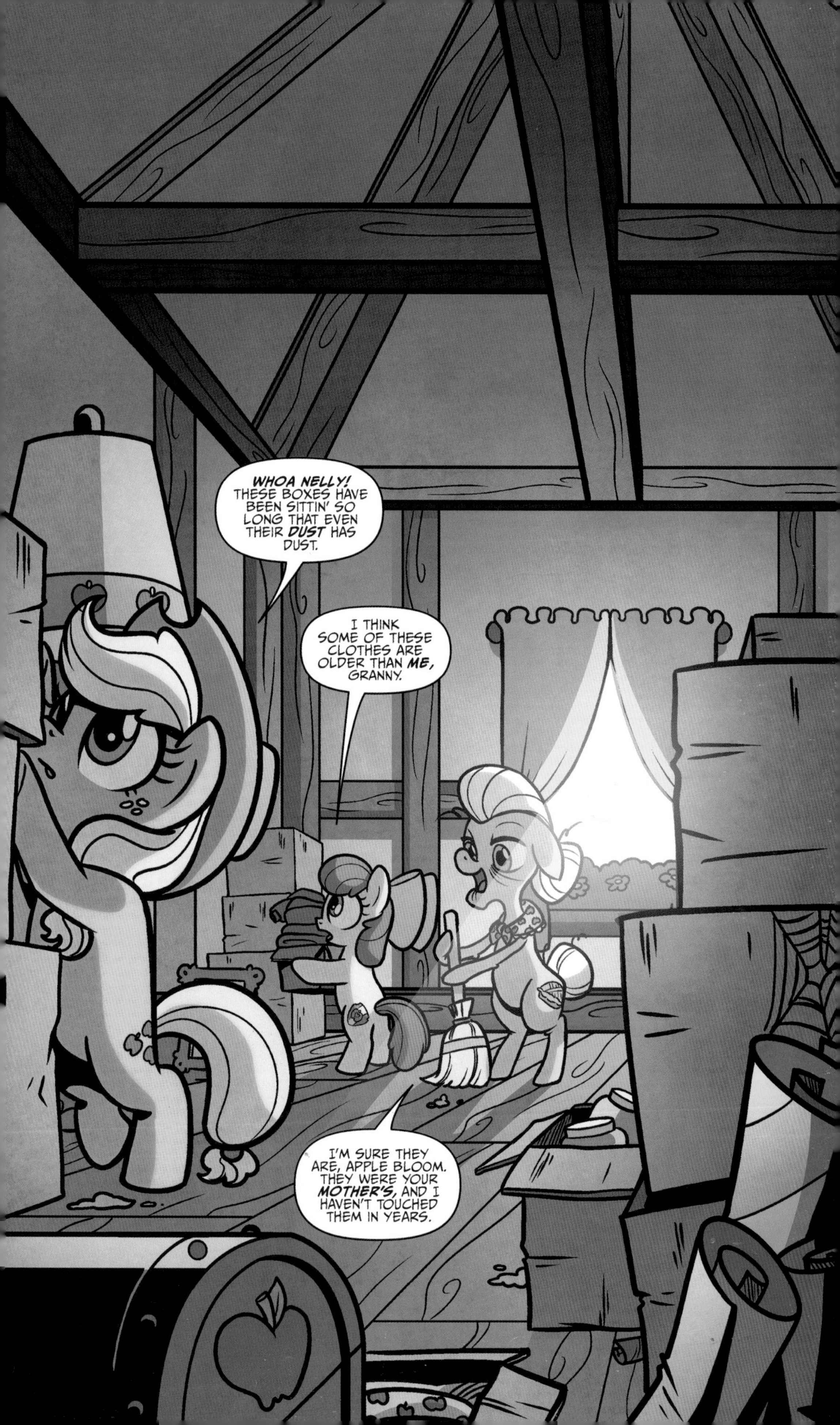
WHOA NELLY! THESE BOXES HAVE BEEN SITTIN' SO LONG THAT EVEN THEIR DUST HAS DUST.
I THINK SOME OF THESE CLOTHES ARE OLDER THAN ME, GRANNY.
I'M SURE THEY ARE, APPLE BLOOM. THEY WERE YOUR MOTHER'S, AND I HAVEN'T TOUCHED THEM IN YEARS.

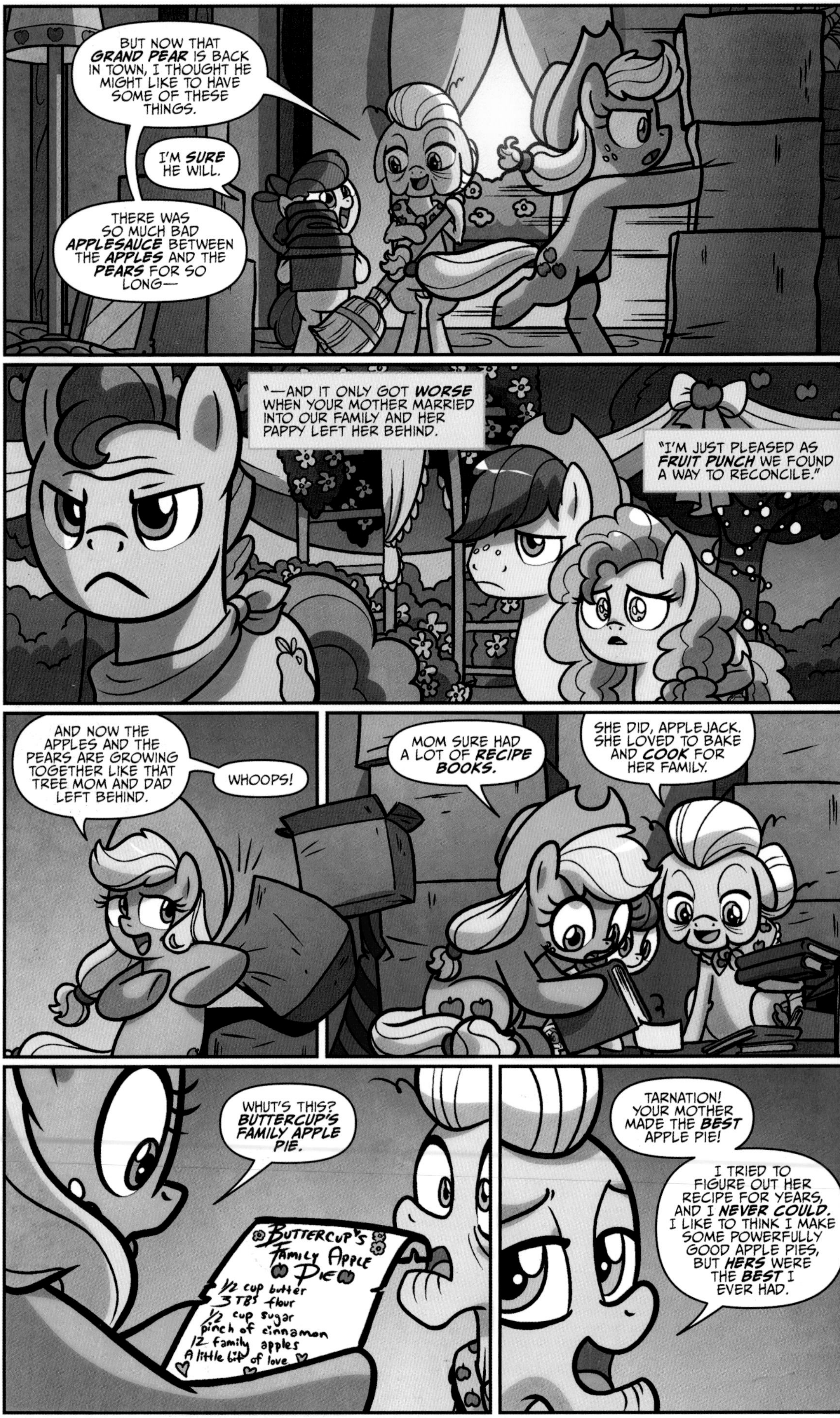

BUT NOW THAT GRAND PEAR IS BACK IN TOWN, I THOUGHT HE MIGHT LIKE TO HAVE SOME OF THESE THINGS.
I'M SURE HE WILL.
THERE WAS SO MUCH BAD APPLESAUCE BETWEEN THE APPLES AND THE PEARS FOR SO LONG—
"—AND IT ONLY GOT WORSE WHEN YOUR MOTHER MARRIED INTO OUR FAMILY AND HER PAPPY LEFT HER BEHIND.
"I'M JUST PLEASED AS FRUIT PUNCH WE FOUND A WAY TO RECONCILE."
AND NOW THE APPLES AND THE PEARS ARE GROWING TOGETHER LIKE THAT TREE MOM AND DAD LEFT BEHIND.
WHOOPS!
MOM SURE HAD A LOT OF RECIPE BOOKS.
SHE DID, APPLEJACK. SHE LOVED TO BAKE AND COOK FOR HER FAMILY.
WHUT'S THIS? BUTTERCUP'S FAMILY APPLE PIE.
Buttercup's Family Apple Pie
1/2 cup butter
3 TBS flour
1/2 cup sugar
pinch of cinnamon
12 family apples
A little bit of love
TARNATION! YOUR MOTHER MADE THE BEST APPLE PIE!
I TRIED TO FIGURE OUT HER RECIPE FOR YEARS, AND I NEVER COULD. I LIKE TO THINK I MAKE SOME POWERFULLY GOOD APPLE PIES, BUT HERS WERE THE BEST I EVER HAD.

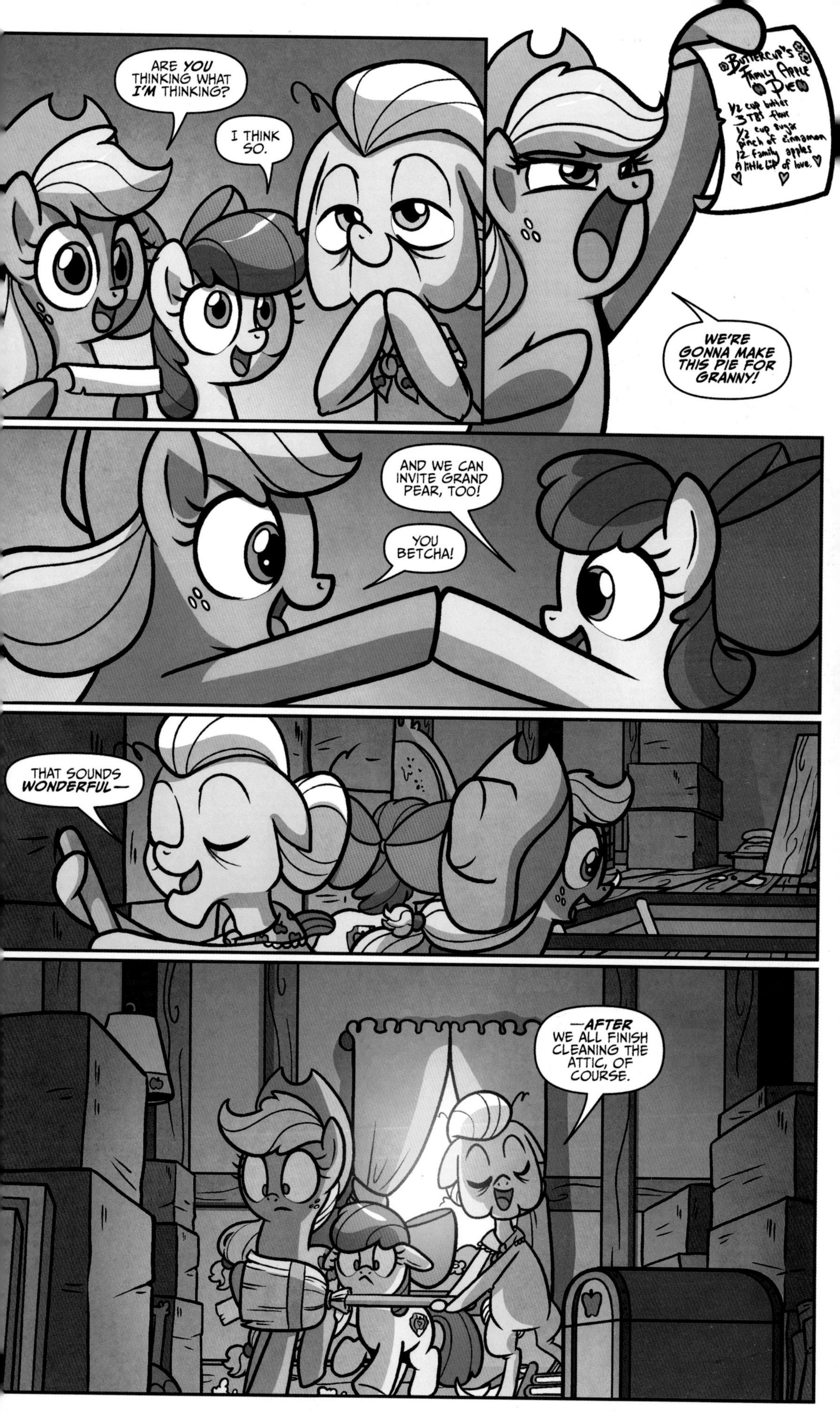
ARE *YOU* THINKING WHAT *I'M* THINKING?
I THINK SO.
BUTTERCUP'S FAMILY APPLE PIE
1/2 cup butter
3 TBS flour
1/2 cup sugar
pinch of cinnamon
12 family apples
A little bit of love.
*WE'RE GONNA MAKE THIS PIE FOR GRANNY!*
AND WE CAN INVITE GRAND PEAR, TOO!
YOU BETCHA!
THAT SOUNDS *WONDERFUL—*
—*AFTER* WE ALL FINISH CLEANING THE ATTIC, OF COURSE.

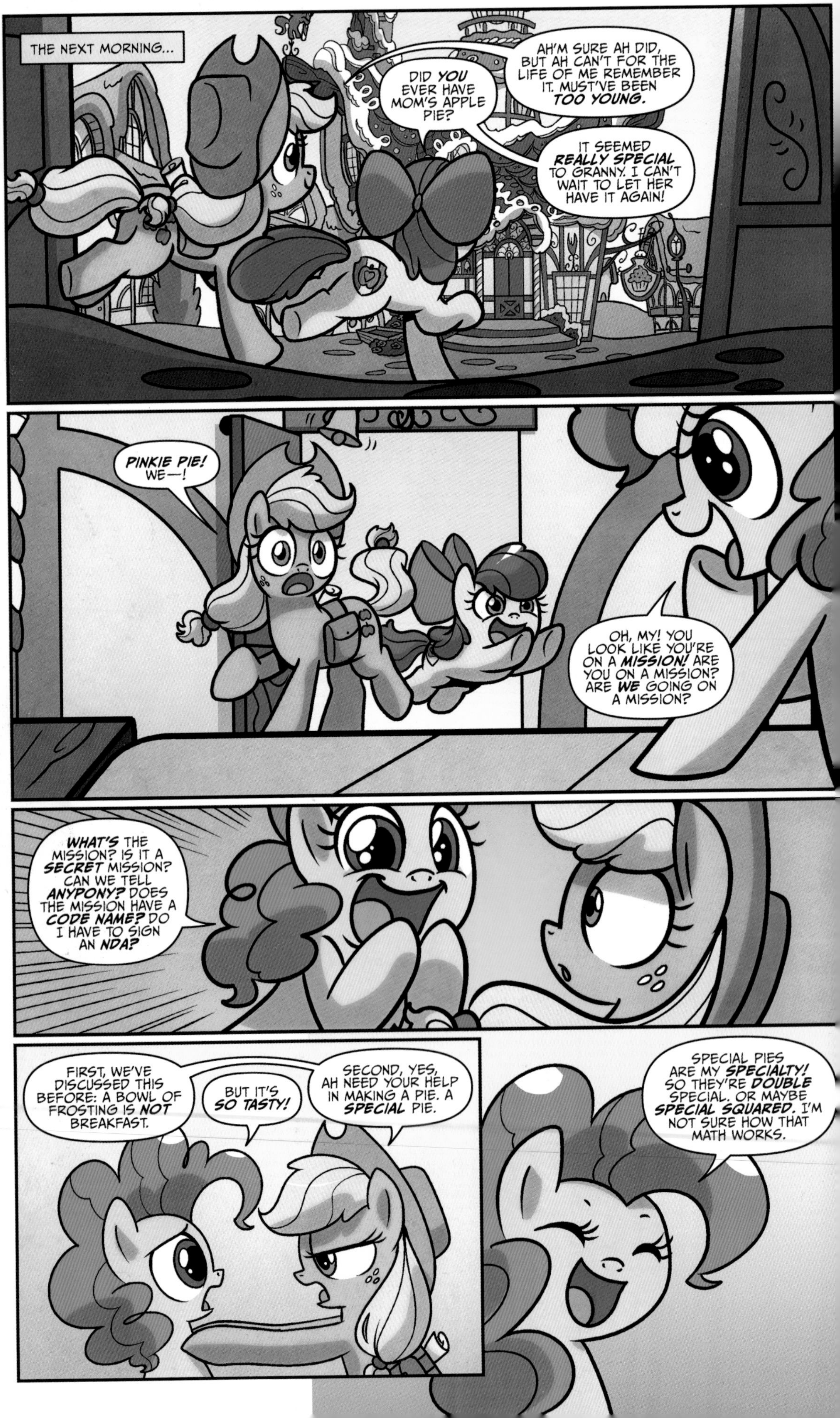
THE NEXT MORNING...
DID YOU EVER HAVE MOM'S APPLE PIE?
AH'M SURE AH DID, BUT AH CAN'T FOR THE LIFE OF ME REMEMBER IT. MUST'VE BEEN TOO YOUNG.
IT SEEMED REALLY SPECIAL TO GRANNY. I CAN'T WAIT TO LET HER HAVE IT AGAIN!
PINKIE PIE! WE—!
OH, MY! YOU LOOK LIKE YOU'RE ON A MISSION! ARE YOU ON A MISSION? ARE WE GOING ON A MISSION?
WHAT'S THE MISSION? IS IT A SECRET MISSION? CAN WE TELL ANYPONY? DOES THE MISSION HAVE A CODE NAME? DO I HAVE TO SIGN AN NDA?
FIRST, WE'VE DISCUSSED THIS BEFORE: A BOWL OF FROSTING IS NOT BREAKFAST.
BUT IT'S SO TASTY!
SECOND, YES, AH NEED YOUR HELP IN MAKING A PIE. A SPECIAL PIE.
SPECIAL PIES ARE MY SPECIALTY! SO THEY'RE DOUBLE SPECIAL. OR MAYBE SPECIAL SQUARED. I'M NOT SURE HOW THAT MATH WORKS.

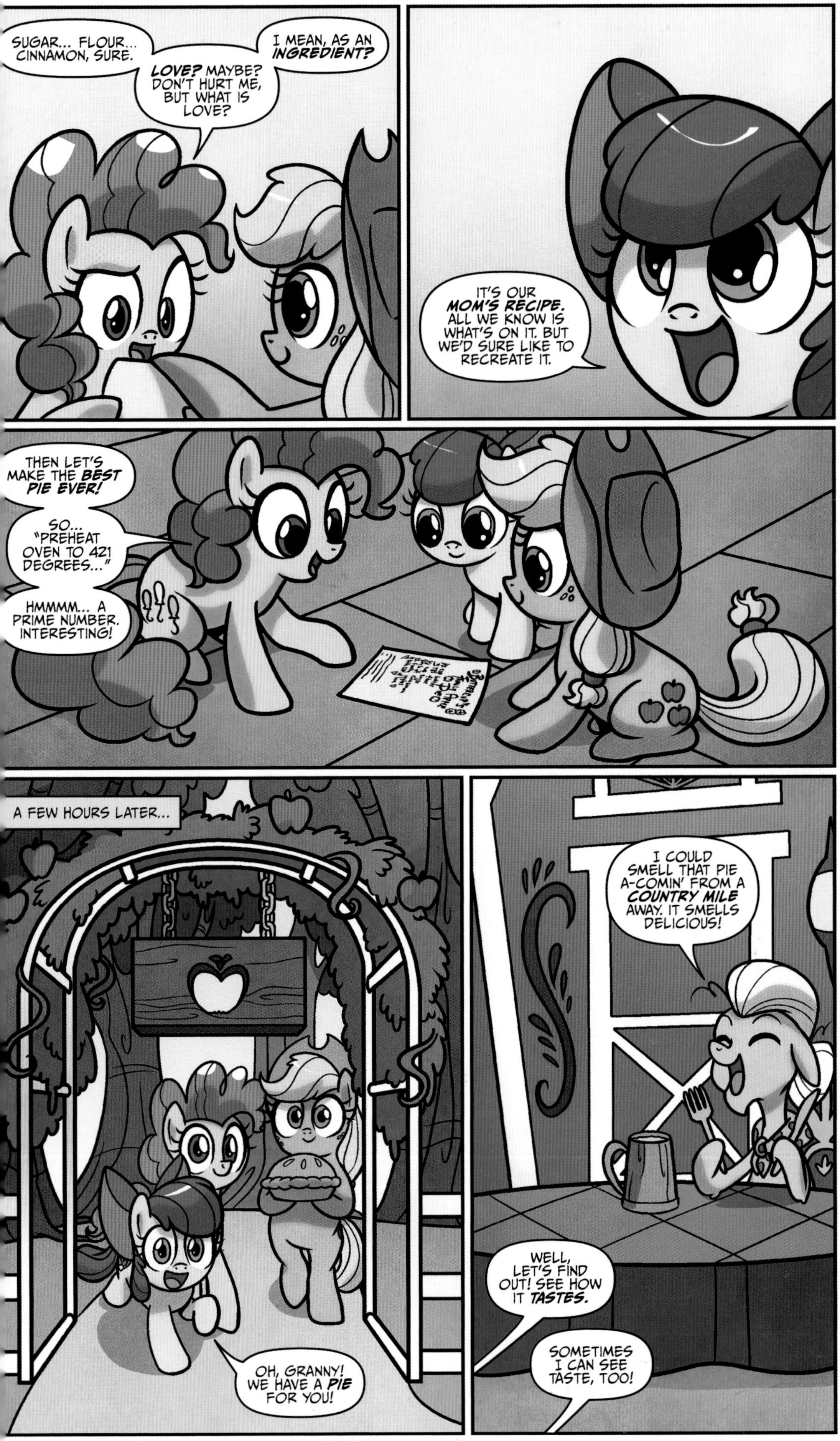
SUGAR... FLOUR... CINNAMON, SURE.
LOVE? MAYBE? DON'T HURT ME, BUT WHAT IS LOVE?
I MEAN, AS AN INGREDIENT?
IT'S OUR MOM'S RECIPE. ALL WE KNOW IS WHAT'S ON IT. BUT WE'D SURE LIKE TO RECREATE IT.
THEN LET'S MAKE THE BEST PIE EVER!
SO... "PREHEAT OVEN TO 421 DEGREES..."
HMMMM... A PRIME NUMBER. INTERESTING!
A FEW HOURS LATER...
OH, GRANNY! WE HAVE A PIE FOR YOU!
I COULD SMELL THAT PIE A-COMIN' FROM A COUNTRY MILE AWAY. IT SMELLS DELICIOUS!
WELL, LET'S FIND OUT! SEE HOW IT TASTES.
SOMETIMES I CAN SEE TASTE, TOO!

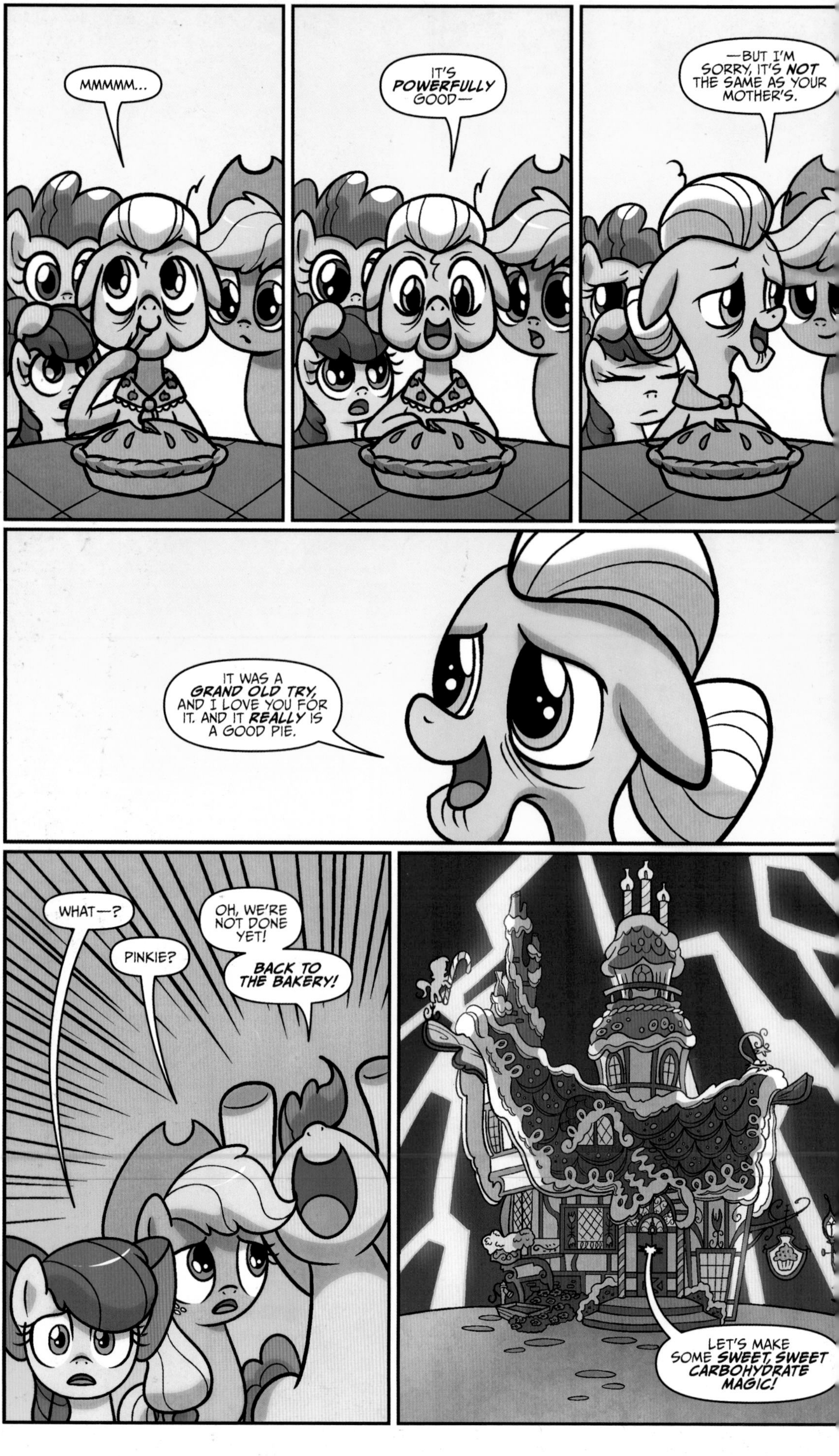
MMMMM...
IT'S POWERFULLY GOOD—
—BUT I'M SORRY, IT'S NOT THE SAME AS YOUR MOTHER'S.
IT WAS A GRAND OLD TRY, AND I LOVE YOU FOR IT. AND IT REALLY IS A GOOD PIE.
WHAT—?
PINKIE?
OH, WE'RE NOT DONE YET!
BACK TO THE BAKERY!
LET'S MAKE SOME SWEET, SWEET CARBOHYDRATE MAGIC!

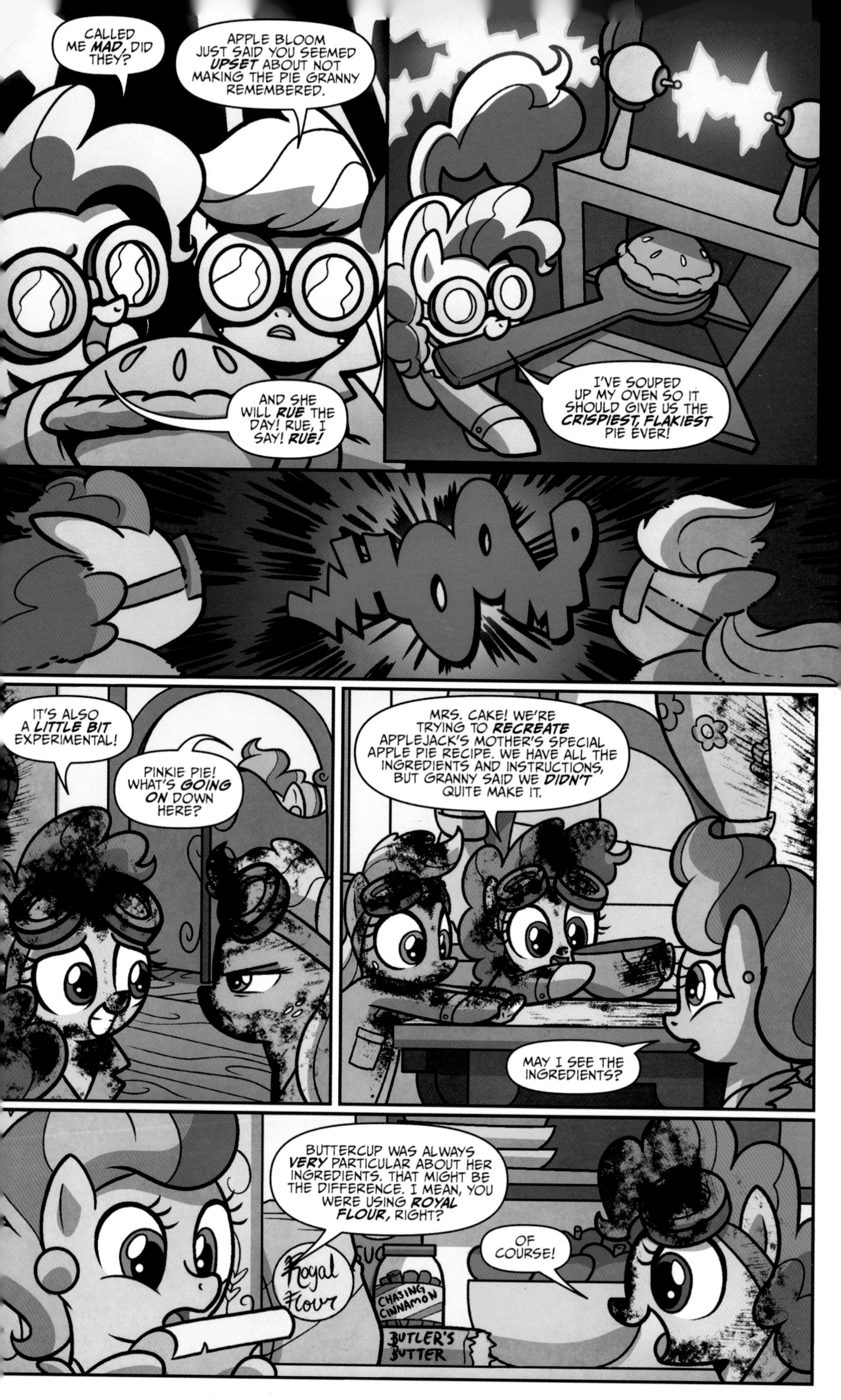

CALLED ME MAD, DID THEY?
APPLE BLOOM JUST SAID YOU SEEMED UPSET ABOUT NOT MAKING THE PIE GRANNY REMEMBERED.
AND SHE WILL RUE THE DAY! RUE, I SAY! RUE!
I'VE SOUPED UP MY OVEN SO IT SHOULD GIVE US THE CRISPIEST, FLAKIEST PIE EVER!
WHOOMP
IT'S ALSO A LITTLE BIT EXPERIMENTAL!
PINKIE PIE! WHAT'S GOING ON DOWN HERE?
MRS. CAKE! WE'RE TRYING TO RECREATE APPLEJACK'S MOTHER'S SPECIAL APPLE PIE RECIPE. WE HAVE ALL THE INGREDIENTS AND INSTRUCTIONS, BUT GRANNY SAID WE DIDN'T QUITE MAKE IT.
MAY I SEE THE INGREDIENTS?
BUTTERCUP WAS ALWAYS VERY PARTICULAR ABOUT HER INGREDIENTS. THAT MIGHT BE THE DIFFERENCE. I MEAN, YOU WERE USING ROYAL FLOUR, RIGHT?
OF COURSE!
Royal Flour
CHASING CINNAMON
BUTLER'S BUTTER

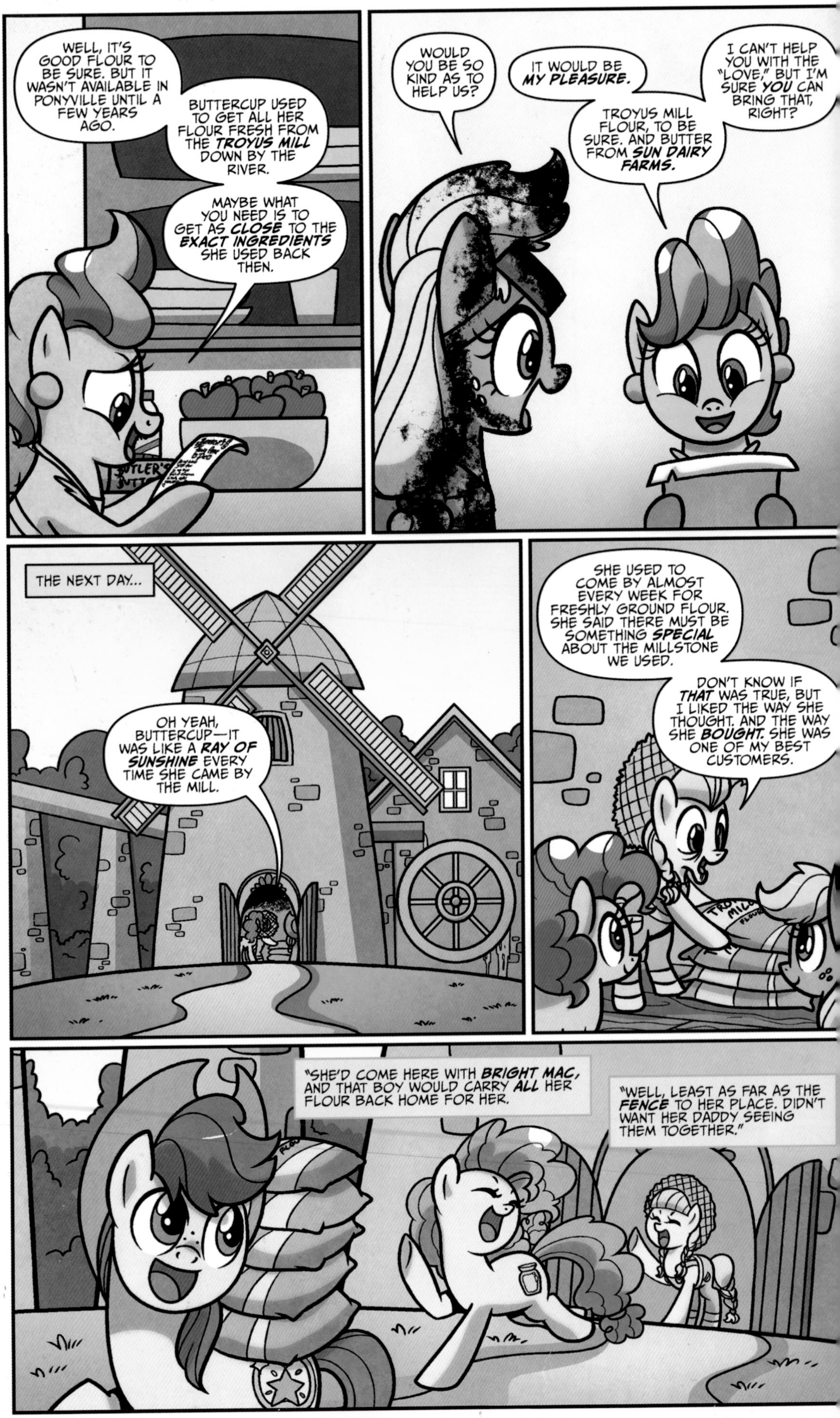

WELL, IT'S GOOD FLOUR TO BE SURE. BUT IT WASN'T AVAILABLE IN PONYVILLE UNTIL A FEW YEARS AGO.
BUTTERCUP USED TO GET ALL HER FLOUR FRESH FROM THE TROYUS MILL DOWN BY THE RIVER.
MAYBE WHAT YOU NEED IS TO GET AS CLOSE TO THE EXACT INGREDIENTS SHE USED BACK THEN.
WOULD YOU BE SO KIND AS TO HELP US?
IT WOULD BE MY PLEASURE.
TROYUS MILL FLOUR, TO BE SURE. AND BUTTER FROM SUN DAIRY FARMS.
I CAN'T HELP YOU WITH THE "LOVE," BUT I'M SURE YOU CAN BRING THAT, RIGHT?
THE NEXT DAY...
OH YEAH, BUTTERCUP—IT WAS LIKE A RAY OF SUNSHINE EVERY TIME SHE CAME BY THE MILL.
SHE USED TO COME BY ALMOST EVERY WEEK FOR FRESHLY GROUND FLOUR. SHE SAID THERE MUST BE SOMETHING SPECIAL ABOUT THE MILLSTONE WE USED.
DON'T KNOW IF THAT WAS TRUE, BUT I LIKED THE WAY SHE THOUGHT. AND THE WAY SHE BOUGHT. SHE WAS ONE OF MY BEST CUSTOMERS.
"SHE'D COME HERE WITH BRIGHT MAC, AND THAT BOY WOULD CARRY ALL HER FLOUR BACK HOME FOR HER.
"WELL, LEAST AS FAR AS THE FENCE TO HER PLACE. DIDN'T WANT HER DADDY SEEING THEM TOGETHER."

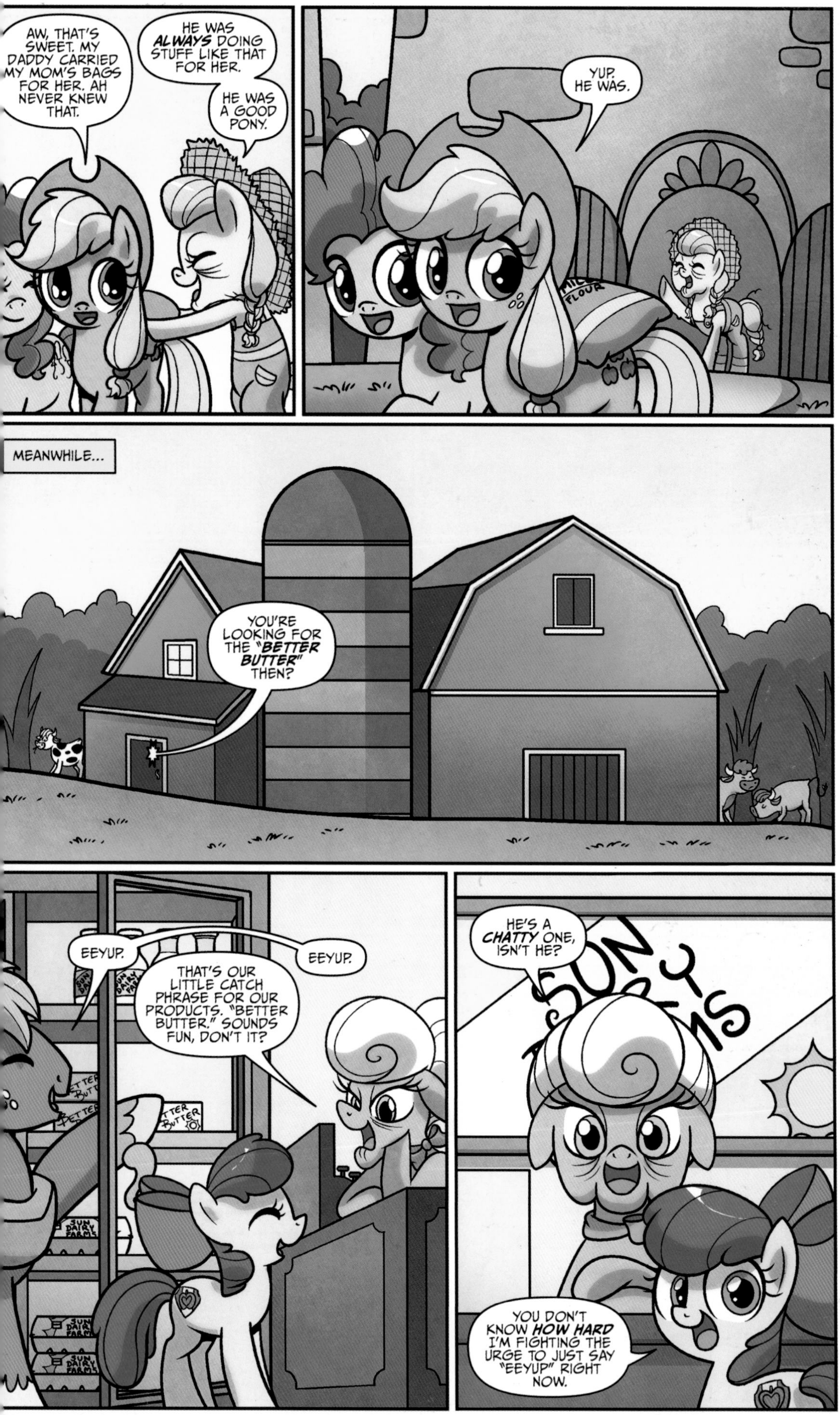
AW, THAT'S SWEET. MY DADDY CARRIED MY MOM'S BAGS FOR HER. AH NEVER KNEW THAT.
HE WAS ***ALWAYS*** DOING STUFF LIKE THAT FOR HER.
HE WAS A GOOD PONY.
YUP. HE WAS.
FLOUR
MEANWHILE...
YOU'RE LOOKING FOR THE "***BETTER BUTTER***" THEN?
EEYUP.
EEYUP.
THAT'S OUR LITTLE CATCH PHRASE FOR OUR PRODUCTS. "BETTER BUTTER." SOUNDS FUN, DON'T IT?
SUN DAIRY FARMS
HE'S A ***CHATTY*** ONE, ISN'T HE?
YOU DON'T KNOW ***HOW HARD*** I'M FIGHTING THE URGE TO JUST SAY "EEYUP" RIGHT NOW.

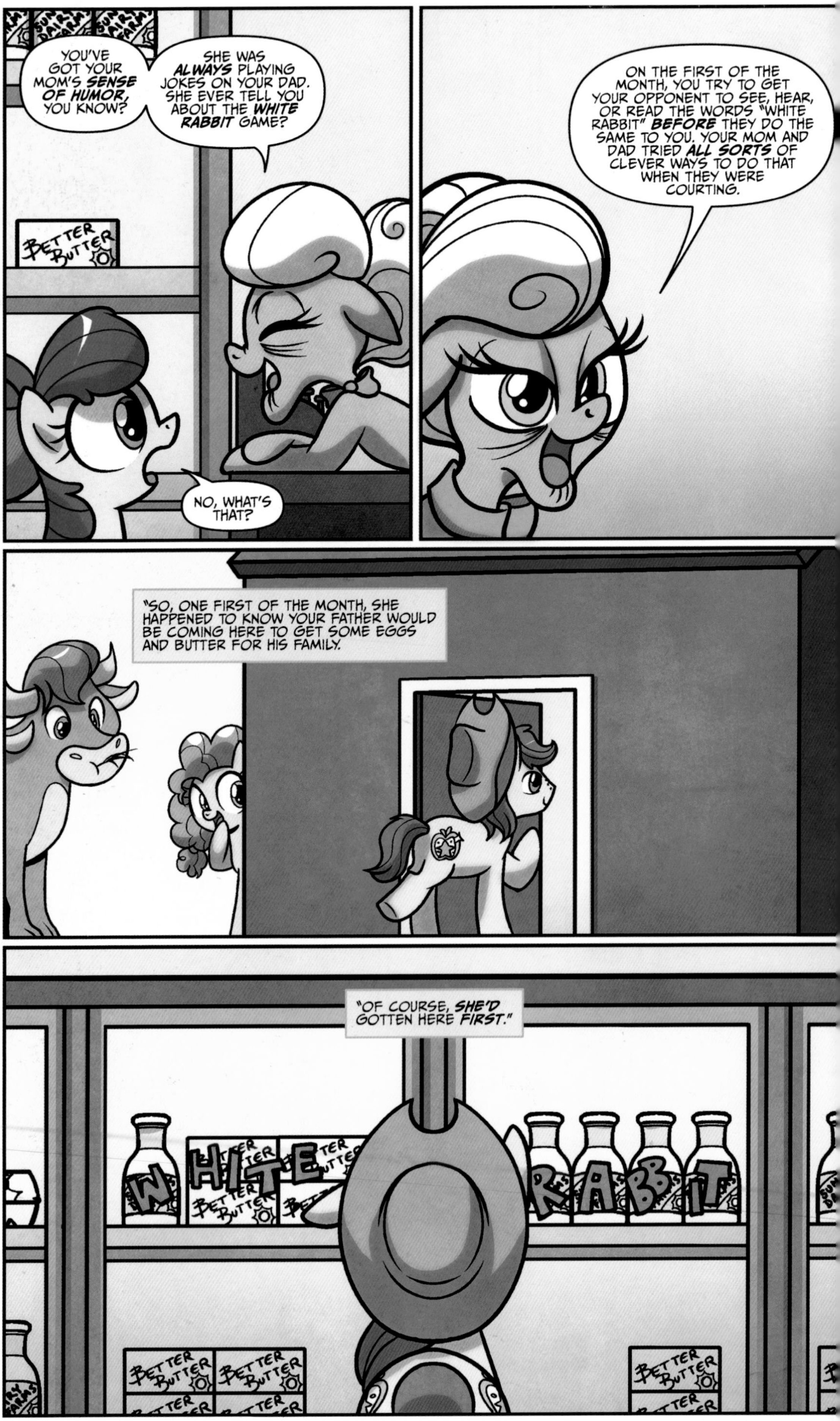
YOU'VE GOT YOUR MOM'S **SENSE OF HUMOR**, YOU KNOW?
SHE WAS **ALWAYS** PLAYING JOKES ON YOUR DAD. SHE EVER TELL YOU ABOUT THE **WHITE RABBIT** GAME?
BETTER BUTTER
NO, WHAT'S THAT?
ON THE FIRST OF THE MONTH, YOU TRY TO GET YOUR OPPONENT TO SEE, HEAR, OR READ THE WORDS "WHITE RABBIT" **BEFORE** THEY DO THE SAME TO YOU. YOUR MOM AND DAD TRIED **ALL SORTS** OF CLEVER WAYS TO DO THAT WHEN THEY WERE COURTING.
"SO, ONE FIRST OF THE MONTH, SHE HAPPENED TO KNOW YOUR FATHER WOULD BE COMING HERE TO GET SOME EGGS AND BUTTER FOR HIS FAMILY.
"OF COURSE, **SHE'D** GOTTEN HERE **FIRST**."
WHITE
RABBIT
BETTER BUTTER

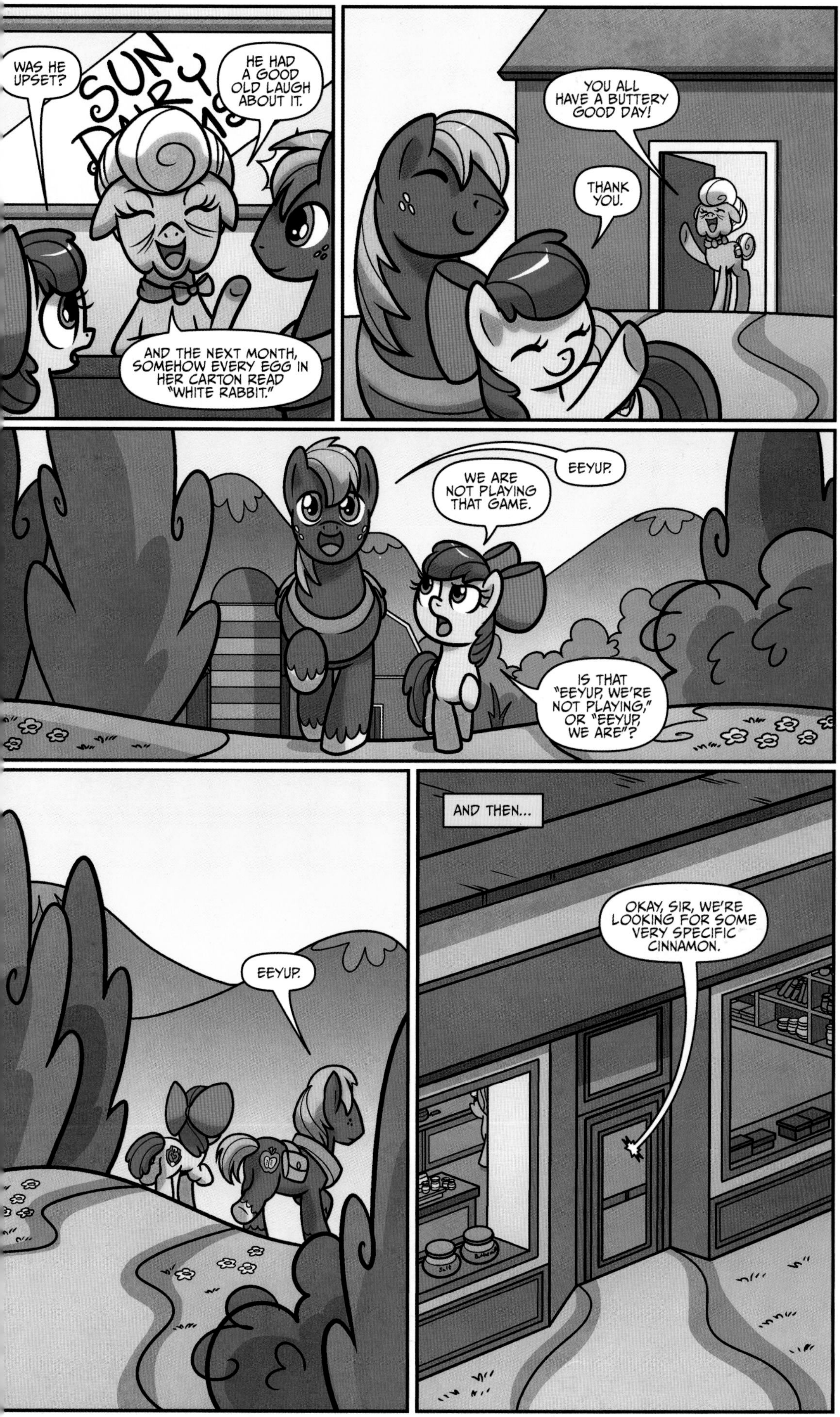
WAS HE UPSET?
HE HAD A GOOD OLD LAUGH ABOUT IT.
AND THE NEXT MONTH, SOMEHOW EVERY EGG IN HER CARTON READ "WHITE RABBIT."
YOU ALL HAVE A BUTTERY GOOD DAY!
THANK YOU.
WE ARE NOT PLAYING THAT GAME.
EEYUP.
IS THAT "EEYUP, WE'RE NOT PLAYING," OR "EEYUP, WE ARE"?
EEYUP.
AND THEN...
OKAY, SIR, WE'RE LOOKING FOR SOME VERY SPECIFIC CINNAMON.

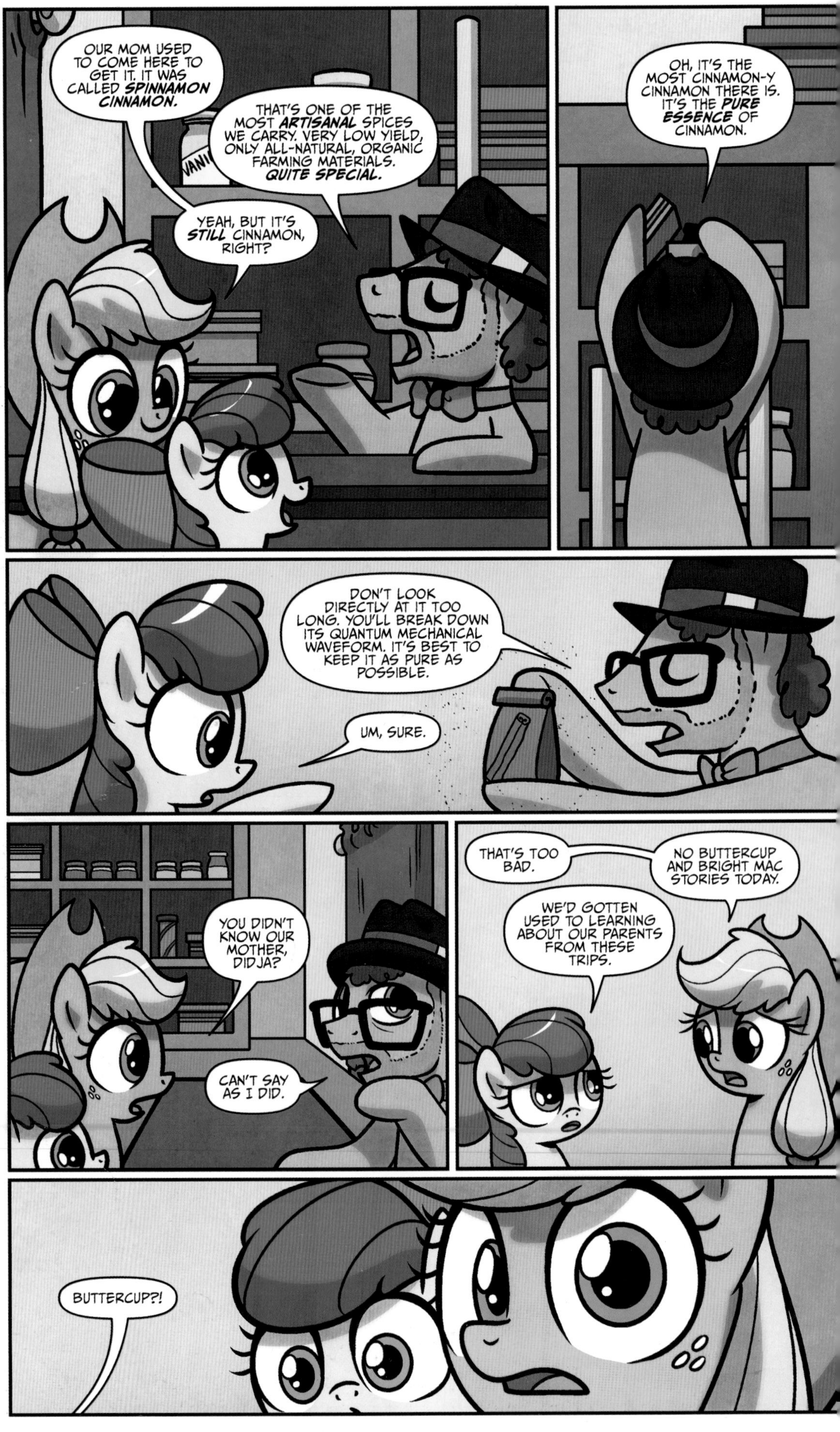
OUR MOM USED TO COME HERE TO GET IT. IT WAS CALLED SPINNAMON CINNAMON.
THAT'S ONE OF THE MOST ARTISANAL SPICES WE CARRY. VERY LOW YIELD, ONLY ALL-NATURAL, ORGANIC FARMING MATERIALS. QUITE SPECIAL.
YEAH, BUT IT'S STILL CINNAMON, RIGHT?
OH, IT'S THE MOST CINNAMON-Y CINNAMON THERE IS. IT'S THE PURE ESSENCE OF CINNAMON.
DON'T LOOK DIRECTLY AT IT TOO LONG. YOU'LL BREAK DOWN ITS QUANTUM MECHANICAL WAVEFORM. IT'S BEST TO KEEP IT AS PURE AS POSSIBLE.
UM, SURE.
YOU DIDN'T KNOW OUR MOTHER, DIDJA?
CAN'T SAY AS I DID.
THAT'S TOO BAD.
NO BUTTERCUP AND BRIGHT MAC STORIES TODAY.
WE'D GOTTEN USED TO LEARNING ABOUT OUR PARENTS FROM THESE TRIPS.
BUTTERCUP?!

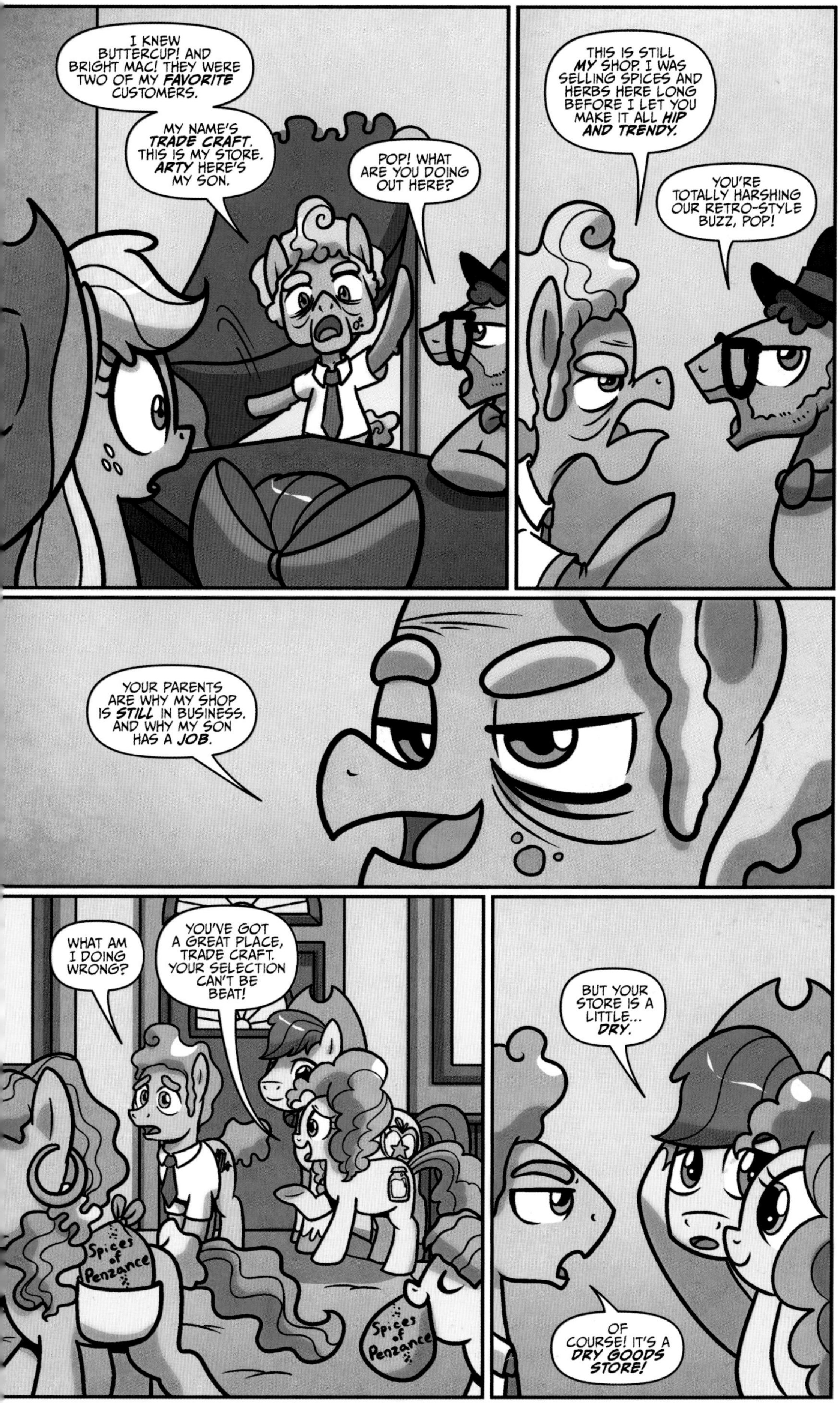
I KNEW BUTTERCUP! AND BRIGHT MAC! THEY WERE TWO OF MY *FAVORITE* CUSTOMERS.
MY NAME'S ***TRADE CRAFT***. THIS IS MY STORE. ***ARTY*** HERE'S MY SON.
POP! WHAT ARE YOU DOING OUT HERE?
THIS IS STILL ***MY*** SHOP. I WAS SELLING SPICES AND HERBS HERE LONG BEFORE I LET YOU MAKE IT ALL ***HIP AND TRENDY.***
YOU'RE TOTALLY HARSHING OUR RETRO-STYLE BUZZ, POP!
YOUR PARENTS ARE WHY MY SHOP IS ***STILL*** IN BUSINESS. AND WHY MY SON HAS A ***JOB***.
WHAT AM I DOING WRONG?
YOU'VE GOT A GREAT PLACE, TRADE CRAFT. YOUR SELECTION CAN'T BE BEAT!
Spices of Penzance
Spices of Penzance
BUT YOUR STORE IS A LITTLE... ***DRY***.
OF COURSE! IT'S A ***DRY GOODS STORE!***

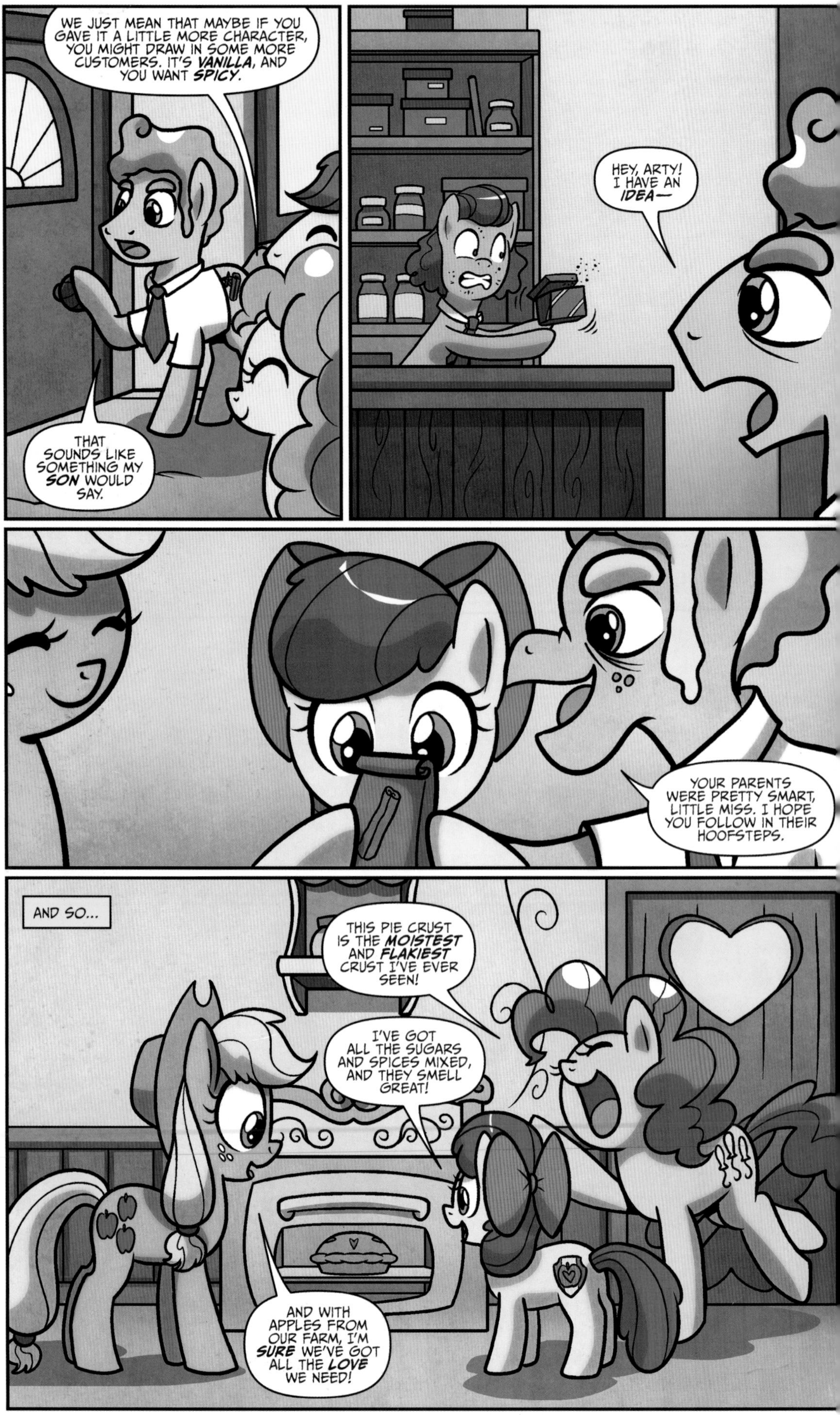
WE JUST MEAN THAT MAYBE IF YOU GAVE IT A LITTLE MORE CHARACTER, YOU MIGHT DRAW IN SOME MORE CUSTOMERS. IT'S VANILLA, AND YOU WANT SPICY.
THAT SOUNDS LIKE SOMETHING MY SON WOULD SAY.
HEY, ARTY! I HAVE AN IDEA—
YOUR PARENTS WERE PRETTY SMART, LITTLE MISS. I HOPE YOU FOLLOW IN THEIR HOOFSTEPS.
AND SO...
THIS PIE CRUST IS THE MOISTEST AND FLAKIEST CRUST I'VE EVER SEEN!
I'VE GOT ALL THE SUGARS AND SPICES MIXED, AND THEY SMELL GREAT!
AND WITH APPLES FROM OUR FARM, I'M SURE WE'VE GOT ALL THE LOVE WE NEED!

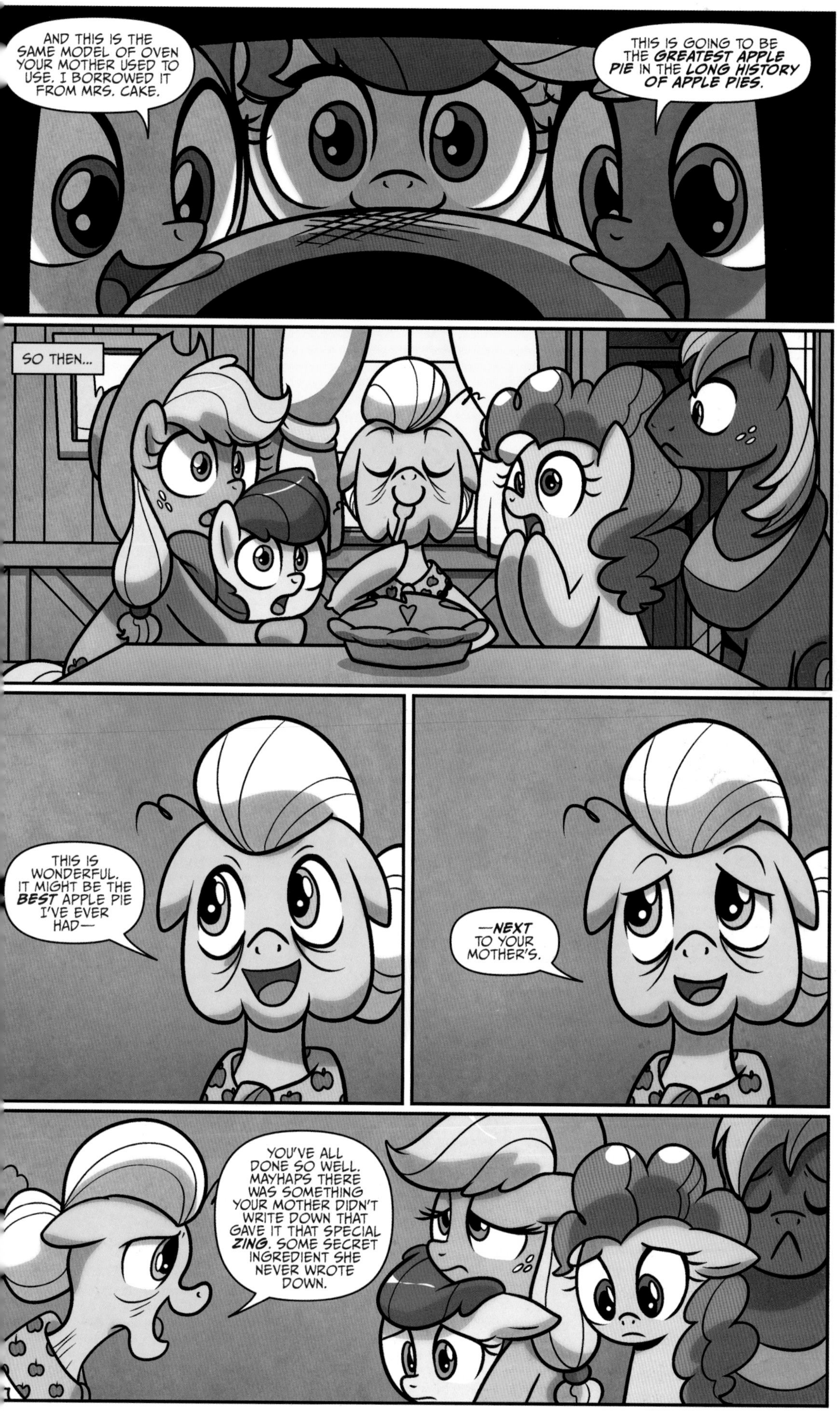
AND THIS IS THE SAME MODEL OF OVEN YOUR MOTHER USED TO USE. I BORROWED IT FROM MRS. CAKE.
THIS IS GOING TO BE THE **GREATEST APPLE PIE** IN THE **LONG HISTORY OF APPLE PIES.**
SO THEN...
THIS IS WONDERFUL. IT MIGHT BE THE **BEST** APPLE PIE I'VE EVER HAD—
—**NEXT** TO YOUR MOTHER'S.
YOU'VE ALL DONE SO WELL. MAYHAPS THERE WAS SOMETHING YOUR MOTHER DIDN'T WRITE DOWN THAT GAVE IT THAT SPECIAL **ZING**. SOME SECRET INGREDIENT SHE NEVER WROTE DOWN.

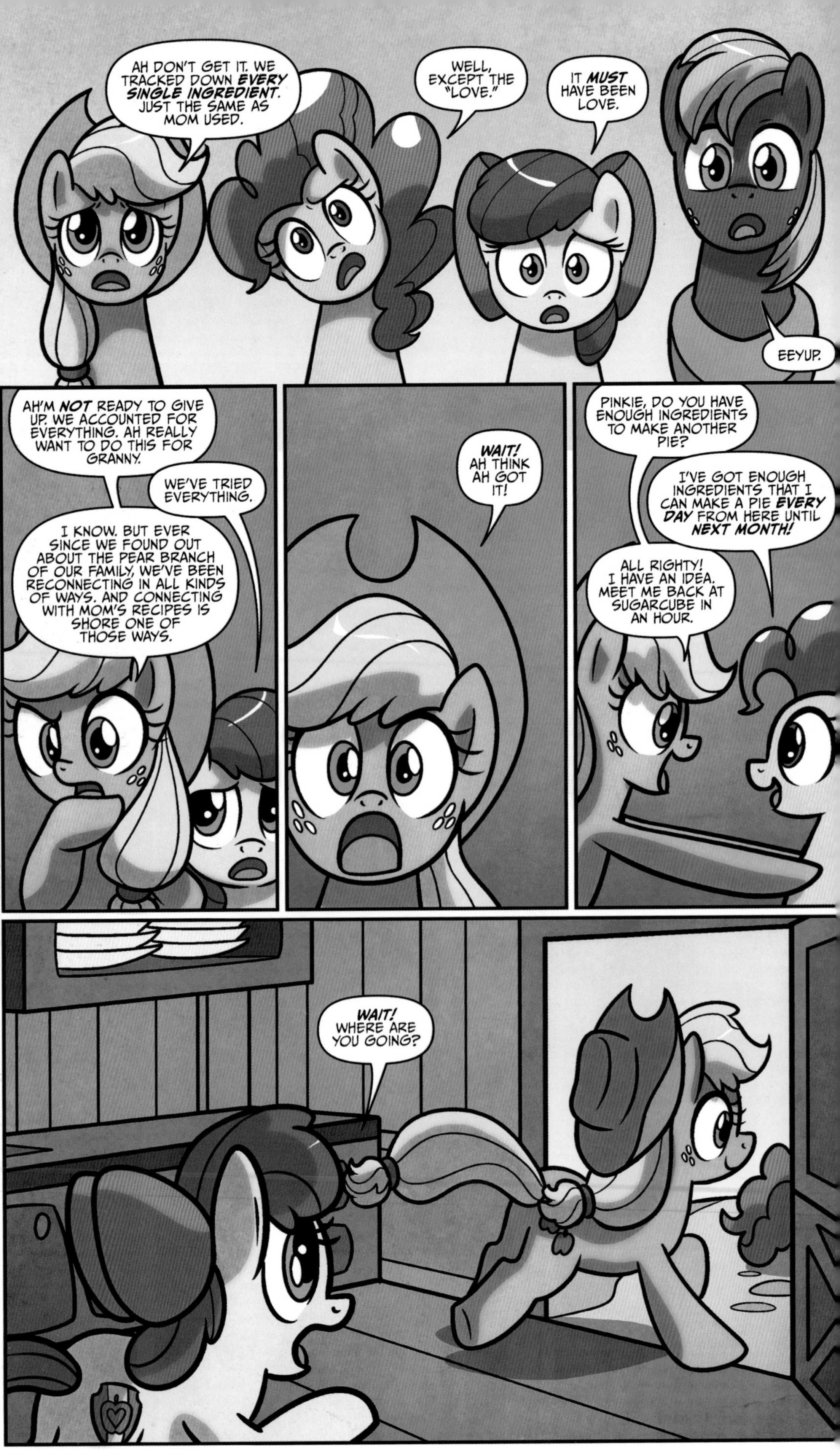
AH DON'T GET IT. WE TRACKED DOWN EVERY SINGLE INGREDIENT. JUST THE SAME AS MOM USED.
WELL, EXCEPT THE "LOVE."
IT MUST HAVE BEEN LOVE.
EEYUP.
AH'M NOT READY TO GIVE UP. WE ACCOUNTED FOR EVERYTHING. AH REALLY WANT TO DO THIS FOR GRANNY.
WE'VE TRIED EVERYTHING.
I KNOW. BUT EVER SINCE WE FOUND OUT ABOUT THE PEAR BRANCH OF OUR FAMILY, WE'VE BEEN RECONNECTING IN ALL KINDS OF WAYS. AND CONNECTING WITH MOM'S RECIPES IS SHORE ONE OF THOSE WAYS.
WAIT! AH THINK AH GOT IT!
PINKIE, DO YOU HAVE ENOUGH INGREDIENTS TO MAKE ANOTHER PIE?
I'VE GOT ENOUGH INGREDIENTS THAT I CAN MAKE A PIE EVERY DAY FROM HERE UNTIL NEXT MONTH!
ALL RIGHTY! I HAVE AN IDEA. MEET ME BACK AT SUGARCUBE IN AN HOUR.
WAIT! WHERE ARE YOU GOING?

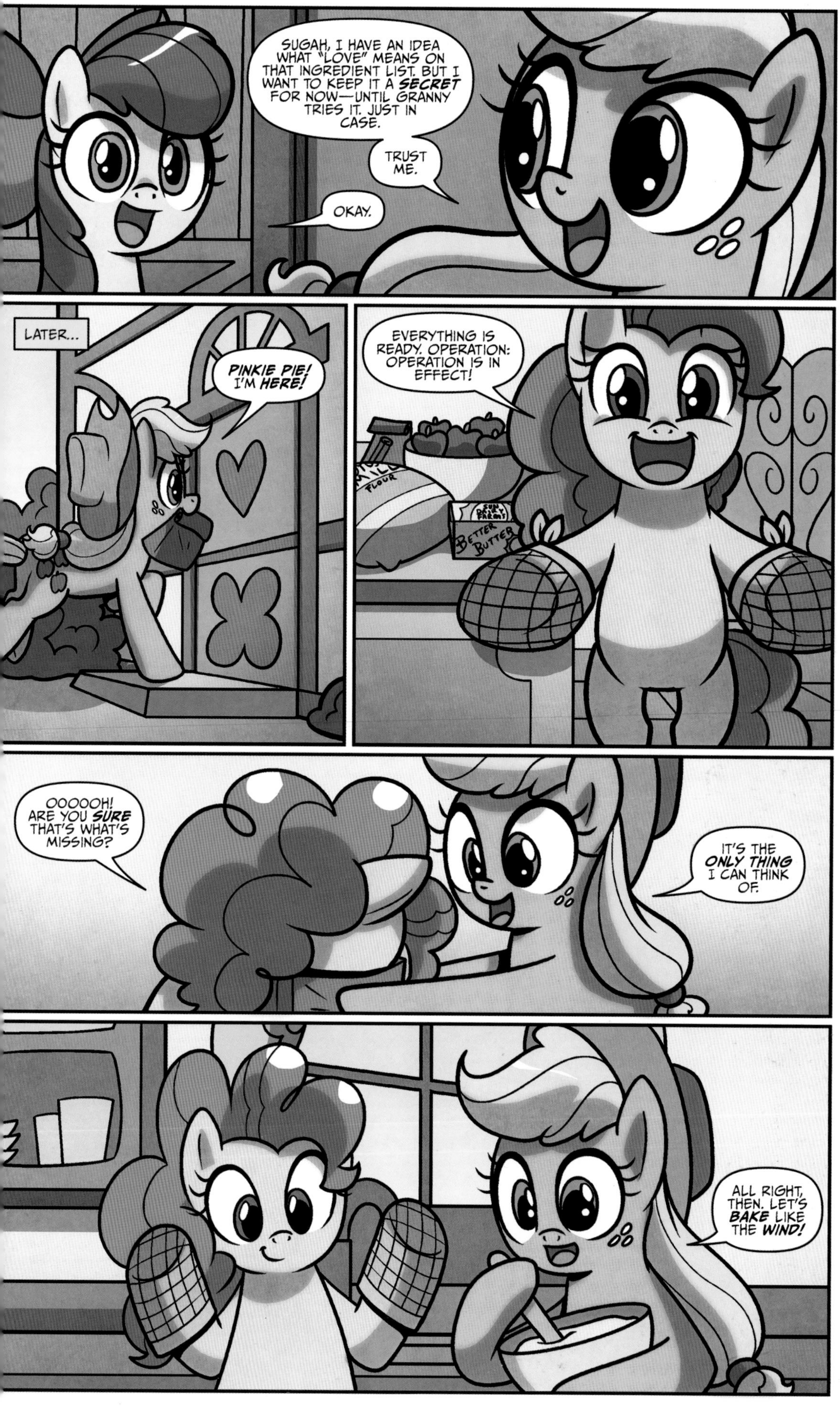

SUGAH, I HAVE AN IDEA WHAT "LOVE" MEANS ON THAT INGREDIENT LIST. BUT I WANT TO KEEP IT A **SECRET** FOR NOW—UNTIL GRANNY TRIES IT. JUST IN CASE.
TRUST ME.
OKAY.
LATER...
**PINKIE PIE!** I'M **HERE!**
EVERYTHING IS READY. OPERATION: OPERATION IS IN EFFECT!
FLOUR
BETTER BUTTER
OOOOOH! ARE YOU **SURE** THAT'S WHAT'S MISSING?
IT'S THE **ONLY THING** I CAN THINK OF.
ALL RIGHT, THEN. LET'S **BAKE** LIKE THE **WIND!**

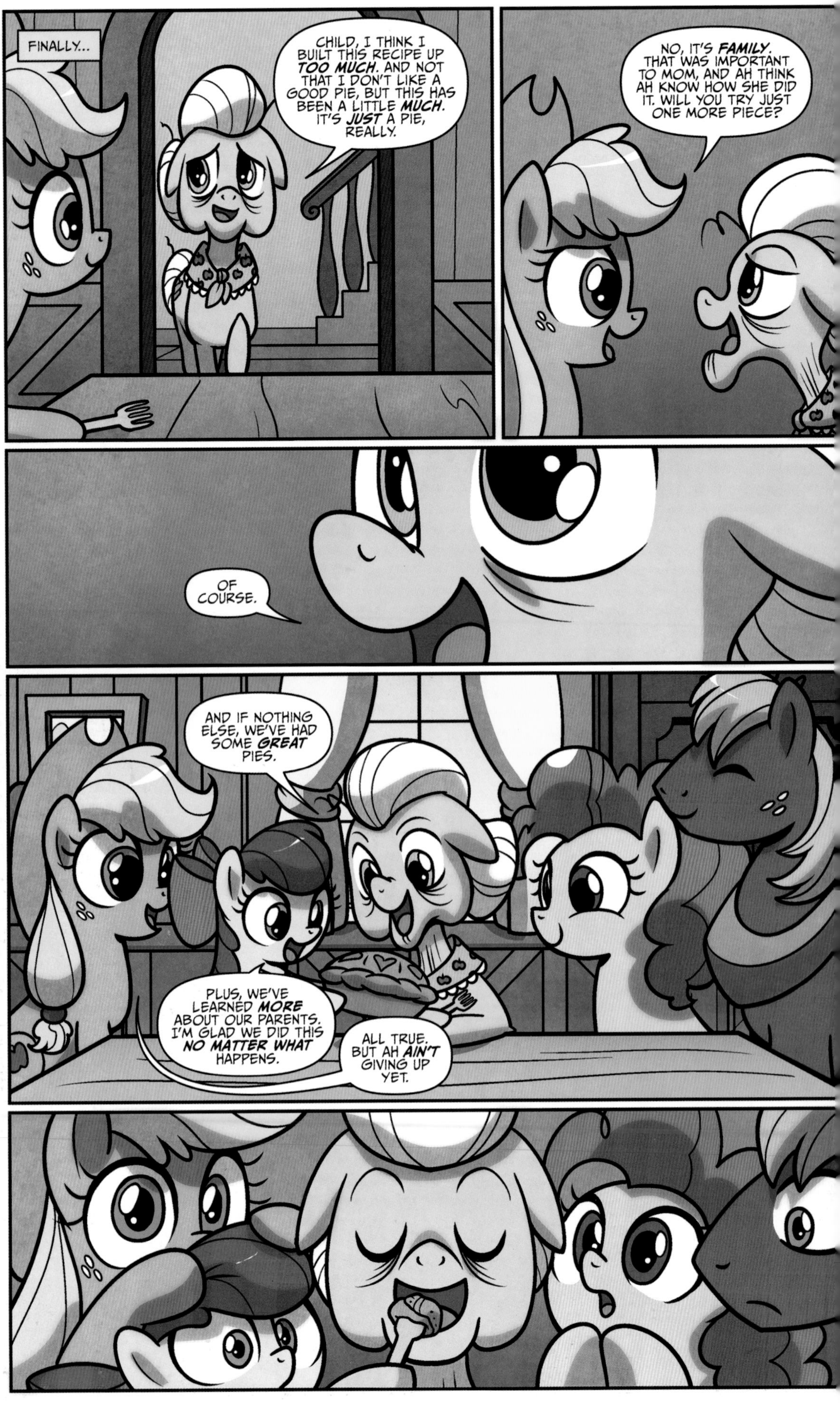
FINALLY...
CHILD, I THINK I BUILT THIS RECIPE UP TOO MUCH. AND NOT THAT I DON'T LIKE A GOOD PIE, BUT THIS HAS BEEN A LITTLE MUCH. IT'S JUST A PIE, REALLY.
NO, IT'S FAMILY. THAT WAS IMPORTANT TO MOM, AND AH THINK AH KNOW HOW SHE DID IT. WILL YOU TRY JUST ONE MORE PIECE?
OF COURSE.
AND IF NOTHING ELSE, WE'VE HAD SOME GREAT PIES.
PLUS, WE'VE LEARNED MORE ABOUT OUR PARENTS. I'M GLAD WE DID THIS NO MATTER WHAT HAPPENS.
ALL TRUE. BUT AH AIN'T GIVING UP YET.

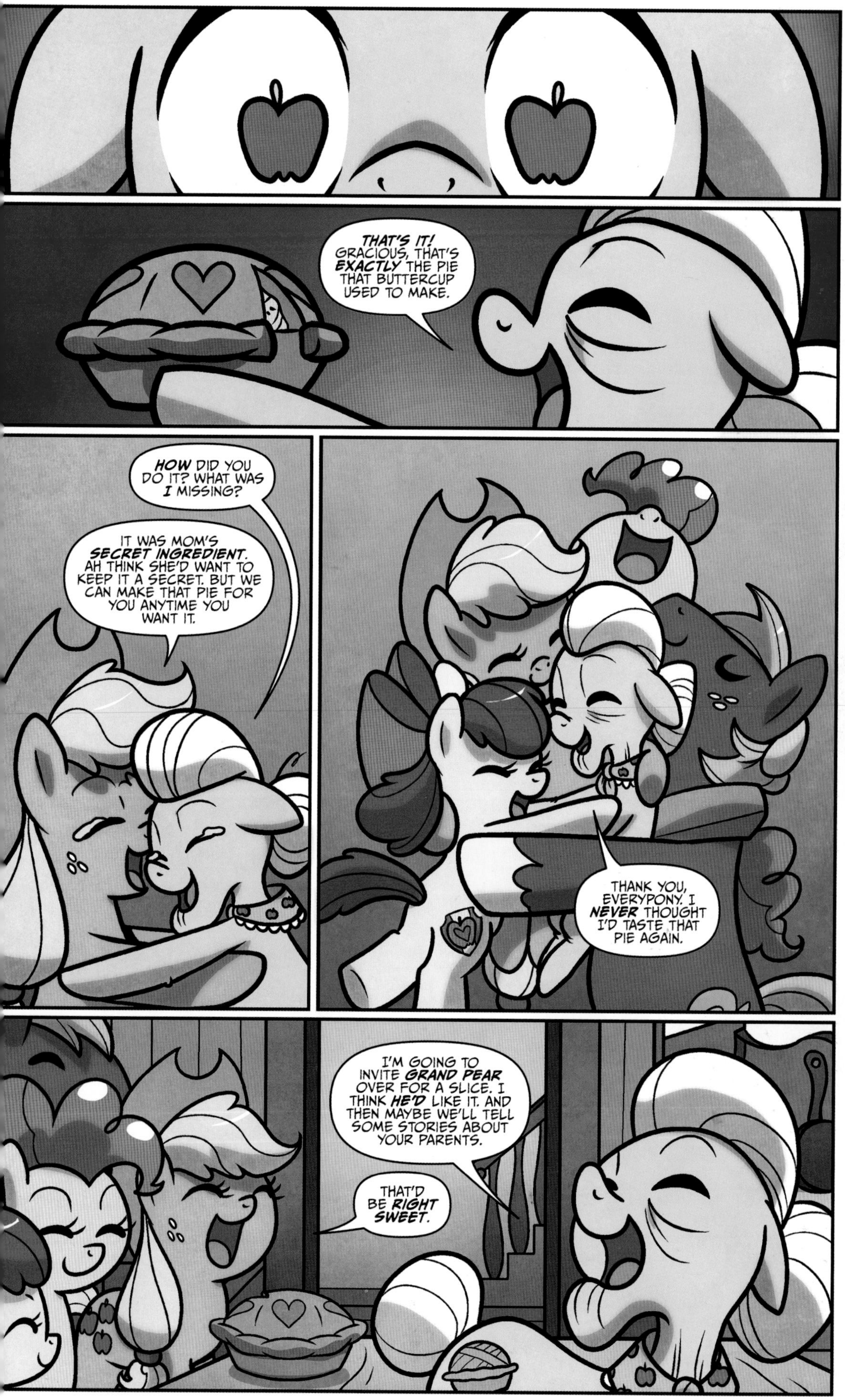
THAT'S IT! GRACIOUS, THAT'S EXACTLY THE PIE THAT BUTTERCUP USED TO MAKE.
HOW DID YOU DO IT? WHAT WAS I MISSING?
IT WAS MOM'S SECRET INGREDIENT. AH THINK SHE'D WANT TO KEEP IT A SECRET. BUT WE CAN MAKE THAT PIE FOR YOU ANYTIME YOU WANT IT.
THANK YOU, EVERYPONY. I NEVER THOUGHT I'D TASTE THAT PIE AGAIN.
I'M GOING TO INVITE GRAND PEAR OVER FOR A SLICE. I THINK HE'D LIKE IT. AND THEN MAYBE WE'LL TELL SOME STORIES ABOUT YOUR PARENTS.
THAT'D BE RIGHT SWEET.

**Panel 1:** YOU'VE *GOT* TO TELL US! *WHAT* WAS THE SECRET INGREDIENT? *TELL US!*

EEYUP.

**Panel 2:** IT WAS RIGHT THERE ON THE LIST. *"A LITTLE BIT OF LOVE."* AND MOM LOVED HER FAMILY. *BOTH* SIDES.

**Panel 3:** "AND *FAMILY* WAS *LOVE* TO MOM. SO A LITTLE BIT OF LOVE WAS A LITTLE BIT OF FAMILY. ONE SINGLE *PEAR*."

**Panel 4:** AIN'T YOU GOING TO TELL HER?

DON'T SEE NO POINT IN IT. MOM KEPT IT A SECRET FOR SO LONG. EVEN SINCE OUR FAMILIES RECONCILED, AH'M NOT SURE HOW SHE'D FEEL ABOUT KNOWING THERE WAS A *PEAR* IN THE BEST *APPLE PIE* EVER.

**Panel 5:** SO LET'S KEEP THAT *MAGIC* GOING FOR HER.

I LIKE THAT IDEA.

EEYUP.

SO KEEP THE SECRET, EVERYPONY! *MOM'S* THE WORD!

The End!

art by Sara Richard

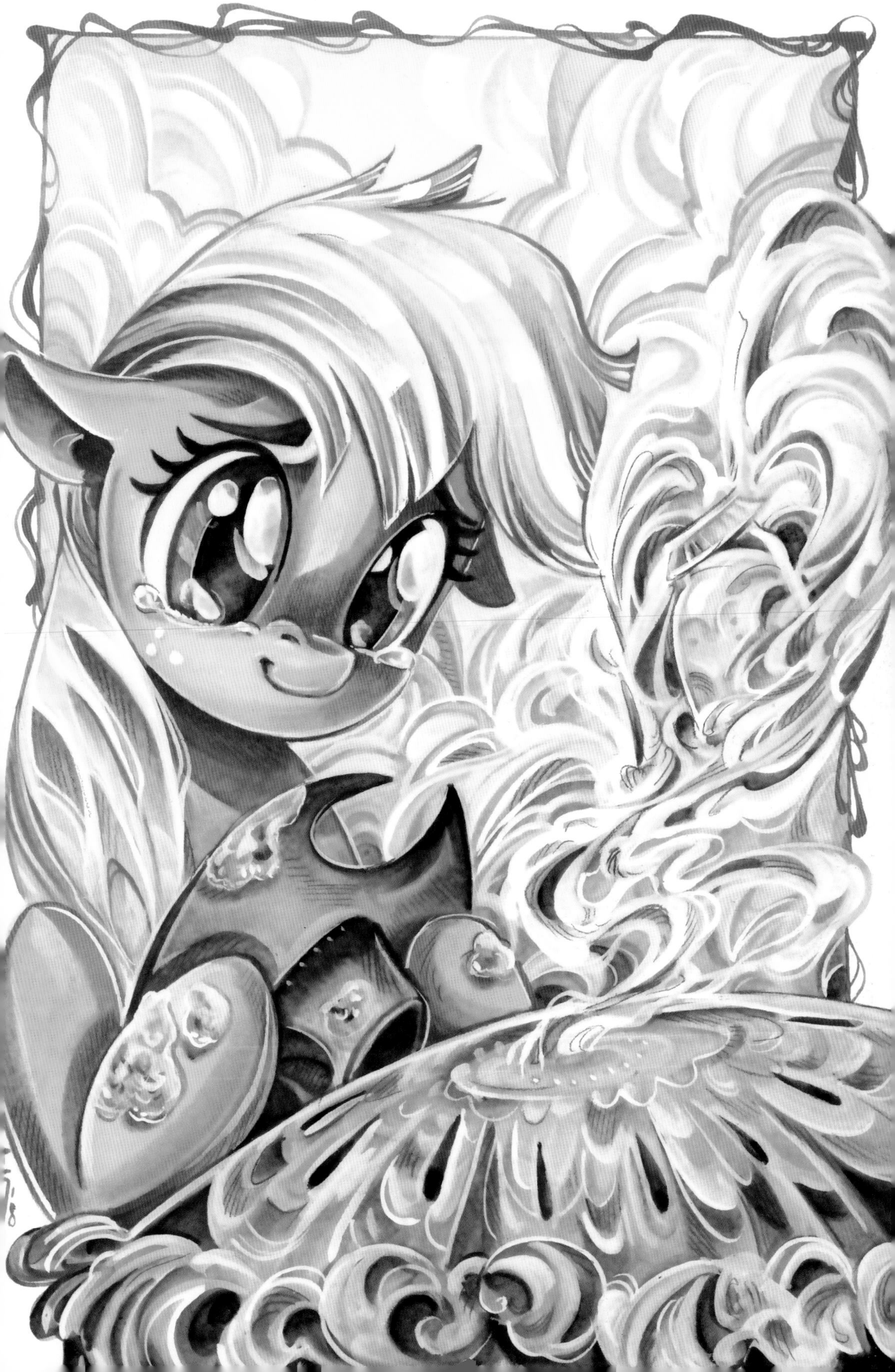

art by Toni Kuusisto

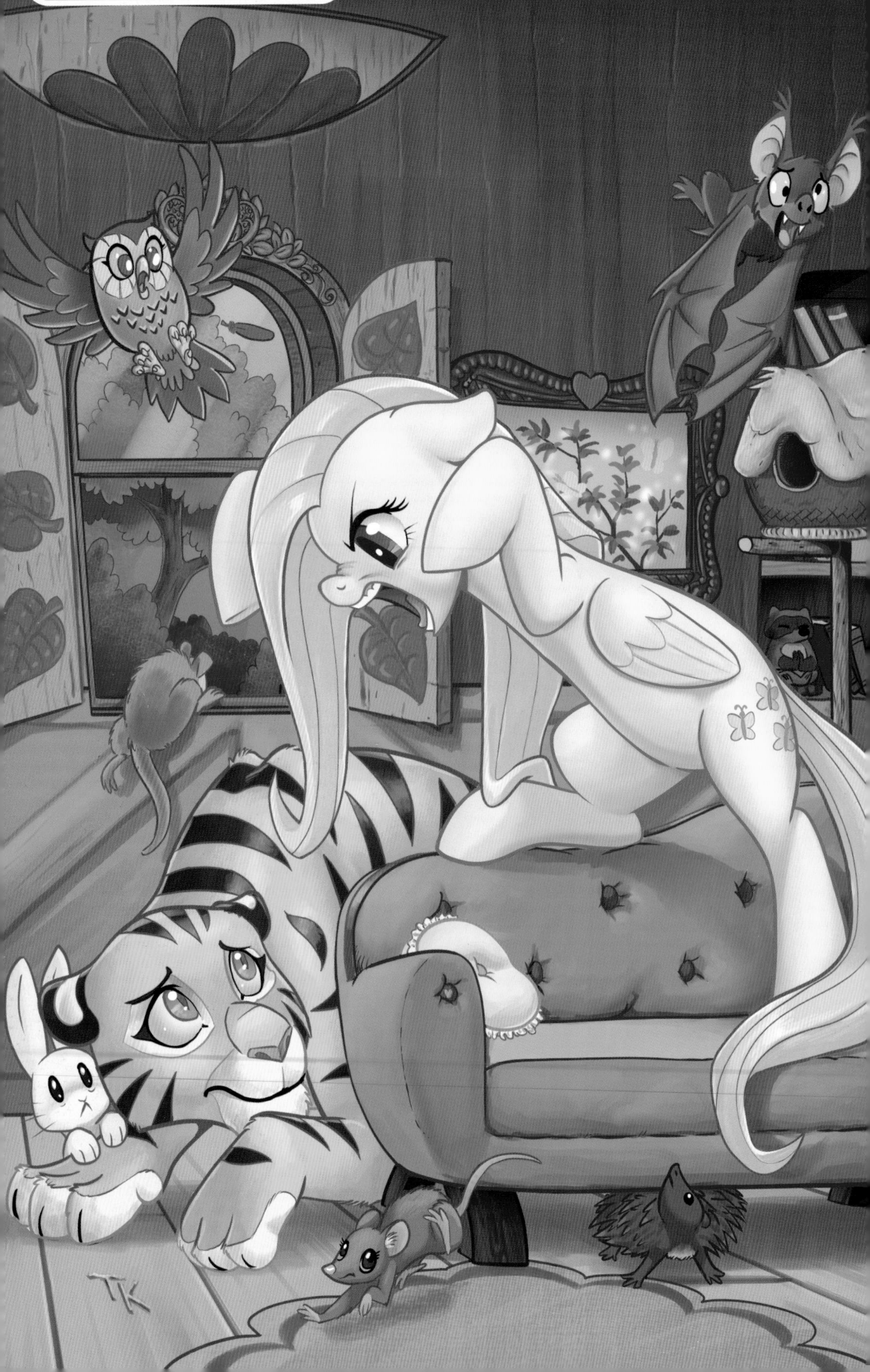

TK

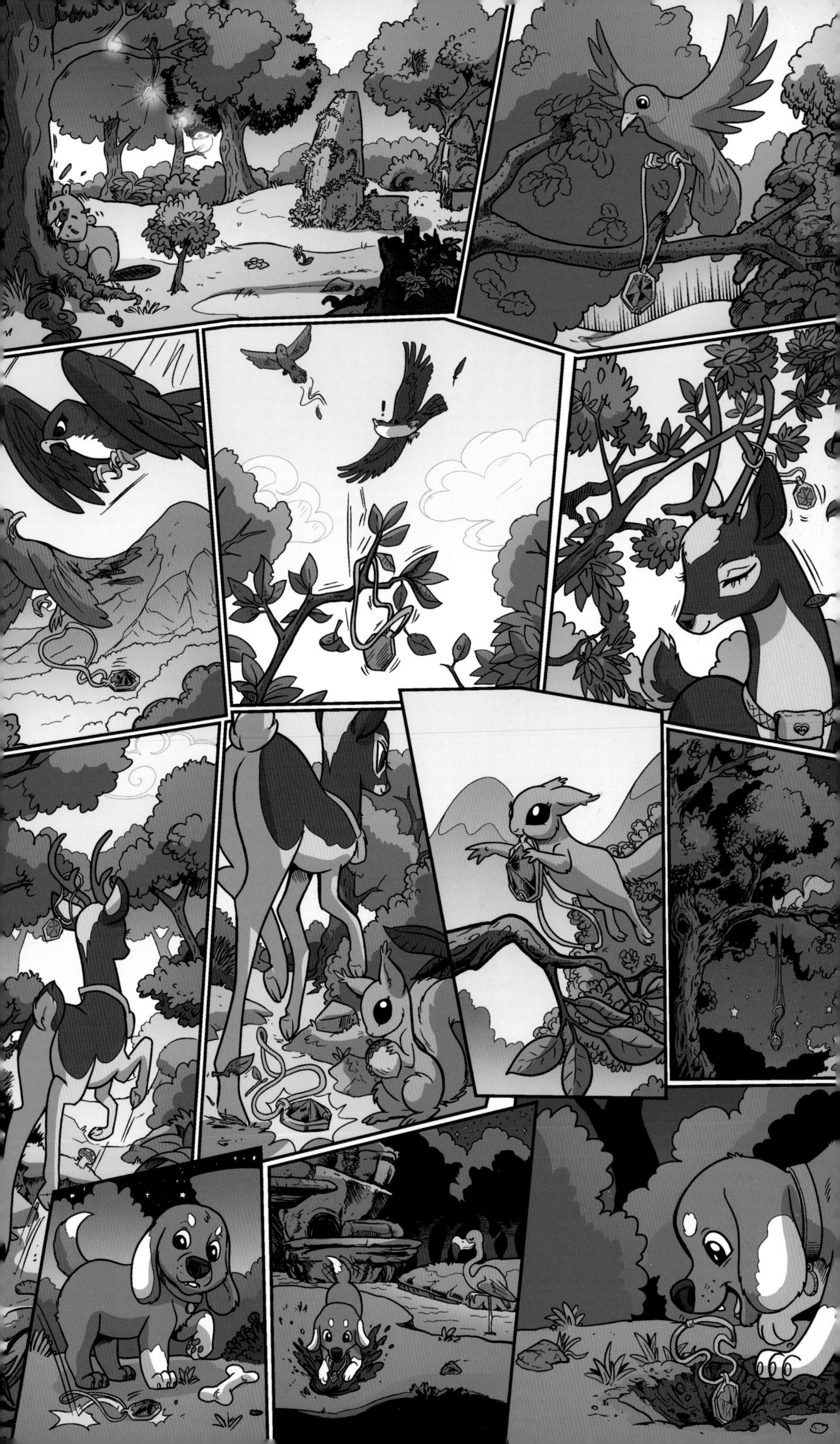

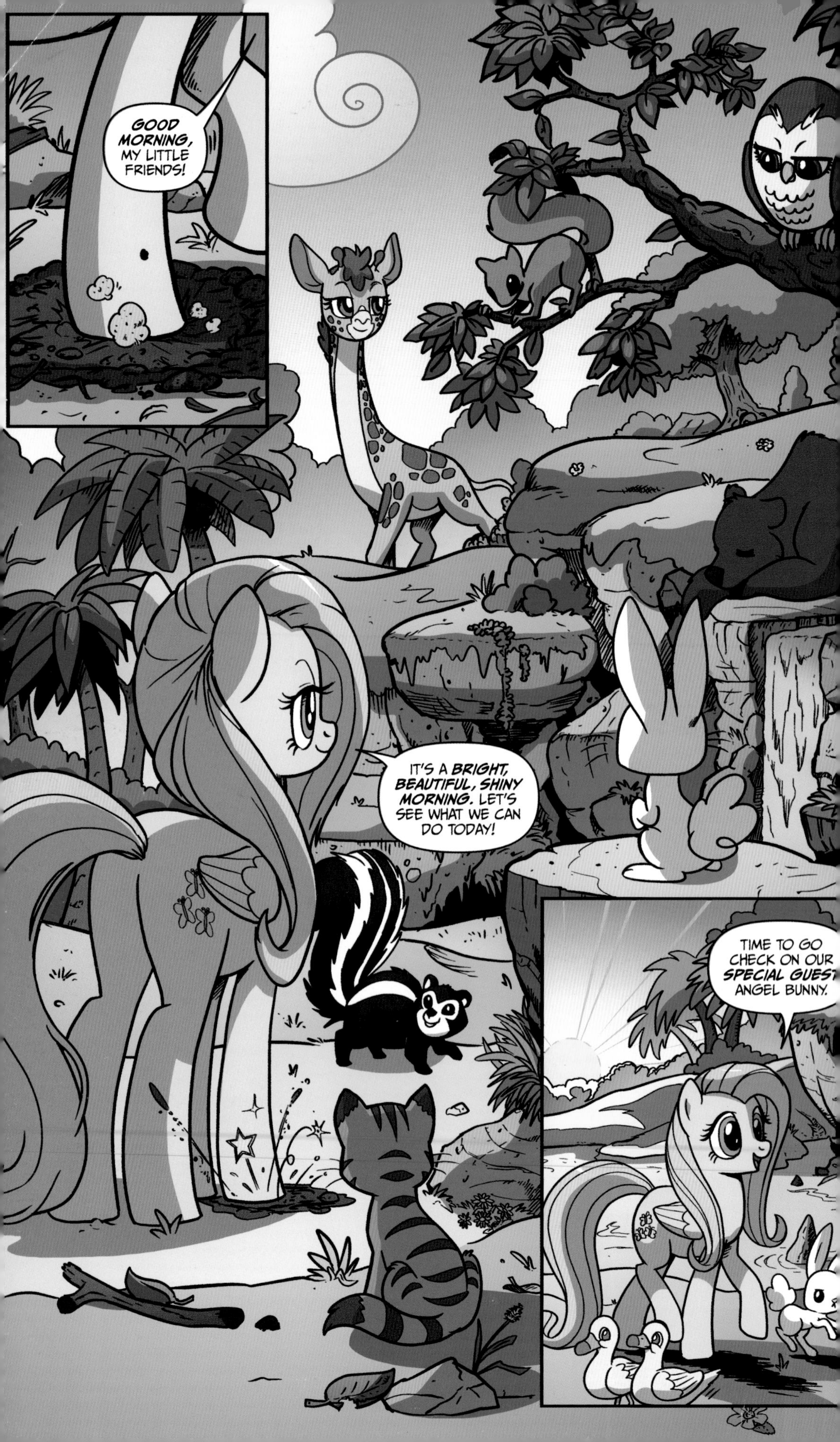

*GOOD MORNING*, MY LITTLE FRIENDS!
IT'S A ***BRIGHT, BEAUTIFUL, SHINY MORNING.*** LET'S SEE WHAT WE CAN DO TODAY!
TIME TO GO CHECK ON OUR ***SPECIAL GUEST***, ANGEL BUNNY.

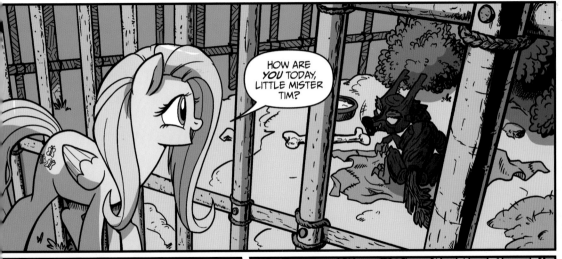

HOW ARE *YOU* TODAY, LITTLE MISTER TIM?

WOW, THAT'S *PRETTY NASTY*, INDEED.

I THINK YOU'RE GETTING *BETTER.*

*DON'T* GIVE ME THAT LOOK, ANGEL BUNNY. THIS PLACE IS FOR *ALL* ANIMALS TO HEAL.

EVEN *TIMBERWOLVES.*

GRRRROWL

BUT I'D SAY IN ANOTHER WEEK OR SO, WE CAN *RELEASE HIM BACK* INTO THE FOREST. HARDHAT SHOULD HAVE THE SPECIAL CARRIER DONE BY THEN, TOO.

YES, YOU'RE RIGHT. WE HAVE *OTHER* GUESTS TO CHECK ON, DON'T WE? LET'S GO SEE LITTLE MAL.

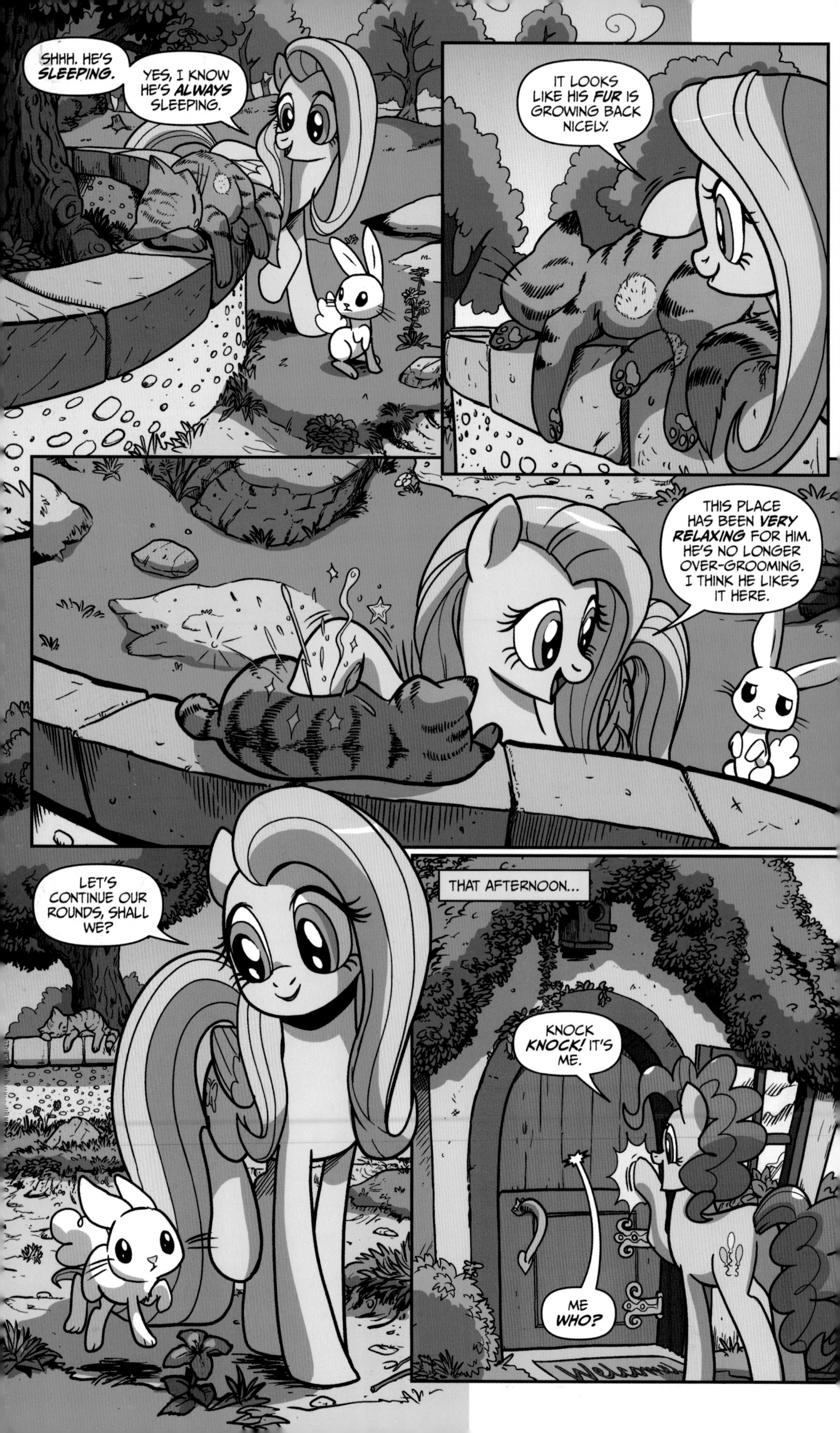
SHHH. HE'S *SLEEPING.*
YES, I KNOW HE'S *ALWAYS* SLEEPING.
IT LOOKS LIKE HIS *FUR* IS GROWING BACK NICELY.
THIS PLACE HAS BEEN *VERY RELAXING* FOR HIM. HE'S NO LONGER OVER-GROOMING. I THINK HE LIKES IT HERE.
LET'S CONTINUE OUR ROUNDS, SHALL WE?
THAT AFTERNOON...
KNOCK *KNOCK!* IT'S ME.
ME *WHO?*

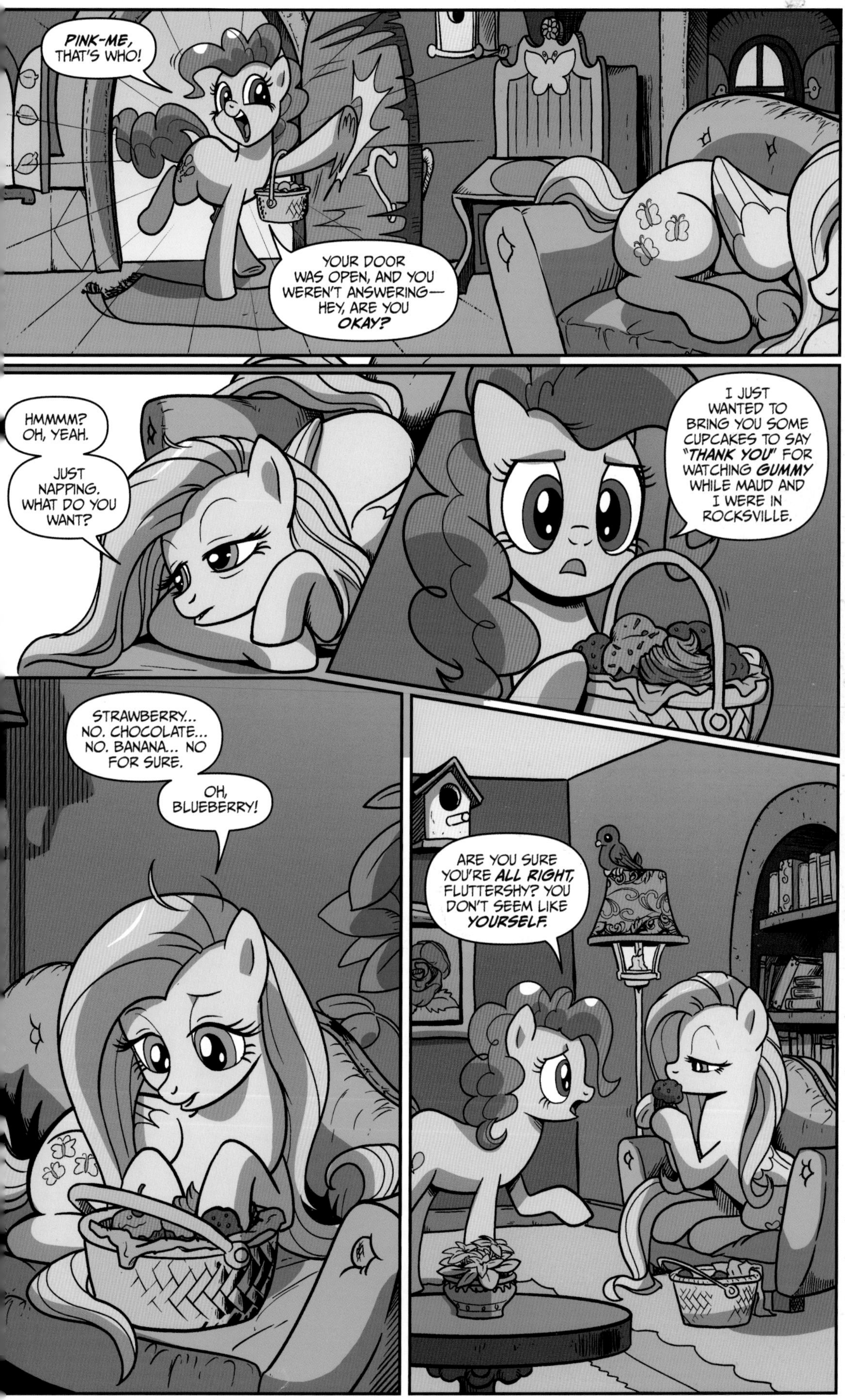

PINK-ME, THAT'S WHO!
YOUR DOOR WAS OPEN, AND YOU WEREN'T ANSWERING— HEY, ARE YOU OKAY?
HMMMM? OH, YEAH.
JUST NAPPING. WHAT DO YOU WANT?
I JUST WANTED TO BRING YOU SOME CUPCAKES TO SAY "THANK YOU" FOR WATCHING GUMMY WHILE MAUD AND I WERE IN ROCKSVILLE.
STRAWBERRY... NO. CHOCOLATE... NO. BANANA... NO FOR SURE.
OH, BLUEBERRY!
ARE YOU SURE YOU'RE ALL RIGHT, FLUTTERSHY? YOU DON'T SEEM LIKE YOURSELF.

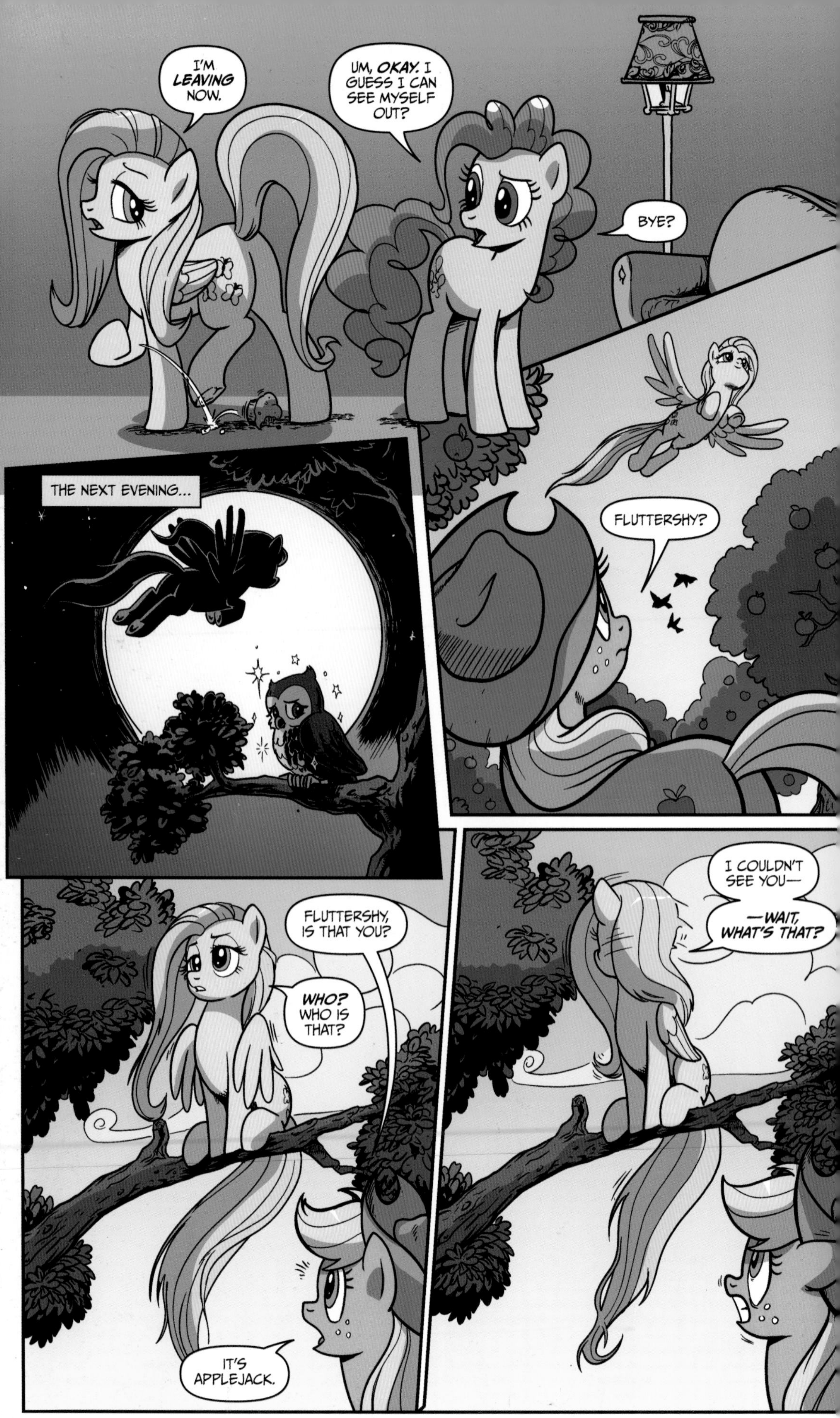
I'M LEAVING NOW.
UM, OKAY. I GUESS I CAN SEE MYSELF OUT?
BYE?
THE NEXT EVENING...
FLUTTERSHY?
FLUTTERSHY, IS THAT YOU?
WHO? WHO IS THAT?
IT'S APPLEJACK.
I COULDN'T SEE YOU—
—WAIT, WHAT'S THAT?

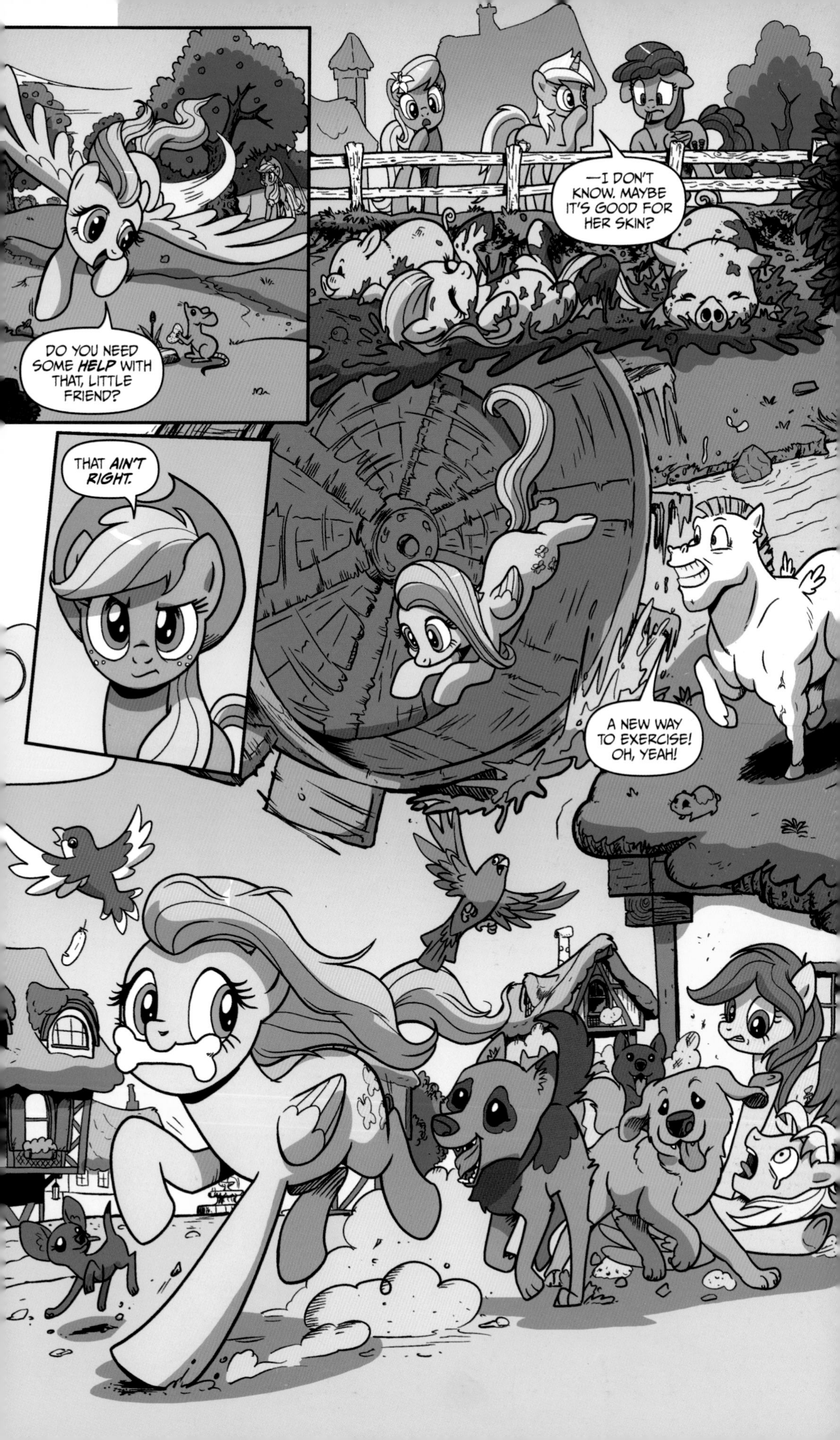
DO YOU NEED SOME *HELP* WITH THAT, LITTLE FRIEND?
—I DON'T KNOW. MAYBE IT'S GOOD FOR HER SKIN?
THAT *AIN'T RIGHT.*
A NEW WAY TO EXERCISE! OH, YEAH!

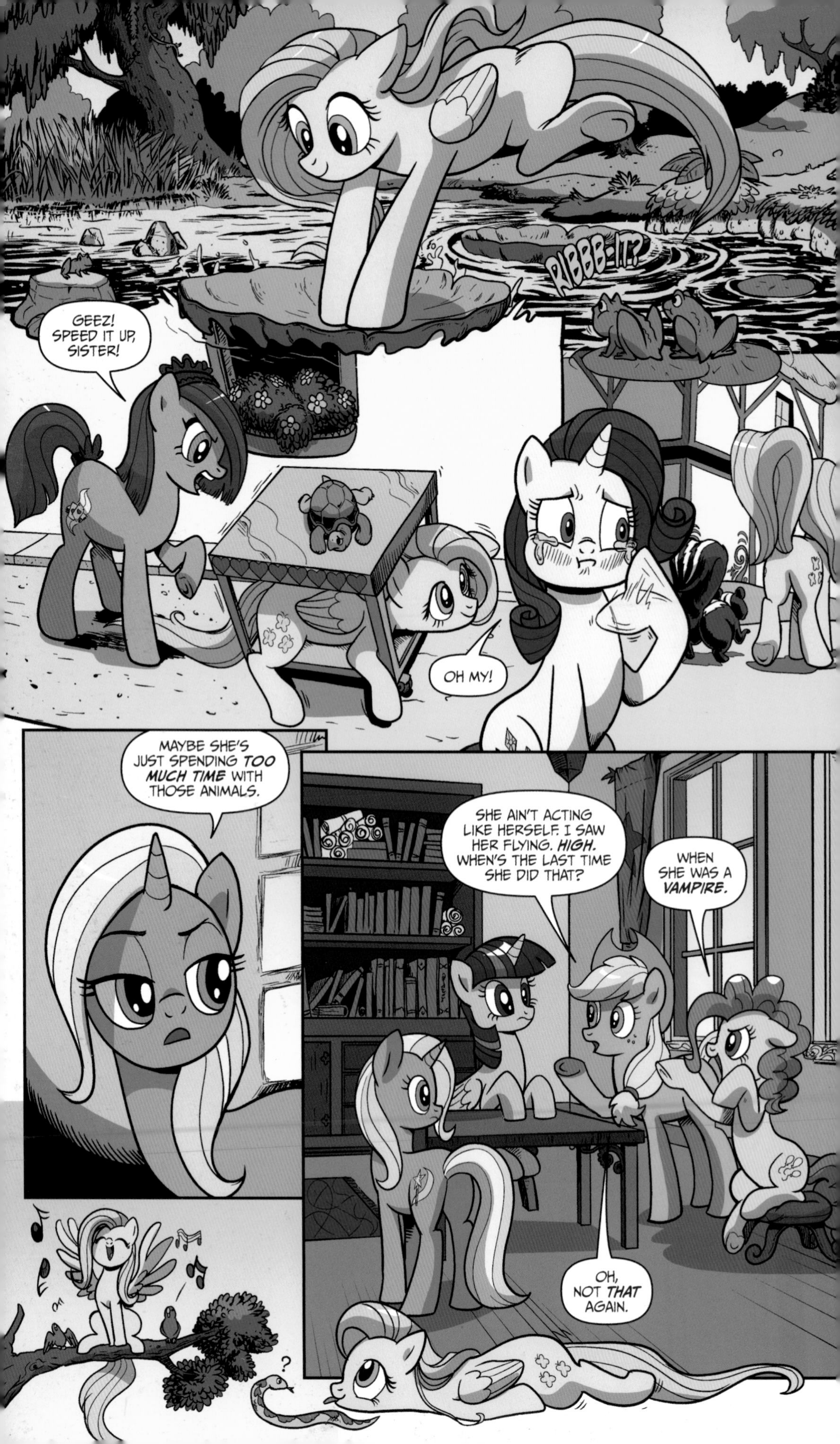
RIBBB-IT?
GEEZ! SPEED IT UP, SISTER!
OH MY!
MAYBE SHE'S JUST SPENDING TOO MUCH TIME WITH THOSE ANIMALS.
SHE AIN'T ACTING LIKE HERSELF. I SAW HER FLYING. HIGH. WHEN'S THE LAST TIME SHE DID THAT?
WHEN SHE WAS A VAMPIRE.
OH, NOT THAT AGAIN.
?

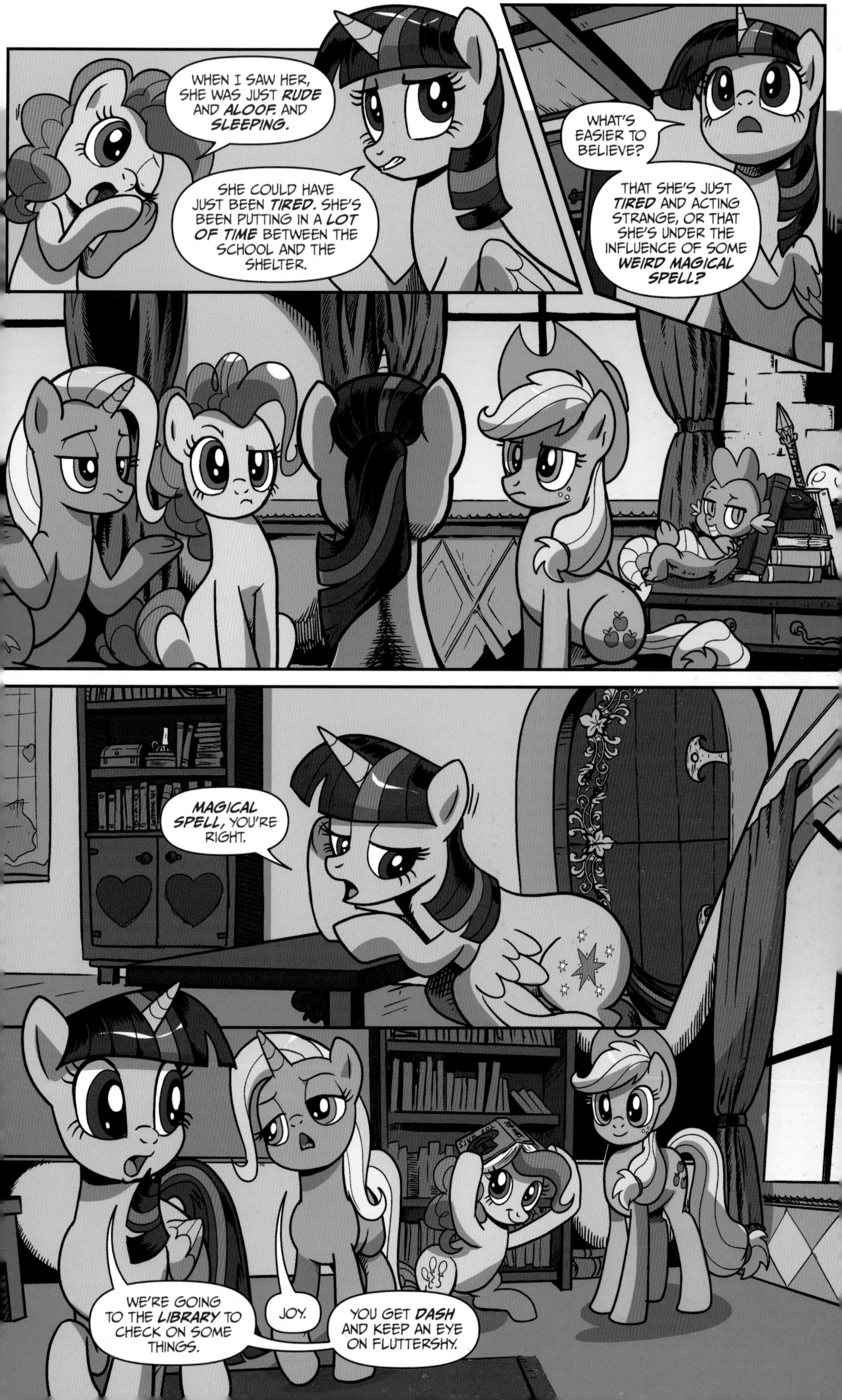
WHEN I SAW HER, SHE WAS JUST RUDE AND ALOOF. AND SLEEPING.
SHE COULD HAVE JUST BEEN TIRED. SHE'S BEEN PUTTING IN A LOT OF TIME BETWEEN THE SCHOOL AND THE SHELTER.
WHAT'S EASIER TO BELIEVE?
THAT SHE'S JUST TIRED AND ACTING STRANGE, OR THAT SHE'S UNDER THE INFLUENCE OF SOME WEIRD MAGICAL SPELL?
MAGICAL SPELL, YOU'RE RIGHT.
WE'RE GOING TO THE LIBRARY TO CHECK ON SOME THINGS.
JOY.
YOU GET DASH AND KEEP AN EYE ON FLUTTERSHY.

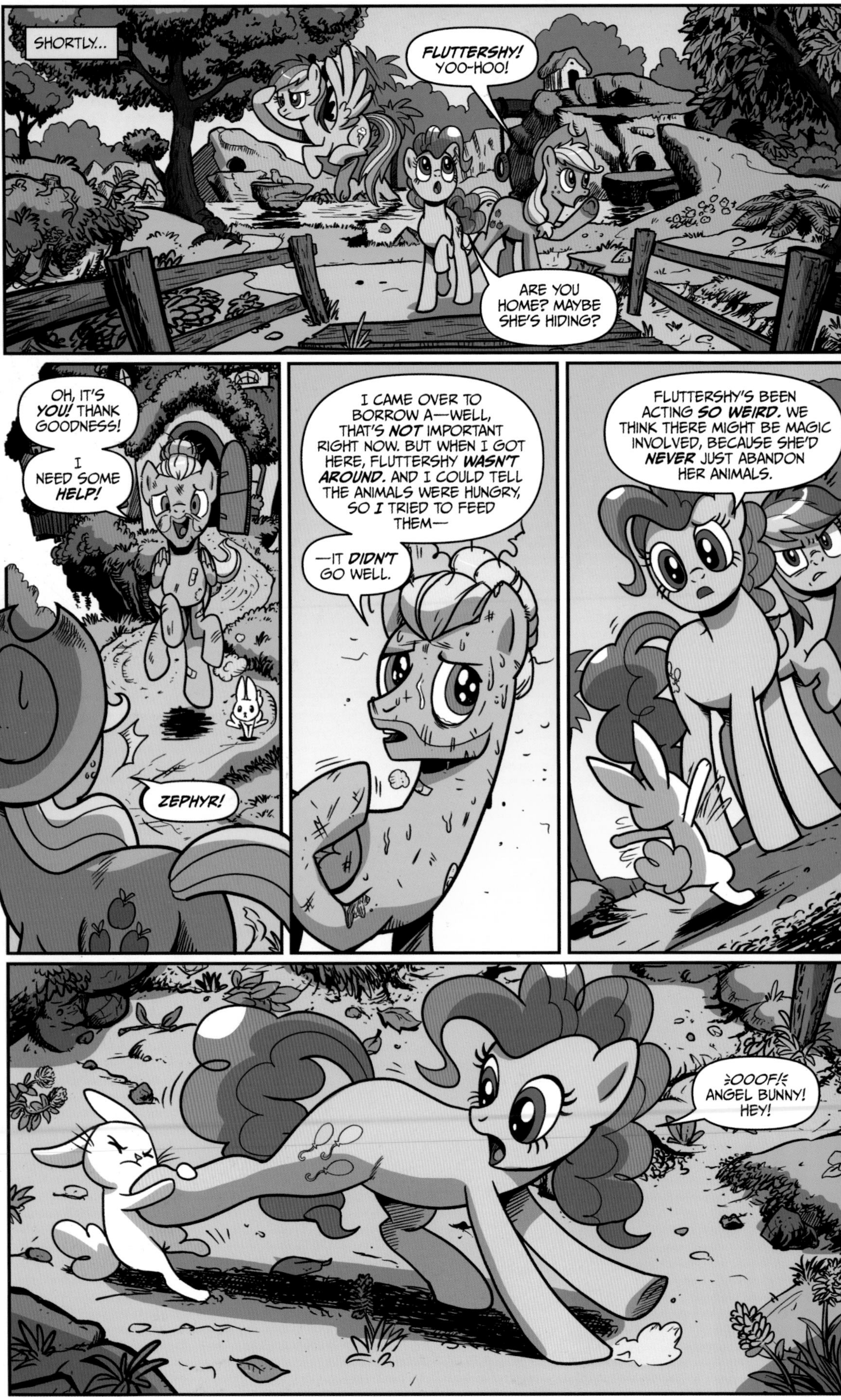
SHORTLY...
FLUTTERSHY! YOO-HOO!
ARE YOU HOME? MAYBE SHE'S HIDING?
OH, IT'S YOU! THANK GOODNESS!
I NEED SOME HELP!
ZEPHYR!
I CAME OVER TO BORROW A—WELL, THAT'S NOT IMPORTANT RIGHT NOW. BUT WHEN I GOT HERE, FLUTTERSHY WASN'T AROUND. AND I COULD TELL THE ANIMALS WERE HUNGRY, SO I TRIED TO FEED THEM—
—IT DIDN'T GO WELL.
FLUTTERSHY'S BEEN ACTING SO WEIRD. WE THINK THERE MIGHT BE MAGIC INVOLVED, BECAUSE SHE'D NEVER JUST ABANDON HER ANIMALS.
OOOF! ANGEL BUNNY! HEY!

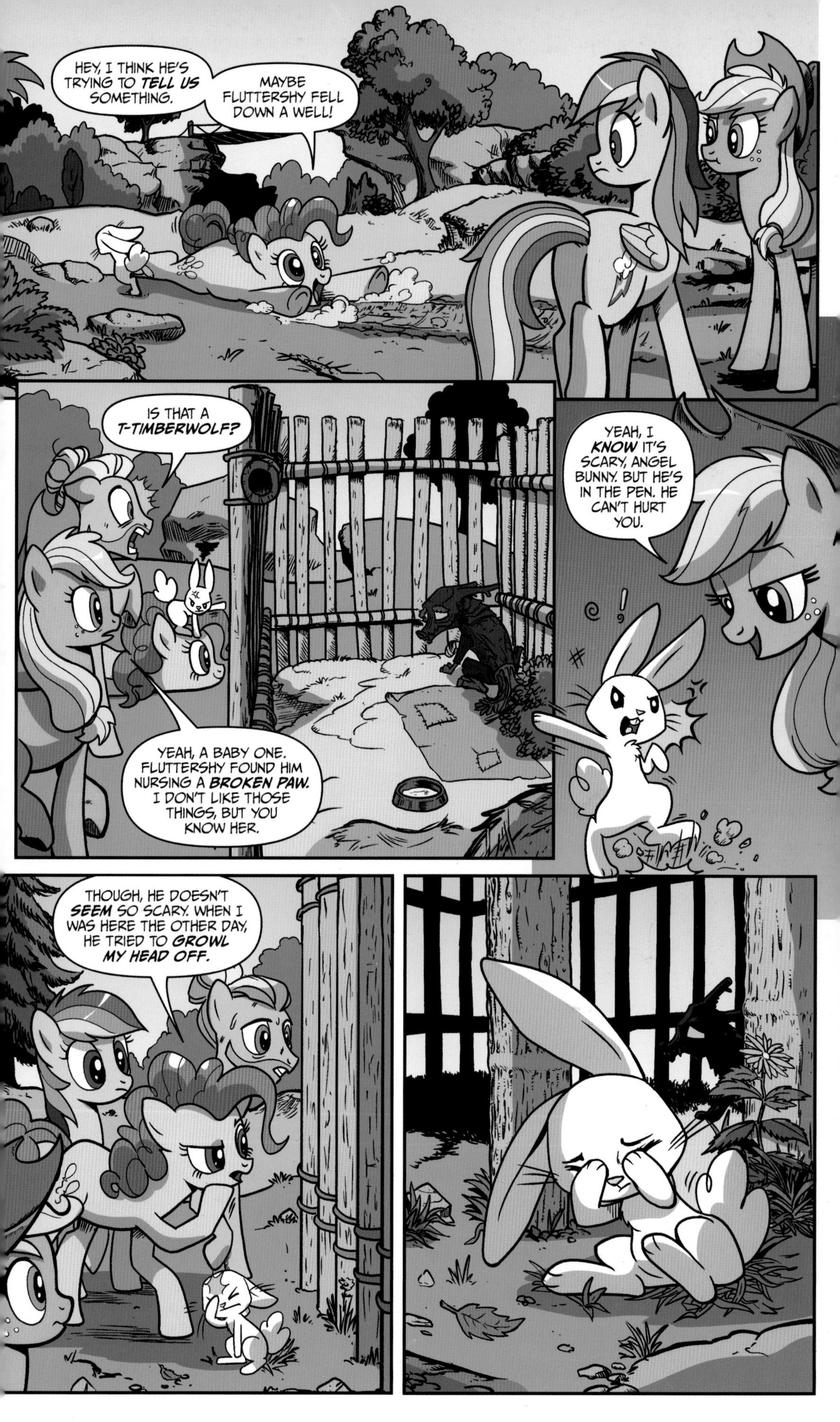
HEY, I THINK HE'S TRYING TO TELL US SOMETHING.
MAYBE FLUTTERSHY FELL DOWN A WELL!
IS THAT A T-TIMBERWOLF?
YEAH, A BABY ONE. FLUTTERSHY FOUND HIM NURSING A BROKEN PAW. I DON'T LIKE THOSE THINGS, BUT YOU KNOW HER.
YEAH, I KNOW IT'S SCARY, ANGEL BUNNY. BUT HE'S IN THE PEN. HE CAN'T HURT YOU.
THOUGH, HE DOESN'T SEEM SO SCARY. WHEN I WAS HERE THE OTHER DAY, HE TRIED TO GROWL MY HEAD OFF.

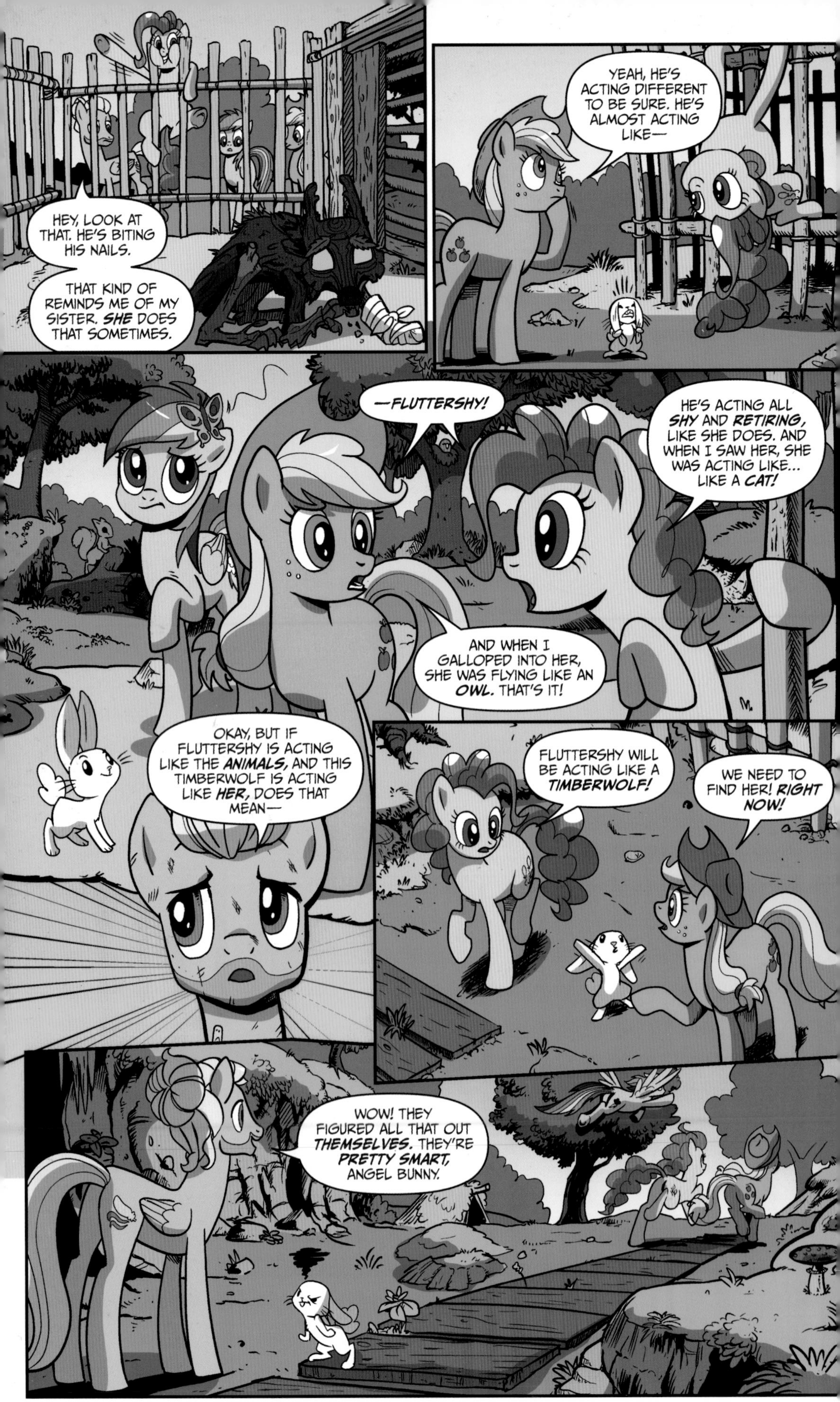
HEY, LOOK AT THAT. HE'S BITING HIS NAILS.
THAT KIND OF REMINDS ME OF MY SISTER. *SHE* DOES THAT SOMETIMES.
YEAH, HE'S ACTING DIFFERENT TO BE SURE. HE'S ALMOST ACTING LIKE—
—*FLUTTERSHY!*
HE'S ACTING ALL *SHY* AND *RETIRING*, LIKE SHE DOES. AND WHEN I SAW HER, SHE WAS ACTING LIKE... LIKE A *CAT!*
AND WHEN I GALLOPED INTO HER, SHE WAS FLYING LIKE AN *OWL.* THAT'S IT!
OKAY, BUT IF FLUTTERSHY IS ACTING LIKE THE *ANIMALS,* AND THIS TIMBERWOLF IS ACTING LIKE *HER,* DOES THAT MEAN—
FLUTTERSHY WILL BE ACTING LIKE A *TIMBERWOLF!*
WE NEED TO FIND HER! *RIGHT NOW!*
WOW! THEY FIGURED ALL THAT OUT *THEMSELVES.* THEY'RE *PRETTY SMART,* ANGEL BUNNY.

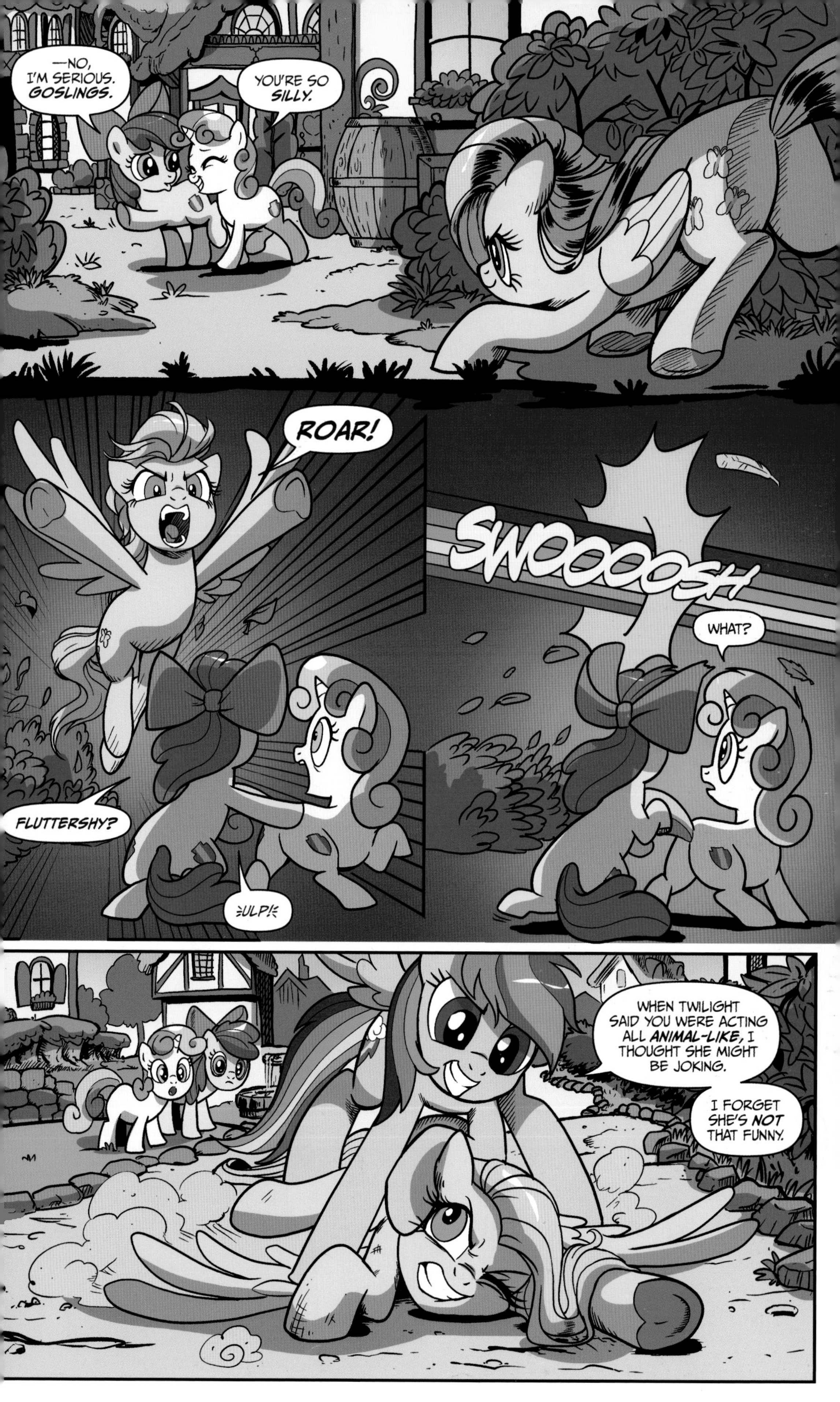
—NO, I'M SERIOUS. GOSLINGS.
YOU'RE SO SILLY.
ROAR!
FLUTTERSHY?
ULP!
SWOOOOOSH
WHAT?
WHEN TWILIGHT SAID YOU WERE ACTING ALL ANIMAL-LIKE, I THOUGHT SHE MIGHT BE JOKING.
I FORGET SHE'S NOT THAT FUNNY.

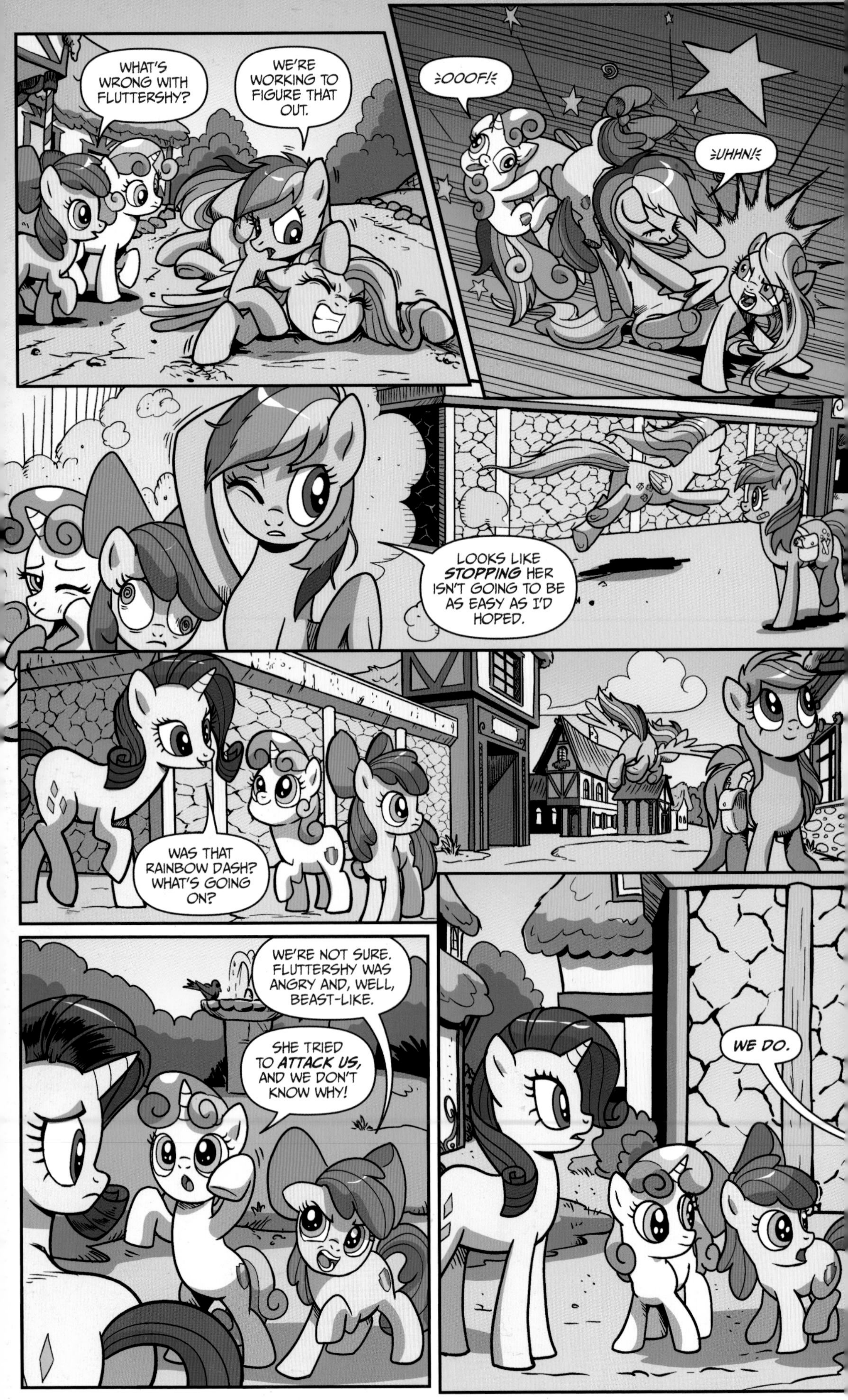
WHAT'S WRONG WITH FLUTTERSHY?
WE'RE WORKING TO FIGURE THAT OUT.
:OOOF!:
:UHHN!:
LOOKS LIKE STOPPING HER ISN'T GOING TO BE AS EASY AS I'D HOPED.
WAS THAT RAINBOW DASH? WHAT'S GOING ON?
WE'RE NOT SURE. FLUTTERSHY WAS ANGRY AND, WELL, BEAST-LIKE.
SHE TRIED TO ATTACK US, AND WE DON'T KNOW WHY!
WE DO.

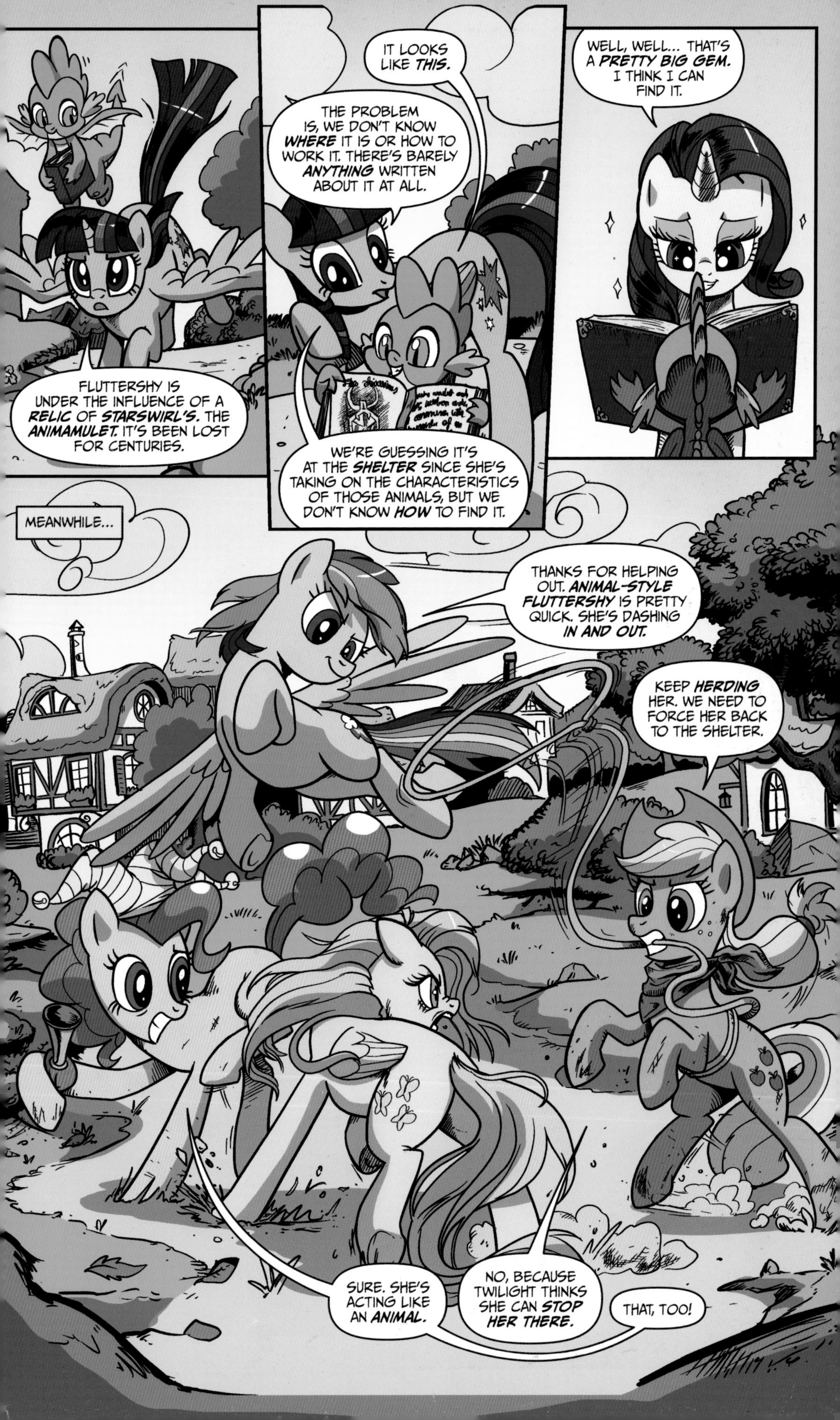
FLUTTERSHY IS UNDER THE INFLUENCE OF A RELIC OF STARSWIRL'S. THE ANIMAMULET. IT'S BEEN LOST FOR CENTURIES.
IT LOOKS LIKE THIS.
THE PROBLEM IS, WE DON'T KNOW WHERE IT IS OR HOW TO WORK IT. THERE'S BARELY ANYTHING WRITTEN ABOUT IT AT ALL.
WE'RE GUESSING IT'S AT THE SHELTER SINCE SHE'S TAKING ON THE CHARACTERISTICS OF THOSE ANIMALS, BUT WE DON'T KNOW HOW TO FIND IT.
WELL, WELL... THAT'S A PRETTY BIG GEM. I THINK I CAN FIND IT.
MEANWHILE...
THANKS FOR HELPING OUT. ANIMAL-STYLE FLUTTERSHY IS PRETTY QUICK. SHE'S DASHING IN AND OUT.
KEEP HERDING HER. WE NEED TO FORCE HER BACK TO THE SHELTER.
SURE. SHE'S ACTING LIKE AN ANIMAL.
NO, BECAUSE TWILIGHT THINKS SHE CAN STOP HER THERE.
THAT, TOO!

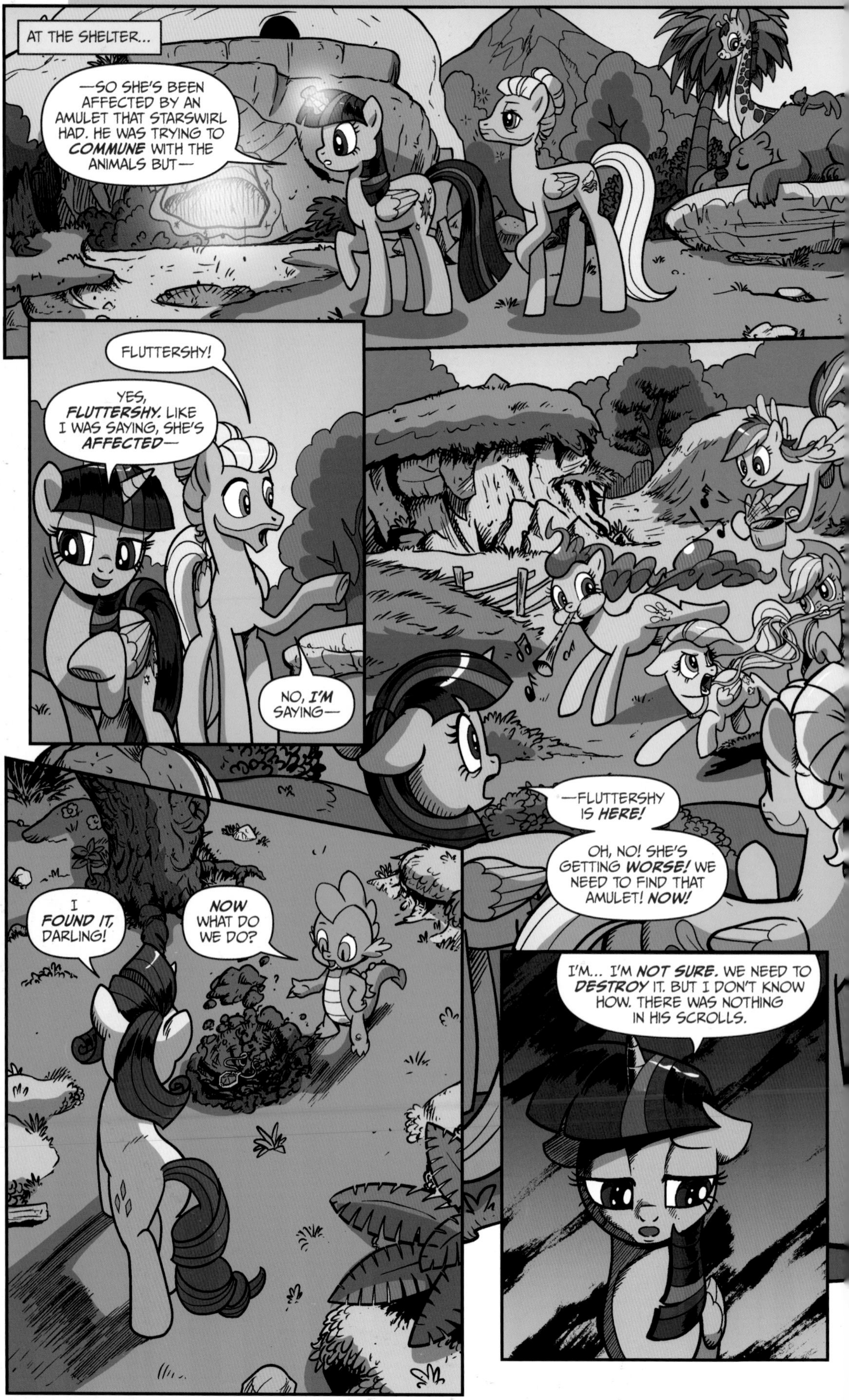
AT THE SHELTER...
—SO SHE'S BEEN AFFECTED BY AN AMULET THAT STARSWIRL HAD. HE WAS TRYING TO COMMUNE WITH THE ANIMALS BUT—
FLUTTERSHY!
YES, FLUTTERSHY. LIKE I WAS SAYING, SHE'S AFFECTED—
NO, I'M SAYING—
—FLUTTERSHY IS HERE!
OH, NO! SHE'S GETTING WORSE! WE NEED TO FIND THAT AMULET! NOW!
I FOUND IT, DARLING!
NOW WHAT DO WE DO?
I'M... I'M NOT SURE. WE NEED TO DESTROY IT. BUT I DON'T KNOW HOW. THERE WAS NOTHING IN HIS SCROLLS.

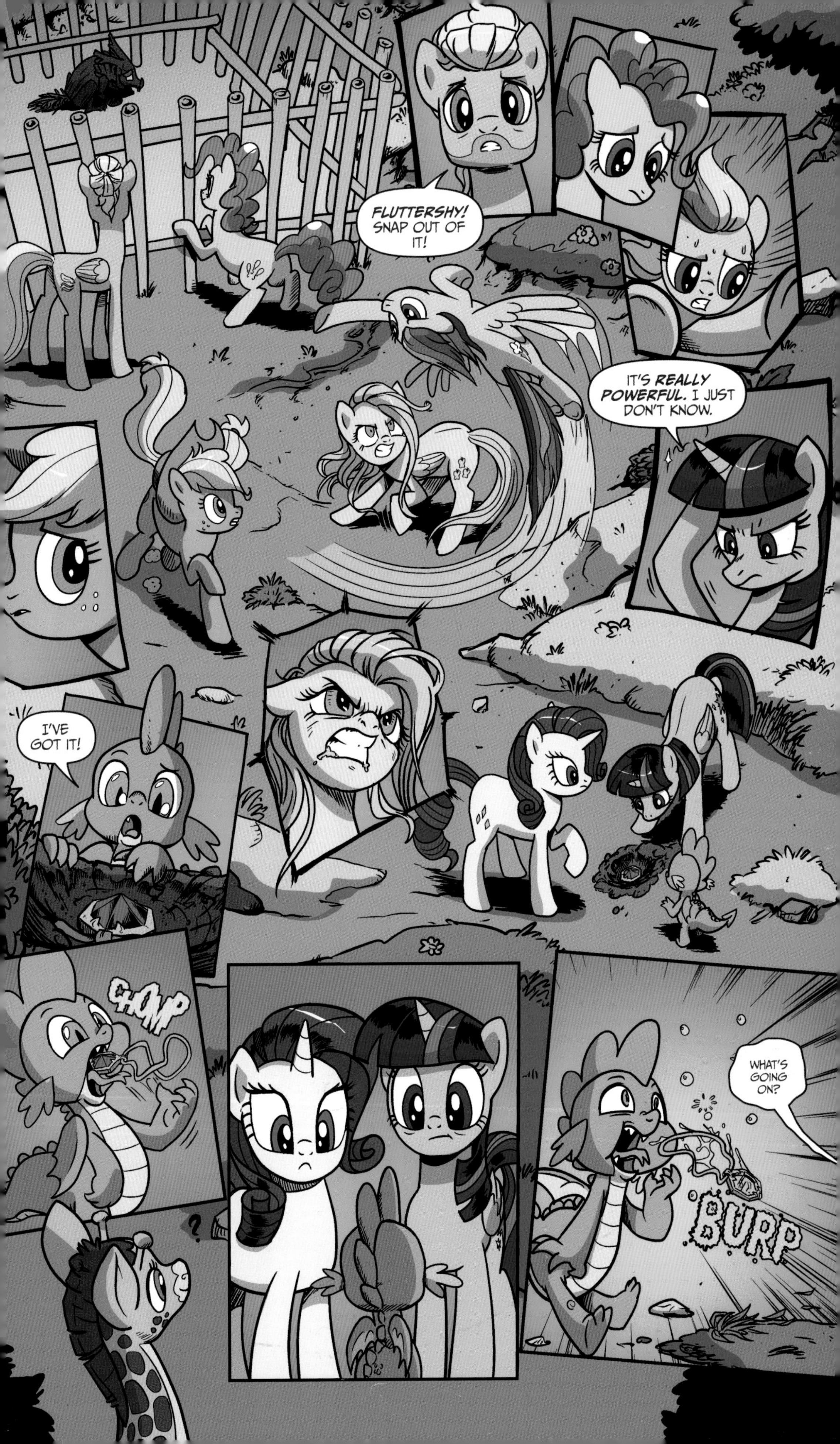
FLUTTERSHY! SNAP OUT OF IT!
IT'S REALLY POWERFUL. I JUST DON'T KNOW.
I'VE GOT IT!
CHOMP
WHAT'S GOING ON?
BURP

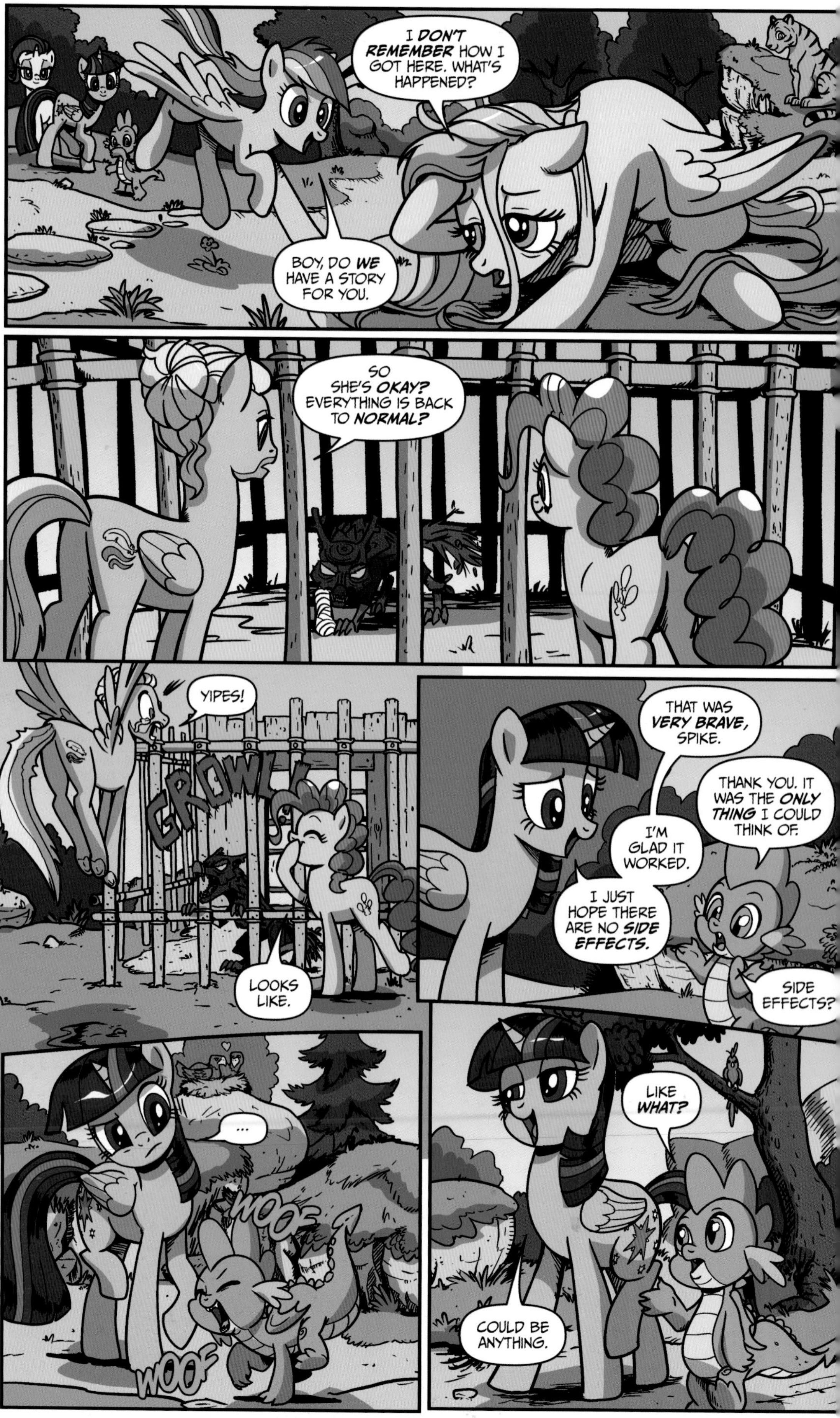
I DON'T REMEMBER HOW I GOT HERE. WHAT'S HAPPENED?
BOY, DO WE HAVE A STORY FOR YOU.
SO SHE'S OKAY? EVERYTHING IS BACK TO NORMAL?
YIPES!
GROWL
LOOKS LIKE.
THAT WAS VERY BRAVE, SPIKE.
THANK YOU. IT WAS THE ONLY THING I COULD THINK OF.
I'M GLAD IT WORKED.
I JUST HOPE THERE ARE NO SIDE EFFECTS.
SIDE EFFECTS?
...
WOOF
WOOF
LIKE WHAT?
COULD BE ANYTHING.

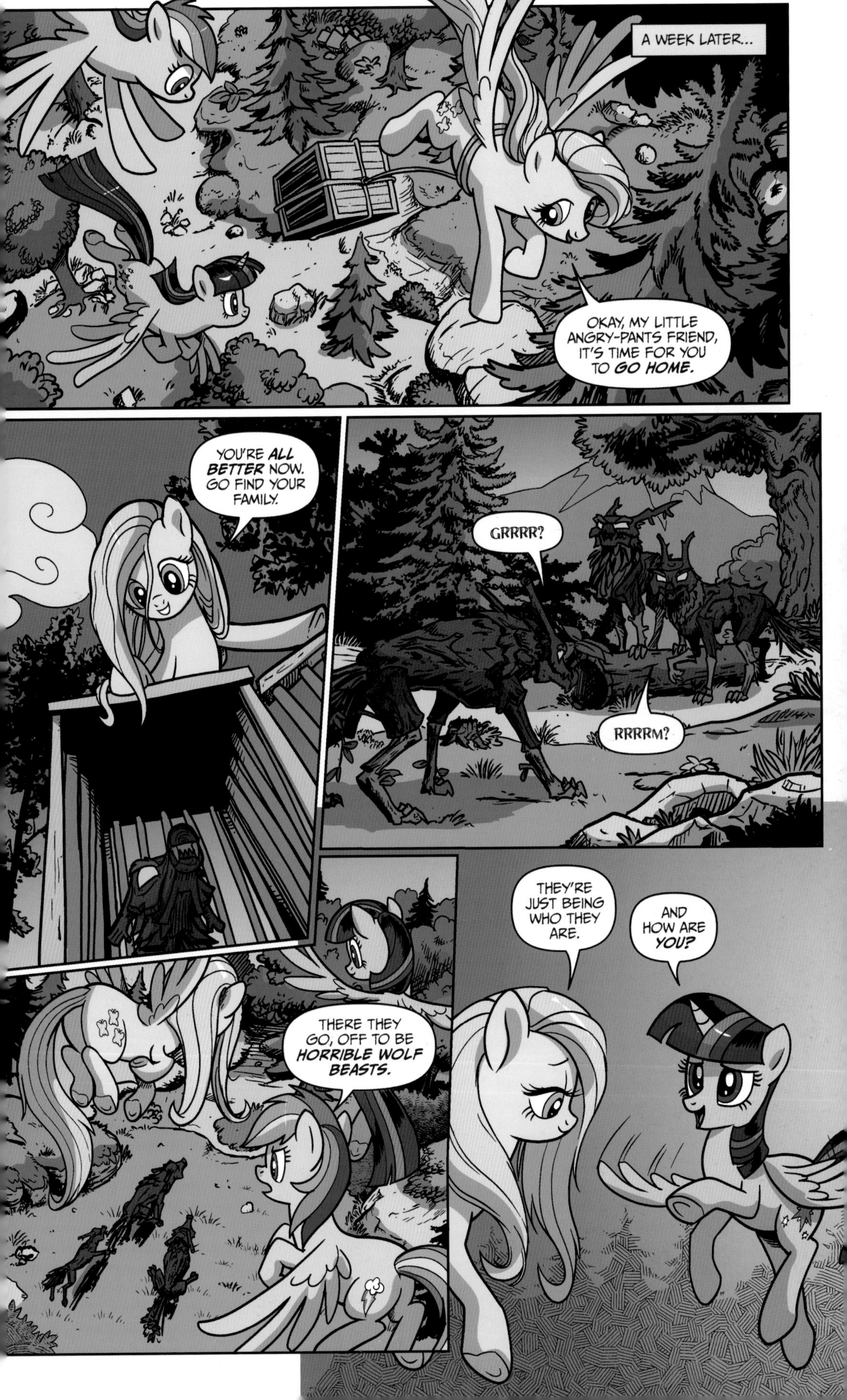
A WEEK LATER...
OKAY, MY LITTLE ANGRY-PANTS FRIEND, IT'S TIME FOR YOU TO **GO HOME.**
YOU'RE **ALL BETTER** NOW. GO FIND YOUR FAMILY.
GRRRR?
RRRRM?
THERE THEY GO, OFF TO BE **HORRIBLE WOLF BEASTS.**
THEY'RE JUST BEING WHO THEY ARE.
AND HOW ARE **YOU?**

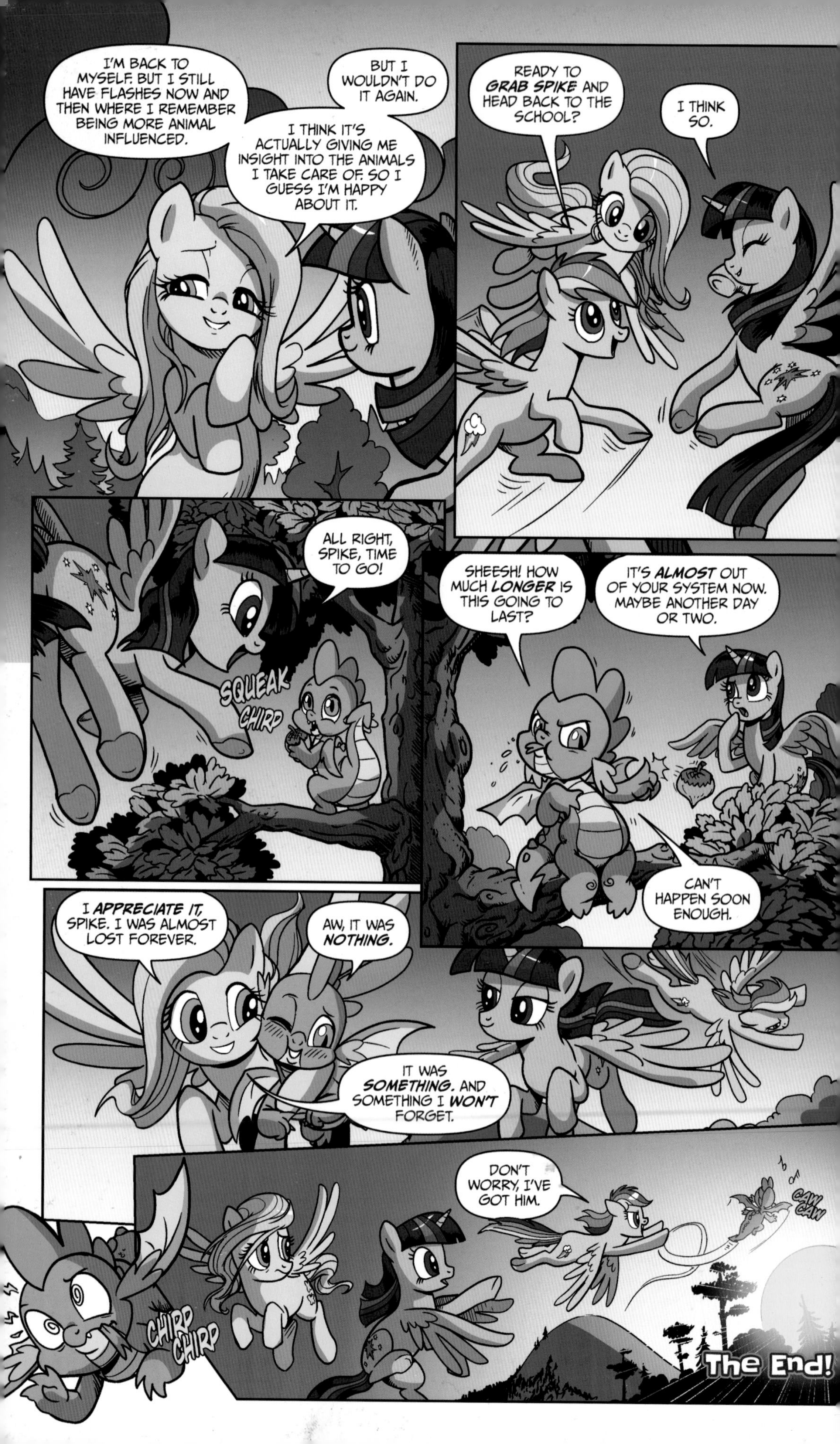

I'M BACK TO MYSELF. BUT I STILL HAVE FLASHES NOW AND THEN WHERE I REMEMBER BEING MORE ANIMAL INFLUENCED.
BUT I WOULDN'T DO IT AGAIN.
I THINK IT'S ACTUALLY GIVING ME INSIGHT INTO THE ANIMALS I TAKE CARE OF. SO I GUESS I'M HAPPY ABOUT IT.
READY TO GRAB SPIKE AND HEAD BACK TO THE SCHOOL?
I THINK SO.
ALL RIGHT, SPIKE, TIME TO GO!
SQUEAK
CHIRP
SHEESH! HOW MUCH LONGER IS THIS GOING TO LAST?
IT'S ALMOST OUT OF YOUR SYSTEM NOW. MAYBE ANOTHER DAY OR TWO.
CAN'T HAPPEN SOON ENOUGH.
I APPRECIATE IT, SPIKE. I WAS ALMOST LOST FOREVER.
AW, IT WAS NOTHING.
IT WAS SOMETHING. AND SOMETHING I WON'T FORGET.
DON'T WORRY, I'VE GOT HIM.
CAW CAW
CHIRP CHIRP
The End!

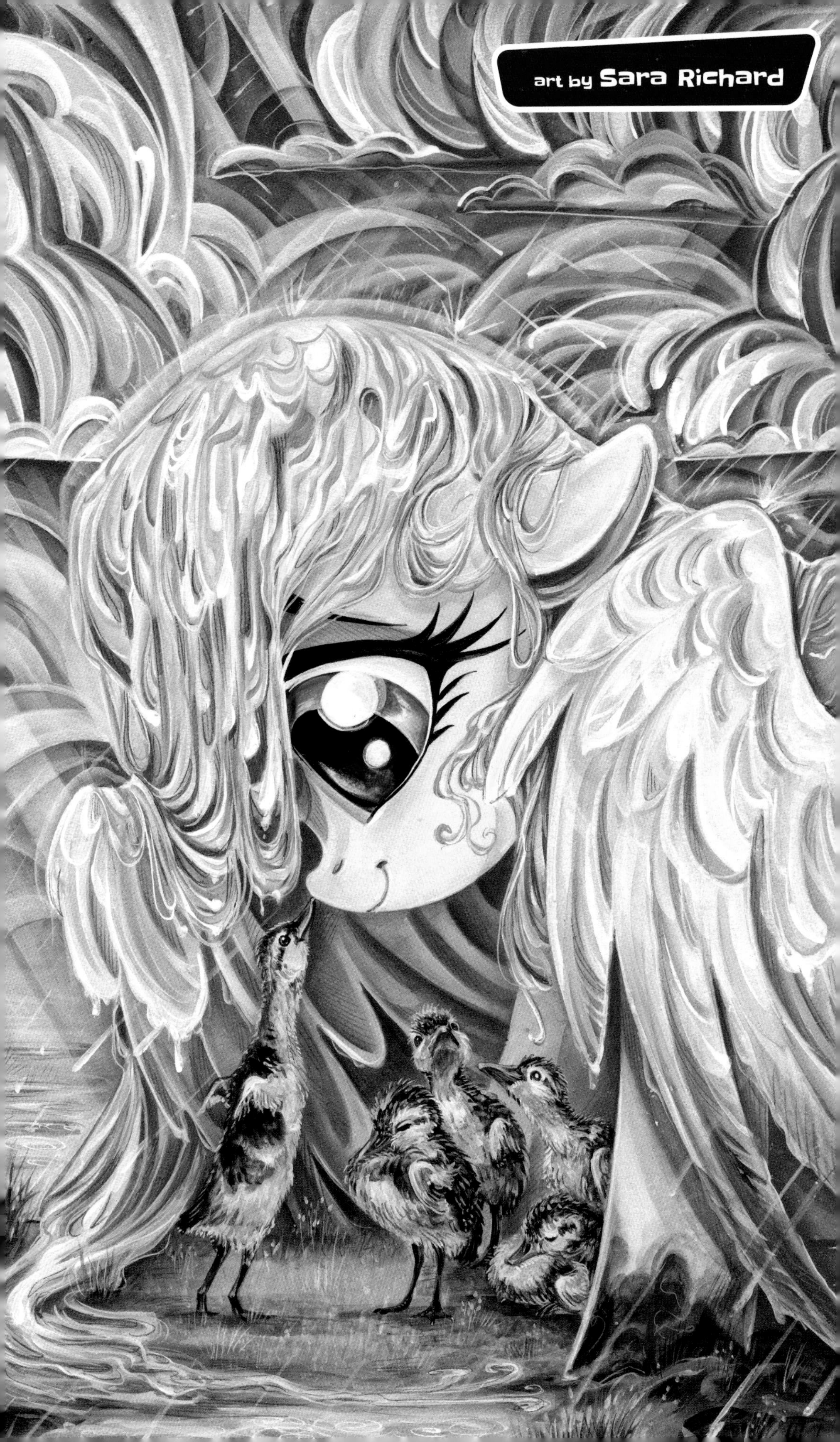
art by Sara Richard

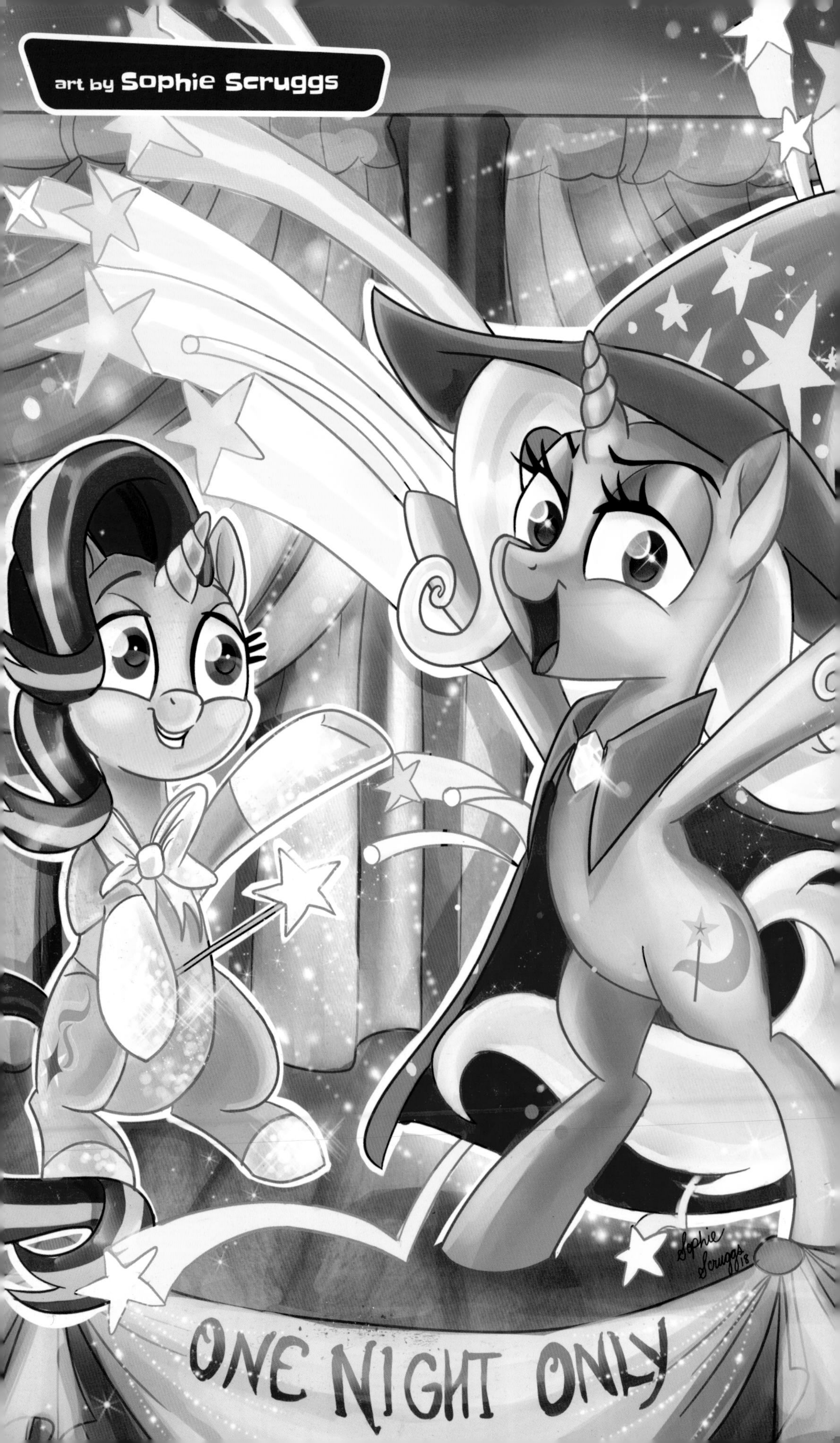
ONE NIGHT ONLY
art by Sophie Scruggs

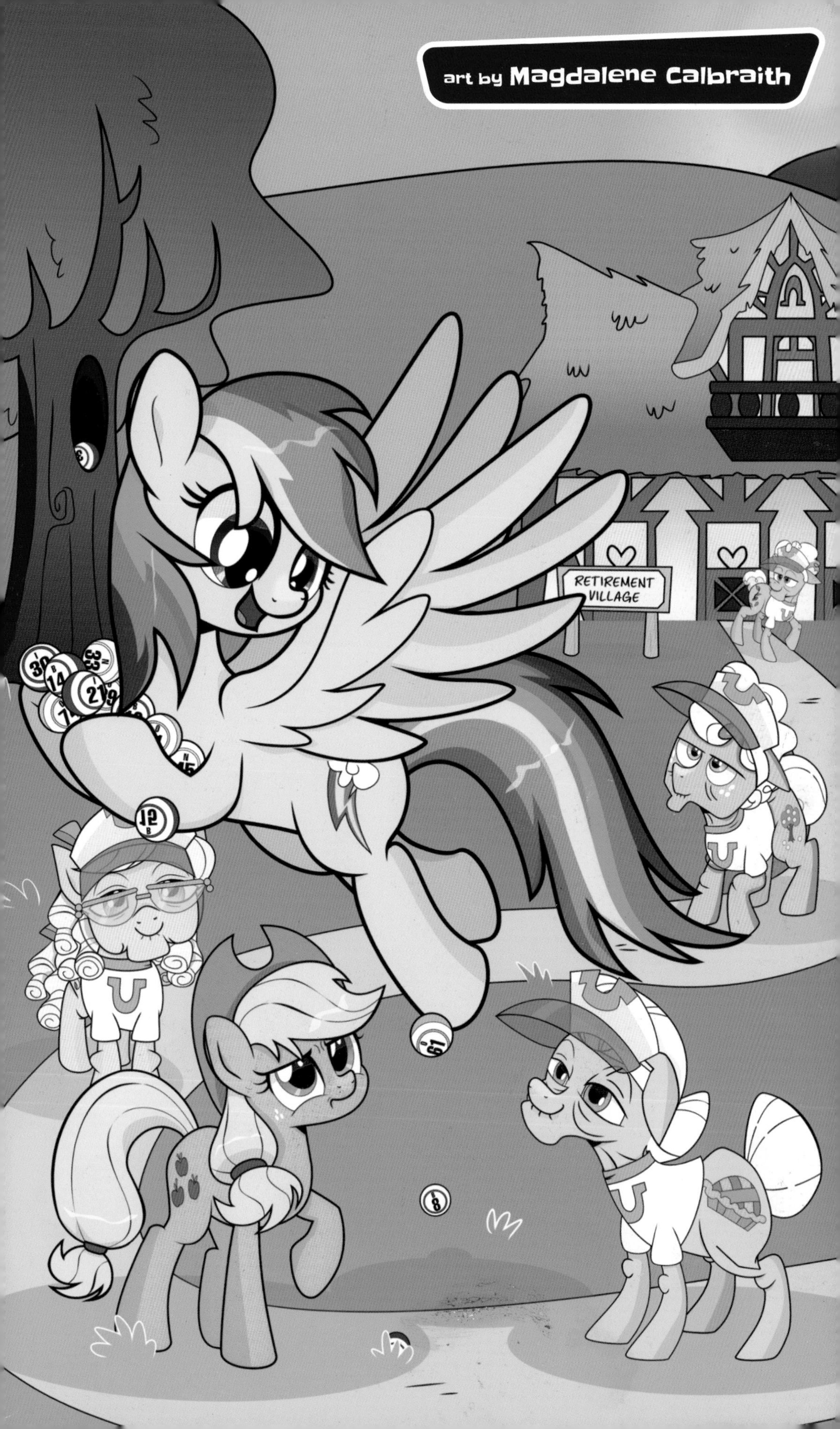
art by Magdalene Calbraith
RETIREMENT
VILLAGE

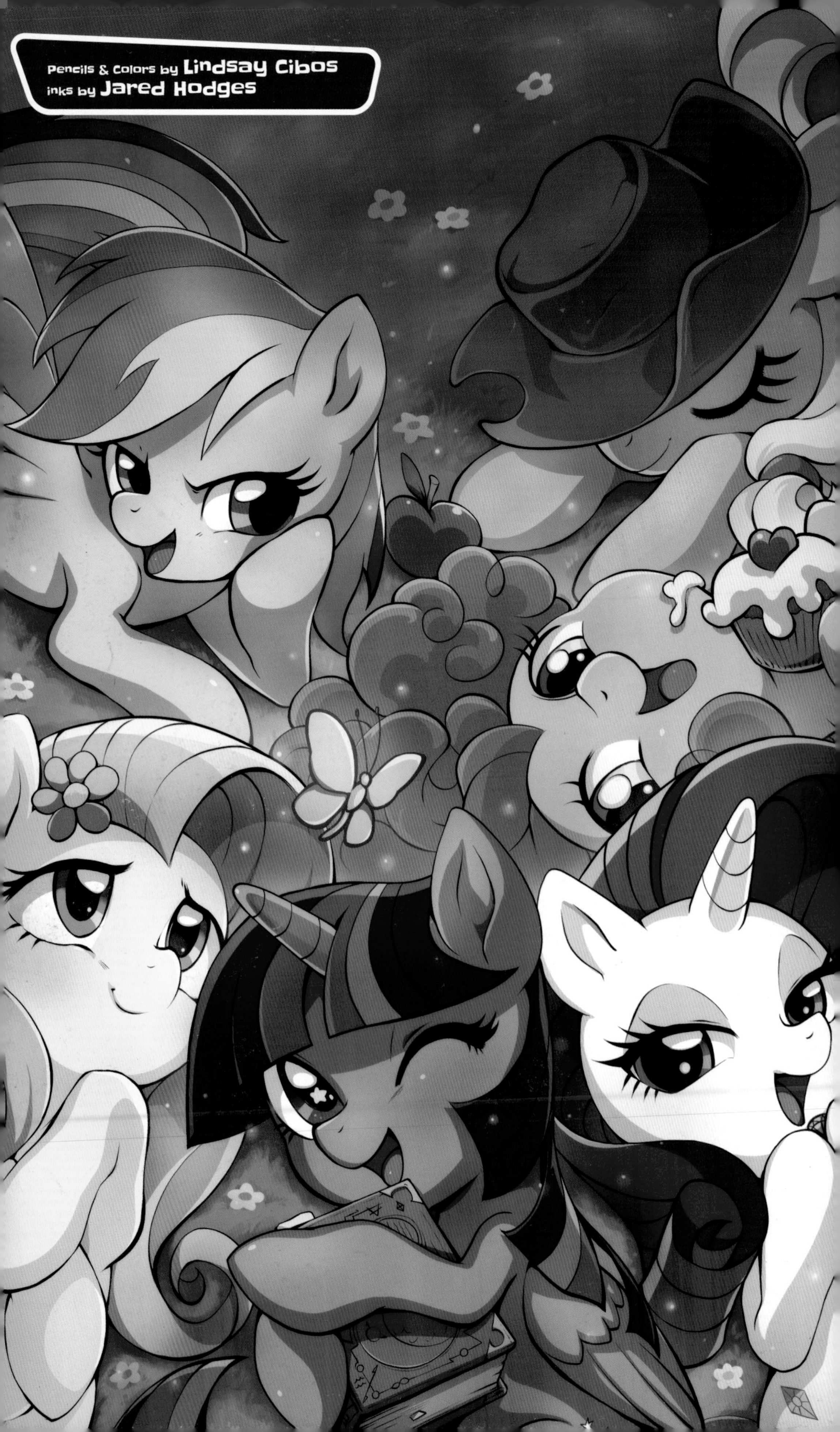
Pencils & Colors by Lindsay Cibos
inks by Jared Hodges

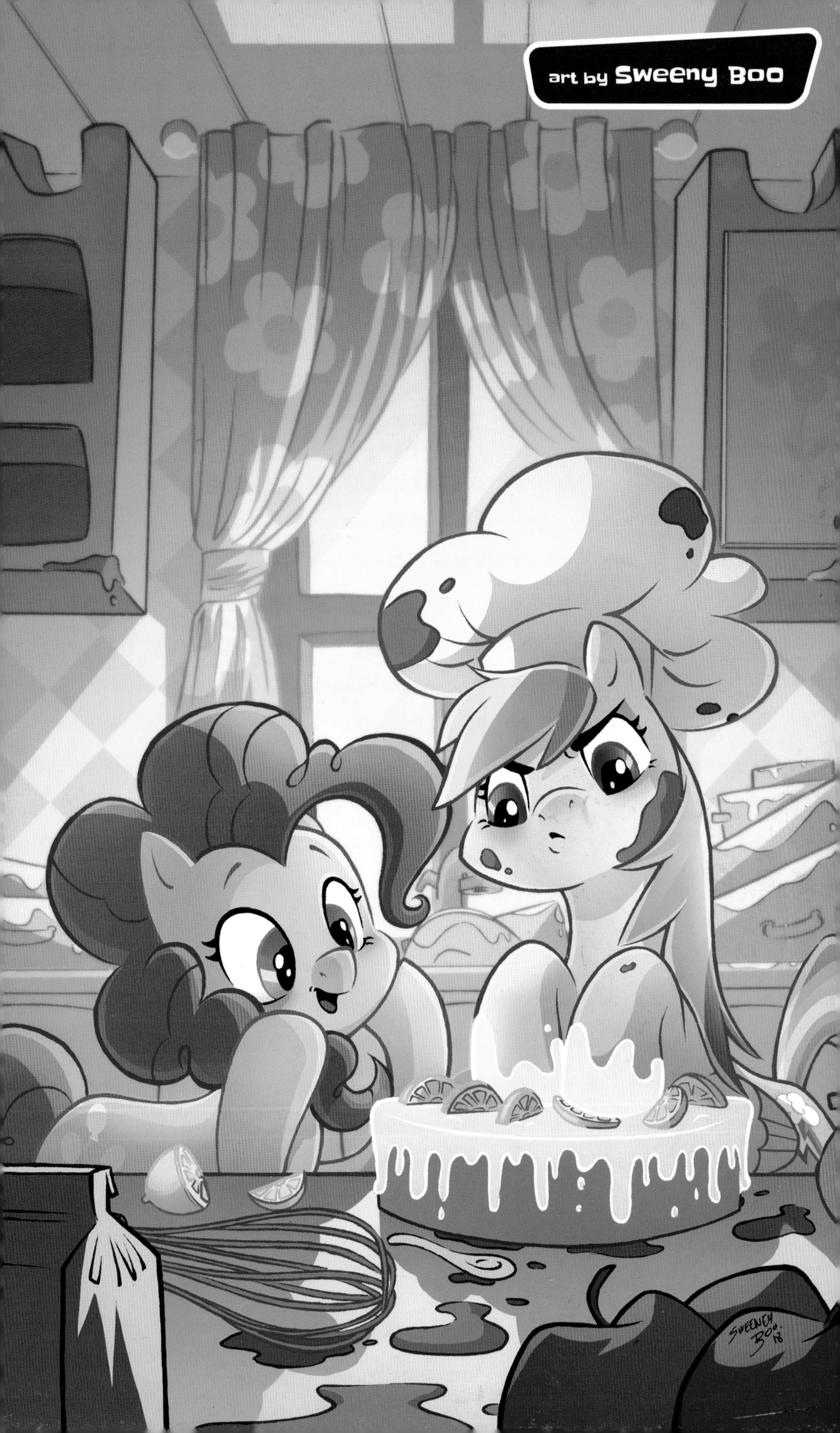
art by Sweeny Boo

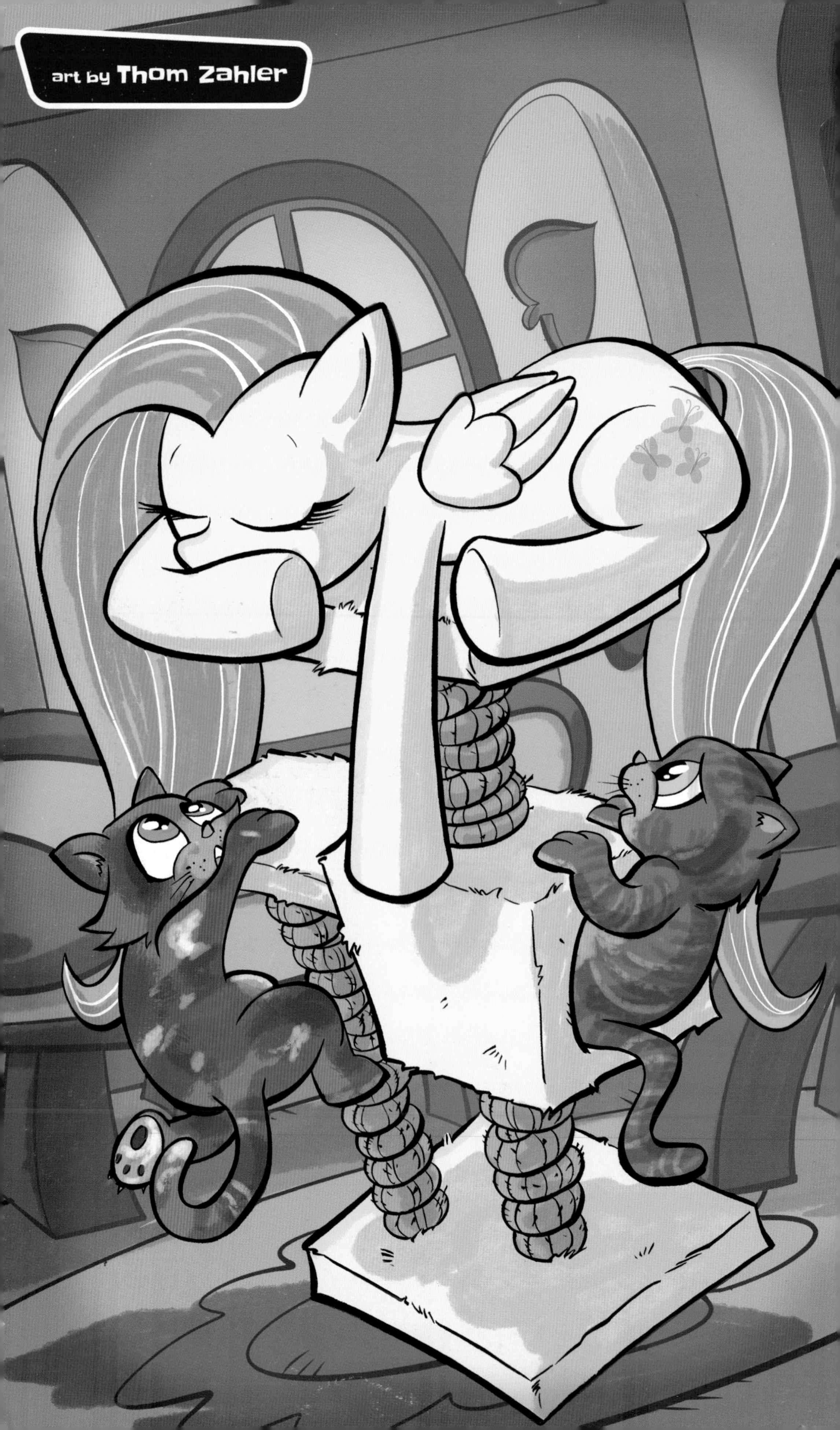
art by Thom Zahler

my LITTLE PONY
Friendship is Magic

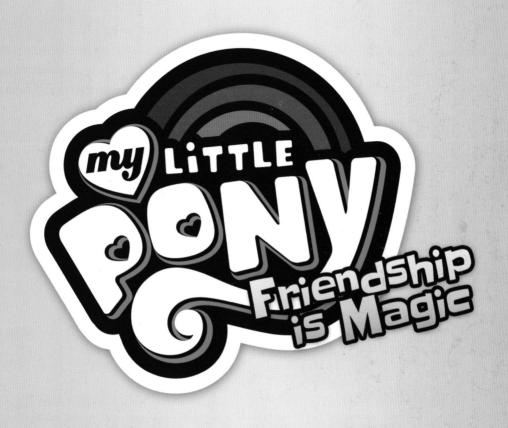

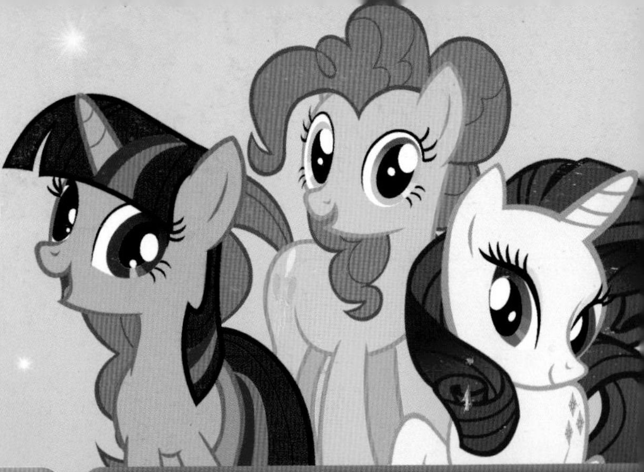

## THE ONGOING ADVENTURES OF EVERYONE'S FAVORITE PONIES!

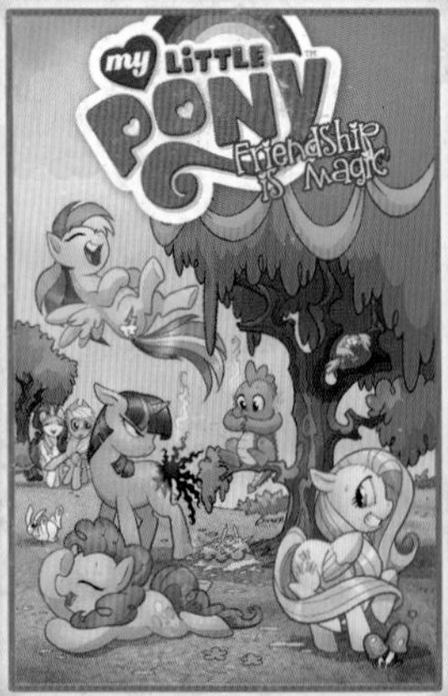
My Little Pony
Friendship is Magic

My Little Pony:
Friendship is Magic, Vol. 1
TPB • $17.99 • 978-1613776056

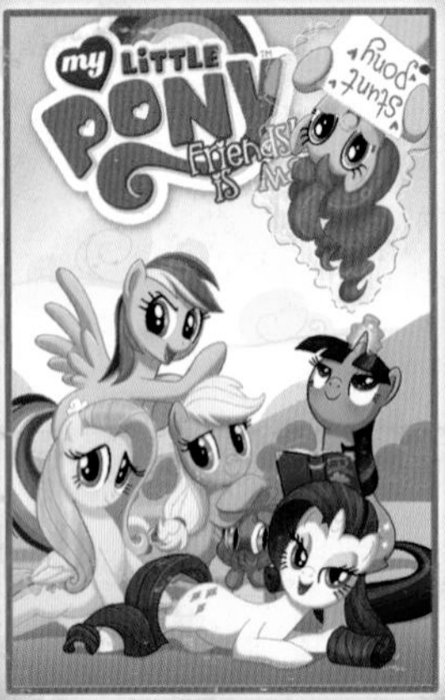
My Little Pony
Stunt pony

My Little Pony:
Friendship is Magic, Vol. 2
TPB • $17.99 • 978-1613777602

## PONIES UNITE IN THIS TEAM-UP SERIES!

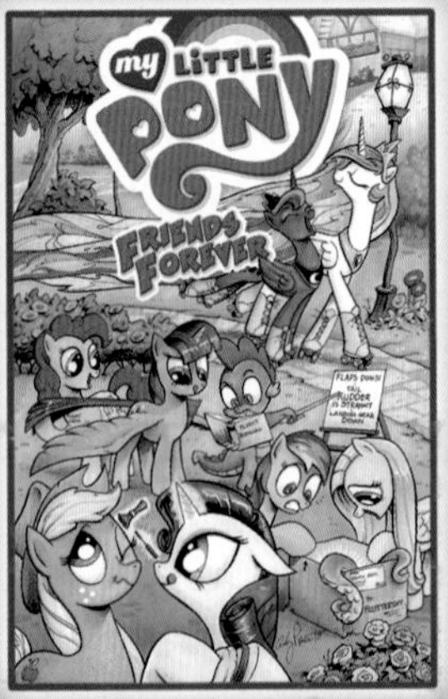
My Little Pony
Friends Forever

My Little Pony:
Friends Forever, Vol. 1
TPB • $17.99 • 978-1613779811

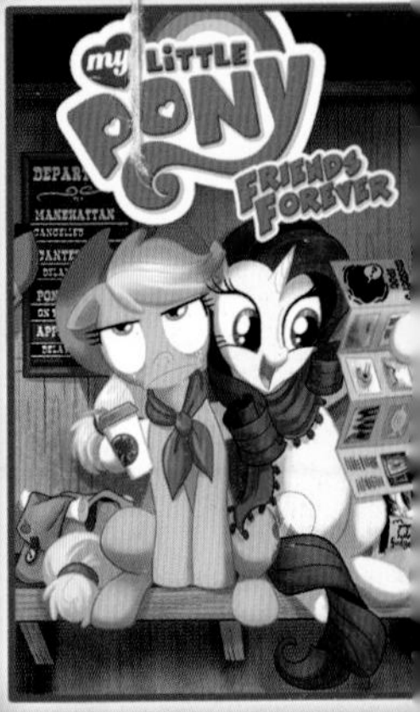
My Little Pony
Friends Forever

My Little Pony:
Friends Forever, Vol. 2
TPB • $17.99 • 978-16314015

## SPECIALLY SELECTED TALES TO TAKE WITH YOU ON THE GO!

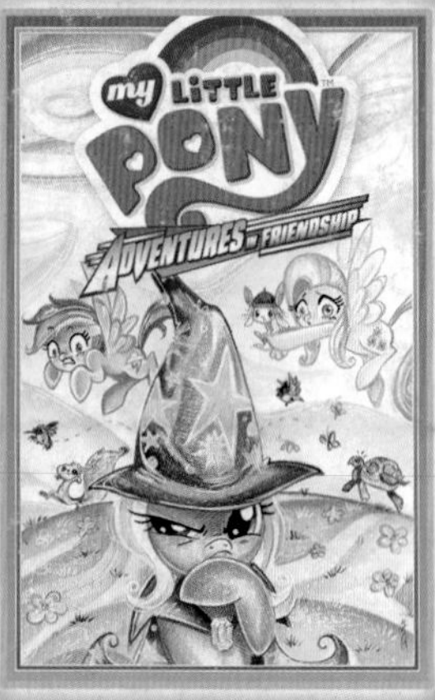
My Little Pony
Adventures in Friendship

My Little Pony:
Adventures in Friendship, Vol. 1
TPB • $9.99 • 978-1631401893

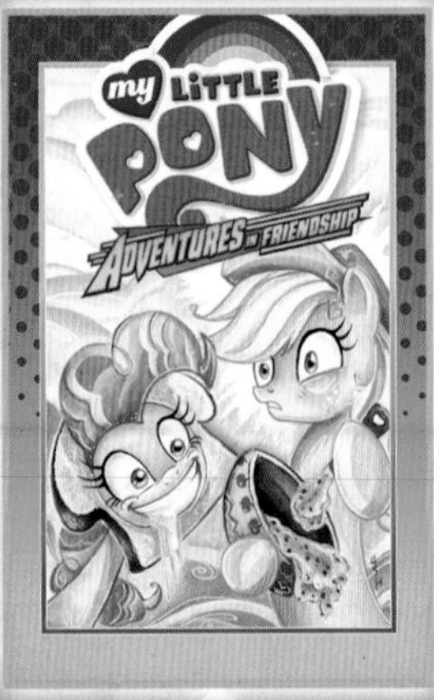
My Little Pony
Adventures in Friendship

My Little Pony:
Adventures in Friendship, Vol. 2
TPB • $9.99 • 978-1631402258

## GET THE WHOLE STORY WITH THE MY LITTLE PONY OMBINUS!

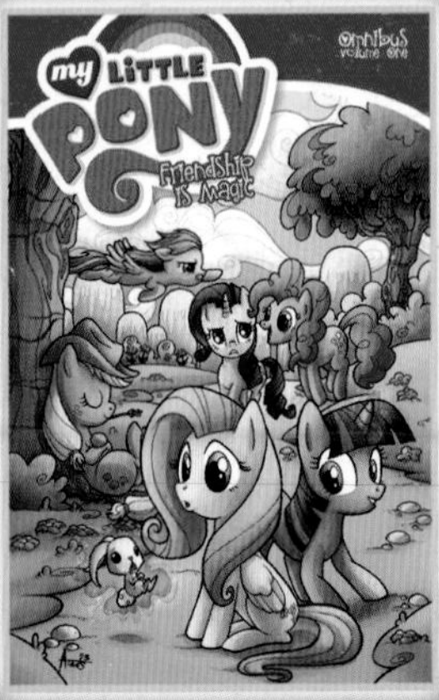
Omnibus volume one
My Little Pony
Friendship is Magic

My Little Pony:
Omnibus, Vol. 1
TPB • $24.99 • 978-1631401404

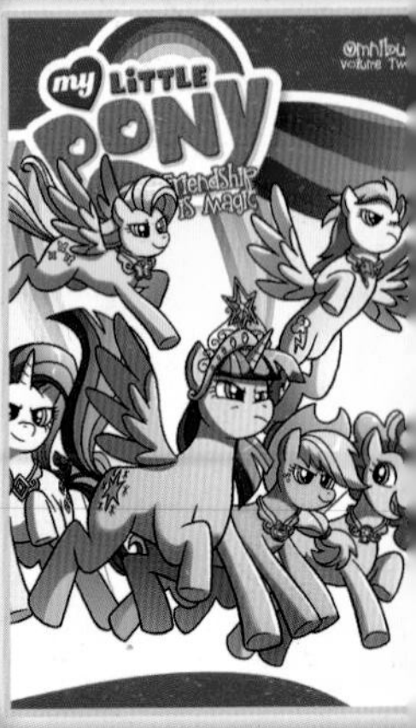
My Little Pony
Friendship is Magic

My Little Pony:
Omnibus, Vol. 2
TPB • $24.99 • 978-16314040

IDW

WWW.IDWPUBLISHING.C